NIGHT
HUSH

NIGHT HUSH

Duty & Honor Book One

LESLIE JONES

WITNESS
IMPULSE

An Imprint of HarperCollinsPublishers

EPub Edition JANUARY 2015 ISBN: 9780062363145

Print Edition ISBN: 9780062363152

10 9 8 7 6

To Kim and Scott, the real centers of my universe,
because without you I'd be lost.

Chapter One

Date: Unknown
Location: Unknown

THE UNCERTAINTY WAS the hardest. The waiting. He would come again, that was a given. He enjoyed her pain, her fear. Her panic. When he tramped into the room, loudly, deliberately, already laughing at her, Heather felt almost relieved to be done with the suspense. Almost.

"Filthy American whore."

She tried to remain strong, she really did.

She rose on shaking legs, lifting her chin with what bravery she could muster. Standing made her feel less vulnerable, but she couldn't stop herself from shrinking back against the coarse mudbrick wall. Her shoulders, numb from being pulled behind her for so many hours, screamed in agony as she tried to use them.

He fell silent, the twisted bastard. Stalking her in the small space. Tacitly urging her to run, to try to escape. She strained to hear what her blindfolded eyes couldn't see. Any inhalation. Any noise.

He gave her a clue. A scrape of a heel. An expelled breath.

When she'd first been captured, she'd been defiant, aiming solid kicks where she thought he stood. When she missed, he laughed. When she connected, he beat her. Now, days later, she merely stumbled away from him, keeping her back to the wall, trying to avoid his fists.

The stink of sour sweat was her only warning before he rushed her, crowded her, pressing his body to hers. His odor penetrated the stench of urine and rotting food that permeated her prison cell. She twisted away from the wall to avoid being pinned. He grabbed her hair, which had long since fallen out of its French braid, then allowed her to wrench away, scalp stinging, dread pulsing with each thud of her heart. Disoriented, hampered by the ropes digging into her wrists and the tight blindfold, she tried to find the wall.

He went soundless again. Circling her. Stalking. Playing with her until she screamed her fear and frustration. Her impotent fury. Her screams were no longer the battle cries of a soldier, an officer in the United States Army. Instead, she sounded desperate, pitiful.

He came for her, his scraggly beard and traditional wool headdress rough against her face as his hard hands bit into her shoulders.

Heather didn't know how much longer she could hold on. She was nearing the limits of her endurance; she could feel it.

How long had it been since she'd been captured? Days and nights of little sleep, little food, little water. No sanitary facilities.

And him. Always him.

August 15. 8:38 P.M.
Kongra-Gel Terrorist Training Site

JACE REED'S ASS had fallen asleep. In fact, he could no longer feel his legs, his feet, or his right elbow. That's what he got, he guessed, for not moving in three hours. Eyes trained on the compound in front of him, he made a minor adjustment to his night vision goggles. The greenish-gray view didn't change. It hadn't changed the entire time he'd been here.

Sighing a little, he pressed his throat mike, and murmured, "Tag."

The almost inaudible response was immediate. "Yeah, boss."

"Let's switch for a while. I can't feel my balls anymore."

"No one'll miss 'em," said Tag.

"Except yo' momma. Get your ass up here."

Sergeant First Class John McTaggert slid silently over the barren ground to the rock outcropping where Jace crouched. Just as silently, Jace descended, forcing his stiff limbs to cooperate. The rock had cooled with the darkness and no longer burned. Once on the ground, he locked the night vision goggles onto his helmet and waited, allowing Tag to wedge into place on the rock as blood returned to his own extremities. He keyed his mike.

"Report."

His other four men, deployed at various strategic points around the camp's perimeter, responded instantly to his almost silent command. No one had gone in or out of the compound in the past twenty-four hours. The roving guards couldn't find their asses with both hands. The aroma of goat stew simmering in the building closest to Archangel's lookout had him weeping for his mother's cooking.

"Roger that."

Their intelligence had Omaid al-Hassid arriving sometime within a twelve-hour window. Jace and his team had now been on-site well over fifteen hours. Looked like their intelligence was wrong. Again. If circumstances forced them to extract before they'd accomplished their mission, his boss would blow a gasket. That wasn't even considering the mammoth sandstorm headed their way, due to arrive in roughly seven hours. Their timeline was fixed.

Jace wriggled himself into Tag's blind, arranging the dusty shrubs so there was no trace of his passage, and resumed his surveillance, this time of the west side of the camp. A broad sweep of desert scrub giving way to rocky hills. A clump of straggling buildings in the shadow of a steep hill; what were probably the mess hall and barracks, three tiny mudbrick houses. A huge tent toward the center of the compound. Two lax guards at the security outpost in the hills, chatting together while they smoked. An old farm truck; and, incongruously, ten bales of hay.

"Contact! Movement at two o'clock." The voice came from Sergeant Alex Wood, the newest member of his team. His whisper was tinged with a quiet, controlled excitement. Finally, something was happening. "Three vehicles. Two Jeeps and an open-bed truck, looks like. I got four warm bodies in the front Jeep, three in the second. Five in the truck. That's two in the cab, three in the back. Truck's piled in the back, too. Cargo."

"Weapons?"

There was a pause. "Can't see yet, boss. They probably have 'em at their feet. But I bet they got the usual assortment of garbage."

"Don't guess. Verify." Jace resisted the urge to shift around the perimeter so he could see for himself. "All teams, eyes sharp."

It would be just their luck if this was a random supply drop. Murphy and his damned law at work again. Still, it didn't get him anywhere useful to believe that. He waited, senses straining, knowing all five members of his team did the same. Information came in low, grim tones as Alex relayed what he saw.

"Confirm automatic weapons on four tangos in the lead Jeep." Tango, the phonetic letter T, used as slang for terrorists. "Confirm automatic weapons on three tangos getting out of the flatbed truck. Movement in Jeep two." Pause. "Three tangos getting out. Two moving forward. One . . . positive ID! I say again, positive ID on our target. It's al-Hassid. I guess we know what's in the back of the truck, yeah?"

Jace let the adrenaline course through his body, recognizing it wouldn't do him any good just yet but knowing he couldn't stop it. "Record where they put it all. Count the boxes, Alex."

"Got it."

Boxes weren't the only thing coming off the truck. The driver also yanked two females wearing loose abaya robes and hijab head scarves to the ground, and shoved them in the direction of a slightly larger building, probably the mess hall. They stumbled inside.

Jace's muscles bunched. Unconsciously, his hand brushed his breast pocket. "Alex, can you get a good look at those women?"

"These two are natives, boss. Not her."

Grateful that the almost subliminal mental connection between his teammates allowed Alex to know instantly the direction of Jace's thoughts, he let his attention flicker even while keeping sharp eyes on the portion of the compound he monitored. To the recent ambush of a military convoy outside of Eshma, at the other end of Azakistan. The taking of an American female soldier.

Not an Azakistani, but a fair-skinned redhead. She'd been in Eshma for the past four weeks, volunteering as an interpreter after someone bombed the Ubadah Government Center, the worst terrorist attack Azakistan had ever seen. If she hadn't been in Eshma, if the convoy she was on hadn't been attacked, she would still be safe on al-Zadr Air Force Base, with him.

He touched his pocket again, where her picture nestled. Well, not exactly *with* him, since they'd never actually met.

The United States Central Command had deployed her likeness far and wide, hoping for information that could lead to her liberation. The probability she'd show up in this part of the country, nearly three hundred miles from the site of the convoy attack, was slim, but that wouldn't stop any of them from looking.

Dipping two fingers inside, he withdrew the battered photo. The darkness couldn't erase his memory of flashing eyes and a stubborn chin, the skin of her oval face looking as soft as peaches. The head shot, clearly a staff photo, revealed long hair pulled back from her face and plaited into some sort of complicated weave. Even the severity of the hairstyle and a military uniform couldn't disguise her beauty. First Lieutenant Heather Langstrom. Jace traced her cheek in the dimness.

He'd seen her around the commissary buying groceries—for just one person—and at the base exchange buying Maui Jim sunglasses and a juicer. Always stared at. Usually shadowed by panting hopefuls, though she never gave her admirers so much as a glance. It was astounding how many male soldiers chose to run at dawn, at the exact moment she laced up her cross trainers and started the ten-mile perimeter loop of the base. They ran in front of her, flexing and posturing, hoping for her notice. They ran behind her, admiring her long legs and tight ass. The braver ones ran alongside, trying to engage her in conversation until summarily dismissed. He, idiot that he was, took his team out of the Delta Force compound at Forward Operating Base Hollow Straw for long, looping runs that crossed paths with her at least once. Pride had kept him from approaching her, fear of being rejected along with the others. Now he wished he'd at least talked to her. Heard her voice.

Wherever she was being held, he prayed her captors treated her with decency. Experience told him, though, it was unlikely. Prisoners of a war declared on the United States by terrorists around the world tended not to be treated with dignity. They were tortured and videotaped. As much war and death as he'd seen, he just couldn't stomach the thought of those pretty blue eyes brutalized.

He glanced up and caught Tag giving him an odd look from his spot on the rock. Shaking his head, he unclenched his fingers from the photo and stuffed it back into his pocket, returning his focus to the trucks. He didn't know her, for God's sake. She wasn't even the first female soldier to be captured. Something about her tugged at him, though. Kept her in his thoughts.

He let out a breath. *Get a grip, Reed.* He'd better get his head in the game, or he'd end up dead. Or worse, captured and in the cell next to her.

The six men of Alpha Team waited through the interminable delay while the soldiers unloaded the boxes and crates and carried them, one at a time, into a small building at the edge of the compound. The soldiers bitched and complained the entire time, dragging out the task past the point where Jace seriously considered going out there and helping them.

"Idiots," murmured Gabriel 'Archangel' Morgan. "They're putting it right under my nose."

Jace agreed. The insurgents, part of the Kongra-Gel, had made a classic mistake. Rather than securing their weapons within reach, they stockpiled them as far away from themselves as possible, in some misguided sense of safety. As though light antitank weapons fired themselves. Their stupidity made his team's job simpler.

The Kongra-Gel, formerly the Kurdistan Worker's Party operating primarily out of Turkey, had expanded its scope from mere armed violence to include drug trafficking in northern Iraq and Europe. Their terrorist tactics included suicide bombings, kidnappings, and targeting tourist sites with violence. They were bad news on a major scale, and the US Special Operations Command and Delta Force had a vested interest in crippling their operations.

His Delta Force team was the best. Hard-core, stealthy, fast. Lethal. Despite the inherent dangers associated with ops deep in enemy territory, this one seemed straightforward enough. Get in. Destroy the rocket-propelled grenades and shoulder-launched light anti-tank weapons al-Hassid had just brought home to his base camp. Get out. Extract in front of the wall of sand blasting toward them. Piece of cake.

But he knew better than most how fast an easy op could go bad. He flexed his left arm, phantom pain flickering through his bones from where a piece of the helicopter's tail boom had broken his arm during the crash in Kamdesh. That mission should have been a cakewalk, too.

"Shit!" Gabe breathed. He clicked his mike twice in succession, a prearranged signal of danger. "More company, guys."

"What is it?" Had he summoned bad luck with his gloomy thoughts?

"Big-ass truck. Looks like it might be . . . holy fuck!" His harsh whisper sent alarm flooding down Jace's back. Gabe was shocked; not something that happened often. "It's a missile transporter. Jace, Holy Christ! They have a SCUD."

Chapter Two

Date: Unknown
Location: Unknown

SHE GULPED DOWN the water, the lukewarm, metallic liquid like manna from heaven. Arms still bound behind her, she shifted on the hard concrete, trying to balance on her knees. Too soon, the tin cup was pulled from her cracked lips. She twisted her head, trying to catch movement from behind her blindfold.

A sliver of dim light. Nothing else.

Did anyone know where she was?

Less than a week ago, she had been merely one of thousands of American soldiers deployed to the dusty, sweaty Azakistani desert. She had two more months before she was due to rotate back Stateside. Heather looked forward to leaving the Air Force base. The high temperatures and long days ground away her energy reserves. As an intelligence officer supporting the 10th Special Forces Group, her every waking hour was dedicated to piecing together bits and pieces of seemingly disparate data, building as clear a picture as possible of what was happening in Azakistan and the surrounding areas. She took her job very seriously. What she did or did not do could cost lives.

But it didn't leave room for anything else.

Someone wrenched her off the ground and onto a hard metal chair.

"Now," the harsh voice said. His English was surprisingly good. "Why do you ask questions about Omaid al-Hassid?"

"Who?"

He grabbed her jaw, squeezing.

Heather suspected her interrogator ranked highly among the group of insurgents setting off bombs at cafés and market stalls inside the capital city of Ma'ar ye zhad. Azakistani police didn't seem able to find or stop them. Fear was starting to sap the city's energy. Showing even the slightest knowledge about them could get her killed.

"Why did you visit Sa'id al-Jabr?"

The current Azakistani prime minister, Uzuri al-Muhaymin, had lost the support of fundamentalist Muslims. His pro-Western stance was good for the free-market economy, good for women's rights, and good for democracy, but there was a growing, festering hatred for all things Western that had many in both the intelligence and the political arenas concerned.

"Who?"

He backhanded her across the face. She crashed onto the concrete floor, landing heavily on her injured shoulder.

Was anyone searching for her?

Heather drifted into her daydream, where pain faded away. A

team of SEALs, swooping in to save her. Their commander, handsome and brave, carrying her to safety in his strong arms. Not straining under her five foot ten frame. Blond, she decided, with a Midwesterner's broad face. He would cradle her with care, press his lips to hers. Soothe away her pain, then take her back to al-Zadr Air Base, far away from this nightmare. They might even enjoy a brief fling, then she would go home. Back to Los Angeles and her family, such as it was.

The fantasy shivered into nothingness.

She was no fainting damsel. Everything she'd earned had been through sheer sweat and grim determination. Heather hadn't needed a man's intercession since she was sixteen, and the boy she'd been crushing on had tried to feel her up in the bathroom hallway of the famous Spago Beverly Hills restaurant. Her daddy had chased him off, then promptly enrolled her in martial arts classes.

No one was coming to save her. She was a soldier in the United States Army, and if she was going to survive this, she must find a way to save herself.

What would be so wrong with a little help, though? Just this once?

"What do you know of Demas Pagonis?" he demanded again.

Nothing, she could have told him. "Who?" No answer at all would just get her hit again, so she forced the word through cracked lips.

His growl sent fear chasing down her spine. She clenched her eyes and waited for the blow. It didn't come; instead, he left her on the floor as he stomped from one end of the cell to the other. Even through her blindfold, she felt his frustration and fury. Heather rested her forehead against the concrete, focusing on breathing. Just breathing.

Three weeks ago, she had been in Eshma, on the southwestern boot of Azakistan, acting as an interpreter for the local civil affairs group. A series of car bombs, strategically placed around the Ubadah Government Center, had taken down the building and left four hundred-plus victims in its wake; the tragedy overwhelmed the meager medical facilities. Government cars, taxis, even rickshaws transported victims to other area hospitals for treatment. Emergency medical supplies had to be trucked in from around the country. Interpreters calmed family members, located relatives, and either reunited them or consoled them in their grief. Heather, fluent in three languages and conversant in two more, volunteered.

After twelve days of relentless effort, the chaos resolved itself into patches of misery, pain, and despair. Heather helped where she could, but began to turn more and more to her job—gathering information. She passed among the women, who spoke to her openly, telling her things she never would have heard from male Muslims. Rumors, gossip, complaints, and praise were all noted, cataloged, and filed away for future reference.

"Dirty slut. My shoe is on your head." Her interrogator kicked her. Heather didn't bother to move or react to the deadly Arabic insult. And she would not—would *not*—scream for him.

August 15. 11:42 p.m.
Kongra-Gel Terrorist Training Site

HEADQUARTERS IMMEDIATELY NIXED the idea of an airstrike to take out the SCUD, a Russian-made short-range tactical ballistic missile. The R-17 SCUD-b's range made it capable of launching an attack virtually anywhere in the Middle East, which made its possession by the Kongra-Gel beyond dangerous. But the Special Operations Command refused to authorize it, even for a threat as extreme as the SCUD.

Jace almost threw his satellite phone out into the darkness. He'd pulled his men a hundred yards or so from the insurgents' camp, to the outcropping of rocks and scrub trees he'd designated as their temporary command post. With the perimeter guarded by the Sandman and Mace, it left the rest of them free to communicate without risk of exposure.

"Damn it!" He knew why, though.

So did Archangel, next to him, who parodied his version of the Azakistani government's inflexible stance on permitting the United States to bomb terrorist targets within its borders. "Jayyyce. While the Azakistani government is well aware that US Special Operations forces operate within our borders, and while we completely rely on you doing our dirty work for us with the clandestine and very dangerous missions you carry out that save our asses over and over again, we will not permit a foreign airstrike on our sovereign soil because that might make us look like the weak-assed dipshits we are."

Yeah, that about summed it up.

Jace stretched until his joints popped, trying to dispel a growing sense of dread. They hadn't been ordered out, which was good, but they hadn't been given the go-ahead, either. They remained on hold, which became increasingly dangerous as the sandstorm advanced. It was due to hit just west of their area early the next morning. They'd been warned that if they missed their scheduled extraction, there would be no air support until the storm passed.

The churn in Jace's stomach grew worse. That wasn't even considering the worst-case scenario—discovery this far into insurgent-held territory.

The weapons cache had abruptly become a secondary objective with the arrival of the SCUD. Now headquarters was bogged down with communications from outsiders, and information trickled slowly back to his A-Team. God damn it! The longer they lingered, the greater the risk of detection. The greater the risk the terrorists might truck in the SCUD's warhead and launch it. And what if they decided to move it, or to use the stack of munitions to attack US soldiers? His Delta Force team had parachuted in to avoid insurgent security checkpoints. If the trucks rolled out, Jace's team would lose them.

How long could it take to get an expert on the line who could tell them how to destroy the SCUD?

Tag came in and nodded.

"What's happening at the camp?" Jace asked. He rotated his head and worked the kinks out of his shoulders.

"Ol' Omaid is getting the royal treatment. Major brownnosing. There's a platoon's worth of men out there now. Thirty-five, maybe forty. There are five on the SCUD. Mostly it's one big party, with lots of opium pipes being passed around. The guys on the SCUD aren't high. They're alert."

Alex held a radio headset out to Gabe Morgan. "Okay, Archangel. HQ got someone on the horn that it says can give us a crash course in SCUD disassembly."

Jace slipped on one headset. Gabe grabbed the other and keyed the mike. "This is Archangel. Who is this? Over."

"I'm Master Chief Kort Van Roekel from the Naval War College, Monterey. How can I assist? Over."

The voice in Jace's ear sounded remarkably clear. Delta Force always got the best. This radio was a state-of-the-art satellite transceiver, originally designed as part of a combat search-and-rescue system. It gave them crystal-clear worldwide secure communications.

Archangel glanced at Jace, who read his mind and gave a small nod. Yes, the Naval War College would have been read in on their mission. He could speak freely.

"Greetings from sunny Azakistan, Master Chief. Figuratively speaking, anyway. It's dark now." Archangel paused. "We have a small problem. We found ourselves a second-generation SCUD-b. No warhead, just the missile. We'd rather not leave it in the gentle hands of the locals. How do we destroy it, or at the very least disable it?"

There was a pause.

"Roger that, Archangel. I'm going to presume you have a search on for the payload, so I'll cut to the chase. So I know how much detail to go into, what's your general knowledge level on short-range ballistic missiles? Over."

Archangel laughed. "Enough to recognize one."

That wasn't strictly true. Delta operators trained in all sorts of weapons systems, especially ones that had been around as long as the SCUD family had been. Still, if Jace had taught his team anything in his time in SpecOps, it was that it paid to listen.

Van Roekel's voice was grave. "All right, then, listen up." Archangel grabbed his notebook and started writing. "What you need to know up front is it's NBC capable. Nuclear, biological, and chemical, gentlemen. It has a range of three hundred kilometers, although the Iranians have reportedly modified some for a greater range." Van Roekel's voice had the rolling cadence of a longtime military trainer. "It can be launched from any transporter-erector launcher, but usually by a Russian-made artillery truck designated Uragan." He gave Archangel its length, width, and cab height. The size of it was breathtaking. Jace knew; he'd climbed all over one early in his Army career. "Will you recognize one if you see it?"

"Affirmative, Master Chief. Big-ass truck."

There was a snort from the other end. "The probability it has a nuke is pretty small, but you have to consider the possibility. The system isn't all that accurate. Whoever has it is probably looking for a large target. A troop staging area, military installation, airport. Maybe an industrial complex. Any idea where it's headed?"

Archangel shook his head. "Negative."

"Okay. The missile will take an hour, maybe as much as ninety minutes, to finish its launch sequence. With me so far?"

"All the way. Give me the bad news."

The chief took in a breath. "Now it gets complicated. So many countries have modified and improved the SCUD family that there are going to be variables you'll have to see firsthand to know. The missile uses an unsophisticated inertial guidance system, three gyroscopes controlling four fins. The fins only fire for the first minute of climb, hence the lousy accuracy. With me?"

"Yeah, I got you. How do I destroy it? Bottom-line it for me, Master Chief."

The line was silent for a few seconds. "An F-15 or A-10 with a thousand-pound bomb will take care of it, Archangel. But you're talking to me, so I'm guessing that's not happening."

Archangel rubbed the bridge of his nose. "You'd be guessing right. What are our options?"

Jace found himself holding his breath, praying that the next words he heard were not, "You don't have a snowball's chance in hell."

"All right," said Van Roekel. "Let's talk specifics on flight control."

Archangel continued to take notes while the man talked.

Chapter Three

Date: Unknown
Location: Unknown

HEATHER HEARD HIS boots stamping back up the hallway. He snarled at his subordinates as he moved away, but she couldn't make out the words. Wasn't trying to. She simply sagged against the wall, her blindfold blocking out all but a shadow of light. Her continued silence infuriated him, and her body bore the proof of his temper. Her bloody wrists pulled against the rope still binding them, but she was, for the moment, beyond caring.

She didn't know how long she drifted in a haze of pain. Minutes, hours? She tried to stand, but her legs refused to cooperate. Her cramping calves and buttocks burned like fire from the caning. When the beatings started, she'd twisted away from the blows. He simply aimed instead at her vulnerable breasts and belly. Her cries, even muffled by the gag, pleased him.

He was growing more desperate; she could feel it. The longer she held out against his interrogation, the more urgent his questions became and the more punishing his abuse. Why had she been in Eshma? What did she know of Demas Pagonis? Who had she told about the lab? About the Kongra-Gel? About the planned attack?

Heather knew too little to be a threat to their plans. She did not know Demas Pagonis. Her tormentor had been one of three men she'd overheard at an open-air market in Eshma, alluding to some sort of attack. Her visit to the Eshma chief of police to report the conversation had convinced her that someone in his office—possibly the chief himself—was in collusion with those three men. The very next day, her military convoy had been attacked, and her tormentor had killed her friends, choked her into unconsciousness, and brought her here.

He wouldn't believe her, though, even if she offered up information. Her silence kept her alive. So she would remain silent.

Her stomach rebelled. It didn't matter. She hadn't eaten in so long there was nothing left to puke up, but even the dry heaves further exhausted her.

She tried again to get her feet under her, and this time succeeded. Stretching up on her toes, she lifted her arms off the crude hook and slid sideways down the rough stone to half sit, half lie against the wall.

Did anyone know she had survived the ambush? Were they looking for her? Where was her handsome rescuer?

She snorted inwardly. Since when had life given her anything she hadn't worked her ass off to get? She had no one to rely on but herself.

For days, the large man had interrogated her. Tortured her.

Taunted her. Degraded her. Beat her. He hadn't raped her. At least not yet. Every time, he told her that when the sheik arrived, she would be punished like the infidel she was, then killed.

Heather believed him.

She had no idea who this sheik was, had made no progress discovering his identity. In fact, she had been struck so hard for asking, her head had bounced off the wall.

The sound of footsteps outside her prison startled her. Why had he returned? The door to her cell rattled an instant before heavy bootheels scraped against the floor, and he entered. His scent hit her nostrils and her head came up, straining to see through the cloth tied over her eyes. She rose to her feet, keeping the wall at her back. Dizziness swamped her, and her head pounded. She had to fight to keep from dry-heaving again.

The man's hated voice spoke. "The sheik has arrived. He will be ready for you shortly. But first, you must be as clean as a filthy infidel can be. You are dog shit under his boots, and your stench would offend him." Hands reached out to grab her, one on each arm. She tried to pull free, but she was weak. So weak. He'd made sure of it.

Her captors dragged her down a corridor and out into the fresh night air. She inhaled it greedily as a guard shoved her across soft ground and into another building. No, not a building. She had been inside enough tents during her time in the Army to recognize the dusty smell of canvas. The sheik's tent? After a few moments, they jerked her to a halt.

The torn and filthy remnants of her uniform were shredded and yanked from her body. The men laughed and jeered, their hands rough. She couldn't help herself; she cringed away from them like a trapped animal.

She heard the man's voice. "Do it," he ordered someone. Heather steeled herself, braced for a blow. Not knowing, not being able to see, made it so much worse. But, to her utter surprise, the cloth was cut away from her head. Sudden light, after so many hours of darkness, blinded her painfully, and she shut her eyes as hard as she could.

Wetness touched her body, along with softer hands. Gentle hands. A woman's hands. She was being washed. Terror flooded her soul.

She opened her eyes a slit and tried to check out the room. Her vision blurred, her eyes tearing from the sudden change. She blinked several times, trying to bring the room into focus. There were two guards. Two, right? Or four. She could hear them across the room discussing what they would do to her, later, after the sheik was through with her. When it was their turn. God help her.

She would survive it. She *would.*

Pushing down the terror, or at least trying to, Heather blinked again. Her blurry gaze found, unerringly, the huge man, the brutal one, who leaned against the doorjamb. He watched her without moving, without blinking. The white strip of tape across the bridge of his nose contrasted with his dark skin. Hatred and fear warred within her.

Her tormentor's eyes burned hot with lust and hatred. They raked her body. His stare slammed into her like a physical blow, and again she had to fight not to vomit. It just made her tremble with weakness. Memories of his hands on her body warred with the fresh terror of knowing, finally, the waiting was over. For better or worse. He would brutalize her. He wanted to; it was there in his eyes. The sheik, the only reason he had not already raped her, waited for her elsewhere in the compound.

The two women bathing her were embarrassingly thorough. They scrubbed her abrasions and scrapes. Many of them started seeping blood again. One *tsked* in sympathy over her wrists, wiping them as gently as she could around the ropes. Heather barely restrained a scream. They pushed her thighs apart and cleaned her there, too. Her eyes darted to the man, face heating. He had straightened from his slouch against the door, watching intently. Heather had no trouble reading his expression. He wanted her to protest, to struggle against the women. That would be his excuse to intervene, to force her legs apart. She made herself be still, not fight. Her breath shuddered in and out. All right. All right. Focus. Think!

They scrubbed her hair clean, rinsing it by dumping a bucket of water over her head. She choked as water rushed into her nose, coughing and blinking to clear her vision.

At last, the bath was over. The women dabbed perfume on her raw wrists. It stung. They patted more behind her ears and knees, which started the guards arguing again.

"Why prepare her like a woman?" one demanded.

The other sneered. "She is an infidel and not worthy of such respect."

The older woman answered calmly. "I follow the instructions of the sheik, who does not wish to foul himself with the woman's filth. She is, therefore, to be as clean as a pig can be."

The arguing stopped.

Wouldn't foul himself. Would only rape her. The sickness of it started her shivering again. Heather sagged against the thick canvas panel. Make them think she was too weak to resist.

Maybe she was.

"I cannot dress her while she is tied."

The big man snarled and threatened, but, in the end, angrily gave his permission for a guard to slice through the rope binding her wrists.

The knife burned against her raw skin. When the rope parted, the guard yanked it off, and a scream ripped from Heather's throat as the skin embedded in the rope fibers tore free. She collapsed to the floor, her legs unable to hold her.

A long moment later, the agony eased somewhat. The younger woman knelt beside her, sympathy clear on her face. She held a cup to Heather's mouth. The fresh, clean water tasted like heaven. It took all Heather's willpower not to gulp greedily. As it was, she had to stop after a few careful swallows. It churned in her empty stomach, threatening to come back up. The woman— hardly more than a girl, really—waited patiently, allowing her to sip again. The man barked impatiently. The sheik didn't care if she was healthy or not. She could spread her legs for him just as well either way.

When she was clean, dry, and dressed in a burkha, the man jerked his head in the direction of the door. The women hurried out. Each guard took an arm, forcing her back out the canvas doorway. Instead of turning left toward her cell, they turned her right. Heather struggled to stay on her feet. Thankfully, it was dark. Her eyes still burned. The younger guard pulled her into a small room, and she knew immediately these must be the sheik's quarters. Tapestries and hangings covered the walls and floors. Not sumptuous by any means, it was nevertheless a far cry from the austerity of the rest of the compound. The guard pushed her through a sitting room and into the bedroom beyond. Unlike her own rusty cot, this room had a real bed. The full size seemed huge to her after the past few days.

"Sit there," the older guard snapped, pointing to a spot near the sheik's bed. He moved his finger up to the younger guard and glared. "Beat her and tie her to the bed if she gives you any trouble."

Chapter Four

August 16. 1:00 A.M.
Kongra-Gel Terrorist Training Site

JACE CHECKED HIS watch, then scanned the area. Beside him,
Archangel did the same. The camp lay still and silent, save for
the lights inside the sheik's enormous tent. They had worked their
way down the mountainside to a point just above and behind the
building housing the weapons cache. The Kongra-Gel cell had
made the classic M&M mistake—they assumed the hard outer
candy shell of the perimeter guard posts would adequately protect
the soft chocolate innards of the camp itself.

Leaving the rocky outcropping and descending toward the
camp, Jace stayed in the deep shadows. Archangel remained
where he was, rock solid and trusted, sniper rifle braced. He
tracked Jace's movements, keeping overwatch. A few times, Jace
slithered like some great dangerous desert snake to the rear of
the ammo dump. It wasn't even a complete building. On the west
side, invisible to their binoculars, part of the wall had crumbled

or been blasted away. He could see two of the guards through the wall at the front of the building, smoking and talking, weapons slung over their shoulders. He backed up to the other corner, set the explosives, then took one of his grenades and wrapped the spoon—the safety handle—with several intricate knots of wire. He fashioned a loop at the other end and carefully pulled the pin, wrapping a knot around the handle to hold it in place. Once he hung the contraption on the inside of the western wall, gravity would start to pull the wire loose. He had roughly an hour at that point before the safety lever lifted, allowing the primer to explode and ignite the fuse. Three to five seconds later, the grenade would detonate.

A scream rent the air, traveling clearly across the still desert air. Jace froze, every nerve in his body suddenly jangling. A female's cry. One of the women who'd come in with the sheik? He recognized suffering when he heard it. She was in serious pain. His fingers brushed against the picture in his breast pocket. Not her. Thank God, not her.

But someone.

One of the three soldiers dedicated to the SCUD walked into view, and Jace melted into the shadows. The man was a mere thirty feet from him; he walked several yards away from the camp and stopped, not even bothering to glance in the direction of that single scream. A pause, then the sound of his pissing. The man finished, but lingered, leaning against a scrub tree as he lit a cigarette. Jace waited patiently while the man puffed. No muscle so much as twitched. At last, an impatient bark from inside the camp had the man flinging the butt into the dirt, grinding it with his heel, and walking back to his post.

Before anyone could take the guard's place, Jace hung his contraption over the inside of a broken part of the wall, lowering it incrementally and laying each section carefully, one eye on the two guards, who had now stepped a few feet away and could barely be seen. When done, he checked it visually one more time, then slid silently back up the hill to Archangel's position.

Date: Unknown
Location: Unknown

HEATHER SAT WITH her knees drawn up to her chest. Her guard stood by the door for a few minutes; then, watching her carefully lest she spring from the floor and attack him, he sat down, laying his rifle across his lap.

Alone in a room with only one guard.

"What's your name?" she asked him in Arabic.

For a long moment, she thought he would not answer her. Finally, though, he said grudgingly, "Ahmed."

"Ahmed, you know, don't you, that they're going to kill me?"

Again, there was a long pause. "Yes."

"Do you have family? A sister?"

It was the wrong question. Hostility flared in his face. "My family is dead, killed at the hands of Alevi dogs as they begged for their lives."

Heather forced herself to stay calm. "I'm very sorry for your loss."

He spat out a curse.

The Alevi, she knew, were a Shia Muslim minority in Turkey. "Wouldn't you have protected your sister from harm? I know you wouldn't have wished her to go through what I have."

Her question was met with silence. Heather knew she was pushing too hard, but she was out of time. "You know what they're going to do to me. Would you want your sister treated that way?"

"Shut up! You are not my sister." He stood abruptly, raising the rifle. "You will be silent now."

Her head throbbed. The boy might sympathize, but he feared the sheik more than he pitied the plight of an infidel. Her young guard pulled a pack of Camels out of his shirt pocket and lit one. He sucked deeply, letting the smoke stream from his nose. No doubt a trick he had learned from his role models, the stone-cold killers who'd undoubtedly cheer the sheik on as he raped and beat her.

As the minutes turned into more minutes, then still more, Heather examined the room. One window, one door. One guard.

She'd never have a better chance.

"Please, I need to use the facilities," she said, feigning embarrassment.

"No."

Great. Now he was sullen and hostile.

"Please, Ahmed." Heather pressed her legs together, eyes lowered. "I don't want to foul the sheik's sheets. Or . . . or his person." Desperation tinged her tone, but it couldn't be helped.

Sighing loudly, the boy jerked the barrel of the rifle toward a smaller opening, the fabric door dangling loosely. "Be quick."

Okay. Okay. She heaved herself to her feet. Made her way into the tent's small bathroom area on alarmingly shaky legs. She started to zip the door closed.

"Leave it open," Ahmed barked.

She could not forget, she reminded herself sharply, that however young, her guard had probably killed by now. The bathroom area was large enough for a claw-footed tub and a wooden seat arrangement. The faint smell told her it had probably been cleaned in preparation for the sheik's arrival. The single window was tiny and covered in translucent plastic. She wasn't getting out that way.

"Hurry!" snapped Ahmed.

She finished rapidly, pouring water from a pitcher into a bowl to wash her hands. Breath hissed from between her teeth as the water splashed over her wrists like liquid fire. She came out of the bathroom and started across the floor. And tripped and fell heavily in the middle of the room. Please, please, she pleaded silently. Have a shred of decency left. She groaned, not entirely playacting. "Oh, God! I think I broke my ankle!"

Hesitation, then steps. A boot came into her vision. She felt more than saw him draw back his other foot to kick her in the ribs. And she exploded into action. She rolled sharply into his approaching foot, pulling her arms in front of her chest, protecting her ribs. She continued to roll, slamming the front of her own body against his knees, pushing him off balance, trapping his lower legs with one arm. He lost his balance with a surprised grunt. As he fell backwards, she continued on, rolling her back entirely onto his lower legs. She let her own momentum finish the turn, bringing her elbow over her body and down into his groin with all her might. Adrenaline coursing through her, she slammed him again, rolling again so they met chest to chest. His eyes bulged in his head as the first wave of agony hit him.

Without wasting any time, she crossed her hands over his throat, sliding her fingers deep into his collar and rotating her wrists into his neck, executing the reverse cross-hand choke she'd learned in judo. His eyes widened as he realized she had cut off his air. He thrashed hard, emitting hoarse, grunting noises. Heather increased the pressure across his carotid artery, keeping herself centered across his chest. She twisted her wrists even further. It seemed to take forever, but the guard's struggles weakened and finally stopped.

When she sensed he wouldn't spring up and grab her, she loosened her hold and finally relaxed. Trembling, she pressed her fingers to his neck. Yes, there was a pulse. She'd knocked him out, but he was alive.

She ran to the plastic window. Soldiers clustered in groups around the compound, chattering loudly, passing opium pipes back and forth. Some simply sat, staring at the stars and not moving, high on poppies.

Shit. Okay. She could do this.

Scrambling back to the guard, she unbuttoned his shirt, wrenching it down his arms. She tore at his pants, her fingers shaking so much it took her three tries to unbutton his fly. Yanking and jerking them off his hips and down his legs, she realized belatedly she'd have to take his boots off first. Mentally cursing, straining to hear any movement from the hallway outside the door, she unlaced them, pulling them off.

The stench of the unwashed uniform hit the back of her throat, nearly causing another round of dry heaves. Heather breathed shallowly through her nose, not hesitating one iota as she pulled on his pants and shirt. Unwrapping his turban, she twisted it awkwardly around her own head, pulling it across the lower half of her face. She stuffed her feet into the boots, then reached down and pulled the socks off his feet. Shoving them into a pocket, she returned to the window. She waited, her heart pounding triple time in her chest, until no guards remained close enough to hear before unzipping the window.

She wanted to freeze. To listen. Instead, she forced herself into action. She had mere minutes to make this work. Someone would check on her, find her gone, and all hell would break loose. She picked up the light assault rifle and popping the magazine. Full. A nice bonus. If she couldn't get clear, she could at least take some of them with her before she died.

Back at the window, she waited, every nerve jumping, until the only guard turned his back to her, and she wriggled headfirst out the window. Tucking and rolling, the action on the rifle neverthe-less smacked her chin, causing a ringing in her head. She came up onto one knee, finger on the safety of the rifle. Nobody shouted alarms or warnings.

So far, so good.

A guard came around the corner, weaving and muttering to himself. He took a drag off the bong in his hand, walked right past her, then wobbled to a halt. Turning, he waved it at her.

"Hey! Want some?"

Quaking from head to foot, Heather stood and shook her head, and made a you-go-on wave with her hand. The guard hesitated for another nerve-shattering moment, then shrugged and continued on. Not long after, he stumbled to another halt and half leaned his head against a building. After a moment, Heather heard splashing as he urinated.

Act natural. One of the guys.

Straightening her shoulders, she stepped away from the build-ing, using every ounce of self-control she possessed to amble. She carried the rifle loosely, barrel down, as she had seen the others do.

Slowly. Don't run. Don't. Run.

She cut a path as directly as she could toward the north end of the camp, away from the enormous tent, toward a scrub of trees.

Keep away from the guard's hut to her left. What looked like a barracks squatted off to her right; stay away from it, as well. Maybe fifteen minutes had passed since the women had washed her. Too much time. Too little time. She needed to be as far away from the camp as possible before the sheik came for her.

Measured steps. Stagger a little, as though high on poppies.

You can do it, she chanted to herself, each step taking her closer to freedom.

At last, she reached the edge of the trees. As she stepped in, she barked her shin. Heather swallowed the cry of pain, forcing herself to stand silent and let her eyes adjust to the night. So far, so good.

The night exploded into chaos.

Chapter Five

August 16. 1:15 A.M.
Kongra-Gel Terrorist Training Site

HIS METICULOUS PLAN to disable the SCUD and blow the munitions sky-high without detection was chucked abruptly out the window as an enraged bellow carried clearly across the compound. A burly man hurtled out of the sheik's huge tent, screaming at the guards, shoving and shouting. A young man wearing nothing but a loincloth as underwear followed much more slowly. Men came onto full alert, scurrying to fix whatever had gone wrong. When flashlights materialized and began sweeping the area, Jace knew they had to act fast.

A handful of insurgents spilled from the main tent and scurried toward the barracks, where lights began to pop on. The compound turned into chaos as soldiers swarmed back and forth like beetles.

Jace clicked his headset twice. "Do it, guys. Do it now."

Refusing to give in to the sudden doubts—uncertainty could

get his men killed—he sprinted toward one of the two insurgents at the ammo bunker. The man never saw him coming. Jace slid up behind him, clamping a hand over his mouth as he efficiently slit his throat. Not far away, Archangel did the same to another guard. Jace let the body drop to the ground as he darted inside the ammo bunker. A quick glance told him exactly where to rig his grenades. Next to their box of hand grenades.

Automatic gunfire ripped through the compound. Their teammates had engaged the enemy.

"Move," he ordered Archangel. "We need to get to the SCUD, now. That's the first thing they're going to try to protect."

The two operators zigzagged their way across the rocky terrain, joining the firefight with Sandman and Mace before breaking off for the SCUD. Behind them, their grenades blew, followed by larger and larger explosions. The ammunition began to cook off, the *pop-pop-pop* almost lost in the racket. Whatever had been in there—rocket-propelled grenades, rifles, and a buttload of ammo, by all reports—could no longer be used to kill American soldiers.

Across the compound, three explosions ripped the air, one on top of the other. Jace wished he could watch fire and brimstone rain down on these terror mongers as chaos exploded in the camp. One charge had detonated near the sheik's tent, setting the heavy canvas ablaze. The other two blew apart the flimsy wooden barracks at the far end of the compound. Five or six insurgents staggered out of the wreckage, disoriented and bleeding, tripping the wire across the door. The Claymore anti-personnel mine fired a curtain of seven hundred steel balls at a velocity of four thousand feet per second. The surviving soldiers fell, decimated by the barrage.

More men charged from buildings and the sheik's tent, half-dressed, searching for their attackers from behind vehicles and other concealment.

Leaving their teammates to engage the enemy, Jace and Archangel raced down the steep incline and over to the SCUD. Jace kept his weapon up and ready as Archangel studied the strapped-on guidance system for a few seconds. They had only once chance at this. Without a guidance system, the ballistic missile could not be launched. However, the missile stretched almost thirty-seven feet long, and the guidance system rested just below where the warhead should have been. Would be, if they did not disable the missile. Jace covered his six while Archangel took the rest of the C-4 and shaped his charge, then clambered onto the vehicle's back wheels to set it.

A vehicle roared to life. It was the sheik's own Jeep. The Sheik and a large man, as well as two soldiers, dove into the vehicle. Another soldier raced toward them, motioning for them to stop, and the vehicle barely avoided hitting him as it roared down the dirt road. Jace and Archangel turned and ran straight up the hill, reaching the lip and tumbling over it just as the C-4 blew. It pushed Jace the rest of the way to the ground as hands grabbed his uniform and dragged him behind the rocks where Alex and Sandman knelt.

"Cut it a little close, don't ya think?" yelled Sandman, pausing to swap out his magazine.

"It was perfection," said Jace, grinning like a maniac. His blood pumped, and adrenaline roared like fire through his body. He peered back down to the SCUD. The flight guidance system lay in wrecked fragments across the desert floor. "Mace, take out the Jeep."

Mace unstrapped the LAW—light antitank weapon—and

snapped it open. If they fired it immediately, it would blow the Jeep, and anyone in it, straight to hell. Mace set it onto his shoulder and sighted through it. Three bullets pinged off the rock next to him in rapid succession. Shards of rock sprayed, one hitting Mace's face. He flinched. His shot went wide, exploding harmlessly near the Jeep, which raced its engine and roared out of sight. He swore, loudly and inventively.

Below them, the insurgents rallied. "Time to boogedy," said Archangel. The four started running east, up the hillside and away from the camp.

Jace keyed his mike. "Break off, guys. Rally point bravo. Let's get the hell out of Dodge."

Chapter Six

UNDER NORMAL CIRCUMSTANCES, Jace would not doubt their ability to evade the enemy soldiers milling in the dark. By the time they organized and began to search in earnest, the A-Team would be safely on board a bird and flying back to Camp Delta.

Still. The terrorists could get lucky. It had happened before.

Before his mind could conjure up an image of his former teammate Dougie's bloodied corpse, he forced himself back into the here and now. Once they left the burning camp behind, he and Archangel snapped their night vision goggles into place.

"We wanna know what they were searching for inside the camp? No way did they make us." Archangel jerked a thumb back toward camp.

"Not our business," Jace answered. "We disabled the SCUD and blew the munitions. Our job now is to get to the landing zone before our ride goes home for dinner."

Archangel looked like he wanted to argue, but finally just shook his head and shouldered his rucksack. In silence, they moved out toward their predesignated rally point. Once they linked up with the rest of their team, who would take a different route to throw off any pursuers, they would hoof it back to the landing zone and meet their extraction helicopter.

Despite his answer to Archangel, the sudden furor in the camp tickled at the back of his skull. His Arabic was barely adequate. Earlier, the guards had gossiped about al-Hassid's latest . . . pig. Maybe. Most Muslims did not eat pork. Maybe he'd gotten the translation wrong. Yes, in retrospect, he probably had the wrong noun; the terrorists later had speculated when it, or a pincushion, would be gifted to them. They probably would not be as excited about a pincushion. Maybe it was pork, after all. Too bad he hadn't seen a bunch of mangy terrorists chasing around after a pig; that would have been amusing.

Thanks to whatever put the terrorists into a tizzy, he could not stick around and watch the detonations, which annoyed him. He loved a good explosion.

Archangel took up the rear, guarding their six. They reached the designated meeting spot and immediately secured it. They settled in to wait for the rest of the team. It would take the yokels a while to get organized enough to search for whoever blew up their precious, newly-acquired munitions.

It therefore seemed only fair to Jace, who was already pissed his flawless op had not gone flawlessly, that one guard had miraculously, or through blind, pig-shit luck, followed them from the compound. True, he floundered through the sparse trees like a blind hippopotamus, but he came straight at them.

Jace's team appeared around him, part of the shadows, and

melted completely into the darkness at his hand signal. They hadn't followed a trail. How could this guy have found them? The moon barely glimmered, and he didn't appear to wear night vision goggles. Jace saw that the man carried the standard-issue AK-47. He winced in sympathy as the man whacked his head against a low branch. He fell over backwards and lay still for a moment. Jace let himself hope the man had passed out. No such luck. He crawled to his feet again, holding his head. It might have been funny if they didn't have a chopper to catch.

The man hobbled forward again. How in hell had he followed them while high? No way, Jace knew. The guy was probably lost, looking for the compound. He grimaced again as the man bumbled toward his spot. The poor sap would pass within inches of him. With Jace's luck, he'd stop to take a leak on his head.

The man swayed again as he came near Jace's patch of earth. And looked right at him.

HEATHER PUT A hand to her throbbing skull. Her concussion roared back to life, vision going blurry and her concentration shot. The starvation and beatings had taken their toll; her ribs ached, breathing hurt, and something in her abdomen burned. That worried her more than anything else. The grapefruit-sized bruise on her left side and the throbbing made her afraid she might have some internal injuries. And between the last log she'd tripped over and the branch that had nearly brained her, her body had become a churn of conflicting miseries. She was stumbling over the landscape, unable to see well, relying on instinct to get her away from the pursuit coming from the compound.

Something made her stop. She peered at the deep shadows, nostrils flaring to catch a scent of the danger she sensed all around her. There didn't seem to be anything there, but she trusted her gut. Backing away, she turned to run.

A muttered curse and a change in air pressure were her only warnings before a heavy weight smashed into her, tripping her and slamming her to the ground. She smacked down forcefully, head bouncing off the hard-packed earth, breath leaving her lungs in a squeaky *whoosh*. Her attacker rode her down, crushing her ability to roll away, his breath hot on her neck. A wave of dizziness washed over her from the blow to her head, her injuries exploding to painful life from the force of the impact.

Before she could recover, her assailant wrapped a forearm under her neck, ruthlessly yanking her head back, exposing her throat. She whimpered helplessly as she felt the cold edge of steel against her throat. Heather closed her eyes, unable to suppress another squeaky noise as she prepared to feel her life's blood leave her.

The blade shivered against her skin, but the pain didn't come. And still didn't come. Finally, the tension against her jugular lessened.

The weight on her back shifted. Heather felt a face push into her neck and heard an inhale. He was smelling her. A flash of hope opened her eyes. Her bath! Beneath Ahmed's filthy uniform, her attacker smelled the sweeter scent of perfume and soap, and it confused him.

He shifted over her, his much larger frame enveloping her. Before he could discount what his senses were telling him, she began to babble in Arabic.

"Please don't kill me! Please don't kill me! I'm not a soldier. I stole this uniform. I'm a woman. I didn't belong in that camp." Blind panic pushed the plea from her throat. She was speaking so quickly that her words ran together, but she didn't care.

Finally, *finally,* the cold steel left her throat. His forearm, still pulling her head back at an awkward angle, tightened, cutting off her breath. His other hand felt along her chest, finding her un-bound breasts through the uniform top she wore. The hand jerked away, hesitated, then fumbled lower, cupping her pubis. The man snatched his fingers away like they'd been lit on fire.

"You gonna take 'im to the prom? Let's go, Jace." A second man had come back and now squatted beside them.

"Holy fuck!" the man on top of her breathed.

"What is it?" the second man asked. "We gotta go."

English! They were speaking English! As she opened her mouth to speak, to reveal herself, to beg for help, the man clamped a hard hand over her jaw and shifted back onto his knees, pull-ing her up with him until her back rested against his front. On her knees, bent back at an awkward angle, she could not gain any leverage. But she wasn't fighting to get away. She struggled to drag air into her lungs past his hand. Spots began to appear in front of her eyes. Panic flared as life-giving air eluded her. Her desperate movements against the man's chest grew fainter as her strength waned. As she struggled, little whimpering noises tore from the back of her throat.

"Hold still," he snapped in Arabic. "Settle down, now. I'll let my hand up, but you need to settle down." He switched to Eng-lish, head twisting to look at his teammate. "I think we found the woman ol' Omaid's so pissed about losing," he said.

The other voice was startled. "Woman?"

He eased his hold on her mouth and throat, and she fell to her hands and knees, great huge rasping gulps of air pulling into her lungs as fast as she could.

"Slow down," the man said. "You'll hyperventilate."

Heather barely heard him through the roaring in her ears. Between her concussion and the choke hold he'd put her in, she struggled just to stay conscious. She stayed on all fours, forearms resting in the dirt and her head on the backs of her hands.

Someone else materialized out of the blackness. "Tick tock, boss."

Heather froze along with everyone else as she heard movement through the woods. Shit. The terrorists had rallied and were now searching for her. And for these men, presumably the ones who'd blown up the camp.

Large male hands touched her head scarf, then withdrew. "Hey," the man said. "You okay?"

Without these men, she was as good as caught. Before she could take a breath to beg, she heard the sweetest words she could imagine.

"We'll take her with us."

"THE FUCK?" SANDMAN expressed it for all of them. "You nuts, Jace? She'll slow us way down. She's just some whore. Cut her loose."

Jace felt a flare of anger at his teammate. But the Sandman couldn't know what Jace did. This woman was no Azakistani, short of stature and broad of hip and shoulder. This woman was tall and willowy. He stood, dragging her with him, keeping her flush against his body, one arm snaked around her waist, the other cupping her chin, thumb across her mouth, tacitly warning her not to make a sound. Despite the mere sliver of moon, despite the keffiyeh—the traditional male Arabic head scarf—Jace looked into her eyes and knew her.

Heather Langstrom. He'd seen those eyes enough times as he

stared at her photo, recognized the body against his from watching her.

He'd found her! Against the odds, against all likelihood, she had appeared as though he'd conjured her with his pipe dreams. His heart leapt and pounded so forcefully she must be able to feel it. He hugged her to him, too late realizing she would misinterpret the gesture. Sure enough, she recoiled from him.

Be professional, Reed. You know what you have to do.

"Stand still. I have to search you. Standard practice." Friendly or not, she was not part of his team and might be carrying God-knew-what without even realizing it. A radio, a tracking device, explosives. Jace tried to remain impersonal and thorough, his hands now feeling carefully what he had merely passed over previously. Her breasts were unbound inside the filthy uniform top, and she wasn't wearing any underwear.

The sounds of pursuit grew louder. Closer. They had to move, and fast. His hands became rougher as he hurried. She clamped her legs together as he felt down each one, small animal whimpers reaching him as she shrank from him. Growling, he nevertheless smothered his frustration and tried to gentle his hands. She had just been through hell. But he needed to search her for everyone's safety, and if they didn't get the hell out of there, he wouldn't be able to protect her. He dug into her pockets and pulled out a pair of socks. He handed them to Tag, who felt through them carefully before thrusting them into his own fatigue pants. Okay. No weapons, no booby traps. She was clean.

Jace relaxed fractionally, suddenly very aware of the way she twisted and flinched. His agitation, the imperative to bolt, evaporated. He abruptly hated making her afraid. What had those bastards done to her? He was a total shithead.

Now that he was done with his search, she stood quietly, her breathing less panicked, but he could feel her heart slamming against her ribs in triple time. She was scared, but he couldn't take the time to reassure her. Explaining who he was would take too long. The enemy was on them.

He gestured sharply for the team to deploy around him. They—good men—obeyed instantly. Jace spun her around in his arms, hands cupping her shoulders as he peered into her eyes.

Aw, hell.

Confusion, fear, and suspicion swam in their depths. Her unfocused look worried him. How bad were her injuries? He put his lips to her ear and whispered, in as commanding a voice as he could, "You do what I say, when I say it. Understand? I promise I'll get you to safety." Hopefully, her military training would force her to react instinctively to his commands.

Her eyes flared in renewed fear, her eyes darting toward the soldiers they could now see. Who could now see them, if they looked in the right direction. The trembling in her limbs increased as she nodded frantically.

"Good. Let's roll."

Without another word, they moved out.

Chapter Seven

August 16. 2:50 A.M.
Somewhere in Sari Daru Province, Azakistan

HEATHER FOUGHT THE waves of exhaustion coursing through her. The adrenaline of her escape had morphed seamlessly into bowel-emptying terror as the man had slammed her to the ground and bared her throat to his knife. To kill her. Without hesitation or mercy. She had tasted utter helplessness as the blade hit her throat, known she was dead. But he'd stopped. Leaned forward to smell her hair. And—her face flushed anew—he had verified for himself what his senses had told him. His search had been humiliating.

So much for a rescue. The man bore no resemblance to her dream hero. No American flag sewn to his uniform's sleeve. No unit patches, no name tag. Dark green and black streaks camouflaging his face and night vision goggles attached to his helmet and snapped into place over his eyes obscured his features. Dark hair, matted with sweat, curled out from under his helmet. Instead of being swept into the arms of her rescuer, she'd been slammed to the ground and had his knife thrust under her jaw, preparing to slash.

But he hadn't killed her.

And he was taking her away from the compound.

For now, that was enough. And she was grateful. But who were these men? What were they doing out here, blowing up the camp like that? They were American, but they didn't talk or act like any military unit she'd ever seen deployed, despite the combat uniforms and camouflage paint streaking their faces.

Thousands of independent security personnel crowded the country, protecting business executives and high-ranking government agents. Fewer but still there, bands of mercenaries infested the Middle East, paid killers for hire. If they worked for cash, they could as easily sell her back to the warlord for a reward once their own lives weren't in danger; or, they could simply kill her for being able to identify them and for knowing where they had been. Her gaze darted back and forth, but she couldn't seem to focus. She was no safer with them than she had been at the compound. Was she? She wrapped an arm around her middle. Confusion swirled through her mind, a fogginess with which she had become all too familiar over the past few days. Her concussion, acting up again. The fall that bounced her head against the ground hadn't helped. The jerky movements as they marched jarred her head, tightening the hard bands around her skull until she thought she might scream from the pain.

All right. She took a deep breath to settle herself. For now, she was putting distance between herself and the sheik, and that was good. They thought she was a Muslim woman. The darkness of night had worked in her favor, blurring her features and turning her auburn hair dark. And the big man—Jace—had spoken to her in Arabic. She could use that to her advantage. She would find out who they were and what they were up to. And, when she found the opportunity, she would slip away from them and make her way back to Ma'ar ye zhad.

She quivered with fatigue and dizziness. The past days of fear, starvation, and abuse robbed her of strength. The pace these men set would have been taxing under normal circumstances. Now, with her bare feet sliding around inside the leather boots she'd stolen from Ahmed, she could barely keep up. Her attacker-cum-savior had tucked her hand into one of the loops of his rucksack. She understood. He knew their destination; she did not. By attaching her to himself, he could move much faster.

Gritting her teeth, Heather stretched her legs and kept up.

SHE WAS DISTRACTING as hell. The perfume he'd detected behind her ears teased Jace's senses even through the funk of the uniform she wore, and her hand kept brushing his arm or shoulder as she fought to keep her balance. Once she grabbed his butt to keep herself upright. She'd wrenched her arm back as soon as she realized what she'd done.

If anything about this had been remotely funny, he would have laughed. At this slow pace, they wouldn't make their rendezvous, which meant delays, recoordination, and a pissed-off troop leader. Once the sandstorm made its appearance, they would be stuck for its duration. Their route took them into the mountains, with the ascent slowing them even more. Shit, even the sliver of moonlight worked against them. They could be detected as they crested the ridges.

They'd only made it three miles from Omaid al-Hassid's training camp. Not nearly far enough to risk stopping. Still, Jace could feel Heather faltering behind him. She stumbled several times and finally lost her grip on his rucksack. Going down on her knees, she simply stayed that way, head bent, hands braced on her thighs as she sucked in air. Then, suddenly, she lurched sideways and doubled over, retching and heaving. Mace, the team medic, knelt beside her, speaking to her in a low voice, holding her hair, taking her pulse. The rest of the team set up a quick perimeter, weapons pointed outward.

Jace gestured for the medic to report.

He came over to Jace, speaking barely above a whisper as he relayed the bad news. "She says she just needs a minute, then can go on, but I doubt she could take another step. Looks like someone's been using her as a punching bag, but I can't see the full extent of her injuries," Mace said.

Jace's shoulders tightened. "Fucking bastards."

"Plus, she says she hit her head in a car accident," Mace added. "She's concussed. We have to get her to a hospital before we cause permanent brain damage."

Concussion. Terrific. Well, that explained the unfocused confusion he'd noted in her eyes. Did she even remember what had happened? Who she was? Memory loss was common with contusion to the head. They needed to be very careful not to traumatize her further. He cursed himself again for his rough handling.

God, what else had they done to her? Fuckers. Did she remember any of it?

"And boss? She's speaking English. Is she . . ."

Jace made a shut-up gesture, and his teammate snapped his mouth closed, a curious look on his face. "Why?"

"We don't know any of the trauma she's been through, or how fragile her mental state is. I'll be damned if we cause a breakdown or some shit. It's possible she has amnesia, and we could just confuse or frighten her. She's trying to pretend, or maybe even believes, she's Arabic. For now, let's just go along with it, okay? Above all else, we need to keep her calm. And thinking only about what we're doing, here and now. Can't afford her to be distracted. Or us, either."

"Roger that. We need to keep moving, though."

"I'll carry her," Jace decided.

Mace returned to Heather's side. "We'll take turns. We'll be able to make up time." He offered Heather his hand.

As she reached up to take it, they heard it. Voices. Lots of them. Then jingling. Lights, faint, moving toward them. As one, the team froze.

And, just like that, their night went from bad to worse.

Whoever they were, they came down the mountain Jace's team was trying to go up. With only shallow gullies and ridges, and a few stubby trees, they had no real cover. Alone, his men could have melted into the night. With an injured Heather . . .

Jace counted a dozen of them. Motioning his men sharply to the left and right, he did not wait to see them scatter. He signaled to their left thirty meters, where he thought he could see a rocky outcropping. The team surged upward, bent over to keep a low profile. A shade too late, they reached the outcropping and saw that the overlapping rocks made a shallow cave, of sorts. Jace heard shouting behind them, the sound of running, a few wild shots.

Jace pushed Heather inside. She wriggled farther into the opening. It was little more than a low hole, longer than it was wide and angled down into the earth. Archangel made a hand signal. *I'll draw them off.* Jace shook his head. He would lead this new band of insurgents away. Archangel leaned forward to speak directly into his ear.

"You make too big a target, Godzilla. And anyway, you're a pussy. My grandmother's poodle is faster than you. I'll lead them in circles for a while. When I get bored, I'll come back and pick you up." With that, he was gone.

Not hesitating now, Jace pulled the quick-release tabs on his ruck, set it in front of the overhang, and arranged shrubbery and rocks around it, creating a blind. Archangel—Gabe Morgan—would die rather than let any harm come to his teammates. Jace and Heather were as safe as it was possible to be under these circumstances. Unslinging his weapon, he went into their hidey-hole feet first, sliding horizontally under the rock overhang. It was a tight squeeze. The overhang gave them a space maybe seven feet across but nine or ten feet deep. The hole sloped slightly; it was like sliding into a sleeping bag. Heather squirmed to one side, but stopped when he began to push in next to her.

"Don't be afraid," he whispered, in Arabic. "I won't let them near you."

She hesitated, and for a moment, he worried she was going to panic. Wouldn't that be just perfect, if she turned out to be afraid of small spaces. But she moved aside, and he slid in beside her.

They lay practically nose to nose, their bodies pressed together in the tight space. Outside, Archangel and the others led the insurgents away. He could hear the shouts, the weapons firing. His teammates yelling and returning fire, just to keep 'em coming. For a brief second, he wished he were out there with them. Then he touched a single finger to Heather's shoulder. She startled and shrank in on herself, and he withdrew it, avoiding her gaze lest he give something away. His men could take care of themselves. But Heather . . . Heather was his to protect.

Gradually, the sounds faded into the distance.

HEATHER LAY STILL, squashed against Jace's body. Maybe she'd die tonight, after all. It seemed impossible these few men would be able to elude the dozens she'd seen coming down the mountainside, no doubt hostile Kurdish guerrillas. If the rebels found them, they might all be killed, or she could be recaptured. And she would be right back where she'd started.

These men, though. They kept her with them; they were protecting her, even now. Something inside her relaxed fractionally. They might not be heroes, but maybe she'd be rescued, after all.

It all caught up with her in an instant. The ambush. Her dead comrades. The pain and fear she had endured while captured, her flight from the compound. Her narrow escape from death. Too much adrenaline, too many times. She began to tremble and couldn't stop. Bringing her hands up to press over her mouth, she tried to stop, tried to regain control. It was impossible. She shook so hard she thought she might break apart. Tears welled up, spilling over so hard and fast she could no longer see. She pressed her face hard into his chest, knowing silence was paramount, that she could not allow any noise to give away their position. They had no idea who might still be out there.

His arms came around her, pulling her in closer to his warmth. Surprisingly, he rubbed over her back in soothing circles. The gentle touch struck her as bizarrely at odds with the camouflage paint streaking his face, which made him look feral and primitive. One hand came up to stroke her hair. He seemed to understand. He put his lips right up to her ear, and whispered in Arabic, "Breathe. From your diaphragm. In through your nose, out through your mouth. That's it. Again. It's just stress. You're all right. Breathe. In. Out. Again."

She latched onto the sound of his voice with thready desperation. She clutched at him. He tightened his hold, murmuring to her over and over again to breathe. He held her until the spasms started to ease.

It seemed to take forever for the trembling to subside. Heather's face suffused with humiliation. *Way to be tough, Langstrom. Prove the assholes right about women being too soft for combat.* Disgust dripped like bile in the back of her throat. And then exhaustion rolled over her like a tidal wave, carrying her under. Against all odds, she fell asleep.

WASN'T THAT THE damnedest thing? Jace couldn't be sure if she'd passed out or fallen asleep. Either way, it made it easier to listen to the night sounds, to make sure none of the little band of miscreants had circled back around to pick up a goat or something. Keeping Heather safe had become his number one priority.

She hadn't made a sound the entire time. Jesus! She was strong. Disciplined. He couldn't help but be impressed that she understood how vital absolute silence was. She'd controlled herself, even in the midst of her meltdown. He rubbed a hand over his face. What the hell had she been through?

He tried to remain professional. Tried not to notice how nicely she fit into his arms. And the fact he couldn't ignore it pissed him off. Now that she slept, her body soft against his, his body came alive. All he could do was grit his teeth and think of his new mission objective. What the hell was he thinking, even having remotely sexual thoughts about this woman?

Fuckers. He wished he could go back and kill them all over again.

Mentally circling back to the compound, Jace tried to puzzle out her presence there. Now that he thought of it, he needed to question her. Something important had been planned, some sort of attack involving the SCUD. She might know something about it. But forcing her to relive God-knew-what could have a devastating impact on her mental stability. He let his head drop back, his helmet thumping against the dirt and stone of their hiding place. Sand trickled inside his collar as duty and compassion warred inside him. What should he do?

As Heather slept, Jace found himself wishing he could see her face. She continued to keep the scarf covering all but her shuttered eyes. His fingers grazed the edge of the keffiyeh. Heather Langstrom. Her name sang softly through his head. Something about her flashing eyes and stubborn chin appealed to him. She had been the source of most of his fantasies since he first saw her at the Base Exchange. Having her nestled against him woke all sorts of protective instincts. Her fingers on his chest, her hair tangled on his cheek brought out the male in him.

He turned his head and put her firmly out of his mind, concentrating instead on the problem of rendezvousing with their ride. It was four in the morning. The sandstorm supposedly would pass south of them, but luck had not been with them on this mission. Assuming it was possible to reschedule a bird to fly them home, could they still get out ahead of the sandstorm? Jace combed through his mental map of the area. If they ended up being stuck here, south toward the coast was the safest egress.

Heather twitched, then began to shiver. Tiny mewls of distress churned from her throat as she slept. He rubbed her back, hoping to calm her into silence. She arched away from his touch, which caused her breasts to press into his chest. As nice as that felt, he shook her awake, placing his hand across her mouth. The insurgents were gone, but screams would carry across the desert.

She jerked awake, crying out beneath his hand, her eyes crazed. She began to flail, striking at his face and eyes with her nails.

"Settle down," he said. "It's me." He said it in English, although that might not reassure her considering he had almost killed her. He switched to Arabic, hoping to calm her. "You're safe. They're gone." He banded his arms around hers and simply held on, ensuring she wouldn't hurt herself or him.

Her breath whooshed out and her body went limp, her head dropping forward onto his chest. He took his hand away. She used the edge of the scarf to wipe her face. All rational thought fled as she lifted her head from his chest. At the same moment, he looked down at her, and their noses bumped. Both froze. Jace's brain short-circuited. The sudden urge to kiss her was intense. What would she smell like fresh from her own shower? How soft would her skin feel against his?

What the hell was he thinking?

He saw his hands reach out to pull the keffiyeh away from her face, and, stunned, had to force his hands into stillness as they gripped the very edge of the scarf. No way was he doing this. His gaze locked with hers, and he knew he'd failed to conceal his sudden desire when her eyes widened. Expecting her to jerk away at any moment, he forced his fingers to release the coarse material. She continued to stare at him, neither moving forward nor back. They lay squashed together, frozen by the impossibility of it all.

Jace raised a finger, gently touching a stray curl at her ear and tucking it back into her scarf. She trembled against him, and he immediately pulled back. He held himself still, afraid of frightening her. She had to know she was safe with him.

His eyes drifted to half-mast as he pressed back against the cave wall, giving her as much space as possible. However, in his imagination, when he leaned back, her hand grazed his chin, tracing his jaw and cheek. He imagined her welcoming his touch, enjoying the press of his lips against the inside of her wrist, then again at her mouth. Their tongues sliding together. His hands tangling in her mass of soft curls. Tracing down the delicate lines of her throat with open mouthed, hot kisses. Her back bowing, head thrown back in pleasure.

A tiny rattle of stones outside their small cave jerked him out of his insane fantasy. Quick as a snake, he coiled onto his back, flipping his rifle up and training it on the opening.

A soft chirring noise made him relax fractionally. He returned the call, only lowering his weapon when his pack was tugged aside and Tag's unmistakable bulk filled the opening.

"We're clear. Let's rock and roll," he said.

Jace took in a lot of air and let it out slowly, trying to get his racing pulse and inflamed body under control. Unable to see her clearly in the darkness, he reached out to touch Heather's shoulder. She seemed to shrink in on herself.

"No," she whispered.

Jace pulled himself out of their hidey-hole and turned to help her. She ignored his offered hand, wriggling out and scrambling to her feet, turned completely away from him as she wrapped the scarf over her nose and mouth, shoulders hunched.

Jace frowned. Was she scared? There was no time to reassure her. She was safe. And they had a chopper to catch.

"We're meeting at the landing zone. Sandman called in for a ride, but we have to hurry. The storm turned north. It'll be here in less than an hour," Tag said.

Jace shouldered his rucksack, his heart still pounding double time. What bothered him more than his intense awareness of

Heather Langstrom was his almost total lack of professionalism. He'd practically forgotten everything—that he was in dangerous territory, surrounded by hostile Kurds, and, worst of all, that he was supposed to be protecting her. Jesus! If the sergeant major could see him now, he'd kick his sorry ass from one end of Fort Bragg to the other. And he'd deserve it.

"Let's go," Jace said curtly. He turned to lead the way and marched several yards before he realized the other two lagged behind. He turned around. Tag guarded their six. Heather struggled over the rough ground, pain etched in her eyes and posture, though, once again, no sound passed her lips. His long strides took him back to her side.

"What's wrong?"

The woman shook her head, speaking in Arabic. "Nothing. I can keep up."

"Well, you're not," he answered in the same language, more gruffly than he'd intended.

She jerked her head up, eyes blazing. "I will," she hissed. "Give me my socks."

And, just like that, he understood. She had grabbed her captor's socks, but had stuffed her feet into the boots and run. Tag had taken her socks when they'd searched her. And then they had dragged her on a three-mile hike over rocky terrain, in the dark, with her feet sliding around, unprotected, inside too-large boots. Her feet must be raw hamburger.

"I'll carry you," he said.

She shook her head, backing away from him. "No."

He swore. Looked at Tag. "How long before we need to be at the LZ?"

Tag checked his watch, unflappable as always. "Twenty-eight minutes and counting."

Jace held out a hand, and Tag dug the socks out of his pocket and passed them over. He pulled the quick-release tabs on his ruck, and Tag did the same. Quickly, efficiently, they sat her down and pulled off her boots. Tag broke open his first aid kit and pulled out a couple Kotex, and they covered her many bleeding blisters with antiseptic and the soft pads. Jace flipped open a knife and hacked a T-shirt in half. Each took one half, grabbed a foot, wrapped it in the cloth, and covered it with two pairs of thick socks. They ignored her protests and laced her boots for her. Tag muttered a quick, "No offense, ma'am, but we can do it quicker." In less than five minutes, they jumped up and continued down the trail.

Heather still moved stiffly, but kept up with the slower pace. Jace did some quick calculations. If they could squeeze some more speed out of her, they would make it, just barely. She had guts, he had to admit. As he increased his pace, so did she, without complaint, though he knew her feet must be killing her. The padding would help, but he knew how painful open sores could be.

They crept to the crest of a large hill, lying flat to scan the valley leading to their exit point. An unearthly hush covered the landscape. The hairs on the back of Jace's neck stood on end. He laid a hand on Tag's forearm. *Wait,* he signaled. Tag stopped immediately.

Jace wasn't sure what nagged at him. Every sense strained, but nothing seemed amiss. He trusted his gut, though, and his gut shrieked a warning.

He heard the wind the same time Tag did. It rose from the eerie silence like the voice of God. They watched with a kind of fatalistic amusement as an enormous wall of sand crested the far mountains and began to swirl at the far end of the valley.

Tag swore. Jace agreed with him, but he didn't waste his breath. "Tell the team to find shelter," he barked. "Go back to the damned Kongra-Gel camp if you have to. We need . . ." He cut himself off as a group of men topped the ridgeline, not fifty feet from them. Weapons out, they swept from left to right, on the hunt. "Shit! They're coming this way." The two operators became part of the landscape. Jace cursed as he realized Heather hugged the ground, but didn't seem to realize she was in the open and visible. He rolled to his feet and gripped her arm. Shouts from behind assured him they'd been spotted.

Jace tugged her to her feet and they bolted, zigzagging across the hard-packed earth until Jace realized this new group was not shooting at them. Instead, they maneuvered to cut them off. Capture them. Oh, no. No, no, no. Wasn't going to happen, not if he had to kill a thousand of them.

Never again.

He increased his pace, dragging Heather behind him like the string on a kite. She matched him stride for stride, the urgency of the situation clear to her. He spared a moment to admire her for ignoring the pain in her feet to do what had to be done.

Behind him, Tag opened up on the enemy, scattering them and giving Jace a precious few seconds. He plunged deeper into the shadows of the brush lining the lower parts of the hillside and pulled Heather to his side. Much more slowly now, they crept through the concealment. Behind him, he could hear her harsh breathing. He slid his hand under her hair to pull her close. She resisted for a moment, then leaned forward. He whispered into her ear, "Slow your breathing. In through your nose, out through your mouth. From the diaphragm, just like before." She nodded, gulping a few times before she got the rhythm.

"What about your friend?" she whispered back. In English.

"He can take care of himself." Hey, now. Maybe her mental muzziness was clearing. Being able to communicate openly with her would be a huge help.

He led her through the brush.

Chapter Eight

August 16. 4:50 A.M.
Somewhere in Sari Daru Province, Azakistan

HEATHER FOUGHT TO BREATHE. Even with Jace's whispered instructions, she couldn't seem to drag enough air into her lungs. Anxiety pounded through her; fear, reduced somewhat since her rescuers started moving away from the Kurdish insurgents, roared back to life. She tried to emulate Jace's sinuous motions through the brush, but she could not manage his silence. It didn't seem to matter, though, because the soldiers above them shouted instructions to each other. Find them. Capture them.

She wanted to cut and run, race away as fast and as far as she could, but she knew the sudden movement would reveal their location. Even Jace's teammate had broken off and vanished. She and Jace flew solo now. Stress and strain and fear jacked all her senses into high gear. She thought she might crack wide open even as she forced herself to accept Jace's slow pace. The soldiers beat the brush, certain their quarry had gone to ground.

When the soldiers' shouts could barely be heard, Jace increased their pace. Heather's legs, frozen into the half-crouch they'd been using, screamed in protest, and she hobbled. Jace stopped and turned, catching her as she staggered again. He wrapped a hard arm around her waist, holding her securely against him. Her legs trembled and shook. She gripped his shoulders helplessly, willing strength back into them. The days of near starvation, little water, and constant fear had taken their toll; their flight had drained her. With a silent sob, she dropped her forehead to his chest. Just for a moment. For strength. Just for a few seconds, wouldn't it be all right to lean on someone besides herself?

"It's all right. I've got you."

The brusque words so surprised her she jerked. His arm tightened, as it had in the cave when he'd looked like he wanted to kiss her. Heat rose in her cheeks. Her own response had astounded her. Rather than feel suffocated or threatened, something had sparked and leapt inside her. The scarf she'd wrapped around her face puffed with her expelled breath. She tucked it back into place, then took a shaky inhale, confused. So who was Jace? Was he the sweet, gentle man who'd cradled her while she broke down in tears back in the cave, who supported her now as though they had all the time in the world for her to get her strength back? Or was he the merciless warrior who'd attacked the terrorist training site?

Heather had trained in small unit tactics during both Air Assault and Jungle Warfare Schools. These men were something different. They moved as one, thought as one, but their methods were like nothing she'd ever seen. He and his team must be freelancers, she thought, not military. Civilians with military or paramilitary backgrounds employed by one of the hundreds of private security firms infesting this region of the world. Heather knew of the atrocities committed by Blackwater and other private security firms. Sanctioned thugs, nothing more. And now, they had been given even more rein, with the mission to locate and kill terrorists. Enemies of the West and whoever got in their way, no doubt.

She gave her head a quick shake, trying to dislodge the buzzing in her brain. Mercenaries could not be trusted. She did not dare put her faith in this one. Yet wasn't that exactly what she was doing?

Life slowly flowed back into her legs, evidenced by furious pins and needles. Heather pulled away, light-headed again. Was it her imagination, or did he hesitate before letting her go? He turned away with a gruff, "Let's go," and the endless trek began again.

Jace led her steadily southwest. He stopped several times to let her rest and drink from his canteen. Each time they stopped, he tried to contact his teammates from both a throat mike and his satellite phone. Despite his failure, he kept trying, betraying no agitation or frustration. She didn't know why he couldn't get through on the sat phone. Maybe the sandstorm interfered?

Thankful for the respite, she eased herself to the ground, pressing a hand over her left side and the peculiar tightness and stabbing radiating from that spot. Jace sat nearby, deep in thought. He turned to her, seeming to be sifting through options until he finally spoke.

"Do you . . . remember how you came to be in that camp?"

It wasn't the question she had anticipated, and the odd phrasing threw her. He had asked it in English; she feigned confusion and answered in Turkish, certain he would not understand her. "My name is Necia Kuzuou. I live in Ma'ar ye zhad. Please, can you take me back there?"

His grim, unsmiling gaze rested heavily on hers, as though he could see inside her head, as though he could tell she was lying through her teeth. "You're Turkish?" he asked. "But you speak English."

She started, realizing she had, without thinking, been either speaking or following his English instructions for miles. Oh, shit! She lowered her eyes, counting on her scarf to hide her expression. Her brain finally unfroze. "Many people speak English. It is only Americans who refuse to learn another language."

There was another long silence.

"Why did you pretend not to understand me, just now?"

Heather's breath caught at the back of her throat. "You frighten me," she said, realizing after the words left her mouth that it was true.

The man said quietly, "I won't hurt you."

"Who are you?" she challenged abruptly, hoping to startle him into revealing something. He only exhaled a soft laugh.

"I'm the guy who saved your ass," he said. "And the guy who's going to take you to safety. To Ma'ar ye zhad."

Keeping her head lowered to mask her relief, she said, "Thank you for your many kindnesses. I did not mean to . . . I am grateful you took me away from that . . . that terrible place." Her voice wobbled against her volition.

He hesitated. "How, um, how did you come to be there? You were a prisoner, right?"

Heather blew out a breath. It was an inevitable question. She chose her words carefully.

"I attend university in Ma'ar ye zhad," she said, in deliberately stilted English. She smoothed her hands over her knees. "I speak out against the atrocities building in this country. I speak out for freedom, for . . . for fairness. Justice for the women who are being forbidden to learn, to be educated. To work, even when they are doctors, biologists, mathematicians, engineers. Many groups do not like when I speak this way. I was threatened, do you understand?" She was lying outrageously, but the sentiment was true. She hated the fundamentalist trend attacking women's rights in this formerly progressive country.

Jace rubbed his chin. "So someone kidnapped you?"

"I was taken against my will to that camp and held there." That much, at least, was true, and it was easy to let her fear show in her voice. "Shouldn't we . . . should we not keep moving?" Heather could feel the trembling in her legs getting worse, and the longer she sat, the stiffer her feet would become. Walking was becoming excruciating. "The sandstorm . . ."

"In a minute. We've got a long road ahead of us." He dug into one of his many cargo pockets and pulled out a couple of power bars. He held one out to her, and she barely stopped herself from lunging for it. It was gone in two bites. He stared at her, his expression unreadable, then proffered the other. She cleared her throat.

"No, thank you. You, also, must eat."

"I think I've eaten a lot more often than you have," he said quietly. "In that camp. What hap . . ." He stopped, shook his head. "Here. You need your strength. I'm sorry I didn't, um, think of it sooner." He handed her his canteen, as well. "We'll rest here for five minutes. I'm sorry I can't give you more time. We have maybe an hour before the storm crosses the valley and reaches us. We have to find shelter. Do you understand?"

"Yes." Heather forced herself to eat the second bar more slowly, trying to give her cramping stomach time to adjust. She uncapped the canteen. Her survival instincts screamed at her to swallow huge gulps as fast as she could; but, as she had earlier, she forced herself to take small sips.

"We'll rendezvous with the guys after the storm passes. They know where." The information was grunted grudgingly; this was not a man who explained himself often.

Heather nodded. "Thank you for the food. And water."

The man searched her face again. Heather knew the scarf covered her. What was he looking for?

"Do you know this area at all?"

"No. I am sorry. You do not?" Heather could have told him she didn't even know where in Azakistan she was, or even if she was still in the country. Her tormentor had choked her into unconsciousness; she didn't know for how long.

"A bit. We're three klicks from our rendezvous," he said. "Um . . . we're three kilometers from where we're going to link back up with my team."

"I understand, but . . . Where are we in Azakistan? You said we are close to Ma-ar ye zhad, but south? West?"

He didn't hesitate. "We're not close to Ma-ar ye zhad. We're three kilometers from Bhunto. We missed our ride."

"Bhunto?" As carefully as she'd studied the maps of the Middle East, she couldn't recall any city with that name.

He laughed. "Yeah. It's a three-goat village near the border. From there, it's eighty miles to Ma-ar ye zhad."

Aw, hell. The middle of nowhere. "We need to get to Bhunto fast. Come on." He rose and held out his hand. Like before, Heather turned away. She pushed herself to her feet, swayed, and barely avoided falling. The pain was bearable, but only just. Her own weakness was now her greatest enemy.

He seemed to know exactly which way to go. Heather could have figured it out, with a map and compass and muscles that didn't shake with fatigue. The wind picked up, swirling around them in warning. She drove herself forward. It seemed to take forever to walk less than two miles. By the time a small collection of mud huts came into view, menacing clouds obscured the moon and stars, and the wind tore at them. When the storm finally hit, hell would seem calm in comparison.

Jace flicked on a flashlight. None of the buildings showed any signs of life. No candles or fires, no movement, no animal noises. It looked like the tiny village had been abandoned. He checked several huts before leading her inside one. It held a table, cupboard and bed, but no dishes, clothing, or decorations of any sort.

Jace dropped his pack on the floor and handed her the flashlight. "I'll be right back," he said, and walked out. Heather ran to the door. She found him right outside, piling rocks into a seemingly random arrangement. She recognized the trick. This way, his team would know which hut they had occupied.

He glanced at her. "I'm not going anywhere. Go sit down."

Pale pink spread over the tops of the mountains to the east. It seemed incongruous that a sweetly gentle sunrise would soon disappear beneath the onslaught of the haboob.

Despite her shaking limbs and fuzzy head, she drew on her training and inspected the walls of the hut for holes, the cupboards for anything useful. Nothing. The tenants had cleared out long ago. She glimpsed his rucksack. He had food and water. They had shelter. They would be fine.

Jace came back inside. "The team'll be along in a bit."

"You spoke with them?"

"Yeah. They ran into some trouble. Nothing they couldn't handle, but they went to radio silence."

"Are they . . . unharmed?" Like a mother hen, she worried about her guys at 10th Group every time they went on a dangerous mission.

"They're good to go. They'll be along."

Was he trying to reassure her she would not be alone with him for very long? Strangely, her fear had evaporated.

"Sit down, Hea . . . here, Necia." He pointed to the bed.

Instead, Heather sat down cross-legged in the middle of the floor. It was possible she would never again voluntarily crawl onto a bed.

Jace made no comment. Setting his weapon against the side of the hut, he opened one of the side pockets of his ruck and tugged out a tan plastic pouch. Heather's mouth watered. Meals, Ready to Eat. Army field rations. Right now, they would taste better than the finest lobster she'd ever eaten. He also grabbed two candles. Lighting both, he turned them so the wax dripped onto the floor, then set the ends into the wax, securing them. The light, though feeble, filled the mud hut. Heather switched off the flashlight.

Tearing open a flameless heater bag and setting aside the enclosed carton, he stuffed the pouch—she couldn't see what it contained—into the bag, added a little water from his canteen, and placed both bag and pouch into the carton. The water generated a chemical reaction inside the bag, producing heat that warmed the food. In a few minutes, she smelled spice and chicken. He found a spoon, cut open the top of the pouch of food, and handed both to her.

"Careful. It's hot. Hold it by the edge."

"Thank you." Heather dug in. The power bars he'd given her earlier had given her stomach time to adjust to the thought of food, and she was able to eat it all, albeit slowly.

Jace removed his Kevlar helmet, setting it atop his rucksack, then went to sit on the bed and untied a boot. He banged the heel against the floor, dislodging a fall of sand. She needed to do the same, but right now she'd fight to the death anyone who tried to take the food from her. It was chicken fajita, and it was heaven. When she swallowed the last bite, she looked up to find him studying her again.

"Better?"

Nodding, she set the empty plastic pouch aside. "Much. Thank you."

He gestured to the canteen. "Drink it."

Heather swallowed exactly half of what was in the canteen. It, too, tasted delicious. Wind now howled around the small hut.

"How long were you in that camp?" Jace's voice was gentle. Again, though, he seemed to be choosing his words with care. "How were you transported there? Do you remember?"

She shivered involuntarily and crossed her arms to hide it. He saw it anyway. He slipped out of his uniform top, handing it to her. She dipped her chin in gratitude, pushing her arms into it over the top of the one she already wore. Jace was so much larger than the young soldier, Ahmed, that it slid onto her thin frame easily.

"Necia . . ." Jace cleared his throat. "You're bleeding at your shoulder and around your ribs. I hate to do this to you. I can't begin to imagine, um, what you might have . . ." He scrubbed a hand through his sweaty hair several times. "But I should see how serious your injuries are. I have a first aid kit in my pack, and some training. It's not much, but . . . Will you let me examine you?"

No, she wanted to say. No way was she giving up the only advantage she had. Her anonymity meant that if she needed to slip away from them, she could make her way, unobstructed, back to her command.

"We have a bit of a wait ahead of us," he added. "God knows how long this storm will last. When it's over, I'll find us a ride, but we have to worst-case it. We're not exactly in friendly territory here. I have to know how badly you're hurt. If you're too injured, we might need to make some sort of stretcher for you."

Heather spoke with more certainty than she felt. "That won't be necessary. I can handle it. I've managed so far." She immediately kicked herself. A Turkish woman would not have used such a colloquial expression.

"I don't doubt it. So far, you've gutted it out more than some guys I know, which is . . . pretty amazing."

Uh-oh. The very lack of expression, either in his face or voice, warned Heather he was suspicious. She thought fast.

"Our country used to be very progressive, Mr . . . Jayyse? I was an athlete."

One corner of his mouth twitched up. "In college. University of Ma'ar ye zhad, wasn't it? You were an amateur triathlete, maybe?"

She rubbed her palms over her knees. He wasn't buying her story. Stick as close to the truth as she could: one of the basic tenets of a good liar. "Long-distance runner. May I sleep for a while?" She gestured vaguely in the direction of the bed. Not that she would go near it. Maybe she could curl up by the door instead.

"Sure. After I check out your injuries."

Heather sighed. His implacability was no different from that of her guys at 10th Group. She wasn't getting any rest until he examined her. Reluctantly, she acceded.

"Very well."

Without a word, he pulled his pack close and reached inside; again, he knew exactly where the first aid kit was. He crouched next to her.

"You'll have to, uh, take off your . . ." Jace gestured up and down her body.

Heather's chest tightened as she nodded, hyperaware of him, of her own vulnerability, of this isolated shack. He scared her, and yet some deep instinct told her he'd been truthful—he wouldn't hurt her. He wanted only to help her. She dipped her chin, eyeing the breadth of his shoulders, the strength of his arms. His large hands, resting on his knees. The planes of his face. The intensity in his eyes. But she couldn't move. She couldn't make her hands reach for her buttons. She couldn't bare herself to him—to anyone.

"I can't," she whispered.

His gaze fixated on the cloth covering the lower half of her face, fluttering slightly with every breath she took. Her lips parted. Jace jerked his head away and busied himself opening the case at his feet, as if she'd unnerved him as much as he had her.

"Look . . . about before. In the cave. I hope I didn't frighten you. You're safe with me."

Heather liked his straightforward approach. No hemming or hawing. No pretending he hadn't thought of kissing her. In fact, she liked his unapologetic leadership, the sound of his voice, the feel of his hands rubbing along her back. He'd protected her with uncompromising skill. No doubt former military, he might even have been Special Forces once. What made him choose to hire on with a private security firm?

But no matter who he was, she felt too raw, too vulnerable to trust herself to anyone at the moment. He met her eyes. She tried to think how a Turkish woman would respond.

"It is forgotten."

Jace nodded. "Thank you." He shifted from a crouch to kneeling on one knee, his back to her. "I'll start with your shoulder, okay?"

She shrugged out of his uniform jacket reluctantly, then did the same with Ahmed's smaller jacket. Suddenly nervous, she crossed her arms under her breasts. "I'm ready."

He swiveled back, his gaze fixed firmly on her shoulder. "I'm going to pull up your shirt, all right?" His voice was soft, reassuring.

Her shoulders hunched. Jace wasn't going to like what he found. He raised the T-shirt carefully from the back, pulling it up to her neck with both hands. A sound chuffed out of him, a sudden exhalation as though he'd been hit.

"Jesus!" Gentle hands traced the welts across her back and ribs. Some had split and oozed blood. Jace swore under his breath. She heard a rustle and a rip, then cold on her back. The antiseptic burned. Heather clamped her lips shut. "Sorry. I'm sorry. I'll be as quick as I can." Jace cleaned the cuts methodically, taping a bandage over each. Moving to her arms, he ran his hands down them, pausing at the obviously hand-shaped bruises on her upper arms. Some of them, the older ones, were brilliant shades of blue and purple. His fingers soothed her skin.

"Who did this to you? Was it al-Hassid?"

Heather shivered. Whether it was from her memories of the big man, or due to Jace's light touch, she couldn't say. "It does not matter."

"Doesn't . . ." Jace muttered a curse. He lifted her wrists, and she hissed. "Sorry." He examined the torn skin. "I'm not going to try to clean these out. The wounds are open. We need to get you to a doctor." Leashed fury laced his tone.

He wrapped them loosely in gauze, then traced the massive

bruise on her left side. "This concerns me the most. There might be blood in your kidneys. If I'm right, you need surgery." He glared at the ceiling as though he could command the sandstorm to vanish. The high-pitched shriek of the wind scratched eerily against her eardrums, along with a heavy pressure that compressed the air inside the hut. "Damn it."

Her head dropped forward. He had a point, but there wasn't a thing they could do about it until the storm passed and they could move again. Although how she was going to keep moving stumped her. She could barely stay conscious as it was.

Jace eased her shirt back down. "May I look at your feet?"

"Yes." Her voice came out as little more than a whisper.

He unlaced her boots and pulled them off, then cut away the crude bandages he and his teammate had tied onto her feet. She flushed when she saw that the soft bandages against her soles were actually feminine napkins. He almost smiled. "They're more absorbent than Army-issue; what can I say?"

He checked her feet thoroughly. "Like your wrists, you need a doctor." He shifted around to the first aid kit. "They're not as trashed as I thought they'd be, to be honest. You've got bleeding blisters and hot spots, but it could have been a lot worse. You're lucky you have runner's calluses." He hesitated, and it seemed as though he was going to say something else, but instead he turned away and pulled several items out of the bag. He covered her feet with the pads and wrapped them in gauze. Finally, he taped them.

A SOFT CHURR from his pocket distracted Jace. He moved away from Heather to answer his phone. She pulled on her boots and laced them. Scuttling to the corner nearest the door, she put her back against the wall and sat down.

"We're outside," Tag said. "Didn't want to surprise you."

Jace went to the door and wrestled it open, and five ghostly bodies tumbled inside. Sand caked every inch of their bodies—heads covered by helmets, eyes protected by goggles, faces wrapped in cloth, and all of it white. They looked like creatures from another planet. They forced the door closed again, shutting out most of the terrible roaring.

Small to begin with, the hut shrunk even more with the addition of five more large bodies. Heather scooted back as far as she could, practically squeezing herself into the corner. There was a lot of stamping and shaking, and sand flew around the inside of the hut.

Alex coughed, pulling down the cloth tied around his nose and mouth and yanking off his goggles, leaving pale rings on his face. "Damn, Sandman, you sure live up to your name," he said, grinning. Apparently, the worse it got, the better the young operator liked it. He was fitting in just fine.

"Oh, man!" Sandman pretended to double over with laughter. "You so funny, man. Oh, wait. No, you're not." He set his rifle against the wall next to Jace's and sat on the floor to unlace his boots, knocking the sand out of them as Jace had done earlier.

Tag and Mace dropped their packs at the foot of the bed, but kept their weapons with them. They brushed off the sand as best they could.

"No more problems?" asked Jace.

There was a lot of headshaking and negatives all around.

"Child's play," said Gabe. He glanced at the woman and away again. They all seemed to understand she needed a few minutes to adjust to their presence.

With a gesture, Jace sent his medic over to check on Heather. Alex stayed on guard. The rest of the team settled around Jace.

"Well, this is a clusterfuck." As usual, Gabe cut to the chase. His bluntness made him invaluable as a second-in-command, even though his lack of tact would eventually hinder his path to promotion. Jace had to agree, though. What should have been a simple op had gone comically awry. They had no vehicle, they'd missed their extraction via helicopter, and they now had an injured Heather to bring to safety. "We contacted HQ. They're happy to come get us when they can fly again, but right now everything in this area is grounded. Pied Piper told me he lent out our ride to ferry around a bunch of damned VIPs for the president's visit to al-Zadr Air Base. Sandstorm better end soon, or Fat Jack might kill someone."

Jace grunted. "I hear ya." Their pilot hated dealing with bureaucrats.

"Best bet is to get to Masrzhad and find a car or truck." Alex spoke up, eager to prove himself. "It's barely five miles from here. And maybe we could get a boat?"

Tag shook his head even while he agreed. "We might not have a choice. We could get lucky. But al-Hassid's gonna send his troops here first thing. It's the closest village. Once the sandstorm's over, we gotta move fast."

Jace grunted assent. "We've lost our lead time. There's no assurance we could get there first. They have trucks." He glanced over at Mace and Heather. "And we have baggage. But the good news is, we found . . ."

A shout from the other side the hut interrupted him. Jace was on his feet and halfway across the floor, weapon out and looking for targets, before he registered what was happening. Mace cradled Heather, who slumped in his arms.

"Report." He knelt beside Mace and pressed his fingers to her neck. Her pulse was strong, but too rapid.

"She passed out." Mace laid her carefully on the floor. "She's been runnin' with a concussion. All our traipsing around made it worse. She told me she was woozy and queasy. Not to mention, she's been beaten. That'll take it out of a person." Mace canted a look at his boss. "Does she remember the convoy attack?"

"Hasn't said yet. Doesn't trust us. Fed me some bullshit story about being a kidnapped university student." Without hesitation, Jace unwound the turban from her face and pulled it off. And stared. Underneath the bruises and cuts, she was unbelievably beautiful. He'd never seen her up close. She took his breath away.

"Hey, isn't that . . ." Alex started. Hadn't the kid been paying attention? A check in the minus column for that.

"Yeah," Jace said. "It is. She's our missing soldier. Lieutenant Heather Langstrom."

Chapter Nine

August 16. 9:12 A.M.
Bhunto, Azakistan

JACE CAME ALERT, completely awake in seconds. Darkness shrouded the hut. His team had hammered the broken shutters shut and covered them with their emergency blankets to keep out the sand. The wind had died down at some point. The storm was over.

Heather stirred. The small noise had woken him. He could barely make out the shapes of his teammates. Four sprawled in various parts of the hut, asleep. Mace perched on the edge of the bed, both keeping an eye on Heather and guarding the door.

She'd been out for about two hours. He'd sat near her almost the whole time, worried she would take a turn for the worse before they could get her airlifted out. Mace had finally shooed him away.

She sat up. "I have to pee," she whispered. Mace helped her off the bed. She picked her way to the door. Mace grabbed the small folding shovel and placed it in her hand.

"Go outside, to the northwest corner of the hut." He pointed. "Dig a hole."

The wooden door seemed hard for her to manage, but Mace was right there, opening it for her and closing it behind her.

Jace checked his watch — quarter past nine. Grit scraped the insides of his eyelids, and fatigue pulled at his bones. "How is she?" he asked the medic.

"About the same. It's a small bleed, I think. They cleared a medevac to take off about ninety minutes ago. It'll be here in sixteen minutes," Mace said.

"Good." Jace stretched and angled himself so he leaned against the mudbrick wall. "We'll need to move fast. Al-Hassid's men will be heading this way." Both men kept their voices muted so as not to disturb the others.

He mentally reviewed the landscape. The helicopter could land just outside the village, on the flat patch of ground to the north. They would be up and out in a matter of minutes.

Seconds ticked into minutes. She should have finished and been back by now.

"Where the hell is she?" The Sandman's low voice was irritated.

"Yeah. She's been gone too long." Jace rubbed a hand down his face. He'd been straining to hear any sign of her return. Why hadn't he told her earlier he recognized her? It was important that she knew they were on the same team. Was she lost, or had she run? Or worse, had she passed out again, unable to call for help?

Sandman uncapped his canteen, tossing the water directly into his own face and hair, then shook his head to dislodge the droplets.

Mace said, "I'll go. She might need medical help."

No one was going after Heather but him. He needed to know

she was all right, and he needed to know now. "Get rucked up and ready to move," he told his team. "I've got this."

Jace saw her the minute he stepped from the hut. The tightness in his chest eased. An old stone wall squatted nearby; half of it had crumbled, and there was nothing to indicate why it had been built in the first place. Heather rested on it, unmoving, head slightly cocked as though listening to something. An unnatural hush had settled over the landscape in the aftermath of the sandstorm, a silence so deep he imagined the desert itself held its breath. Heather released a breath slowly, as though unwilling to disturb the stillness.

He parked himself on the wall next to her. She tilted her head his way.

"We notified your command we had you," he told her. Even if she didn't remember the ambush, even through the trauma of her incarceration, she knew who she was. "They're sending a medevac."

She tried to hide a start of surprise.

"Yes, we recognized you. It'd be hard not to. Your face has been plastered all over the news for days." He tapped a finger against the pocket carrying her photo, then withdrew it and handed it to her. "Part of my mission out here was to find you." Why had he said that? It wasn't even true. They'd wanted to find her, but had never expected to run across her so far from the site of the attack. He was angry with her for her suspicion, he realized, however unreasonable it might be. "It would've saved a lot of time if you'd just trusted me."

If he had not recognized her, if he hadn't known who she was, they might not have . . . what? It really wouldn't have changed anything. They still would have missed their extraction. They would still be bringing her to safety. Only their destination had changed.

Still, it irked him that she had lied to him. Assumed he was a gun for hire.

He couldn't explain his reaction to her, not even to himself. When he'd realized the hardy woman he'd almost killed, then saved, was his Heather, it had thrown his entire world out of whack. His precious photo come to life. He wanted her to rely on him. To turn to him, as she had in his fantasies. To lie warm against him, as she had in the cave.

She took a lot of air into her lungs. "You've been kind to me. Truthfully, I'm not sure what I'd've done on my own," she said. "I haven't been able to think clearly since the ambush. I banged my head pretty hard."

"All the more reason to get you to a hospital." It would make life simpler if he could just tell her who he was. His own government still did not acknowledge the existence of his unit, though, and secrecy was part and parcel of belonging to Delta Force. Did she still think he was some sort of mercenary? "We really are the good guys, Heather. American Army, okay? That's all I can tell you, but, honestly, you can trust me. I'm going to get you home."

Chapter Ten

August 16. 9:30 A.M.
Bhunto, Azakistan

HEATHER HEARD THE helicopter a shade before Jace. She knelt and shaded her eyes, watching the speck grow larger as it approached. Soon, the racket drowned out everything else. The team circled up to defend the Blackhawk medevac as it came in for a landing. The rotor wash nearly knocked her over. Almost before the wheels touched down, Jace wrapped an arm around her, lifting and supporting her weight as they approached the red cross on the door. Two medics hopped out and took over, guiding her inside and directly onto a litter. The rest of the team piled in, and the bird lifted into the sky.

One of the medics, a fresh-faced, freckled woman, inserted a large-bore peripheral IV into the back of her hand and taped it down, checked the drip of the saline, and then hooked her up to a monitor. Her vitals began to appear on the screen. Blood pressure, heart rate, oxygen levels. The medic frowned at the monitor and placed an oxygen mask over Heather's nose and mouth.

Now that she knew she was in good hands, everything inside Heather relaxed. That also meant she could no longer compartmentalize the pain of her battered body, which became a seething mass of misery. Her vision began to blur again.

"I'm going to start you on morphine," the flight medic said. "Scale of one to ten, how bad is it?"

The pain came in at a killer solid ten, but Heather managed a shrug, avoiding the other woman's gaze. "I'm all right."

The medic squeezed her shoulder. "That you are, Lieutenant. That you are." She produced a syringe, checked it, and slipped it into a vein.

A tingling glow spiraled through Heather's body, softening the agony until it vanished under a wash of weightlessness. Time slowed. She stared at the ceiling, grateful to whoever had developed the drug, drifting in a cocoon of warmth. The medic checked her other injuries, pronounced herself satisfied with Jace's handiwork, and updated her patient's status on the rugged combat laptop bolted to a shelf.

Jace came over, hunched so he wouldn't hit his head on the equipment stored above him. He peered down at her, worry flickering in his eyes. "How is she?" he asked the flight medic. The interior of the medevac was relatively noiseless, so she heard him with ease.

"Stable. We won't know the extent of her injuries until we get her to the Emergency Department. They'll need to run tests," she said. Eyes bright, she added, "It's great you found her!"

Apparently the crew knew who they'd flown out to retrieve.

Heather frowned, uncomfortable. What had Jace said? She'd been on the news?

Jace grinned at the flight medic. "Damned straight. It's freaking amazing. Is it all right if I sit here?"

"Sure. Holler if anything changes." The medic strapped herself into a jump seat a few feet away.

Jace squeezed himself into the narrow seat next to her litter. Heather rolled her head toward him, scrutinizing him for the first time without trepidation. He'd told the truth. He was one of the good guys. The relief felt more intense than it should have.

She allowed her gaze to run from his face to his shoulders, then all the way down his body to the sturdy combat boots planted on the metal plating beneath him. The fact was, even with sweat-matted hair and streaked camouflage face paint, he was gorgeous. From his high cheekbones to his strong jaw and hard body, he was sheer male perfection.

When she peeked at his face again, she found herself ensnared. The intensity in his eyes unnerved her, but she couldn't seem to look away. She fumbled for his hand. He scooped hers up, cupping both of his around her fingers.

"Thank you," she whispered.

A tender smile softened his features. "My pleasure," he murmured back.

JACE CHECKED HER VITALS. She remained stable, which was a relief, since they were still an hour and a half from the trauma center at al-Zadr Air Force Base. A quick survey of his team showed most of them dozing. He should be getting some shut-eye, too, but he could not seem to force himself away from her side. She watched him out of eyes unfocused from the morphine running through her bloodstream, as though afraid he would vanish if she closed them.

He'd found her, or rather she'd found him, but she'd relied on him to get her to safety. The buds of trust had bloomed. There was nothing more to the look. It was wishful thinking on his part to believe there might be anything more.

How could she know how many hours he'd spent mooning over a stupid photo? And if she did know, why should she care? She had people waiting for her, a family, a . . . a . . . Oh, shit.

"Are you married?" he blurted out. Why hadn't he ever considered the possibility that she had a husband waiting for her back Stateside?

"What?" A tiny laugh escaped. The throaty sound mesmerized him. She reached up and took the oxygen mask off. "No. I'm not."

"Boyfriend?" Why was he asking her that?

"Not at the moment, no. You might say I'm married to my career." Pride and conviction rang in her tone. "I'm going all the way. And I'm doing it my own damned self. Nobody's given me shit."

He didn't doubt she could do it, either. She'd shown herself to be strong, capable, and cool under pressure. "The survivors from your convoy reported you'd been kidnapped, but no one had any idea where you'd been taken."

News media coverage had been ferocious. Heather Langstrom was a national celebrity, with vigils held around the country for her safe return. The intelligence community and 10th Group had been frantic for any word. The White House had made her liberation a priority.

"There were survivors?" Heather's face lit up. "Oh, I'm so glad!"

Just as quickly, her face clouded. "I'm . . . I forgot to ask about them." Genuine distress laced her tone. "God, I'm . . . I never meant to forget about them. I didn't know if I was alone in that camp, or if there were other prisoners. Even when I escaped, I didn't think to . . ." She tensed, starting to sit up on the litter. Jace placed a hand on her shoulder to prevent her from raising any higher. After a moment, she gave in and eased down, but both hands fisted in her hair. "What kind of soldier . . ."

"Stop that!" Jace made his voice sharp. He knew where this was heading. There was no room in their line of work for second-guesses. "You were a lone female prisoner snatched from a convoy and taken to the middle of nowhere. Given how you escaped, there's no shame . . . good God, Heather, you barely made it out of there alive. You know that, right? You might not have been released for years. Maybe never. Most likely scenario is they would have killed you. And that's the nicest they would have done. Or did." She flinched, and he knew he'd hit a nerve. His fists clenched. What, exactly, *had* they done to her? "Heather, I . . ." He leaned forward, ready to comfort her, to erase the self-condemnation he could see simmering in the depth of her gaze.

She jerked away as though she knew his intention, raising an arm to keep him at bay. "No. I didn't do what I—" Her breath hitched, her voice filled with self-loathing. "What I was supposed to do. I only thought about my own situation. I didn't even consider that there might be more prisoners. So much for my training." Her arm dropped as though she no longer had the strength to keep it aloft. Jace knew the sudden movement triggered a wave of morphine-induced muzziness by the way her eyes slackened and glazed. He relaxed back into the seat. She wasn't ready to hear anything he had to say at the moment.

"How many survived?" she asked after a moment, voice slurring.

"Four dead. Seven wounded."

"Four? Who? Do you know?" She tried to catch his gaze, but her eyes no longer focused. Jace stroked a gentle hand over her head.

"Relax, now, Heather. Everything will be all right. Shh, baby. Sleep."

Chapter Eleven

August 16. 8:15 p.m.
Near the Samarra Mosque, Ma'ar ye zhad, Azakistan

THE ENGLISHWOMAN, CHRISTINA Madison, was in trouble. Aa'idah peeked through the kitchen curtains, watching her walk through their tiny wrought-iron gate and turn left, into the after-dinner bazaar. Straight toward Aa'idah's brother Shukri and the imam, Salman Ibrahim, who would be returning from evening prayers. That was not good.

Maybe they would not see her?

Aa'idah raced to her mother's sewing room, which looked out onto the bazaar. Her ballet flats whispered along the ceramic tile, past the cutting table to the counter with the brand-new sewing machine. She wedged herself into the small space between the sewing table and the window, raising her veil across her nose as she pushed the window open and peeped through the sheers.

Christina stood out among the Muslim men and women, her fair skin and lack of head scarf setting her apart. Aa'idah herself had the typical dark hair and brown eyes of the region, although her nose was a shade longer and her face was perhaps a bit more square than others.

Christina had passed the storefront piled high with baskets of every imaginable size and construction and eased around a cart stacked with tomatoes, cucumbers, and lumpy brown potatoes. She paused for a moment next to the two carts filled with soccer balls and lifted her nose into the air, inhaling deeply. Aa'idah mimicked the move. The air had cooled and was now spiced with an aroma of roasting lamb and falafel. Delicious.

The brunette Englishwoman stood almost directly below her open window. Aa'idah's heart began to pound as she saw her brother and the imam cutting a path straight to her. Yes, they had seen her leave the Karim household. This was not good.

Christina picked up a brass water jug and appeared to admire the wide bottom, tapered top, and swirled handle. Her fingers traced the intricate design and rubbed across its scratchy surface, but the glances she darted toward Shukri and Salman Ibrahim spoke a different story. She knew who they were, and their approach made her nervous. Which meant the timing of her visit to Aa'idah had been no coincidence, as she had suspected.

The vendor approached eagerly, speaking in halting, broken English. "You like? Very beautiful. For flow the water, yes?" Aa'idah knew the merchant. His English, like her own, was nearly flawless. For some reason, he believed Westerners bought more expensive pieces from him because they saw him as poor and needy.

"I give special to American. Good price." He named a price that probably represented a hundred percent profit for the man, but would seem low enough to Christina.

"I'm with the British Education Foundation," Christina said, her London accent firmly in place. "We're here rebuilding bombed-out schools. Great Britain. Not American. English." Aa'idah's brother and Salman Ibrahim drifted closer. Aa'idah hoped they could hear Christina. She hoped they believed her.

"Good price. American," the merchant said stubbornly.

Sighing, Christina pulled a few crumpled bills from her pocket and offered the money to him, spreading it out to show the amount, clutching it with both hands. The merchant hesitated a moment, then reluctantly nodded and took the bills. He wrapped the jug in paper and handed it to her, face still registering disappointment. Christina nodded her thanks, trying and failing—to Aa'idah's eyes, anyway—to appear contrite and grateful. The deal had been a good one for both parties. Aa'idah knew the moment Christina turned, a smug look would appear on the merchant's face.

But Christina did not have the chance to turn, and the merchant did not have the chance to gloat. Shukri reached her, roughly grabbing her arm and yanking her around to face him. The self-proclaimed English relief worker tensed. Aa'idah thought she might fight, but instead she shrank away and clutched the paper-wrapped jug as though she thought she was being robbed.

Shukri, wearing the dark pants and tunic hanging past his knees he always wore to Friday prayers, muscled Christina out of the street and into the space between the brass seller and the carts piled high with soccer balls. She eased back, anxious that neither her brother nor the imam catch her eavesdropping. Christina pulled and twisted, uttering cries of distress. Aa'idah's heart fell. The action would not garner her sympathy. Shukri pounced on weakness like a cat after a dormouse. True to form, he shoved her against the stucco wall. The light material of Christina's blouse caught on the rough surface. Both Shukri and the imam faced her now, twin lasers of hostility and anger in their gazes.

Christina shrank back, one hand flat on the wall behind her, the other clutching the jug to her breast like a shield. "Who are you? What do you want?" she rasped.

Salman Ibrahim jabbed a finger at her, voice venomous as he upbraided her for strutting in the marketplace as though she were an empress, then in the next breath accused her of being a shameless whore. Aa'idah's cheeks heated with embarrassment for the other woman, even though the stream of angry words issuing from the imam's mouth was clearly too fast for the Englishwoman to follow. Christina shook her head, a bewildered look on her face; but Aa'idah knew she got the gist of it loud and clear.

"What do you want? Who are you?" Christina asked again. Shukri put up a hand, and Salman Ibrahim subsided.

"Why did you speak to my sister?" he asked, in clear, British-accented English. The evening shoppers maneuvered around the confrontation, heads down, pretending they saw nothing. Christina straightened, looking Shukri in the face. Aa'idah's heart hammered against her rib cage. In this ultraconservative section of Ma'ar ye zhad, the imam could beat her to death right in the street, and no one would interfere.

"Your sister?" Christina asked. "I'm very sorry, but I don't know you."

"I am Shukri Karim." His voice swelled with arrogance. "My sister is Aa'idah Karim."

"Oh, yes. I talked to her just now. She is a teacher at the Thenoon al Fattah school for girls," Christina said, voice puzzled but respectful. "The school is nearly fully rebuilt. When it reopens, the children will need their teachers back. I asked her to return to teach. That's all."

"You spoke to her alone," he said accusingly.

In fact, Aa'idah remained convinced Christina had arranged the timing very carefully, approaching her door just after Friday prayers and on a day when her mother had gone to visit her aunt. And yes, they had spoken of the school, and the girls who urgently needed an education. But they had spoken of so much more. Things Shukri must never hear.

Christina continued to look up at Shukri, her brows pulled together. "No one else was home."

"This is not permitted. A male member of her family must be present."

The imam grabbed Christina's arm, looming over her as he shook her. His fist clamped so tightly around her bicep that Aa'idah knew Christina would carry the bruises for a week. Shukri translated as the imam snarled. "Salman Ibrahim is a Shi'ite cleric, imam of the Samarra Mosque. He says you have behaved in a disrespectful manner, shaming the home of Mahmoud Karim. He says you are brazen and not of good character, that you walk outside with no male escort to ensure your virtue. He says you do not lower your eyes submissively, as a woman should. He's going to beat you to teach you to behave properly."

Blood pounded through Aa'idah's head. If Salman Ibrahim followed through on his threat, did she dare interfere?

Christina pinned her gaze to the cleric's feet and gripped the water jug tighter. Aa'idah imagined the other woman's hands were probably shaking as badly as her own. "Please tell him no discourtesy was intended." Christina's voice cracked. "My group is staying at a hostel near the school. Your government places no restrictions on us. I'm a British citizen. Please call the consulate. I'm sure this is just a misunderstanding." Her voice became pleading. "I'm a relief worker. I'm here to help you." Tears gathered at the corners of her eyes.

"We do not wish your help," Shukri said harshly. "Your corrupting influence has spread far enough. My sister will not be returning to teach."

Aa'idah's heart sank even further. She had suspected as much. Her father seemed to be fading, allowing his eldest son to make decisions for the family. And Shukri had become angry. Bitter. And determined to force his traditionalist ideals onto his family whether they wanted it or not.

"All right. I'm sorry." Christina tried to disengage her arm from the cleric's grip. He growled something, his voice too low for Aa'idah to hear. When he glared into the woman's face, yanking her closer, a cold frisson of fear slithered down Aa'idah's spine.

Shukri spoke, sounding neither sorry nor concerned. "Salman Ibrahim says," he reported, "that you are under arrest."

This was very bad.

Chapter Twelve

August 19. 2:30 P.M.
Base Hospital, al-Zadr Air Force Base, Azakistan

THE STEADY BEEP of the heart rate monitor was driving Heather crazy. The tubes running from her arms to various drips annoyed her. She'd been swarmed the moment the helicopter touched down. In short order, she'd been whisked from a rapid bedside ultrasound to a CAT scan, and in less than an hour she'd been in surgery. The doctor had taken one look at her battered body and been generous with the pain meds; the first days had passed in a blur.

This time when the doctor made his rounds, she would be coherent enough to get some answers. She pressed the button that raised the head of the bed so she could sit up, wincing as her bruises made themselves known, and drummed her fingers against the bed rails.

Finally, Dr. McGrath came in, followed by a straggling group of interns. He picked up her chart and flipped through it, then handed it to the closest one. "Dr. Sottile, run down the history for me."

The intern cleared his throat, glancing at Heather and away again. He ran quick fingers over his trimmed beard, the red in his face matching the red of his hair. "Patient is a twenty-six-year-old female presenting with a grade three blunt trauma splenic injury, causing intra-abdominal bleeding in the retroperitoneal space. Failed observation with dropping hemoglobin . . ."

Heather tuned the intern out. She wasn't interested in what had happened; she wanted to know when she could get out of the hospital. Finally, his litany and the subsequent questions died down, and the group turned to leave.

"Dr. McGrath," she called.

The group stopped and turned as one, staring at her with mild curiosity. Dr. McGrath came back to her bedside and gave her a gentle smile. "What is it, Lieutenant?"

"When can I go home?"

The smile turned into a grimace. "I'll move you from ICU onto the medical-surgical floor tomorrow, but only if your vitals remain steady and the infection in your shoulder starts responding to treatment. If you continue to improve, you might be released as early as Friday or Saturday. Just so you know, though, the base Public Affairs Officer approached me about moving you into an inpatient room to control media access when I feel you're fit enough for that particular impending circus."

Four more days. Heather groaned. Military health care was much more conservative than its civilian counterparts; in the civilian world, she would probably be home already. Still, she was not a hundred percent yet. A lethargy that had nothing to do with the morphine running through her veins tugged at her. Her skin felt hot and dry.

Dr. McGrath checked her wrists, rewrapping them in soft gauze. "These are healing nicely."

Heather frowned. "Can you at least make that beeping noise go away?" she grumped.

"Sure. The danger's past. Try to get some rest." He patted her hand and left.

As soon as Dr. McGrath closed the door behind him, it opened again. Expecting the nurse, Heather sat up, ready to yank the leads off her body.

"Hello."

Her head swiveled around in surprise. The broad shoulders filling the doorway sent an immediate wave of relief through her. Jace.

"Hi."

"You're awake," he said.

"For the first time in days, I think. I've been pretty much out of it."

"I know." He entered, glancing around a room that suddenly seemed smaller. He rolled his shoulders, looking uncomfortable. "So, ah, how are you?"

"I'm doing all right."

The banal chitchat felt odd to her, as though somewhere in the past week her veneer of civilization had slipped.

"They still have you on pain meds. That's not the same as being all right." He pointed to the IV in her arm. "Demerol, right?"

She nodded. Her head felt too heavy, so she eased it against the pillows.

"Can I, uh, get you anything?"

"A little water, please." Her skin prickled as he came closer and filled her small cup from the pitcher on the table beside her bed. Instead of handing it to her, he leaned over her, one arm braced near her head and the other holding the plastic cup to her lips. His gaze snared hers, and she found herself lost in his eyes as she sipped. It felt surreal. Her vision tunneled and grayed around the edges.

Jace set the water aside. His hand came up to cup her jaw, carefully, and he brushed her lips with his mouth; just a whisper of sensation that she felt to her toes. He came back again, just as softly, and Heather deepened the kiss without conscious volition, tracing his lips with her tongue. He made a soft sound of pleasure, but then straightened. Heather looked up at him, confused, her throat already dry again. A headache seemed to have banded itself around her head.

He smiled down at her, but his hand slid away. "Sorry. I know you're still hurt, but I've wanted to do that for a while."

"Ahem."

Heather jerked away guiltily. Jace was slower to move back, glancing over his shoulder at the nurse without embarrassment or apology. The nurse came farther into the room, her eyes twinkling.

"Your EKG showed a sudden spike. I now see why." She grinned. "The doctor says we can unhook you. I'd say I have to agree. You seem healthy enough." She made a shooing motion with her hands, and Jace obediently stepped back. "Now just let me unhook the electrodes."

Face heating with embarrassment, Heather turned her face

away as the nurse whisked the small round pads off her chest and back. Thankfully, the *beep-beep-beep* finally stopped. The nurse left with a stern admonition not to tire Heather. Silence descended in the room.

"They're being ultracautious with me," she finally said.

Jace eased himself into the blue plastic visitor's chair. "I know. I've been checking up on you."

Heather didn't know what to say to that. "Why?"

He leaned forward, resting his forearms on his thighs. "I always check on damsels in distress once I rescue them."

Dismay coursed through her, but there wasn't much she could say. He *had* rescued her. She *had* relied on him to get her to safety. Her relief at seeing him turned to chagrin.

"What did I say?" Jace cocked his head. "I didn't mean to offend you."

Heather shook her head, not looking at him. "I'm just . . . used to making my own way. I don't rely on people. They let you down." It wasn't his fault. He had been doing his job, the same as she had been doing hers when she had been taken. He couldn't know the many disappointments of her childhood as her parents ignored her pleas to go to space camp or join the Civil Air Patrol—anything meaningful—in favor of their own ambitions, nor the subtle or open contempt of male soldiers as she struggled for acceptance and respect.

She'd proven herself strong and capable time after time; yet, in her first real test, she'd been dependent on someone else to save her. It galled her.

"Not a team player, eh? Odd profession you chose, then."

Heather's chin lifted of its own accord. "I work with others. Intelligence people share information, at least in the Army. Dealing with the alphabet agencies is a nightmare. The CIA is the worst. They won't tell you the sun is shining half the time."

Jace laughed. "We have the same problem with them."

"We? We being . . . ?"

Jace waited, silent.

Heather shrugged, obscurely disappointed. "Fine. Just tell me you stopped those insurgents from attacking US personnel."

His brows rose. "Nobody told you? The Azakistani Air Force sent two fighters out to the compound. Bombed the shit out of the place. It doesn't exist anymore."

Heather's breath left her in a whoosh. "The people? There were women . . ."

"Virtually deserted. Once al-Hassid beat feet, the rest of the troops pretty much deserted." He paused. "We bumped into a . . . surprise while we were there. Do your intelligence resources have anything on SCUDs in insurgent hands?"

Heather's vision cleared and her eyes widened. The headache grew worse. "What? They had a SCUD?" Then, in a breathy whisper, "Please God tell me you destroyed it."

"We destroyed the inertial guidance system. The Azakistanis took care of the missile itself. There was no warhead on-site that we saw."

Her breath whooshed out. "Who knows about this?"

"It went to the Tactical Operations Center at Forward Camp Gryphon. I'd bet my last dollar Central Command has it now." He assessed her. "There's nothing you need to be worrying about right now except healing."

The tension left her body. "Who were they? It seems odd that I still don't know who they were."

Jace grimaced. "You were the special guest of Sheik Omaid al-Hassid, of the Kongra-Gel. That name mean anything to you?"

Heather fluttered a hand, startled. "Yes, actually. That makes . . . a lot of sense. I think that's why I was taken prisoner." Since she couldn't seem to lift her head, she pressed the button and raised herself a little more erect. "I overheard a conversation in one of the open-air markets in Eshma. Three men, one of whom—the leader—was the man who . . . questioned . . . me at the camp." A quiver ran through her. Jace reached for her, but stopped and let his arm drop.

Disappointed, Heather forced herself to continue. "It's my job to listen, to eavesdrop, to figure out how things fit together. You never know when small grains of sand will clump together to form a real, live piece of intelligence information." She traced her fingers along the blanket covering her lap. "I heard part of a name. Omaid something, and you've just given me the rest of it. They were concerned because one of their group members had died, but not worried enough to stop their plans. Based on the questions I was being asked, I'm betting it's someone named Demas Pagonis. Also, they were using a boy—I didn't catch his name—to do part of their job. He was having second thoughts, and the leader threatened to kill him if he didn't cooperate. It wasn't a whole lot, but enough to get me thinking."

Heather stilled her fingers. "I got a couple of decent photos with my iPhone. We went to the chief of police, guy by the name of Sa'id al-Jabr, with the pictures. He said he didn't recognize them, but I'm pretty sure he lied. The next day, our convoy was ambushed." She shivered, suddenly chilled.

Jace shifted closer. Heather stopped herself a fraction before she reached for his hand.

"I'd say we stopped them, at least for now," he said. "The rest can wait until you're stronger. You've been through enough."

"I guess." She twisted her fingers together. "I just feel . . . help-less. There's something going on out there, and I need to figure it out before people get hurt." The sheik's henchman wouldn't give up so easily. His crazed eyes . . . she shuddered. Real evil lived in that body. She knew in her gut that he had escaped with the sheik. She finally turned her head to meet Jace's gaze.

"Look," he began. What had they been talking about? She couldn't seem to focus. His voice trailed off, his gaze tracing over her face. His brows snapped together. Pushing himself to his feet, he took two steps and bent over her. His fingers were cool as they cupped her face. She leaned into them, welcoming the relief from the heat that coursed through her body. "Shit." Jace grabbed the nurse call button and pushed it several times. He pressed the inside of his wrist against her forehead, which had beaded with perspiration. She shivered harder.

"She's running a fever," Jace said, his voice far away. A lighter voice answered. Pain pulsed in her joints, unconnected to her bruises or the site of the surgery. She sensed the bustle around her, but couldn't seem to muster the strength to lift her head.

"Out, now." Heather didn't like that voice. "We need the room cleared, stat."

For a brief moment, Jace leaned over her, smoothing her hair away from her face. He pressed a brief kiss to her forehead. "Stay strong, Heather. Fight it."

She thought she might have answered him, then gave in to the swirl of confusion in her mind, closing her eyes with a tired sigh.

Chapter Thirteen

August 24. 8:00 P.M.
Ma'ar ye zhad, Azakistan

AA'IDAH SHIFTED HER abaya's sleeve so she could grasp the frozen yogurt her father handed her. The abaya was light and comfortable, though fitted loosely enough to hide the shape beneath it. Blue satin edged the sleeves and front hems, with a second edging of pale sequins. Her scarf covered her hair, but left her face visible. Her mother and two younger sisters dressed similarly, while her little brother wore trousers and a button-down shirt. He had already smeared the frozen treat over his face.

The sun had set long ago, and cool breezes wafted through the causeways. She strolled with her family down a wide bricked path between shops and under an old walled arch. Stopping with her sisters to look at dresses, she exchanged pleasantries with the proprietress, a young woman wearing a long skirt and blouse. Her head scarf swirled purple and pink flowers. An old man dozed in a chair at the back of the shop.

"Your hijab is lovely," Aa'idah murmured.

"I have another." The young woman slid her hands under a stack of head scarves and pulled one free, draping it across her arm to show it off. Aa'idah fingered the soft chiffon. Her own hijab was a conservative gray silk.

"How much?" she asked.

"For the daughter of Mahmoud Karim, seven thousand *tenge*."

"Five thousand." Roughly twenty-seven US dollars. US dollars had been much on her mind lately as she transferred sums back and forth per her father's instructions. Sometimes dollars, sometimes *tenge* or Iranian rials.

"Six."

Normally Aa'idah enjoyed bartering, but this evening her thoughts were elsewhere. She paid the proprietress and waited while the purchase was wrapped. Her family had moved to the next boutique, her sisters fingering necklaces and brightly patterned belts.

"We will sit and enjoy a coffee," her father said, gesturing to a café with an outdoor patio.

Wooden tables with red chairs littered the area. Most were full. A slew of young Azakistanis chatted together. Others scrolled through their phones, sipping glasses of Persian tea as their thumbs tapped across phones or iPad screens to text or reply to email. A young couple bounced two babies on their knees. Four college students played Pasur, a card game that had them laughing raucously as they won or lost a round. Aa'idah heard at least three languages swirling through the throng.

Shukri pulled three tables together. Her mother and the girls sat at one end, leaving the males together. Her father pulled her to a middle seat next to him. Unease shivered through her.

That was seven. Who were the other seats for?

A server hurried to them. Her father ordered for them all: Syrian coffee for five, and fragrant rose tea and bitter almond biscuits for the rest.

The guests arrived before the coffee. Three men approached the table. One loomed over the others, shoulders seemingly wide enough to block out the sun. White tape covered his hooked nose, which had clearly been broken recently. His five o'clock shadow gave him a sinister mien. He wore a brown, ankle-length tunic and red-and-gold sandals. His white cotton *ghutrah* headdress was banded by a black cord doubled around to keep the *ghutrah* in place.

The second, shorter and older, wore the traditional white cotton tunic. His *ghutra* had red and white checks, and his beard was long and bushy. He must be a sheik, Aa'idah decided, an elder and a leader. The third, much younger, dressed like Shukri in jeans, T-shirt, and sneakers.

Her father rose and shook hands all around. "Peace be upon you."

"And unto you, peace," replied the sheik. He sat at the head of the table as though it were his due. The hulking man sat to his right. The third one sat next to Shukri, and her father resumed his place next to her.

Her father made no introductions. The server arrived with a tray and served the three visitors, Shukri, and her father the strong Syrian coffee, then distributed the tea and biscuits for the rest of the family.

"I should get to drink coffee with the men," her little brother complained. Her mother quickly shushed him.

"Things went well in Eshma?" her father asked.

The big man with the broken nose inclined his head. "A great success. Shukri was very helpful."

Shukri straightened, beaming with pride. "It was my honor, sir."

Shukri had been gone for days on a trip that even their mother knew nothing about. A bad feeling began to churn in her stomach. The bombings in Eshma had been headline news for weeks. Please, please let it be coincidence. Please let her brother not be involved in anything illegal.

"One minor inconvenience," the sheik said, frowning. "Zaahir was careless. But our friend the chief of police in Eshma warned us in time, and we removed the problem."

The big man with the broken nose glowered. "It will not happen again, I assure you."

"What problem?" her father asked.

"Apparently an American woman overheard Shukri, Rami, and me. It was my fault; I do not deny this." It seemed to gall him to say the words. "We were in a public place. After the Ubadah bombing, we had nowhere private to talk."

Aa'idah bent her head over her tea, blowing across its surface to hide her expression. Was it Christina? Was she the woman they discussed? What had happened to her after the imam, Salman Ibrahim, dragged her away?

"Removed the problem how? Is she confined?" Her father lowered his voice. "Dead?"

Aa'idah couldn't control her start of dismay, causing the big man to glance her way. Their eyes met and held, hers wide and fearful, his fierce and his sharp as daggers. Then, amazingly, he smiled. It didn't make his any less frightening, but Aa'idah dropped her eyes, relieved anyway.

"Escaped. But no matter. She knew nothing." Zaahir's fingers clenched around the coffee cup. "To the problem at hand, which is serious. The filthy infidel dogs bombed our home in the hills. We will need to start reconstruction."

Her father nodded, a bit reluctantly, it seemed to Aa'idah. "Of course. Do you have a cost estimate?"

"Four million *tenge*," the sheik said, shrugging carelessly. "That is the easy one."

Aa'idah pretended to nibble a biscuit as she calculated the amount in her head. Twenty-six thousand American dollars, give or take, would buy many guns in this part of the world. And would also buy the hands to hold them. Did her father not understand that he was condemning hundreds of young men and boys to death? Terrible to consider, but was he actually in charge of sending millions of Azakistani *tenge* into the countryside, to terror-training camps?

"The difficult problem is that our special item must be replaced."

Her father set his coffee cup down and dabbed his lips with a napkin. "I see. It was not easy to locate."

"And expensive to acquire," Zaahir said. "We understand. My contact in Tehran is trying to find me another as we speak. He says it will be at least four million."

Her father grew very still. "Euros?"

"Dollars." Zaahir narrowed his eyes. "Is this a problem?"

"No, only . . ."

"It will come through the usual sources," the sheik said over him. "Some from Zaahir's international business company, some from our friend in the government through one of his holding companies."

Aa'idah bit her lip. Shell companies to funnel hidden capital into the sheik's pockets. Who was their 'friend' in the government? What would happen if she asked?

She wasn't brave enough to find out.

But she couldn't pretend or plead ignorance. Though she did not understand what they planned to do, it was clear they meant harm. Where? Against whom?

What should she do?

Her thoughts settled on the British aid worker, Christina Madison, who she suspected was an agent for the CIA, given how her accent came and went. Should she report what little she knew? Betray her father, her brother.

No. Aa'idah felt unclean just thinking the thoughts. But . . . what if she did arrange to be alone with Christina?

If the woman was not dead already.

Chapter Fourteen

August 26. 1:00 P.M.
US Embassy, Ma'ar ye zhad, Azakistan

JACE FOLLOWED HIS boss and Ken Acolatse, the Troop Command Sergeant Major, into an opulent conference room with sophisticated everything. An array of sandwiches and fresh fruit, drinks, and even alcohol filled the sideboard. A dozen people milled about, filling plates or nabbing bottles of expensive artesian water.

A slender woman with high cheekbones and dark hair curling over her ears and forehead set up at the front podium. A Poindexter type near her messing with cords and a projector sent her a worshipful look, which she either didn't see or ignored. Her large brown eyes snapped with intelligence. She hooked up her laptop and flashed a slide announcing a political threat briefing. Poindexter disappeared.

Lieutenant Colonel Louis Jowat, commander of the 214th Security Forces Squadron, lounged against the podium. Several times, he leaned forward into the woman's personal space, a smirk in place and nothing good on his mind. The oily colonel had a reputation that included sexual harassment, intimidation, and coercion. As he was the senior cop on the Air Force Base, grievances mysteriously vanished and complainants found themselves on the receiving end of traffic tickets and other blowback. The woman shifted away from him and even turned her back, irritation showing in the set of her shoulders. She finally whispered something to him sharply enough that he scowled and straightened.

Gradually, the men and women settled into the thick, padded-leather executive chairs. Jace found his name at the table and planted himself. Jowat sat opposite him, arms crossed and face sullen. Jace doubted he'd be much use during the meeting.

The unpleasant colonel would provide the initial perimeter security to the parade grounds where the president would address the troops. Jace was here because the Secret Service wanted to use one or more of Colonel Granville's teams as support and extra eyes, a second perimeter around the president's podium. The president's protection detail would surround the president himself.

Because Delta Force operated outside of the conventional military hierarchy, they often supported other branches of service and alphabet agencies like the CIA or FBI. Every day something new and different, just the way Jace liked it. Bo Granville plunked himself down beside Jace, juggling a plate and three cups of coffee. He shoved one of the cups in front of Jace, flicking away the hot liquid that splashed onto his fingers, and gave the other to Ken. He waved his hand over the food, tacitly telling his men to share in the bounty. Jace grabbed a turkey club, setting it on a napkin near the folder at his elbow.

Across from Jace and two chairs down, a British Army officer scrutinized the woman with laserlike intensity. Jace assessed
him automatically. He could tell just from watching that he was
a special operator. The way he sat; slouched, but prepared to
launch full tilt in a nanosecond. The way he held his hands open
and ready. His eyes. It always showed in the eyes. A nonoperator
wouldn't see it. Maybe an intensity, maybe deep pools of experience. But to Jace, it was as obvious as if the man had waved a
semaphore.

Jace glanced at the beige beret thrown carelessly onto the table.
The insignia showed the flaming Sword of Damocles, which made
him Special Air Service. The SAS was almost as elite, and almost
as secretive, as Delta Force, and the two organizations worked together regularly. The officer turned that laser focus to the three
Delta Force operators and inclined his head solemnly. Despite
their civilian clothes, he had summed up the three just as easily
as they had him.

Delta operators rarely wore uniforms or adhered to required
protocols or military grooming standards. As often as not, they
ignored rank entirely and addressed one another by first name.
They enjoyed a level of autonomy found nowhere else in the Armed
Services. It helped keep their identities secret. But operators recognized other operators. He raised a single finger in greeting.

Ready, the attractive woman up front cleared her throat.
"Ladies and gentlemen. If we could begin."

They immediately quieted and turned their attention to her.
The Brit cocked his head, glancing around the table at the clear
respect offered to her, then studied the woman even more closely.
Evidently, she was more senior than her age would suggest.

She clicked the device in her hand, and "Upcoming Presidential Visit" flashed onto the screen. Below it, September 11.

"Good morning. For those of you who don't know me, I am Deputy Political Counselor Shelby Gibson. I'd like to take this opportunity to welcome Mike Boston and Brian Seifert of the US Secret Service. They'll be coordinating all aspects of President Cooper's visit and will be joined by more agents shortly. Obviously, we will give you any assistance you need." She smiled warmly at them, then cleared her throat as she turned to the Brit. "Also, may I introduce Major Trevor Carswell, of the 22nd British SAS, Counter-Terrorism, here in Azakistan on temporary duty."

There was a murmur from around the table. Shelby Gibson's gaze sharpened, landing on Trevor with curiosity. The Brit's lips twitched. Jace watched the exchange, amused. Did they realize how transparent their mutual interest was?

"Glad to have you, Major Carswell," said a tall, thin man. He adjusted his glasses so he could peer along the table. "Nice job in Iraq." He got up and came around the table, putting out a hand. "You saved my agent's ass. I'm Jay Spicer. I'm the CIA station chief here."

Trevor rose to shake the man's hand. Colonel Jowat glowered and remained seated. The thin, severe-looking woman across from Trevor asked, "Were you part of the SAS team that pulled those two pilots out of Afghanistan a few months ago?"

Trevor gave the woman a blank look. "I'm sorry. I don't know wh . . ."

Shelby interrupted. "Major Carswell, everyone here is read in at the Top Secret level, and then some. You may speak freely. May I introduce everyone?"

She went around the room. The three Delta Force operators were introduced by name, with no military designation. The Secret Service agents understood; it glimmered in their eyes. The buttoned-down woman across from Trevor turned out to be Dr. Harriet Pangbourn, Director of Cultural Relations (Middle East) at the Institute for International Progress. Jace had never heard of it.

Shelby directed their attention back to the projection screen. "This morning, I'm going to give a general overview of the current political climate here in Azakistan. I know you're getting separate economic and intelligence briefings, so I'm going to cover high-end trends within the government, all right?"

Brian Seifert nodded. "We're only trying to get a sense of where things stand. Right now, we're just gathering information."

Shelby gestured around the table. "We're all here to answer any questions you might have. I'll assume for the moment you don't know much about Azakistan. Most people don't. We're smaller than both Kyrgyzstan and Tajikistan. The Islamic Republic of Azakistan has had democratic elections since 1998. The prime minister draws his legitimacy from Parliament, and is subject to their confidence. His term is for five years."

She clicked to the next slide, a map of Azakistan. "We're located east of Iran and south of Turkmenistan. There are marshes and lakes in the northeastern regions, including here in the capital city and around al-Zadr Air Force Base, which is about twenty miles from Ma'ar ye zhad. The central corridor is primarily long, low stretches of emptiness and scrub brush, ending in the high mountainous regions of the Afghan border to the south. That's just to orient you. Now let's get to the heart of Azakistani politics."

Jace found himself listening as attentively as the rest of the room as she outlined the shift away from a pro-democratic stance toward a fundamentally traditionalist view. The dynamism in her presentation, her voice, her body language, all spoke of a woman passionate about her work. As she outlined the political aspirations of various members of Parliament, he scanned the brief in front of him. It included a section on politicians deemed friendly to the West and those who opposed Western influence. It was thorough and well written, and she'd grasped nuances of the conflict that had taken him years in the field to understand fully.

"Obviously, the shift toward conformism concerns us. Pashtuns abhor every Western influence as evil. We're starting to see Pashtun imams in outlying cities, and some within certain sections of Momardhi and Tiqt, enforcing some of the, shall we say, less appealing aspects of an otherwise peaceful religion. The Pashtun Nationalist Party could very well gain a majority in Parliament during the next election."

Jowat leaned forward and rapped his knuckles on the table. "Doubtful. All the political analysts agree the Reformists will win reelection. Don't stir up trouble. Keep your pretty little head on the slides you're supposed to read, sweetheart."

Shelby's face reddened and she glanced down at the podium before meeting Jowat's condescension head-on. The SAS major shot Jowat a dirty look and opened his mouth.

"Yes, but if it does happen," Shelby said, narrowing her eyes at Trevor. Her message couldn't have been more clear—*shut up and let me handle this*. Jace watched her, curious. What would she do? "We need to consider the ramifications. *I* wrote *my* briefing after consulting numerous sources." She sent Jowat a bland smile. "As I was saying, if the Pashtuns control the government, there could be an increase in ethnic and racial discrimination. Diminished rights for non-Pashtus and women. Pressure to reduce or eliminate Western influence. American businesses could be boycotted. There will probably be bans on imports. It just gets worse from there."

Shelby clicked to another slide. "There are two main concerns as far as the president's visit. One is the people with whom he'll come into contact."

Mike Boston held up a hand. "All attendees will be thoroughly vetted. You don't have to worry about that part."

"Yes, of course," Shelby said. "I just meant that I know that some former warlords, in particular, are virtually flocking to the opposition party's side. I've outlined who they are, as far as we know. One of these is the opposition party leader's chief of staff, Ali Bin-Muhammad al-Rashid." Click. "He rose from being a government-sponsored enforcer to the Tiqt chief of police before shifting into politics. He personally placed many of the new city police chiefs, loyal to him alone."

She clicked to another photograph. "Yesterday, he attended a meeting with a powerful businessman, a staunch conservative who believes Western influence is diluting Islamic culture. He has a history of repressive conduct. We don't know the substance of this meeting. We're trying to find that out now."

"What's so important about this particular meeting? Was it here?" Mike Boston asked.

Harriet Pangbourn smacked her coffee cup onto the mahogany table. "The meeting was at the Laleh Hotel in Tehran," she said. "We're worried the conservative movement might be contemplating more direct action against the government. Violence, bombings, up to and including assassination of key political figures. We suspect al-Rashid might have ties to terrorist training camps."

"Yes," agreed Shelby. "If he is sponsoring or importing terrorist leaders, perhaps even placing those leaders within local police forces, it could undo all the good we've done in reducing terrorist capabilities in this country."

What?

"In the past two years," she added, "special missions in this country have located and destroyed a large number of weapons caches held by various insurgents and terrorist units. Incidents of terrorist or armed protest are down sixty-seven percent from when the special missions started. Attacks in industrial centers, in the capital, or in other large cities are poorly thought out and largely ineffective."

"So as things stand right now, you consider a direct threat against the US president to be low?" Boston asked.

"Yes. It could change over time, but right now, the US and Azakistanis have substantially reduced the threat of terrorist attack."

Jace sighed. However well-intentioned, the men and women in this room remained bureaucrats. He glanced toward his boss. Should they correct her?

Just as Bo Granville jerked his chin for Jace to proceed, Trevor spoke up. "Your statistics are undoubtedly correct, Ms. Gibson, but I'm afraid your conclusions are off base."

Suddenly, the British officer was the focus of ten pairs of eyes.

"All incoming reports having to do with the frequency and intensity of insurgent attacks say their capabilities have been greatly reduced, Major," said Shelby coolly. "After only a few days on the ground, what do you know that they don't?"

Jace saw Trevor bite the inside of his cheek to keep from laughing. "It's not a novel theory, I regret to say," the SAS officer said. "Your statistics only see the front end. The fringe groups, the barely equipped ones. One-shot wonders, as I believe you Americans say. They blow up a car, there's some property damage, maybe someone gets hurt or killed. I'm not saying that's acceptable; far from it. But I'm speaking of the more organized groups. Al-Qaeda. Abu Nidal. The Kongra-Gel."

Jowat snorted. "So now you're an expert on Azakistani military operations?"

Trevor's eyes narrowed on him. Jowat had the good sense to sit back in his chair. "The special operations missions are succeeding, as far as it goes. But what's happening out there isn't what you think. Instead of finding a bunch of antiquated AK-47s and a couple of hand grenades, they're finding antitank weapons, wire-guided missiles, and other high-tech, NATO weapons."

The two Secret Service agents exchanged bewildered looks.

Jace bottom-lined it for them. "You smack a bull on the nose, it backs up for a minute," he said. "You may think you've scared it, but then it charges. All you've done is make it more dangerous."

Silence settled in the room.

The CIA station chief cleared his throat. "So what I'm hearing you say is they haven't gone away. They're just getting more sophisticated weapons to attack us with?"

"Yes."

"How, then, do you explain the reduction in the attacks against US interests?" asked Dr. Pangbourn.

"Obtaining that type of weaponry is costly," Trevor said. "Most of the rabble-rousers in this part of the world are disorganized, decentralized, and don't have that type of cash." He tugged on his earlobe. "There's another theory, of course. I and my teams are seeing evidence on the ground that some of the more extreme groups are organizing. That they have more on their mind than a few car bombs. Possibly even a major objective."

Brian Seifert sat up. "The president?"

Jowat huffed. "I'm in charge of securing the parade grounds. No one is getting through my security. The president will be safe, I promise you that."

Seifert threw him an annoyed glance. Trevor shrugged and spoke directly to Seifert. "Perhaps, although that would be extremely difficult to pull off. The Secret Service, who, as I understand it"—he twitched his lips—"is *solely* responsible for the safety of the American president, happen to be extremely good at their job."

Mike Boston put a hand on the other agent's arm. Seifert sat back, still glowering.

Jace leaned forward to snare Boston's attention. "They would need a significant amount of funding, training, and weapons," he said. "Things we believe some of the groups have. The Kongra-Gel is the biggest threat here in Azakistan." He thought about the SCUD and its capabilities. "My guess would be something less well guarded, but still very important. Critical infrastructure. A power plant. A Western-style mall. Prime Minister al-Muhaymin's home, maybe. It depends on the group's objectives. Do they want Westerners out? Do they want the current government to fail? Do they just want to cause mayhem in the name of jihad?"

Shelby fiddled with her pointer. "The State Department intelligence group created summaries of the various terrorist groups in the region, outlining the major players and their objectives," she told the Secret Service. "Would you like a copy?"

Mike Boston cleared his throat. "Let's take that a step further. Major Carswell, Mr. Reed, would you two be willing to get with our intelligence assets here? Vet what they suspect against what you know?"

"Yeah, sure. Whatever you want."

"It would be my pleasure."

Chapter Fifteen

August 27. 8:45 A.M.
Ma'ar ye zhad, Azakistan

AA'IDAH KARIM WATCHED Shukri with the sheik from her safe position behind her desk. The three men stood in the glass-enclosed conference room. It felt odd that they did not sit.

Her brother's stiff shoulders and tight mouth broadcast his anger. He did not dare shout at the sheik, though, and Aa'idah knew with a sinking certainty he would take it out on her, later, at home. He disapproved of her working here at their father's asset management firm, even as a temporary receptionist. Perhaps this time he would convince their father his younger sister ought to remain at home, sequestered with their mother and her two younger sisters, as a proper Muslim girl should be. Never mind that Aa'idah was twenty-six years old, or held a master's degree in Education. She had been teaching Grade 11 at a girl's school for the past year. Her students loved her.

The more Shukri kept company with the Salafists, the angrier he became.

Aa'idah had been heartbroken when her school had been closed, the girls told to return to their homes and stay there. The imams, particularly Salman Ibrahim, preached there was no need for them to receive an education. Men should have that privilege, because it was a man's sacred duty to provide for and protect the women of his family.

Most of the other teachers had taken it badly. Aa'idah, however, knew it was a blessing from Allah, because scarcely five weeks after it had been closed, an American bomb had missed its target and damaged the school. It had been in the evening, after hours, but her heart still shuddered at the thought of tiny bodies buried in the rubble.

The conversation with her brother and the sheik ended. The sheik sailed majestically out of the conference room and into her reception area, followed by the brawny man at his side and a sulking Shukri. The large man, whose name was Zaahir al-Farouk, frightened her. The Salafist jihadists, of which her stupid brother was now proudly a member, frightened her as well, but Zaahir's zealotry bordered on lunacy. He intended to strike at the heart of the infidel, whatever that meant. His seething hatred of all things Western was idiotic, but she dared not say so. Not to her brother. Not to her father.

Zaahir stopped at her desk, offering her a gentle smile that made her want to hide. "Good morning, Aa'idah. How are you today?"

Aa'idah could not force herself to return the smile. She kept her gaze lowered, afraid he'd see her thoughts in her eyes. "Good morning to you, as well. I was just about to get a cup of tea." She winced, realizing too late her words might be misconstrued as an invitation. Fortunately, the sheik barked at Zaahir to hurry. With a lingering, pensive look, he nodded to her and left.

Aa'idah let out a slow, shaking breath. Each time she saw the big man, his interest became more blatant. Her brother would see it as an honor; perhaps force her into accepting Zaahir's interest. And then what would she do? She shuddered with revulsion and fear.

When had her life become so complicated and fraught with danger?

If either her brother or Zaahir were to learn that Christina Madison wanted her to spy on her family, she would be punished and sequestered. Christina hadn't come right out and said that's what she wanted of Aa'idah, but Aa'idah was not stupid. Nor was she ready to betray her loved ones, no matter how misguided her brother had become.

But at the same time, she could see what waited in her future. First they took the right to education away from Muslim girls. Then they took everything else. She could not simply stand by and watch that happen.

Whatever her brother and his cohorts planned would be dangerous, and doomed to failure. Yes, they might strike a blow. Bloody some noses. But long-lasting peace could not be achieved through violence. And Aa'idah wanted peace for her country. She wanted an end to the constant presence of NATO soldiers, the constant fear of bombs exploding and killing her friends, her family. She wanted a return to how things had been, when a Western influence had been considered beneficial.

She didn't hate Americans. She just wanted them to leave.

Without the constant American presence, her brother and the other jihadists might relax.

But with the increased influence of the imams, she could very well end up a virtual prisoner in her own household.

The thought of her gender declining into the equivalent of a Dark Age, banned from government, from careers, their vision and perspective ignored, flooded her with repugnance. Her stomach churned. It was happening here in Azakistan as surely as it had happened in Afghanistan and Iran.

She would help end this, Aa'idah decided. She would discover Zaahir's plan and find a way to pass the information to Christina Madison. It would be worth it, if she could help stop the insanity in some small way.

And maybe, in the process, she could save her brother's life.

Chapter Sixteen

August 27. 11:00 A.M.
Base Hospital, al-Zadr Air Force Base, Azakistan

THEY GATHERED AROUND her hospital bedside like so many shadowy mongrels. No group of people could have been more dissimilar: the starched-and-pressed commander of 5th Battalion, 10th Special Forces Group, wearing a blue service uniform and a chestful of ribbons; the jittery CIA station chief, Jay Spicer, in his rumpled plaid shirt and flip-flops; a Secret Service agent wearing a cheap black suit; and a lawyer from the Judge Advocate General's Office, on hand to assist her with whatever she needed. Even the FBI legal attaché put in an appearance because she had been a kidnapped American. An impossibly young soldier in an Army combat uniform sat off to the side with his stenograph machine.

"Just take your time," the lawyer said, crossing her legs. "Take us through the events of August 10 and 11."

Heather pushed back against the pillows propping her up, trying to get comfortable. This debriefing would be much easier if she were properly dressed, she reflected. But no, she wore a hospital gown and fuzzy pink socks. She sighed. Where to start?

"Well, I was in Eshma, as you know. They were desperate for Arabic speakers after the bombings. I was there for about two weeks." She drew her knees up to her chest and ran her palms over them. "I was in a market plaza grabbing some lunch. Wearing a full burkha, as requested by the mayor when relief workers started arriving on-site. I sat under a tree and read my book while I ate.

"Three men were already at table close by. I couldn't hear everything they said, but they were quarreling. Angry. The man in charge was . . . was the man who questioned . . ." *Call it what it was, Langstrom.* "Tortured me. While I was being held, to find out if I really knew anything."

She focused on the water pitcher by her bed. Anything was better than seeing their pitying expressions.

"What was his name?" Jay Spicer asked. His foot tap-tap-tapped against the floor.

"I never found out. The soldiers just called him sayyed. Sir."

"Can you describe him?" asked one of the Secret Service agents. Brian something. He gripped a stubby pencil as he prepared to jot down notes.

"Yes." She would never forget him. Never. "Big. Broad shoulders. Six-two, maybe? Definitely five or six inches taller than most Arab men. Swarthy. Strong nose with just a slight hook. Short hair with a bit of gray at the temples, but I doubt he was any older than forty."

The lawyer tapped her pen onto her yellow legal pad. "What happened then, Lieutenant?"

"I called my company commander, who was in Eshma with

me. I asked him to get us in to see Sa'id al-Jabr, the Eshma chief of police. I wanted to see if the men I saw were known criminals."

"Were they?" Jay Spicer asked. Now his knee bounced. The man seemed incapable of sitting still.

"Sa'id al-Jabr claimed he didn't know them. I could tell he was hiding something, though. He didn't seem concerned when I tried to warn him about the possibility of another attack, like the one at the Ubadah Government Center." That had turned out to be her last day of freedom.

Her battalion commander shifted his weight. Unlike the others, who sat or leaned on various surfaces, he stood with legs shoulder-width apart and arms at his sides. "At this point, Captain Bernoulli contacted me and gave me a full report."

The lawyer looked up from her notes. "And Captain Bernoulli is . . . ?"

"My company commander," Heather said. "Was. He died in the convoy attack." Her throat tightened. She grabbed the pitcher and poured herself some water to cover the sudden rush of emotion.

Jay Spicer gave her a reassuring nod. His knee finally stilled. "Colonel Neal passed that report on to me." He gestured to the battalion commander, glancing to make sure the lawyer understood. "We followed up on that, Lieutenant. Sa'id al-Jabr got his position through political connections. If he has ties to the Kongra-Gel, we couldn't find it."

"We don't believe at this point the convoy attack had anything to do with the Eshma police," added the FBI legal attaché, "or the mayor's office. We think it was a target of opportunity."

Brian of the Secret Service looked up at that. "Sorry, what? There's no way that was coincidence."

"I didn't say coincidence," the attaché said. "I said opportunity."

The battalion commander, Lieutenant Colonel Jerry Neal, turned more fully to face Brian. "He means that the men Lieutenant Langstrom saw acted on impulse to ambush the convoy."

Brian's brow furrowed as he shook his head. "And took her? Only her? Lieutenant, were you the only woman in the convoy?"

Heather put a hand to her aching head. "I think so. Maybe. I honestly don't remember."

"So they were looking for whoever wore the burkha, I guess," Brian muttered, scribbling something into his notebook.

Jay Spicer scratched his cheek, then just left his fingers where they were, as though he'd forgotten what he was doing. "Hate to ask you this, Lieutenant," he said. He looked at the floor, then ran a finger under his lip. "You said 'questioned.' The man who questioned you. What did he ask?"

Heather froze. She *so* didn't want to go there.

"Lieutenant?" This time it was her commander, his tone calm but authoritative.

She took a deep breath. "He wanted to know why I was in Eshma. Something about a lab. Who I'd told about the Kongra-Gel attack. I didn't know anything."

"There will not be an attack," Colonel Neal. "Bomber planes destroyed the missile they had on-site. They no longer have the ability to attack us."

"I'll have you write everything out in more detail," the lawyer said. "We're just trying to get the basics here."

"What happened after your visit to the Eshma police?" Jay Spicer asked.

She began to breathe again. "Captain Bernoulli decided we should head back here, to al-Zadr. We'd done everything we could in Eshma. A convoy was leaving the next morning. He wrangled us a ride on it." She rotated her head, trying to alleviate some of the tension in her neck. "The trucks were empty. They'd brought medical supplies, food, and water to Eshma."

The next part would be tough. Heather forced herself to continue.

"The convoy consisted of an empty flatbed truck and two deuce-and-a-halfs." She glanced at the Secret Service agent. "That's a two-and-a-half-ton truck. It's a cargo-slash-personnel transport. Two wooden benches run the length of the truck bed, one on either side, butting up against a heavy canvas canopy. Looks kind of like a modern-day covered wagon."

Brian nodded and gestured for her to continue.

"We also had the required armored Humvees front and rear, with infantrymen to guard the convoy. Armor plating reinforced the trucks, and all of us wore flak jackets and Kevlar helmets. We were armed." She was stalling, and everyone in the room knew it. Heather cleared her throat.

"We'd been on the road for about forty minutes when the convoy slowed. I was in the back of a deuce-and-a-half and could see the turret gunner in the trailing Humvee start to yell and point. There was an explosion—it had to have been a roadside bomb. Next thing I knew, the truck was practically upside down in a ditch." Heather had been slammed against the metal siding hard enough to see stars. A heavy body had smashed into her. Cries of surprise and fear around her had turned to groans of pain.

"RPGs exploded in and around the convoy . . ."

"I'm sorry," Brian interrupted. "RPGs? Rocket-propelled grenades?"

"Yes. There was a lot of confusion, yelling, gunfire." She had struggled to lift the dead weight off her before she saw who it was. The young corpsman's face had been a bloody mess, his eyes open and staring. "I got free of the truck, then I could see maybe two dozen Arab men coming down the hillside, firing at us. I had my sidearm, so I returned fire."

"What were the others doing?" her commander asked.

"We were all fighting, sir. But there were too many of them. We were overrun."

"You surrendered?" Distaste colored the commander's tone.

"Yes, sir. We had no choice." She smoothed the blanket over her legs. "The leader—the sayyed from the camp—grabbed me. I fought, of course." Her fist had smashed his nose. She had the satisfaction of seeing his blood spurt before he growled and hit her alongside the head with a meaty fist. "I went down."

She crushed her empty paper cup in a fist. "Next thing I remember, I was in a prison cell in a terrorist training camp."

Chapter Seventeen

August 29. 11:30 A.M.
Base Hospital, al-Zadr Air Force Base, Azakistan

"I'M FINE," HEATHER said, for the four-thousandth time. Dr. Mc-Grath merely smiled, drat him. "Look, the bruises are fading. The infection in my shoulder is practically gone. I'm eating, and I'm hydrated. Why can't I go home?"

Dr. McGrath checked the tubes and made a minor adjustment. "I'm concerned about a lot more than your bruises, Lieutenant. Between the surgery, infection, the high fever, and the concussion, I feel we still need to keep you under observation. Add to that the interviews and statements you're giving, I'm not willing to risk a relapse. It's taking more out of you than you realize."

She didn't want to admit it, but the debriefing two days ago had exhausted her. Since then, she'd been moved to a private room on the medical-surgical floor, but access to her had been restricted by the base Public Affairs Office. They coached her before each public statement and interview, and wrote press releases on her behalf.

She was more than happy to let them take the lead. The sooner they were done with that nonsense, the better. Dr. McGrath supervised it closely, but he was right; it tired her.

"I'm keeping you here for another few days, at least. If you had a roommate or someone who could monitor you, I might be persuaded to release you early." He waited, kindly and patient, and Heather gave a tiny groan.

"You know I don't."

"Then ask one of your visitors to bring you some books or magazines to help pass the time. Don't think I don't know what will happen. As soon as I send you home, you'll be pushing to go back to work. They will get along without you for a few weeks."

Heather gaped at him. "A few *weeks*? What am I supposed to do for a few *weeks*?"

The doctor snorted a laugh. "Rest. Recuperate. Rest some more. Sleep. Watch a soap opera. And then rest again."

As he left, he turned sideways to avoid a figure leaning against the doorjamb.

Jace.

Once again, the room shrank with his presence. He was all broad shoulders and hard planes and strength. His short hair was curly; she itched to run her fingers through it, to discover if it was soft or wiry. She realized she'd been hoping that he would come, waiting, no matter how foolish the pipe dream was. He glanced her way and caught her gaze trailing over him. His smile held both knowledge and promise.

And that was the problem.

A woman who wanted a career in the Army had to hold herself to the highest standard. And that meant keeping her social life separate from the job. Keeping personal details personal, so nothing could be used against her. Not sharing, not dating, not making friends with the men with whom she worked. She'd learned that the hard way at Fort Campbell, Kentucky, just before she'd come to Azakistan. By dating the brigade's logistics officer, she'd opened herself up to smirks and leers. She hadn't realized until far too late that the louse had spread and embellished the details of their liaison. Taking her for the kind of woman who earned promotions on her back, the brigade commander promised her a glowing performance review in exchange for special favors. She'd managed to extricate herself, but it had taught her an important lesson. Never again would anyone be able to sneer that she'd gotten where she was on her knees. She could and would do it on her own, without help from anybody. Vowing then and there to eliminate even the slightest shred of overlap with her personal life, she threw herself into her career and requested deployment to Iraq or Afghanistan. The Army sent her here instead.

Straight into a situation that made her want to throw all her preventative measures out the door. It wasn't fair that men like Jace could smile like that. She dropped her gaze to the plastic-wrapped bundle he carried, avoiding his eyes.

Jace stepped over to her hospital bed and handed her the flowers.

"Thank you. They're lovely." Heather settled the bouquet into her arms. Her room was, in fact, littered with vases of blooms. The al-Zadr base command, members of her unit, the news media, her coworkers, people she didn't even know. Flowers had poured in. She'd sent most of them to other wards. The truth was, with all the hoopla, she'd barely had a moment to herself. But somehow *these* flowers were prettier and smelled sweeter than all the rest.

Good grief, Heather. Get a grip.

Jace glanced at the tubes still in her arms with a concerned frown. "So, how are you?"

Heather glowered. "Well enough to go home, but Dr. McTorture won't release me unless I have a chaperone."

Jace grinned. It completely transformed his face, making him look younger and verging on carefree. Heather caught her jaw dropping and snapped it shut, but she couldn't stop the flush that heated her face.

"Bored, huh?" he said.

Shrugging, Heather bent her head to sniff the flowers. The medley of wildflowers smelled heavenly. "I haven't really had time to be bored. The media rigmarole is a nightmare. I'm as famous as Lady Gaga, so they keep telling me. I've been to press conferences, meetings, debriefings. And these newspapers and magazines keep calling for interviews. They're relentless."

Jace pulled the visitor chair as close as the hospital bed would allow. "You're a hero. A captured female soldier who not only managed to escape, but also gave the Azakistani Air Force enough information that they bombed the terrorist stronghold where they kept you."

Heather laughed, shaking her head at the same time. "And we both know what a bunch of baloney that is. I did nothing of the sort. That was pure politics."

"Yeah." Jace glanced at her and smiled. "But it gave the Azakistanis a decisive victory and wiped out a terrorist training camp. It mollified the Americans who wanted retaliation for the attack on your convoy, and Washington can point to it as progress in the War on Terror. A win all around."

"It's embarrassing."

Jace chuckled. "It'll pass. Some politician will be caught cheating on his wife, or another Wall Street company will ask for bailout money, or there'll be a safety recall on power scooters. Give it a week. The sharks will move on."

Heather folded the blanket between her fingers, then smoothed it out. "Look . . . I never really got the chance to thank you. For saving me. Saving my life. Because whatever the media says, we both know I'd never have made it without you."

"Mace will be crushed."

"I meant all of you, of course." Laughing, Heather glanced up at him. And couldn't tear her eyes away. His warm gaze moved over her features, and in his eyes she caught the glimmer of the banked desire that had been burning inside her for days. Her smile faded, and her breath caught in the back of her throat. She couldn't mistake the heat. She caught herself shifting toward him and managed to stop herself, just barely. Frowning, she stared determinedly out the window. Still, she knew it was too late; he had seen the longing in her eyes.

He rose abruptly, putting the width of the room between them. Two seconds later, he returned to the blue plastic chair, perching on the edge of it. "Heather . . ."

She shifted the wildflowers, intending to set them on the table next to her bed. The long stems and wrapping paper tangled in her IV, flipping the bouquet over and sending it sliding toward the edge of the bed. They both reached for the flowers, hands meeting on the plastic. Faces mere inches apart. She froze, eyes widening. Moistened her lips with the tip of her tongue.

His gaze zeroed in on that small gesture, and Heather's will to resist stuttered along with her heart. Slowly, Jace took the flowers from her unresisting fingers and leaned over her, bracing one hand beside her head and the other near her shoulder. For a moment, he simply stared at her, taking in each nuance of her expression. He seemed to see straight through her skin to what she thought, what she felt. And what she wanted. She might regret it later, but right now, in this moment, what she wanted was Jace.

Jace tilted his head toward the ceiling, groaning and closing his eyes. "Christ," he muttered. "I can't."

Heather pulled her knees in to her chest, smoothing the blanket over them. Her heart was pounding overtime, and she wanted to jump out of bed and into his arms. Not good.

You don't date soldiers, Heather. Remember?

Jace captured her hand and pressed a kiss to the inside of her wrist. On top of the bandages. "You're still stiff and sore. You're still on pain meds." He cleared his throat. "And . . . that's ignoring the other . . . injuries."

Ah.

But he kept going. "And there's the whole Become-Attached-to-My-Rescuer thing."

Heather had to laugh. "Is that what this is?"

Jace scratched his nose, looking uncertain. "Well . . . emotions can flare while on a mission. And then, when things settle down . . ." He toyed with her fingers. "You are one tough lady. I admire the hell out of you. And once you heal . . ." There it was again, the heat in his eyes. "But not until you heal, and . . . have time to process what happened. And, you know, get help."

"Jace," she said softly. "I wasn't raped."

His eyes flared with relief. "Thank God. I was . . . I wasn't tiptoeing around it. Well, I was, but not because . . ." He scrubbed both hands down his face. "I can't even imagine what it might be like for a woman, held prisoner and tortured. Because you were tortured. I saw the evidence."

She turned to look out the window. "Yes. I was slapped around and burned and humiliated. But I wasn't raped." She shivered. "I would have been if I hadn't escaped. That man . . ." She stopped, embarrassed by the rush of tears. The hospital psychologist had warned her she would be hypersensitive for a while. She took a few deep breaths. "You saved me from that. And I'm grateful. But don't think it's any different for a woman to be captured than a man. You're subject to the same things."

"Maybe. But I've been trained to handle it."

She shot him an incredulous look. "No one is trained to handle it. You find out what you can endure. I've done Survival, Escape, Resistance, and Evasion training—SERE—and I know you go beyond what you think you can bear. And you also find your breaking point. Because everyone has one. Everyone."

Jace stared at her for a long moment. "You're right. I'm sorry. That was . . . sexist of me, wasn't it?"

Heather smiled. "Very. But I forgive you. You can't help yourself; it's that Y chromosome."

Laughing a little, Jace shook his head. "I'd better get going. Let you rest."

Disappointed, Heather's shoulders drooped as she focused on the television, mounted high on the wall. CNN played in the background, sound muted. "Sure you don't want to stay for lunch? The cart comes by in a few minutes. I think we get green goo today."

"I'll pass."

Heather forced herself to meet his gaze. "Well. Thanks for the visit."

His gaze traveled from her hair down to her mouth and seemed to get caught there. She moistened her lips. Jace swallowed. The voices in her head cautioning her not to let him get close became a purr in her head, urging her to meet him halfway, consequences be damned. He leaned over her again, his head tilted and his eyes closed, and when he captured her mouth, he didn't hesitate. Parting her lips with his tongue, he explored the inside of her mouth. The rough velvet slide electrified her. His mouth tasted of cinnamon and heat. She wanted to stay like this forever, wrapped in his scent of warm-honey fire. His hand slid down her throat, fingers pressed to the thudding pulse there.

And still he kissed her.

She slid her hand up his arm and around his shoulder, pulling him closer. As he gathered her into his arms, his hand tangled in the tubing, accidentally pulling on the IV needle taped to her arm. He cursed under his breath, freed himself, and straightened, looking down at her with a confused frown.

Silence descended in the room.

Heather broke the awkward silence. "Well . . . thank you for the flowers."

Thank you for the kiss. Do it again, please.

"I should go. You need your rest." But Jace didn't move.

Heather nodded. Before she could say anything, a sinewy figure filled the doorway, and her room shrank again.

Jeremy, the lean, muscular man who'd entered, chatted as he came in. "Hey, hey, LT. I figured you'd be about ready to, like, chew your arm off by now . . . oh, hi." He barely stopped as Jace stepped in front of Heather, craning his neck to look around Jace's impressive stature. He gave her what she thought of as his adorable-puppy look, devoted and worshipping. But he also noticed her guilty flush and bright eyes, because his brows pulled down. "I brought you some books," he said, sounding less genial. "I wasn't sure what you dig, so I grabbed some of mine, and, like, looted a couple from Stevie. Who are you?"

The once-over he gave Jace was not altogether friendly. Heather grimaced. That's all she needed. Jeremy was young, still growing into his green beret, and had a crush on her, to boot. Jace gave him a fixed stare, simmering with subdued raw male energy. Jeremy tried and failed to stare him down.

Neither had the right to stake a claim in her room.

She cleared her throat. "Jace, this is Private First Class Jeremy Wahl. Jeremy, this is Jace Reed. He led the team who rescued me."

Jeremy bobbed his head several times, smiling, though it didn't reach his eyes. "You *totally* have our thanks."

Jace did not crack a smile. "It's Captain Reed, actually. Good to meet you, Private."

Jeremy just kept talking as though he had not heard. "We weren't there when the lieutenant needed us. Let me just tell you how pissed we were. Everyone in our unit, they're ours, you know? We protect our own."

The threat, challenge, whatever it was, again zinged in Jace's direction. Heather sighed. Jeremy wasn't the youngest of the Special Forces soldiers of 10th Group, but he'd barely hit twenty, if that. And no matter how she'd tried to discourage him, he imagined himself in love with her. He had a baby face and California surfer-dude bonhomie, but like all Special Forces, he was a highly trained, highly skilled warrior.

And Jace would mop the floor with him.

Jace, bless him, did not laugh at the youngster or patronize him. He simply nodded. "I'd feel the same if I were in your shoes, Wahl. I'm glad I could bring her back safely." He stepped back, allowing Jeremy access to Heather's bed. She glanced at him with amusement, but he was scrutinizing Jeremy. He'd been about to leave, but had apparently decided Jeremy needed monitoring. Not an entirely bad idea. Maybe Jace's hanging around would discourage Jeremy's crush.

Jeremy pulled the visitor's chair close to the bed and handed Heather the paper bag in his hand. "So your replacement is due to arrive in country in, like, two weeks. Top says you'll probably still be on quarters. We're all supposed to keep you away from the TOC." Still on bed rest, God help her, restricted to her quarters.

The Tactical Operations Center was the central hub of activity for the Special Forces assigned to al-Zadr Air Base. At least, she'd thought so. Evidently, Jace's unit operated autonomously. And anonymously. She no longer had the slightest doubt that he belonged to Delta Force. "Tell Top I'll be back as soon as I can." Master Sergeant Tom Hines, the senior—or top—sergeant in Jeremy's company, tended to hover protectively over her. Sometimes she found it amusing; other times, annoying. And always unacceptable.

She opened the paper bag and pulled out the books. The latest Dan Brown, two political thrillers, a book featuring vampires, and the history of the Bataan Death March. The last one made her wince.

"This should be light reading. Was this yours, or Stevie's?"

Jeremy grinned, unabashed. "Mine. It's only that my great-uncle survived it, and he's coming to visit in a couple of months, after I rotate back Stateside. My father sent it to me."

She set the books aside. "Thank you. I'm stuck here for another day, so this is good." She looked at Jace, standing by the window, one hand clasping the opposite wrist at his waist in classic bodyguard pose, looking calm and steady and like he never intended to move.

Heather groaned inwardly. While she couldn't deny her attraction to him, she had worked long and hard to be accepted as an equal in this man's army. Even sitting in a hospital bed, she wasn't about to risk losing that, and Jace's sudden territorial attitude brought home the realities his kisses had banished. She didn't need a bodyguard, and having one would undermine the foundation she'd laid. Her men respected her. The women looked up to her. She wasn't about to trade that in for a man, no matter how much his kisses made her want it.

Jeremy chatted on about the various happenings within the company, and Heather smiled and nodded in the right places, while her mind worked on the problem of what to do about Jace. She snuck a glance at him. Feeling her eyes on him, he straightened and came to stand by her bed, suddenly radiating authority . . . and danger.

"Okay, Junior. Visiting hours are over."

Predictably, Jeremy rose, bristling . . . and once again, they stood toe to toe.

"I don't answer to you. I'll go if the lieutenant wants me to."

"She wants you to."

Jeremy got bigger, getting right in Jace's face. Jace was more experienced, harder, more dangerous. Couldn't the younger man see that Jace would tear him in two? Or didn't he care?

Of course he didn't. Why did men have to be so stupid?

"I have every right . . ."

"Shove off, Junior."

Heather clapped her hands together sharply, as though to disobedient children. "Both of you. Stop it. Stop it now."

The crack of authority in her voice broke the tension long enough for both of them to look at her. Good.

She pointed toward the door. "I think it's time for you both to go," she said. Wishing it could be another way didn't change the fact that it couldn't.

Poor Jeremy looked like a kicked puppy. She forced a smile. "Jeremy, thank you for the books. It was a lovely thought, and I will enjoy them. I need to rest, now, though, okay? Please?"

Jeremy nodded, his reluctance clear. "All right. Whatever you say, LT. I gotta get to training, anyway. I'll see you later." With one more hostile look at Jace, he left.

Jace moved to the chair Jeremy had vacated. "Finally."

Heather tossed the bag of books onto it before he could sit. She was suddenly angry with him, and equally angry with herself for letting it get this far. "And you can get out, too."

Jace had the grace to look contrite . . . or maybe the look was contrived, designed to get on her good side. Well, right now, she didn't have one.

"What the hell was all that about? Posturing and puffing like a couple of morons. Like I'm going to fall into the winner's bed, just like that?"

His eyes lit. "I'm good with that. As long as it's mine."

Heather was good with that, too. A sudden vision of them tangled together in his sheets . . . No, wait. She wasn't good with it. The answer was no. The answer had to be no. She fought his magnetic pull, fought her own attraction.

"You and Jeremy, the whole whip-it-out-and-measure-it thing. I can't allow that." She tried for brisk, professional, but her voice came out croaky and glum. "Seeing you two reminded me why I don't do relationships with military men.

It never ends well. No matter the temptation, I can't act on it. I won't."

"That's not even on the table until you've healed," Jace said.

Heather grabbed a double handful of blanket and tried to strangle it. "Jace. I am and always will be grateful for the rescue. I will always owe you my life. But." She let her head slump back onto the pillow, feeling a headache coming on.

Jace crossed his arms over his chest, the smile wiped from his face. "I don't want your gratitude. Not like you're implying."

"I'm not implying anything. I'm telling you flat out. You wouldn't be beating your chest like a caveman if you'd rescued a man. You'd accept his thanks and move on. That's what I need you to do for me."

Jace took in a lot of air and exhaled slowly. "You're not a man."

She chose her words with care. "As a woman in a male-dominated field, I have to work twice as hard to be considered half as good. And a significant percentage of the young, cocky men I work with take one look at me and don't take me seriously as a professional. As a potential girlfriend, sure. But that's not what I want. I'm not a part of this man's army to date. I'm good at what I do, and I intend to be the next female three-star general."

"So?"

"So-oo . . ." She drew out the word. "I don't date soldiers."

Jace looked displeased.

"Never?"

She shook her head.

"You must not have much of a social life. How long have you been stationed here?"

"Twenty-two months."

Jace looked puzzled. "So, what? You're a hermit? That's no good. People need people."

Heather lifted her chin. "I have my work. And it's not like I never go out. I just don't date military."

Jace leaned against the wall, crossing his ankles together. He studied the toe of his boot with apparent fascination. "No exceptions?" A dull red crept over his cheeks.

Heather made an exasperated sound. "This was a classic example of why I don't. You were ready to tear Jeremy apart just for being here. But guess what? I'm not property that needs to be guarded. I don't need your protection, or your jealousy, or your posturing."

Jace didn't move. He didn't blink. Finally, he nodded.

"You're right. I acted like a jerk. I just . . ."

He stared at the door, and she heard the words he didn't say. He'd been jealous. Of Jeremy. It would have been laughable if any of this was funny.

"Yes." She pointed at his chest. "I'm just a soldier you brought home. Same as any other. No more, no less."

Jace lapsed into that peculiar stillness again. Heather could practically see the gears working in his head.

"What?"

One side of his mouth tipped up. He straightened, and came back to her bedside. Leaning down, he used his thumb and forefinger to tilt her chin up. He dropped a hard kiss onto her mouth. "You can bet your ass I didn't kiss Mace when I saved his bacon."

And he was gone.

Chapter Eighteen

September 3. 6:10 P.M.
Ma'ar ye zhad, Azakistan

AA'IDAH HEARD THE voices as soon as Shukri opened the front door and preceded her inside. Shukri went immediately into the parlor. Aa'idah sighed, anxious to unwind her hijab, but that would have to wait until their guests departed. She had no desire even to see who pontificated so animatedly to her father, much less join them. All she wanted was a hot cup of tea and maybe to read a book for a while in front of the fireplace.

The day had been long and stressful. Her father had directed her to transfer sums from multiple sources into a company account she believed must belong to the sheik. She did not like it one bit. Her heart ached for the young, impressionable men—boys, really—recruited from tiny villages all over Azakistan, particularly from the southwest mountains of Badikh Rawasi Province, butting up against Afghanistan and so poor a few *tenge* a week seemed a fortune. Terror mongers filled their heads with nonsense, winding them up with their bastardization of the peaceful precepts of the Qur'an until they strapped bombs to their bodies and sent their souls to Allah before their time.

Her mother came into the hallway, motioning her to hurry into the kitchen. Aa'idah complied, nose wrinkling. Her mother tended toward the dramatic, with crises around every corner. True to form, she wrung her hands.

"We are running so low on tea," she said. "I hardly have enough."

Aa'idah made a soothing gesture. "But you do?" She looked over at the central island, at a tray laden with porcelain teacups and bread. "How many are here?" She noted the pastries on the counter with a sinking feeling. "They are staying for supper?"

"Yes. There are two, plus your father and Shukri, now he's home. Take this in to them." Her mother poured the tea into the fancy teapot and set it onto the tray. "Go. Do not make your father wait."

As Aa'idah entered the formal parlor, conversation ceased. Her heart sank. The odious man, Zaahir al-Farouk, reclined near her father, while the other man, slender and rather pale, sat opposite. Astonishingly, al-Farouk rose to take the tray from her. His fingers brushed along hers as he smiled warmly into her eyes. It would be rude to react otherwise, so Aa'idah returned the smile, moving to clear magazines from the side table so al-Farouk could set the tray down.

"My thanks, honored sir," she said, lowering her eyes modestly. It was expected of her. She hated it, and all the other little so-called proper behaviors which marked her as lesser.

He nodded and returned to his seat, but Aa'idah sensed him watching her as she poured the tea. A fine trembling seized her.

He noticed, for he cupped her hand in his much larger ones as he accepted the teacup. He sipped and gave an approving nod. "It is excellent."

"My mother will be pleased."

Zaahir al-Farouk settled back in his chair and focused back on her father. "You are truly blessed to have such a beautiful daughter, Mahmoud."

As Aa'idah left the room, she heard him ask, "She is unmarried, correct?" Her palms moistened, and her heart pounded. Please, no. Please, let her father reject him. Surely Allah would not be so cruel to her.

Dared she listen to their conversation?

Telling her mother she wanted to change out of her work clothes, she stepped into the hallway and tiptoed closer to the parlor door. Their voices rang clear. As she listened, her face lost all color.

Chapter Nineteen

September 5. 6:03 A.M.
Bachelor Officer Quarters, al-Zadr Air Force Base, Azakistan

THE HAIRS ON the back of her neck prickled a half second before her doorbell rang. She closed her book and carried it to the door, already knowing who would be waiting on the other side.

"I'm here to liberate you."

A smile tugged at her lips even before she twisted her head to watch Jace enter her tiny apartment. "Say again?"

"I wasn't sure you'd be awake this early." Jace crossed to the single window and nudged open her plain white window blinds. "Parking lot. Excellent."

"I specifically requested it when I first arrived."

Trying to control her silly grin proved impossible, so Heather tossed the book onto the couch and plopped down next to it. His gaze followed the movement.

"Dan Brown. Good choice."

"It seemed a little less intense than the Bataan Death March."

Jace fidgeted with the blinds, pressing the plastic until it bowed, then letting it snap back into place. "Yeah. So. How are you feeling?"

"Almost back to normal. They discharged me five days ago. Sixteen days in the hospital was fifteen days too long, but they were being extra cautious because of all the media attention. I'm restricted to quarters, though. No work, no running. Just sleeping and watching soap operas"

"I'm not surprised. You feel up for a ride?"

Heather sat forward, resting her hands on her thighs near her knees. "Really? Hell, yeah. You're really here to spring me?"

Jace scratched his chin. His gaze moved over her face and body, apparently trying to assess her condition through her nightgown and robe. "Only if you're up to it."

She pushed herself upright again, trying to hide her winces. "I'm up for it. Let's go. Where are we going?"

Jace chuckled. "Whoa, there. Let's get you dressed first, okay?"

She shot him an amused glance. "I'm even going to shower." She went into the bedroom and selected a change of clothes, then stepped into the bathroom.

She washed, ignoring the parts of her body that still protested, mostly around her ribs. Once dressed in jeans and a loose top, she grabbed the garment bag that held her newly-laundered dress green uniform. She'd lost her wallet along with her uniform—she would *not* dwell on that now—but the Public Affairs Office had provided her with a new military ID, which she slid into her front pocket.

Jace took the uniform bag from her. "Not sure you'll need this, but it's safer to have it than not."

"Okay, I'm ready. Let's go," she said, heading for the door.

He chuckled as he followed her out. "I have a car waiting."

Sure enough, a silver BMW Z4 was illegally parked just outside the staircase exit. She slid onto butter-soft leather seats. "Nice wheels. Typically male."

Jace laughed, a deep-chested burst of amusement that kicked shivers down her spine. "My other car's a minivan."

"Yeah, right."

"Okay, maybe not." He threw the car into reverse and executed a smooth backward-facing U-turn. Impressive.

"So where are we going?" Heather asked, not really caring about the answer. She was out of her quarters and spending time with Jace. A double win.

Jace left the bachelors' parking lot and turned onto Black Saber Road, wending his way north to avoid the senior enlisted housing area. Al-Zadr sat on more than twenty square miles of land, boasted two runways over seventy-five hundred feet, and hosted more than sixty-two hundred soldiers and airmen, plus a small Marine detachment. The Department of Defense provided primary and secondary education for dependent children. An indoor strip mall attached to the Base Exchange boasted a Starbucks, McDonald's, and Quiznos, as well as the flower shop and car-rental counter. Al-Zadr was a self-contained town.

Jace slowed at a light, then turned left onto Constitution Boulevard, which would take them out to the airfields. "We're taking a hop to Ma'ar ye zhad, the capital city. You been?"

"Couple of times," she said. "Mostly for training. Um . . . why?"

"Why are we going? Your language skills are needed. There was an accident. One of the embassy's classified-document couriers is in the hospital there. So you're kind of going to another hospital." Jace's smile had disappeared, replaced by a look of serious concentration. "It's a twenty-minute hop. They're hold-ing transport for us."

"Surely the embassy has interpreters?"

"For Arabic and Kurdish, even Pashtu. You speak Turkish. And you have the Top Secret security clearance they need. Some-one up there remembered you from the news and suggested you be brought in."

"Don't the foreign national couriers have to speak English?"

Jace frowned. "I don't have any more details. Here we are." He pulled into the airport's parking lot and killed the engine. Twist-ing in his seat, he faced her, face solemn. "If you're not up for this, you tell me, and I scrub this mission. No questions asked."

"No, I'm good." No way was she being shut out of the action. She stiffened her spine and squared her shoulders.

He continued to scrutinize her. "You sure?"

Heather put an end to the conversation by opening the car door and carefully climbing out. "I'm sure."

Jace hesitated for a long moment, as though he were having second thoughts. Finally, though, he emerged onto the pavement and clicked the car locks. "We're this way." Instead of entering the airport proper, he led her across the street, to a small fleet of cargo planes. He bypassed the two FedEx planes and the C-130 cargo transport, and stopped beside a Blackhawk helicopter. The pilot was under the rotor, making a notation on a clipboard. He raised a hand in greeting. "Go on in," he called. "Wheels up in two."

Her brow furrowed. "They're going to a lot of trouble. What's the rush?"

He lifted a shoulder and dropped it. "This was all arranged by Shelby Gibson at the State Department, which is inside the US Embassy in Ma'ar ye zhad. It's one of her couriers."

The side doors were locked back, leaving the interior open. Jace hopped on board, then turned to offer a hand. She considered ignoring it and climbing in herself, but it seemed petty, so she placed her palm in his and took the large step up into the helicopter. They sat in two jump seats at the rear and fastened the over-the-shoulder safety belts. In short order, the pilot climbed on board, started the rotors, and lifted into the air. Heather felt a familiar thrill. She'd ridden in helicopters many times, particularly during Air Assault School. She leaned over so that she could see the ground dropping away beneath her feet, absently rubbing her bruised ribs.

The chopping roar of rotor wash and air rushing past made talking nearly impossible, so Heather settled back and watched the world fly past. In about fifteen minutes, they dropped down onto a landing pad at the Kenneth L. Peek Army Air Field. An embassy car and driver waited for them.

A lump of dread settled in Heather's gut. What the hell merited this kind of VIP treatment?

Traffic snarled the streets as workers tried to beat the day's heat. As comparatively small as the capital city was at a mere half a million people, it packed too many into too small an area, causing overcrowding. Similar problems existed in the larger cities of Momardhi and Tiqt. Even Eshma, as remote as it was, filled daily as the poor flocked to the cities in search of a better life.

Pedestrians and vehicles alike ignored the embassy logo on the car. Their driver stood on his brakes several times to avoid an accident. The third time he swerved, laying on the horn, the force threw Heather against Jace. Her head landed in the middle of his chest, an arm wedged between them the only thing preventing her from being plastered against him chest to chest.

"Sorry," she mumbled into his chest. Bracing a hand high on his thigh, she pushed herself upright. The muscles under her hand corded, causing her to peek up at him.

"Don't move on my account," he murmured. A hard male gleam in his eyes told her where he really wanted her hand. She rolled her eyes. Men. She snatched it back, pushing deeper into her own seat.

"Aww." He gave her a lopsided grin that made her melt. "Put it back."

An answering smile tugged on Heather's lips. To quash it, she cleared her throat and rubbed her hands briskly over her knees. To distract him—and herself—she focused on their mission.

"Do you work with the State Department often?" she asked. "The helicopter, the car. Is this normal for you?" Or was this a personal favor from the State Department employee, Shelby Gibson? Surely that burning in her chest was from her breakfast of eggs and toast, not from any kind of jealousy.

"We work together from time to time. We're technically not part of any branch of service, so we get loaned out to do specialized jobs." Jace's eyes lit. "This time around, we're supporting the Secret Service for the president's visit."

"Nice," she said. "It's good morale for the troops that he's coming for Patriot Day." It always struck her as strange that the commemoration of the 9/11 horror seemed to center around the military, when none had been involved in the Twin Towers collapse.

"Yeah." His Adam's apple bobbed as he swallowed. "Hey, I was thinking . . ."

Uh-oh. Something about his expression, the tension in his body, his voice . . . Heather did not want to know what he'd been thinking. It was probably close to what she was thinking, and she could not go there with him. "So what brought you into the Army?" she cut in.

He hesitated for a long moment, during which Heather held her breath. The trouble was, she wasn't entirely certain if she was hoping he would take her hint or if he would ignore it. Finally, though, he dipped his chin and settled back onto the seat. "Never wanted to do anything else," he said. "My grandfather was an Airborne Ranger during the Korean War. I grew up on his stories. I wanted to honor him and have stories of my own to tell. He would have disowned me if I'd joined the Navy, so the SEALs were out."

Heather made a sound of agreement. The rivalry between Army and Navy stretched back two hundred years.

"Anyway, SEALs are good, but Delta's the best. I made Selection, and I've never looked back."

"Your family must be proud."

He looked away, shoulders suddenly tight. "Granddad, you bet. My old man had his hands full with . . . other stuff. My little brother. He, uh, didn't make it. He had substance abuse problems."

Heather felt herself soften with compassion. He would not welcome her sympathy, though. She didn't know how she knew that; she just did. She kept her tone brisk. "What about your mom?"

"She's the only reason the rest of us survived into adulthood." Genuine affection laced his tone. "I have two other brothers."

"Oh, my God," she said. "Five men and one woman in your house?"

Jace grinned. "My mother kept us in line."

The car slid to a stop in front of the Prince Nasser Hospital, which turned out to be a modern building of glass and concrete.

Heather pushed open her door, more than ready to put an end to the mystery and find out why she was here. Jace leaned forward to speak with the driver, then followed her through automatic doors and to the information desk.

"Morning," Jace said. "A man was brought in last night. Car accident. What floor's he on? Na'il Fakhoury."

The man tapped a few keys on his computer. "He is on the critical care ward, sir. Floor seven. The lift is on your right."

The elevator whispered open as though it, like the helicopter and car, had been waiting for them. It whisked them up.

As soon as she stepped out onto the ward, she saw the Marine guard, positioned with his hands clasped behind his back, stiff as a board. He stood alert, his gaze landing on them as they trekked down the corridor.

He nodded a greeting. "Ma'am. Sir."

Heather pulled her military ID from her pocket and handed it to the Marine.

"I'm Lieutenant Langstrom. Someone called me up here to talk to an embassy courier?"

He examined her ID and consulted what was clearly a faxed form, probably a list of allowed personnel. Finally, he looked back at her and returned her ID. "Yes, ma'am. Follow me to the prisoner." He moved far enough to look into the room and give a nod.

Heather's brows pulled down in confusion. "Prisoner?"

The man's grim expression didn't change. "The classified documents pouch was open when the kid was brought in, Lieutenant. With that and his refusal to answer any of our questions, we have reason to believe Na'il Fakhoury is a terrorist."

Chapter Twenty

September 5. 7:20 A.M.
Prince Nasser Hospital, Ma'ar ye zhad

"UNTIL THERE IS an investigation, he will remain in custody."

Jace stepped forward. "Can you run us through the timeline? We're a little behind the power curve here."

The Marine's eyes slid to Jace. "And your name, sir?"

Jace pulled his ID out and handed it over. "Captain Reed."

The guard—Gunnery Sergeant Bisantz, according to his rank insignia and name tag—checked his security clearances list. "Yes, sir. Your command faxed over your clearance an hour ago."

Heather was not surprised. Delta always got the best. Their clerical support must also be top-notch.

"What I can tell you is that the courier from Tehran was on his way to the embassy at around four in the morning when another vehicle ran a red and T-boned him," Bisantz said. "They found the kid's courier ID, their call got routed to the embassy agent on duty. He authorized the Marine Security Guard to dispatch me to the hospital because of the classified pouch."

"You said the pouch was open," Heather said. "Anything missing? Any documents recovered from the car?"

"No, ma'am." The Marine's voice was completely neutral. "The contents appeared to be intact on cursory examination."

She peeked into the room, where another Marine stood near the door, watching a nurse adjust some tubes running into Na'il Fakhoury's arm. The young man looked so small, so pale, lying in the hospital bed. His head had been bandaged. He had bruises and cuts on his face. Tubes and wires hooked him to various machines. Gauze covered what little she could see of his chest and arms. One thin wrist was handcuffed to the side rail of the bed.

What was going on?

A slim brunette sitting off to the side stood as Heather came in. "Heather? Are you Heather Langstrom?"

Heather crossed to her and shook her hand. "Yes. And this is Jace Reed."

"I'm Shelby Gibson. I'm sorry I dragged you out of bed so early. Thank you so much for coming."

"I'm happy to help. How is he?" She gestured to the injured man. When Shelby just shook her head, Heather went to the bed. The nurse looked up as Heather repeated the question in Arabic.

"I will fetch the doctor for you, miss. He will be able to tell you."

Heather went to Na'il's bedside. The sharp scent of antiseptic and detergent invaded her nostrils. His eyes remained closed, and his breathing seemed labored.

"Hello," came a lightly accented voice from behind her. She turned to see a man in a white lab coat, stethoscope slung around his neck. "I am Dr. Ramzi Alam." He came forward to shake her hand.

"Thank you for coming to talk to me. How is he?"

Dr. Alam shook his head. "Not well. His injuries are quite serious. His spleen ruptured, and his liver was bleeding rather extensively. There is swelling in his head. The surgeon has stabilized him, but he is still in critical condition."

Heather swallowed, feeling sick. "Consciousness?"

"He is in and out of it." The doctor checked the chart at the foot of the bed, made a notation, and went out.

Almost immediately, another man entered. This one was fiftyish, with a rapidly receding hairline. He crammed half a powdered donut into his mouth, barely bothering to close his mouth as he chewed.

"Jed. Finally. What took you so long?" Shelby Gibson's voice was sharp.

Jed brushed powdered sugar from his blue shirt and wiped his hands on his trousers. "Traffic."

"But I called you hours ago!"

"Where's the courier pouch?" Jed ignored Shelby's protest. Seeing it on the table by the window, he brushed past the brunette and went over to it, glancing at Jace without interest. Heather joined Shelby.

"Okay, so why does the Marine Security Guard think this guy is a terrorist?" she asked.

"Holy shit!"

Heather whirled around, immediately regretting the action as her still-sore body protested. Jace straightened, coming forward. Jed stared at a small, open case next to the misnamed security pouch, a boxy contraption with metal buckles and straps and a cypher lock. His mouth hung open and his face paled. The other Marine, Corporal Landry by his sleeve stripes and name tag, actually took a step back.

"That's why." Shelby pulled a worried face.

Heather moved so she could see, shaking off Jace's restraining hand. Nestled in the metal case, in individually padded pockets, were five sealed, opaque vials and some sort of large metal syringe. She tipped her head toward the case. "Drugs?"

"No, ma'am," said Corporal Landry. "Please be careful."

"Then what . . . ?" And the significance of the tubes clicked. She flashed hot, then cold. "Oh, my God! You think these are some sort of biological weapon. Like anthrax?"

The Marine nodded. "It's possible, ma'am. We need to get them tested to be sure. They are intact; the accident didn't rupture them. But, ma'am," he said, "we found them inside the pouch."

Heather blinked. "But why assume the courier was smuggling them? Come on. For all we know, it's a compound for the chemical guys at al-Zadr. Some controlled substance. What does the paperwork say?"

Jed shuffled through the list of contents. "Nothing," he reported. "It's not on the manifest."

And that was the reason for the two Marine guards and the handcuffs. Not to protect the classified data inside the pouch, but to guard a suspected terrorist carrying a possible biological weapon. Sweet Lord in heaven.

Shelby scraped her hair behind her ear. It immediately fell forward again. She looked to Jed. "What do we do?" she whispered.

He brushed a hand over his thinning hair. "We call DTRA—the Defense Threat Reduction Agency. Turn these over to them. And

notify the Regional Security Officer, unless you guys called him?"
He directed his question to Corporal Landry.

The young Marine nodded. "Our orders are to take Na'il Fakhoury into custody and safeguard the classified pouch until an
authorized representative picked it up." Someone with the proper
security clearance, he meant.

Heather put a hand to her head, which spun a little. "What's a
Regional Security Officer?"

"Our boss," Corporal Landry said. "The Marine Corps Security
Detachment reports directly to the Regional Security Officer. He's
the senior security advisor to the ambassador. By now, he's probably
briefed Ambassador Stanton. He'll be looking for answers, and fast."

Jed clicked through his Blackberry. "Need the number for
DTRA," he muttered. "It's not here."

Heather rubbed her arms, feeling cold. What if those vials were
anthrax, and they leaked? All of them could get sick. Or even die.
Without being able to see what was inside, they couldn't even be
sure if the vials contained a liquid or a powder.

Why had it taken so long for someone at the embassy to react?
"Were you the duty officer, Shelby?" Heather asked.

Shelby gave Jed a disgusted look. "No. Jed was."

So Jed apparently had opted to order Marine embassy guards
to the hospital last night rather than come himself. The Marines
must have updated Jed at the same time they briefed their boss.
Lacking further orders, the Marines had remained at their post,
guarding both the classified data and their prisoner, waiting for
someone from the State Department with a Top Secret clearance
to come pick up the pouch. That Jed had not come was unprofes-
sional in the extreme.

"Did you know this last night?"

Jed didn't look up. "Nothing happened. Don't make a federal case out of it."

"For the love of God, Jed," Shelby nearly shrieked.

That earned her a glare. "No, I did not know about the vials. We had a conversation on an unsecured landline. The Marine just told me the pouch was open, and there was an irregularity."

And had, no doubt, told Jed to get his butt down to the hospital as fast as possible. The irresponsibility of it sucked the air from Heather's lungs.

"You better believe I'm going to make a full report of this," Jace snapped, snaring the odious man's attention.

Jed opened his mouth, shot a glance toward Corporal Landry, scowled, and resumed searching his phone directory.

Shelby wrapped both arms around her middle. "What is DTRA, Jed?"

He scrolled to a different area on his phone. "They're the experts in weapons of mass destruction. We don't have one here. I think the nearest might be in Kazakhstan."

She shivered again. "But that could take hours, for them to get here. What do we do in the meantime?"

A soft moan from the bed got their attention. Heather and Shelby both hurried to his side. Na'il. He muttered something, tossing his head from side to side.

"Get the doctor!" Shelby called to Jace.

The nurse came in, taking Na'il's pulse and feeling his forehead. The doctor wasn't far behind, pressing his stethoscope to the boy's chest. He apparently didn't like what he heard, for his brow furrowed, and he moved the stethoscope to another spot.

"We need to talk to him," Heather said "Is he conscious enough for that?"

The doctor shook his head. "He must rest."

Shelby's phone rang. The doctor gave a disapproving frown. "You must turn it off, miss. Our equipment can't be compromised. You may use it in the lobby."

Shelby silenced the phone and powered it off. "I'm sorry, Dr. Alam. About Na'il . . . we won't make things worse, I promise. But if it's at all feasible, it really is vital we talk to him."

The Marine from the hallway came inside. "My boss authorized me to conduct a preliminary investigation. Ambassador Stanton wants an update."

Dr. Alam nodded. "His condition is still critical, but speak with him if you must. Try to limit to your questions to five minutes. I would be happy to translate."

The Marine shook his head. "I'm sorry, Doctor. This is a classified investigation." He looked at Corporal Landry. "Man the door. No one in or out."

"Yes, Sergeant Bisantz." The corporal disappeared.

Shelby planted herself at Na'il's side. The doctor gave a warning glare all around and departed. Sergeant Bisantz leaned over the bed.

"Mr. Fakhoury. Can you hear me?"

Na'il focused on the Marine. Hostility flared in the younger man's gaze, his mouth tightening and twisting as a spate of words flew out of his mouth. Heather's cheeks reddened.

"Not a compliment?" Sergeant Bisantz asked, deadpan.

Heather nearly choked out a laugh, but the seriousness of the situation focused her. "Uh, no. Not unless your mother really did copulate with a camel."

Sergeant Bisantz lowered his gaze to the man in the bed, face expressionless. "Mr. Fakhoury, I need you to answer a few questions. What are those vials? Where did you get them? Did someone give them to you?" The sergeant asked the questions as though he had all the time in the world, with an air of patience that clashed with his impassive face and stiff posture. Heather translated in the same calm tone.

The young man pressed his lips together, face shuttered and sullen.

Sergeant Bisantz posed more questions over the next few minutes, but Na'il refused to speak. Finally, the Marine slapped his own leg with a hand and rose. "We'll try this again in a bit. We'll just have to keep at him until he talks."

"But that could take hours." Jed said. "We may not have hours." He glanced meaningfully at the case containing the vials. "We may not have minutes." He ran his palm over his thinning hair several times. A drop of perspiration slid down his temple.

"Now, Jed," said Shelby. "Let's not get ahead of ourselves. Obviously, nothing has happened. The vials are intact. Let's not panic."

Ignoring her, Jed turned to the Marine. "I want this room quarantined. I want decontamination units sent here. Do you understand?" His voice quavered as he gave the commands.

Heather rolled her eyes. Jed was working himself into a state. Across the room, Jace snorted with derision.

Ramrod straight, the Marine blanked his face. "Mr. Callum, please don't overreact. Corporal Landry and I have been here all night. The doctor believes we're safe. I think the first step is to contact DTRA, as you suggested. How 'bout if you do that now, sir." He maneuvered Jed out of the room, pointing down the hallway. "The nurses' station has a telephone you can use. The sooner we get some concrete information, the sooner you can update the ambassador."

Clever. The prospect of briefing the US Ambassador to Azakistan finally got the man moving in the right direction. Away. Heather exchanged an amused look with Jace and the Marine.

Heather sat at Na'il's bedside, trying to coax the young man into talking to her. He just shook his head and glared. The utter hatred and contempt he levered at her stunned Heather. Could he really have agreed to transport the case of vials inside the classified pouch? No one would stop or question a courier for the Embassy of the United States. It was the perfect cover; and, she had to admit, the perfect way to transport hazardous chemical weapons without being detected. If the vials were really dangerous, where had Na'il been taking them? And for what purpose?

After a few moments, he slipped back into unconsciousness. That, or he pretended to sleep, to avoid her questions.

Sergeant Bisantz ran a hand along the back of his virtually nonexistent buzz cut. "Damn it. We're not getting anywhere." He gave his attention to the woman from the State Department. "Are there any other irregularities in the morning pouch, ma'am?"

She grinned. "Call me Shelby, for heaven's sake. If we're going to die of anthrax poisoning, we might as well be on a first-name basis, right?"

Amusement glittered in the other man's eyes as his lips twitched. "Then you better call me Hugo." He crossed the room and lowered his voice. "Is it inappropriate for me to tell you that I'm impressed with how you're handling this? You're keeping your cool. Not overreacting."

Shelby's eyebrows shot up to her hairline. Heather smothered a smile and looked away, at least giving them the illusion of privacy.

Unbidden, her gaze sought out Jace, who leaned against a wall with his arms and legs crossed. He watched her, concern in his eyes.

"You okay?" he mouthed. She nodded, wishing he would stop asking her that.

"I've seen you around the embassy," Hugo said. "People like you. And, well, me, too. Would you have dinner with me some night?"

Shelby clapped a hand over her mouth as a giggle escaped. "Aren't you the king of poor timing? By tonight, we could both be drooling and puking."

As he opened his mouth to respond, a shadow at the door sharpened his attention there, and he was abruptly once again the rigid Marine. Corporal Landry poked his head in.

"Sergeant, we lucked out. DTRA says there's a biochemical weapons expert in Ma'ar ye zhad right now. A Brit. He's on his way in now."

Shelby's face whitened, and her hands tightened into fists. Heather moved to her side and whispered. "You okay?"

"Not really."

Chapter Twenty-One

CONFUSED, HEATHER PULLED Shelby aside. "You know him?"

Shelby swallowed. "Yes. He's part of the team supporting President Cooper's 9/11 visit." She ran both hands through her hair, gripping the ends hard. "I could just go back to work. Leave this to the experts. Where's Jed?"

Corporal Landry grimaced. "He went back to the embassy."

"What? Why?"

The younger Marine shrugged. "He said he would check back later, when we knew something for sure."

"But he's the one who suggested the quarantine!" Shelby cupped her own cheeks, lines forming between her brows. "And he was my ride back. I came in a taxi."

Hugo straightened even more, something Heather would have thought impossible. "We'll make sure you get back in one piece, ma'am."

She sighed and groaned, pressing her hand to her forehead. "All right. Thank you, Hugo."

With a flick of his head, Hugo sent the other man back out

into the hall. "Listen, I hope I didn't cross any lines. By asking you out . . . ?"

Heather went back to the hospital bed. Na'il still appeared to be unconscious.

Shelby rammed the sheaves of paper back into the courier case, face bright red. "No, no lines," she said. "But you have to understand how hard it is, being a woman in a country like Azakistan. Even inside the embassy, everything I do is scrutinized, cataloged, and judged." She pushed her hair behind her ear. "I appreciate the invitation. But I have to say no. I'm sorry."

"Me, too. But I understand."

With Na'il out of it, Heather found herself without anything to do, but unable to leave in case he regained consciousness and talked. Jace left, with the promise to return with food and coffee. Hugo helped to pass the time by relating stories of some of his adventures on this assignment, which had Shelby and Heather laughing helplessly.

" . . . and I swear to God, he weighed four hundred pounds. We tried to get him onto the helicopter . . ."

The rest of Hugo's words disappeared as a man in uniform appeared in the doorway, tan beret in hand. Shelby took one look, then deliberately kept her back to him as Hugo popped to attention.

"Good morning, sir. Ma'am. I'm Gunnery Sergeant Hugo Bisantz, Embassy Security Group."

"Major Trevor Carswell, 22nd SAS, Counter-Terrorism."

"Christina Madison. British Education Foundation."

The female voice snapped Shelby's head around.

Curious, Heather gave her a once-over, then stared. The woman standing next to Trevor was maybe four or five inches shorter than her own five foot ten. Her hair crackled and moved around her head like a living thing, curling down past her shoulder blades. Her face, though—minus the hair and narrow shoulders, the woman was a dead ringer for the crown princess of Concordia, Véronique de Savoie. Heather remembered a news spot from her time in the hospital about the princess's goodwill visit to Mali, and her subsequent return to Europe to raise awareness for hunger in Africa.

The woman in the hospital room, however, wore an oversized T-shirt and sweatpants that swam on her slender frame. Christina Madison turned her hands over to show empty palms to Hugo. Paper rustled as the British major gave Hugo a copy of his orders, which would also carry his clearance level. He wore a desert-camouflaged uniform, pressed and crisp, with trousers tucked into tan boots. The princess clone looked around, nodding to Heather and Shelby.

"Ma'am, I need you to wait in the hallway with Corporal Landry," Hugo said. Christina left without protest.

Hugo nudged his chin toward the silver case and filled Trevor in. It didn't take long. There was too much they didn't know.

Trevor's eyes gleamed with intelligence and understanding. Rather than open the case, however, he took three steps to stand in front of Shelby. She tucked her chin and crossed her arms, grasping each elbow with her fingers.

"Major," she said coolly.

"Good morning, Shelby." His tone was soft and questioning. "All right?"

"Just fine." She dismissed him with a nod, turning toward the case with studied nonchalance. "What do you think it is? Anthrax?"

Trevor hesitated for a long moment, simply looking at her. Finally, he moved to the silver case. He took each vial out, checked the seal on the stopper, held it up to the light, and sniffed it. "Doubtful. These are almost certainly liquids." He paused, then elaborated. "These types of opaque vials are generally used for chemicals in liquid form. You would have to swallow anthrax in its liquid form to come to any harm from it, so if it does turn out to be anthrax, none of you are infected. Even if the courier was exposed, you can't catch it, like a virus."

Heather exhaled a breath she hadn't known she was holding. Good to hear.

"That's . . . a relief. What is it, then?" asked Shelby.

Trevor's somber voice seemed to echo in the room. "Polio. Cyclosarin. VX, or another nerve agent. Without testing them in a lab, I have no way of knowing." Trevor replaced the vials in the case. "These are solidly sealed, so we're all safe for now. I'll have to take them to a facility equipped to deal with potentially hazardous substances. Given the circumstances, we have to fear the worst, I'm afraid."

Hugo had taken up a post just inside the door, much as Corporal Landry had earlier. "I'm told that might be in Kazakhstan, sir. If that's true, I'm fairly certain the Regional Security Officer, Special Agent Johns, would authorize a helicopter to get you there as fast as possible."

Snapping the case closed, Trevor took possession of it. "That would be helpful. The sooner the better, I should think."

"Yes, sir." Hugo started for the door, but Shelby beat him there.

"I'll make the call. That way, you can guard your prisoner." She smiled brightly at him. "And I can update my boss." She turned to leave.

Heather shook her head. Clearly, something had happened between the two. This was a solid example of why she didn't date
people with whom she worked. It never ended well, and the drama
and heightened emotions disrupted professional interaction, as it
did here. It was good that Shelby was leaving.

But Trevor followed her out into the hallway.

"Shelby, wait."

Chapter Twenty-Two

September 5. 10:14 A.M.
Prince Nasser Hospital, Ma'ar ye zhad

JACE STEPPED OUT of the elevator, juggling a tray piled with food and two cups of coffee. He needed to ensure that Heather had the chance to eat. Something about her made him want to care for her, to whisk her away to some private spot, just the two of them. And keep her there for a week. Make that two weeks. Preferably naked the whole time. He paused to savor the erotic images swimming through his imagination.

"Shelby, wait!" The SAS officer from the Secret Service briefing, Trevor Carswell, hurried down the hallway, trying to overtake the woman with swishing dark hair and war in her eyes. "*Miss Gibson.*"

The sheer command in his voice made her stop and turn.

"Yes, Major Carswell?" Her voice was glacial.

"I'm sorry I didn't wake you this morning. There was an emergency . . ."

The woman slashed the air with a hand. "Don't give it a second thought, Major. It's a matter of supreme unimportance."

Jace almost felt sorry for the guy. He clearly didn't know what to do. Obviously the two had acted on their mutual attraction in the time since the briefing and had spent the night together. It also plainly meant more to Shelby than she let on.

"Shelby, let me explain . . ." the Brit started.

She glared at him and stepped closer. Jace nearly missed her next words. "Is that woman wearing your clothes?"

"Well, yes, but . . ."

"And was she in your apartment this morning?"

Trevor sighed, clearly frustrated. "Yes, but . . ."

"Then there is absolutely nothing more we have to say to one another." She turned on her heel, brushing against Jace as she pushed past. "I have work to do, and so do you."

The man hesitated, torn. In the end, though, he squared his shoulders, swept an assessing gaze over Jace, and turned away. Jace didn't take it personally. He obviously needed a few moments.

He followed the sound of voices back to the critical care room. A woman, this one shorter and with very curly hair, lingered in the corridor. God, how many people did it take to question one Azakistani national?

"Hi. Are you feeling as useless as I am?" the unknown woman asked. "Fetching lunch?"

Jace did a double take, looking at her closely for the first time. "You look just like . . ."

She rolled her eyes. "I know. Princess Véronique of Concordia. Been hearing it my whole life." She stuck out a hand. "Christina."

"Jace. Good to meet you." He tried to shake with the hand holding the coffee, and nearly spilled it on her.

"Right. Sorry. Stupid of me." Christina dropped her hand. "I don't suppose that's for me? I sure could use some caffeine."

"Sorry, no. Cafeteria's on the second floor." He twitched his head at a sandwich, then jerked his chin at Corporal Landry, who scooped it up.

"Thanks!"

"Not a problem." He cast a look at Christina. "Not letting you into the fun house, huh?"

"I'm not really a part of this," Christina said. "I'm just waiting for a ride."

"I'm sure we'll all be done soon."

Jace set the tray and coffee cups down and handed a sandwich to Hugo Bisantz, who accepted it with a surprised look. "Thank you for thinking of us, sir."

Heather sat beside Na'il, speaking to him in a quiet voice, her body language open and encouraging. Jace took a few moments simply to look at her. Long auburn hair hung down her back, with enough wave to make his hands itch to run his fingers through it. Her amazing blue eyes were serious as she listened to the injured man. Her oval face was classically beautiful, her nose adorable. Casual jeans and a stretchy top accentuated her long waist and those long, long legs he wanted wrapped around him. And just like that, he was hard again.

Trevor finally came back inside. He spoke quietly to Gunnery Sergeant Bisantz just before the Marine guard disappeared out the door. "The sergeant is finding us a room where we can talk." He thrust out a hand. "Trevor Carswell. I'm with the 22nd Special Air Service. Don't know if you remember me from Shelby's briefing last week."

"Jace Reed. First Special Forces Operational Detachment-Delta."

"That's what I thought. What's your connection here?" Trevor's gaze followed Jace's to land on Heather. "Ah."

"I'm escorting Lieutenant Langstrom, that's all." But he looked hard at the other man.

The Marine came back into the room. "Ladies and gentlemen. If you'll follow me, please." The three of them, followed by Christina, trooped out of the critical care area and into an unoccupied private room. "The prisoner will stay in my custody until I'm instructed otherwise," Sergeant Bisantz said. "From this point forward, only authorized personnel will be permitted into his room. This space is for your use indefinitely." He left.

"Well," said Heather. "Na'il is definitely hiding something. He won't answer any questions about the case with the vials. He insists he didn't open the courier's case. He is distant and hostile." She looked at Trevor and Christina. "Where do you fit in?"

Trevor introduced himself again. "Biochemical weapons. I'm taking the vials to the lab in Almaty, Kazakhstan. The helicopter will be here in thirteen minutes."

Christina stepped forward and offered her hand. "Christina Madison. CIA, but currently on assignment with the British Education Foundation, so if you could avoid mentioning me at all, that would be good."

Heather shook it and turned to Jace. "He's in bad shape. The doctor isn't certain he'll survive the night. Whatever information we get from him, we'll have to do it fast. So far, he's not cooperating."

Jace thought for a moment. "Who does he know at the embassy that we can talk to? Can we compile a list of friends and associates? Talk to his family?"

Trevor cleared his throat. "Shelby can probably help us with that. She's one of the deputy political counselors. She should still be in the hospital."

Jace doubted that. More likely, Shelby had made a beeline out of there after she ended her argument with Trevor. He slid an assessing glance over Christina. Yep, those were definitely men's clothes. Amusement glittered in his eyes as he considered various scenarios that could have landed Trevor in his current predicament.

Christina intercepted his look and grimaced. "For the past two weeks, I've been a guest of the conservative Ma'ar ye zhad secret police. Keepers of the old ways, which is another way of saying repressive, oppressive, misogynistic control freaks."

Heather blanched.

Jace was instantly at her side, gripping her arm lightly. "You okay? You need to sit down?"

Heather shook her head and pulled away from him. "No, I'm . . . I'm fine."

Christina cocked her head, puzzlement flitting across her face. It cleared quickly. "Hey, I recognize you now. You . . ." She stopped, clearly ill at ease.

Taking a deep, fortifying breath, Heather forced a laugh. "Was also a guest, of sorts. Two weeks? I was only a prisoner for four days, and it seemed like a lifetime."

Christina whistled between her teeth. "Hey, they just detained me. I was never charged. Someone didn't like who I was talking to. That's not the same as being a POW. I listened to the interview you did for NPR. It was . . . well." She blew out a hard breath. "I at least got three squares and a reasonably comfortable cot."

Heather's face lost even more color, and she swayed. Ignoring the others in the room, Jace pulled her into his arms and held her. Something Christina had said made her react—the cot? Was that it? The implication had Jace gritting his teeth, the urge to hunt down and kill every man who had touched Heather strong enough to make him tremble with the force of it. She'd insisted that she hadn't been raped, but he still didn't know exactly what had happened while she'd been held captive. He swallowed hard.

Christina said something about not being allowed to use the telephone until someone decided to wake her in the middle of the night and return her cell phone to her. "I need to maintain my cover as a British aid worker, but I can't involve the Foundation in any way. Their reputation here has to be spotless, or they won't be invited back in. That was the deal . . . if I ran into any trouble, I was on my own. You know—'the secretary will disavow any knowledge . . . ?'" She raked long fingernails through her curls, fluffing her hair. When she was done, it looked exactly the same to Jace. "So I called my old buddy Trevor for a local contact. I couldn't believe it when he said he was here. My lucky day!" She beamed at Trevor, who smiled back at her with affection.

Jace realized he was staring down at Heather's mouth, moving closer. She stopped him with a slight headshake and gently pulled out of his arms. He immediately missed her warmth.

"I'm fine," she whispered to him.

Fine? No, she wasn't. But he couldn't take the time to probe for more information. They had a puzzle to solve.

Trevor picked up the mysterious case. "Time for me to head for the roof. Let's get some answers." He started to leave, then stopped short, a strange look crossing his face as he looked at Christina. "Uh . . . where do you need to be, princess? Back at your hotel?"

She looked surprised. "Oh. Yes, eventually. But if it's all right . . . that is, if either of you are going anywhere near the embassy, I sure would be grateful for a ride." She divided a hopeful glance between Heather and Jace. "I should check in with Jay."

Jay Spicer, the CIA station chief. Jace remembered him from the Secret Service briefing. "We have a car. The driver can drop you there," he said. "We might be here awhile."

Christina exited with Trevor. It was quiet in the room after they left. Jace kept an eye on Heather. "Are you all right?"

She rotated her neck, trying to work the kinks out. "I wish people would stop asking me that."

He grasped her shoulders and turned her. When he settled his hands on her shoulders, she tensed, then calmed. He kneaded her trapezius, pressing the muscles to loosen them. It took several minutes, but she finally relaxed, allowing him to massage her neck and the base of her skull. A tiny moan slipped out, and his heart leapt in triumph as she melted against him.

"You have magic hands."

"And don't you forget it." He kept his tone light, teasing, knowing she remained one touch away from bolting. It was too soon after her desert experiences. Still, he couldn't stop himself from stroking his fingers through her hair. It felt amazing, soft and supple and almost alive. He dropped his nose to her neck to inhale. She smelled like cherry blossoms. His mouth watered.

Her head tilted forward, giving him better access. "I should get back to Na'il," she whispered.

"In a minute," he murmured. "Let me hold you." He slid his arms around her waist and spooned her, surrounding her as much as he was able with his strength, his warmth. He rested his chin on her shoulder.

She turned in his arms, surprising him. For long moments, they simply stared at one another, awareness sizzling between them. She cupped his cheeks with her palms, but made no other move. He covered one of her hands with his own, bringing it down to rest over his heart.

"Heather . . ."

"Shhh."

Her other thumb stroked against his bottom lip. He turned his head, capturing it and drawing it into his mouth. He sucked gently, scraping his teeth across the sensitive pad. She shivered. The naked longing in her eyes nearly undid him.

It took every ounce of self-control he possessed to let her go when she stepped back. She looked down, her cheeks reddening. "You should go back to base."

"I'm not going anywhere."

When she met his gaze again, the soldier was firmly in place, the warm, desirous woman nowhere to be found. "You're a distraction I don't need, and even if you have nothing better to do at the moment, I have a job to do."

Stung, he slouched back, lips tightening. He jammed his hands into his jeans pockets, then immediately yanked them out again. "I'm also doing a job, Lieutenant," he bit out. "In case you haven't been paying attention, that man in there"—he jabbed a finger in the general direction of Na'il's room—"might be planning an attack against the President of the United States. And my unit is supporting the Secret Service for the duration of his visit. I'm here as their representative."

He pushed past her and started out the door, smarting from her sudden turnabout. "Let me know if you learn something."

Chapter Twenty-Three

September 6. 9:00 A.M.
US Embassy, Ma'ar ye zhad, Azakistan

HEATHER'S GUIDE BROUGHT her to Na'il Fakhoury's cubicle and left her there with a cheerful farewell. She probably shouldn't have presumed to come to the embassy to investigate Na'il's belongings. Her contribution to this mission lay in her Turkish language skills, nothing more. But she'd had nothing else to do with her time, and no way back to al-Zadr without Jace.

She frowned. He'd disappeared after Na'il died this morning. They had barely spoken during the hours she'd sat at the courier's bedside. At one point he'd brought her food; another, insisted she shower and change into fresh clothes. She wished now she hadn't shut him down so hard yesterday. He'd done nothing wrong; her own fear had caused her retreat. Fear of liking him too much. Fear of getting involved with another soldier. It never ended well.

Heather sifted through the contents of Na'il Fakhoury's cubicle. Like the dozen others on the first floor of the embassy, the six-by-six space was walled on two sides, with a half partition on the third. It boasted a computer on an L-shaped desk, a wall shelf, a small filing cabinet tucked underneath, and nothing else. No posters. No plants. The boy had been obsessively neat. A few personal pictures—a group shot, and two of a girl who was most likely his sister, based on their strong resemblance—and a calendar, detailing his work schedule. Nothing in the filing cabinet except napkins and ketchup packets.

There wasn't a shred of anything useful to be found. Hopefully, there would be something in the computer itself. She logged in using the administrator password she had been given.

Again, there was very little on the computer. No personal files, no documents conveniently entitled, "Plans to blow up the president." His email was, likewise, virtually empty. Most of the missives tended to be general embassy notifications.

His browser's home page was set to Yahoo mail. On a hunch, she called up to IT security.

"Fellars, here."

Heather identified herself. "Can you crack the username and password on a Yahoo mail account?"

"No, ma'am. We don't usually run a keystroke logger. At least not on every machine. But . . . where did you say you were?"

She told him.

"We've monitored that system for two months, maybe three," Fellars told her. "For contract fraud. Money being funneled out under pretense . . . Let me check. Yes, among other things, we installed a keystroke logger. Give me a second to search through . . . here we go." He read off a user name and password combination. "It repeats a number of times. Is that it?"

Heather typed it in. Don't get too excited, girl, she told herself.

Someone as careful as Na'il probably wouldn't leave anything incriminating. An inbox icon appeared. "Yes. That's it. Thank you."

She disconnected and scrolled through a number of emails in the inbox. Direct-mail medications, low mortgage rates, Viagra. Natural male enhancement. Sexy, hot girls looking for a good time. How did this junk get through the spam filters?

On a hunch, she clicked over to the Drafts folder. And struck gold.

There were four messages.

One immediately caught her eye. It was addressed to Na'il. The Sent From field was blank. She clicked on it.

"Delivery to Zaahir al-Farouk on 5 September at 0600, at the Starbucks at Kahraba Almarkiz." That was it. A lowercase letter N had been typed in below the message.

It was an old trick.

Christina joined her at the desk. "Found anything?"

"Oh, hey," said Heather. "Where did you come from?"

Christina settled a hip on the desk. "Looks like we had the same idea. I'm here to talk to Jay Spicer about the SCUD's warhead your rescue team decommissioned. He can't see me for a bit, so I thought I'd take a chance and see what I could ferret out here. How's Na'il?"

Heather just shook her head. "He died two hours ago."

"Damn it! Did he say anything?"

Heather blew out a breath. "Nothing except terrorist rhetoric." A heavy weight settled onto her shoulders. "A confession would have been too easy, I guess. On the good-news end, I found something interesting on his computer. A free mail account with draft messages. Four of them."

Lines appeared between Christina's brows. "Huh? Drafts?"

Heather pulled the other woman over and showed her the screen. "Since rumors of Echelon, it's become a trick terrorists use to communicate securely with one another. Terrorist Cell A sets up a free email account. Rather than use it to send messages back and forth, however, every member of the cell has the same user name and password. Since sent email is subject to interception, no mail is ever sent. Instead, Cell A leader types up messages for each member and saves them as drafts. Each member of the cell logs in, reads his or her own instructions, and puts an initial or a word or whatever at the bottom, or in the subject line, to tell the cell leader he's read and understands his instructions." Heather grinned. "And I just found four of them."

Christina's eyes lit up. "Do they give us a plan?"

"One is for Na'il. A date and time for a meet-up. He missed it."

Christina pointed to the red light blinking on the telephone, indicating new voice mail. "We'll have to check that out, too."

"Good call. I didn't see that." Heather called back the security guy. "Can you send someone up who can retrieve a voice mail?"

"Sure."

While they waited, Heather opened the other three messages. All of them listed dates, times, and a contact name. All but one had an initial typed in at the bottom. The dates ranged from three weeks prior all the way to Na'il's meeting yesterday morning. The presumably unread message's date was for five days hence, the day of the president's visit: *Pick up transportation vehicle on September 11 at 9:00 A.M. Link up with me by 11:00 A.M.,* the Arabic symbols read.

Heather's eyes widened. "That's proof! They were planning an attack on the president!"

Christina fluffed her hair with her nails. "We'll need to get this to the Secret Service ASAP. What vehicle, and where is he picking it up from? And linking up where? The base?"

"It has to be. They must have found a way to get onto al-Zadr." The possibility the vehicle might contain the warhead for the SCUD intrigued Heather, but she discarded the idea after a moment of thought. "When was this email written? Maybe they don't know the SCUD is out of commission."

The communications tech arrived. He lifted the telephone receiver, punched in a long stream of numbers, listened for a moment, then handed the receiver to Heather.

A male voice snarled into the phone in Arabic. Heather pressed the speakerphone button, and the harsh voice resounded through the tiny cubicle. She blanched and gripped the edge of the desk with both hands.

"That's him. The man from the Kongra-Gel training camp." She took in a lot of air and exhaled hard. "Run it back."

Christina restarted the message.

"Where the hell are you?" Heather translated. "You missed your delivery. You better meet me tomorrow, same time, or you will meet Allah earlier than we planned." The sound of a receiver being slammed back into its cradle, then silence.

The two women stared at one another.

"Well," Christina finally said. "How about that."

Heather shivered with excitement. She had a chance to catch the cell leader! Then she sobered. The odds of her being allowed anywhere near this were slim. Technically, she should be at home resting. Still, she *was* involved now. She could still be of use.

Heather realized Christina was speaking, and forced herself to listen. " . . . where they're supposed to meet. If we can get local police there, surround the place . . ."

"We don't know where the meet-up was supposed to be," Heather interrupted. "And even if we did, that won't help us. We lose control immediately. The Azakistani police would want to question him themselves, and we'd be shut out."

Christina sighed. "I have to brief my boss anyway. Let's bite the bullet and see what he says."

JAY SPICER SIMPLY looked at them.

"Sir," Christina Madison tried again, "the SCUD, the vials the courier carried, and now these messages. I think we have to acknowledge the Kongra-Gel terrorists might have a Plan B. It merits an investigation, surely."

Spicer threw his pen down onto his desk. "I appreciate your enthusiasm, Madison. And I know your reputation, Langstrom." He sighed. "I also know what you've been through. Some distrust and suspicion is natural after your ordeal. But I think you're barking up the wrong tree with this one."

Heather bristled. "You have no idea what I've been through." She worked hard to keep her voice steady. "I was questioned because my captors wanted to know what I knew about an impending attack. And they specifically wanted to know what I knew about Omaid al-Hassid, and he was in charge of the camp I was held at. I'm simply suggesting we look closer at this."

Spicer bobbed his head. "I get that. I do. But the threat's been neutralized. The Azakistani Air Force took care of the SCUD. We know Omaid al-Hassid wasn't there when they bombed his camp. But alive or not, he's been incapacitated for the moment."

Heather couldn't shake the nagging sense the CIA station chief was wrong. The danger still existed; she could feel it in her bones.

"What if there's a backup plan?" Christina asked, fidgeting in her chair.

The station chief pinned her with a look that had her clasping her hands together. "Have you forgotten your screwup in Iraq six months ago? Your misjudgment there could have cost us several lives, including your own. If the SAS hadn't pulled you out of the fire . . . well, let's just say I assigned you here with me to give you time to gain some experience. And perspective. This isn't really helping me believe you've learned anything."

Heather blew out an irritated breath. Spicer turned to her. "What has 10th Group said?" he asked.

She hated to admit it, but. . . . "I haven't run this past them. I'm still on medical leave. Truthfully, I'm not exactly certain leaving the hospital was sanctioned." Sitting back, she met Spicer's gaze squarely. "The new regimental intelligence officer at 10th Group doesn't know me, and I'm in limbo pending reassignment. After the docs clear me to go back on active duty, I'm due to rotate back Stateside." She smoothed her hands along her thighs. "But the SCUD's warhead is still physically out there, and we don't know what they plan to do with it. Look, what would it hurt to let us poke around a little?"

Spicer rubbed his chin, leg jiggling under the desk. He tapped his fingers against the chair's arm. "The SCUD's dead, and so is the courier. We have the vials, whatever they turn out to be. Whatever meeting they planned is over. The last email gives no clue where or what, but the Secret Service has it and is investigating. We'll support them, but it's their baby. Their call. They need me, they ask. Meanwhile, I got half a dozen ops running. I have better things to do with my resources. Including you." He jabbed a finger at Christina. "What progress have you made with Aa'idah Karim?"

"None, sir," Christina mumbled. The young agent managed to keep her face blank, which was more than Heather was able to do.

They were wasting their time here. Heather pushed herself erect.

"Thank you for your time, Mr. Spicer." She held out a hand.

He rose and took it, tilting his head forward. "Bring me something more concrete than obsolete emails, and I'm all over it, Langstrom. But resources only stretch so far."

Heather sighed. "I understand, Mr. Spicer. I'll be back."

"Call me Jay." He shot a glance at Christina. "Madison, get out of here before I bust you back to trainee."

Chapter Twenty-Four

THE SILENCE BETWEEN Jace and Heather persisted on the trip back to al-Zadr Air Force Base. She mulled over how to bridge the distance between them. Finally, she just blurted, "I'm sorry for how I acted."

"Forget it," Jace said gruffly.

That didn't sound forgiving, but Heather didn't push it. How would she feel if, in the end, he dropped her at the bachelor officer's quarters and simply left? Relieved, of course.

Wistful.

"I asked Dr. McGrath if he felt you were capable of making this trip," he admitted. "He asked me to bring you by the hospital so he could check you out."

"No. I'd rather you take me home."

"Let's wait till we get closer, then we can fight to the death about where I take you."

That sounded a little better, maybe a little bit teasing. Heather held her breath, but he didn't say anything more. With nothing else as a distraction, memories flooded her. Her prison cell, her captor, and that rusted, creaking cot. She shuddered.

Heather had not been able to open up to the psychologist the Army had insisted she see. The man had extensive experience with post-traumatic stress disorder. The soldiers of 10th Special Forces Group lived for weeks or even months in the field, accomplishing virtually impossible tasks in the war on terror. They were encouraged to seek counseling; but unless it was directly ordered, they didn't go. Heather had always thought the man-code forbade such a perceived weakness. She now realized it was not machismo, but an inability to put words to what they had seen and done. As long as they kept on keeping on, memories could be compartmentalized or suppressed. As much as she knew the psychologist was only trying to help her, she just couldn't face talking about it. Not yet. Maybe not ever.

She just wanted to forget.

The embassy's VIP treatment had ended with the courier's death. No Blackhawk waited to fly them back to al-Zadr. The car and driver drove them east all the way to the Air Force Base's airfield, where Jace's car waited exactly where they'd left it the previous day.

Jace held the door for her, then hopped in and started the engine with a roar. Strangely unsettled, she stared out the window as he put the car in gear. The sudden coughing backfire of a nearby truck startled her; Heather jerked back. Farther down the tarmac, a plane fired up its engines. For a moment, she found herself back in the Kongra-Gel training camp, in the middle of the chaos as she tried to escape under cover of explosions and automatic gunfire as

Jace's team attacked the compound. She found herself grabbing for the door handle, her pulse slamming in her throat, choking her. Her vision blurred, and she couldn't hear over the thunder of her heart.

"Heather. Listen to me. You're safe. Hear my voice. You're in a car. It's just a plane engine. There's nothing wrong." The voice was calm, soothing, persistent. It cut through her panic. Her vision cleared.

Jace slowed and pulled to the side of the road. His hand hovered at her shoulder without actually touching her. Her eyes wide, Heather stared at him, breathing hard. Jace lowered a single finger to her shoulder, touching her so softly she barely felt it. It served to ground her back to the here and now.

"You're safe," he told her again.

Heather turned away to hide her sudden rush of tears. "I know. I'm sorry."

"Don't be sorry. It happens."

Heather wiped both hands down her face, then clasped them in her lap to still the trembling. "Not to me."

Jace slipped his finger under her chin, nudging her face around. She leveled a defiant glare his way.

"To everyone, Heather. You're not the only soldier to experience PTSD."

Heather focused for a moment on breathing. Inhaling and exhaling. She flashed back to the small cave in the mountains, of Jace holding her against his body, rubbing circles on her back, telling her to breathe with him. In and out. Over and over.

God, she wanted him to hold her.

He had been so strong in those mountains, sure and confident. He'd led his team with unapologetic competence. He hadn't sneered at her weakness or her tears.

Jace slid a hand to the back of her neck and up under her hair, massaging her scalp. She leaned into his touch. Was it weakness to let him affect her? Maybe. At the moment, though, nothing mattered but the slide of his fingers through her hair. Her skin prickled, hot and tight, and her breath hitched. It was a small sound, but he heard it, and used the hand at the back of her neck to pull her to him. She expected him to kiss her. Instead, he pressed his forehead to hers, and spoke, his voice low and rough.

"You should never have had to go through that. Your convoy attacked, seeing your friends get shot. None of it. You should never have been . . . I want to kill the man who put that fear into your eyes."

Heather jerked in his arms. "Man?"

Jace pressed his lips to her temple. Heather had to fight not to turn her head, to search out his mouth, to let him kiss her until her memories disappeared. "You said in the hospital that . . ." His voice trailed away. "Was it more than one?"

What had she said? What had she admitted, in a moment of weakness? Shit. She pulled away from him and stared ahead, out the windshield. "It was nothing."

Jace sighed. "Heather . . ."

"Let's just go. Please."

She could feel his gaze, resting heavily on her. Finally, *finally,* he put the car in gear and pulled onto the road that would take them away from the airport. Scenery rolled past; she didn't see it. All she could see was *him,* above her, straddling her. Her stomach churned.

"No matter how well trained we are in Delta, and we are the best-trained force in the world, there comes a point for all of us—*all* of us—when something happens we can't put into perspective," Jace said, as if he'd read her thoughts. "That just . . . defies justification. So horrible, you have to stuff it away just to stay sane. But, eventually, at some point, you have to bring it out and look at it. Some don't. Probably a lot don't. But if you don't, the black place inside of you just . . . gets bigger. A tiny piece of you dies every day until you're just, I don't know, empty. Not quite human anymore." He sighed. "By the time an operator hits that point, everyone's clued in, and the guy just retires. But every once in a while . . . there was one guy, guy named Harvey, just snapped one day. Not part of my team. Not even from my squadron. But out on a mission, he just started shooting. There was no enemy, but he couldn't see that. I guess he just couldn't see anything anymore. He killed an old man and a little girl, just out getting some fresh air."

Heather sucked in a breath. "That's awful!"

"Yeah." He gripped the steering wheel until his knuckles turned white. "As bad as it is, you can't just keep it inside. I'm sure they sent you to a shrink. Talk to him. Please."

No. No way.

"What happened to Harvey?" she asked, in an attempt to distract him.

Jace was silent for so long she was sure he wasn't going to answer. Finally, though, he dragged in a breath. "He died. On that mission." He grimaced. "Delta prides itself on never, ever taking out the wrong target. Never killing an innocent. Never."

Heather put a hand over his and patted it awkwardly. "I'm sorry."

He squeezed the steering wheel so tightly she was surprised it didn't shatter. "I almost killed you." His voice was bleak. "In the desert, when you were dressed like . . . I could have killed you."

Oh, Jace. "But you didn't. You saved me."

He didn't answer her. The car slowed, and she looked around. The major intersection would take them either back to the hospital or over to the rest of the base.

"I'm not going back," she blurted out, turning to challenge Jace. "I'm fed up with that place. They're nice and all, but enough is enough. I'm not an invalid, and I don't need round-the-clock care. I'm sick of hospitals."

"Okay."

She stared at him. "What happened to the fight to the death?"

One corner of his mouth kicked up. "If you can fight to the death, then you don't need a hospital. I did make Dr. McGrath a promise, though, in exchange for his permission."

Uh-oh. Something in his expression . . . it was at once contrite and gleeful.

"And that was?"

"I promised him you wouldn't be alone."

Heather started to laugh; she couldn't help it. "No. You're not coming home with me."

Wisely, he didn't argue with her. Instead, he squinted into the midmorning glare, an arm draped casually over the steering wheel, and turned right.

"Not going home with you it is."

But before they reached the bachelor officer's quarters, he turned onto an unmarked road. She knew she should protest, should insist he take her back. Instead, she let her head thunk onto the seat back in tacit acceptance. They drove several miles, ending at a remote area and a fenced-off compound she hadn't even known existed. A grizzled old sergeant with an M4 carbine slung over his shoulder guarded the gate. No wonder no one knew Delta Force operated out of al-Zadr. Probably only a select few even knew of this remote area, and even fewer were allowed inside. The guard logged her in, using her military ID card to jot down information on a clipboard.

"Have a good 'un, Cap'n," he said to Jace, opening the gate for them. Jace waved and pulled through. He weaved through a collection of buildings, none of which had any identifying signs or symbols. Clearly, Delta valued its anonymity.

Jace pulled up in front of a small house, on a dirt street lined with identical houses. Popping the trunk, he pulled her dress green uniform bag out by its hanger.

He came over and opened the passenger side door. "Well, come on," he said, holding out a hand. She just looked at him.

Undaunted, he grabbed her hand and pulled her from the car. She laughed and steadied herself. "Jace, you know I can't stay here."

"Why not?"

She gave him an exasperated look. "You know why not. There are a zillion reasons why not, and you know all of them."

He pretended to think it over. "Okay. I'll take you back to the hospital."

Heather reached for her uniform. "How about you take me home? To my home. My quarters. And drop me there."

He held her belongings just out of reach. "Nope. I made a promise to the doc. It's here or the hospital."

Looking around, Heather verified no one watched. Not at this time of day, but one never knew, and the last thing she needed was to become more of spectacle than she already was. Lord, she was tired. The excursion to the Prince Nasser Hospital to talk to Na'il had sapped her small reserves. "Fine. For a little bit, but then you have to take me home."

Jace led the way up the tiny walk to the house and unlocked the door. He stood back to let her go in first. He had not, she was amused to note, promised to take her home later. She forced her head up and her shoulders back as she stepped into the foyer. Be strong, Langstrom.

The house was typical Army-issue. To the right was the living room, with the dining area at the far end. The kitchen would be around the corner. In front of her, the staircase stretched impossibly far. Please, don't let her have to go up. To her relief, Jace walked into the living room and draped her uniform over the back of a dining room chair. She dropped onto the sofa with a sigh. It, like all the furniture, was also Army-issue. She could have commented on the sterility of what was obviously bachelor's quarters, except her tiny apartment looked the same. She lived in a four-story walk-up, no different from her bachelor officer's quarters Stateside. Ten one-bedroom apartments to a floor, forty officers living in proximity and mostly eating in the chow hall. The long hours she put in didn't leave her much interest in cooking.

Jace disappeared up the stairs. Heather let her head drop to the back of the sofa. Just one minute. Just let her rest for one minute.

His voice drifted down to her. Was someone else here?

Jace came bounding back down the stairs. His energy preceded him like a battering ram.

"Here." Something soft was thrust into her hands. She opened her eyes to find a well-worn olive green T-shirt. "Crap and double crap. I got called in to the office. Make yourself at home. Shower. Take a nap if you want. Grab some lunch . . . damn it! Why didn't I go to the commissary last week? I'm so sorry. Rummage in the cupboards—there might be something edible. Have that pizza place deliver. The number's on the fridge. I should be back in a few hours. I'll take you to dinner, okay?"

She managed a wan smile. "What happened to not leaving me alone?"

Jace stopped short, a comical look on his face. "God, I . . . might have stretched the truth a little on my promise to the doctor. Shit. Do you need . . . I can take you to the hospital? Are you in pain? Feeling dizzy?" He came over to kneel next to her, turning her face side to side as he examined her pupils and felt her forehead.

Heather batted his hands away. "I was just kidding. I'm fine. Go. Just . . ." Her voice wobbled. "Just come back, okay?"

Jace sat back on his heels, a gentle smile on his face. "You can bet on it." He brushed his lips across hers, just a whisper of sensation. "Be back before you know it."

But she did know it, as soon as the door closed behind him. The sad truth was, she didn't want to be alone. Too many thoughts, jumbled and frightening, rolled through her mind. Too much confusion, and memories she did not want to examine. Still, she couldn't stay here. It was inappropriate, and would reflect unfavorably if someone found out.

The devil on her shoulder scoffed at her. Inappropriate for whom? They were both officers, and he wasn't in her chain of command. There was absolutely nothing that said she could not spend time with Jace Reed. Nothing.

Except her own fear. What if she spent time with him? Other soldiers would notice and start pestering her. She'd been cowardly at her last duty station. Rather than report her boss's inappropriate behavior, she'd requested a transfer and run away to the desert. Never again, she vowed. I will not back away from what is right out of cowardice.

And what about her no-dating rule? Was she willing to throw away her principles and beliefs because of . . . of lust? Well, she allowed, he was an exceptionally good kisser. But, no. As tempting as he was, she would not get involved with him. Nope. No way.

She lifted the T-shirt to her nose. It smelled like him, kind of spicy and woodsy. Well, it wouldn't hurt anything to stay for a bit. He wouldn't be back for hours. And Heather would feel so much better after a shower and a nap.

She dragged herself off the sofa and up the stairs. The bathroom was right where she expected it to be, but she bypassed it to peer into the other two rooms. One was an office; the other was the master bedroom. It was surprisingly neat. The bed was made. No piles of clothes on the floor or shoes scattered around. There were, however, books. A lot of books, on the dresser, on the night table, even two on the bed itself. Heather took a tentative step inside, then laughed at her timidity. She was an intelligence officer, after all. She was expected to be nosy, wasn't she?

Driven by a curiosity she couldn't explain, she picked up a few books and read the titles. There was one on white-water rafting, and another on rock climbing. Two histories of the Peloponnesian War. Two? How interesting could that war have been?

The bed looked inviting. She drifted closer, and even trailed her hand along the plain blue bedspread. Maybe if she just lay down for a moment?

No. Jerking away, she forced herself to turn and walk back into the hallway. She had absolutely no business snooping in Jace's home. Determined to grab a shower while she could, she locked the bathroom door and turned on the water. Stripping out of her clothes, she sighed with relief as the spray sluiced over her body. More than two weeks in the hospital with restricted shower time had given her an appreciation for unlimited water.

She stayed under the spray until the water cooled and her skin pruned. Finally, she turned it off and used the towel hanging on the rod to dry herself. It also smelled of Jace. She rubbed her hair as dry as she could, then looked at her jeans. There was nothing wrong with them. They had been clean when she put them on this morning.

But Jace's well-worn shirt looked much more enticing. She slipped it over her head and breathed in his masculine sent as it cascaded toward her knees.

Leaving her jeans and T-shirt where they lay, she borrowed his comb and went back downstairs to sit on the sofa. She flipped on the television in time for the two o'clock broadcast. As she detangled her long hair, she caught up with local and world news.

There was an update on her own condition, to her embarrassment. An interview with the chief medical officer at the base hospital, whom she had never met; comments by a public affairs officer on local insurgent activity; a medical analysis of prison conditions in third world countries, as if that had any bearing on her experience. They did their utmost to keep the drama alive. She wished they would move on.

Finally, her hair was, if not dry, then at least manageable. Sliding down a little, she swung her bare feet onto the cushions, glancing out the window at the afternoon sunshine. After another moment, she laid her head onto the couch's arm. Her eyes fluttered, and closed.

Chapter Twenty-Five

September 6. 12:12 P.M.
Ma'ar ye zhad, Azakistan

AA'IDAH SAT STIFFLY, legs pressed together, hands clasped in her lap to stop the shaking. This time, her father had given permission for her to eat with Zaahir al-Farouk. They sat inside, which was a shame because the noontime weather was mild and enticing. The ceiling-high windows flaunted rich orangish curtains, which were swept back and tied. Traditional low tables, inlaid with intricate geometrical patterns and polished to a high gleam, waited in front of long seats to be filled with dishes: chelow kabab, Tah-chin rice, appetizers, bread, condiments, and side dishes. It was much too fancy for lunch.

Her father and Zaahir sat at right angles to her, and she sat beside Shukri. Zaahir beamed and nodded and seemed very pleased. She felt his eyes on her frequently as he spoke with her father. The men discussed politics, which inevitably led to complaints against Prime Minister al-Muhaymin's government and his pro-Western leanings. Zaahir pontificated, her father and Shukri attended him, and Aa'idah wretchedly tried to find a way to derail the catastrophe bearing down on her.

She could not—*would* not—marry him.

Zaahir was a monster. She had eavesdropped when he and the slender boy she thought must be Rami had visited her home. Zaahir had lamented the loss of a ballistic missile, cursing the government as spineless dogs. He had intended to use that missile against the Americans. Now, though, he planned something else. Some way, and she did not understand how, he had devised a way to make an explosion on the American military base look like an accident. This "accidental" explosion would have so incensed her people and her government that Najm al-Najib, the conservative party leader, could force early elections and take control of the government.

Her father and brother worked in tandem with Zaahir's vile machinations; she could no longer ignore their complicity. Allah condemned the wanton murder of the innocent. Anxiety crawled through her innards. She needed privacy to dial the number Christina Madison had left her.

"Is the food not to your liking?" Zaahir asked. "You're not eating. Shall I order you something else?"

She jolted, having been caught up in her thoughts. "The food is delicious, honored sir. I simply did not wish to eat greedily."

Her answer pleased him. He glanced at her father for permission, who gave it with alacrity, then reached past him to take her hand in his. Zaahir's palms were warm and dry, his touch confident. He was handsome, in a rough sort of way. If she could not see the monster crouching within him, she might enjoy his attentions.

But she did see it.

Her entire body trembled and shook. Repugnance clenched her gut and threatened to bring the food right back up. "Please release me."

"It would please me for you to call me Zaahir. I like you very much, Aa'idah. We shall become well acquainted, you and I."

Aa'idah nearly gagged on a bite of lamb. Taking a swift sip of water, she tried to ease her hand from his. He tightened his grip.

"I'm unworthy, honored sir," she choked out. "Truly. This is not false modesty. I would not suit you. I have many faults."

"You are beautiful and young enough to learn. Your father and I have similar interests and beliefs. Shukri works with me toward our noble purpose. It is good that we join together."

Aa'idah yanked her hand from his. "No. I will not."

Something ugly flashed through his eyes, gone so quickly she might have imagined it. "You will do as your father tells you." Zaahir turned his gaze to her father, challenging him.

"It is a good match, daughter," he said. "He is an honorable man with many fine qualities. I have given my permission for Zaahir to court you."

Uttering a cry of despair, Aa'idah stumbled to her feet, backing away from the nightmare. Ignoring Shukri's sharp command, she turned and fled.

Chapter Twenty-Six

September 6. 12:50 P.M.
Forward Operating Base Hollow Straw, al-Zadr AFB

JACE PULLED INTO the Tactical Operations Center at the same time as Gabe Morgan. He swung his long legs onto the gravel and slid out, lifting a hand to greet the junior officer. Placing his palms at the small of his back, he stretched, grateful Delta focused on action rather than pomp and circumstance. They very rarely had to wear the starchy and uncomfortable Class A uniforms the rest of the Army had to endure. The two walked to the plain, unmarked building together.

"Where'd you disappear to yesterday? I'd complain, but it meant we could slack off at PT this morning," Gabe said.

He would have given Gabe a chiding look, but he knew in his absence, the young lieutenant, if anything, pushed the A-Team even harder at physical training than its commanding officer. "I went to see how Heather Langstrom was doing. Turns out she got called up to go talk to a detainee, so I drove her over there."

Gabe cut his eyes toward Jace as he pulled off his sunglasses. "Uh-huh." He tucked the dark glasses into the front of his "I'm having a good day—don't screw it up" T-shirt. "You doggin' 'er?"

Jace pushed into the Tactical Operations Center and swung the door back hard. It banged into Gabe's quickly outstretched hand. The other man, with his overlong blond hair and hooded eyes, always looked to Jace like a fallen angel. The Archangel Gabriel, Messenger of God. Women flocked to him, apparently drawn by the intense look in his eyes and the symmetrical perfection of his features. Jace wasn't going to go so far as to describe Gabe as great-looking, but the constant stream of women throwing themselves at him must mean they liked what they found.

Gabe came inside and mimed zipping his lips and throwing away the key, then made a production of brushing his hands together. "Message received," he said, amusement dancing in his eyes. "Subject off-limits."

The Tactical Operations Center, or TOC, bustled with activity twenty-four/seven. Terrorists and insurgents did not stop at sundown, and neither did the US Special Operations Command. Two rows of computers lined each side of the room. Four flat-panel monitors mounted above the computers displayed CNN, enlarged maps of the area, and a complex battlefield assessment system. More conventional paper maps and a number of diagrams covered the back wall. A huge table took up the center of the room, around which sat the other members of his team. Jace and Gabe joined them. The ribbing started immediately.

"Jace, you gone soft? Sleepin' in to all hours?" Thomas 'Mace' Beckett's Cajun drawl matched his relaxed slouch. He slung an arm across the back of the chair. "I think I want to be an officer. The hours are better." His black T-shirt, straining across his chest, had the sleeves torn out to show off the barbed-wire tattoo across his upper bicep.

The Sandman wagged his tongue and made an obscene gesture. "Bet he's balling some sweet hoochie. Give us the blow-by-blow . . ."

Jace didn't see it, but by the sudden silence he knew Gabe had made a shut-up gesture. They shut up. Just as well, so he didn't have to beat the hell out of Scott Griffin. The Sandman had grown up rough, in a run-down, blue-collar neighborhood in Pittsburgh. He was vulgar, crude, and went through women like other men drank coffee. He was rock solid in the field, though. There was no one Jace would rather have at his back.

The downside to the silence was that he was now being treated to speculative looks.

"Tag, what's the latest word on the president's visit?" he asked, trying to steer the conversation away from himself. "Is my team supporting the Secret Service or not?"

The sharp rap of bootheels on plank flooring preceded the arrival of their boss. "Another team will be assigned to that mission," said Lieutenant Colonel Bo Granville. The squadron commander yanked out a chair and spun it around, straddling it as he smacked his arms onto the backrest. "Thanks for the update on the situation with the biological agents." He held up a hand to forestall any comments. "Yeah, we'll all be relieved if it turns out to be someone's piss to fake a urine test. Meanwhile, I found out this morning that the National Security Agency's Signals Intelligence guys came across an interesting conversation. Guy by the name of Demas Pagonis, a Greek scientist working in Turkey for Galatas Chemicals, had a conversation with one Omran Malouf, who works for a major politician here. Subject was a delivery of some sort. Shrouded in doublespeak and euphemisms, of course. Two things make this interesting. One, Malouf has known ties to the Salafist jihadists, a loosely knit group of terrorists who believe the only way to purify Islam is to kill all nonbelievers. Al Qaeda are Salafist jihadists. So are the Jund Ansar Allah and the Kongra-Gel.

"The other thing that makes this conversation worth note is his assistant found Pagonis dead in his lab on August twelfth, almost three weeks ago. Reason we tied it together was the vials on that embassy courier. What's-his-name. Fakhoury. With Pagonis dead, they poked around a little and found out he was working on a little project on the side." He stopped and looked around the table. "Well? Isn't anyone gonna ask me?"

Jace slouched back in his chair. "Why don't you enlighten us, sir?"

Granville pulled a cigar from his breast pocket and stuck it into his mouth. Chewing around it, he said, "Phosgene." He yanked the cigar out and pointed it around the table. "Specifically, weaponizing phosgene by loading it into a warhead. And guess what killed the poor bastard? Phosgene poisoning."

Holy shit. Jace bolted upright. "What?"

Granville jerked his finger behind him, and a female soldier materialized. She flicked a single-paged document across the table; it landed directly in front of Jace. She did the same six more times, each page landing in front of a member of his team.

"Hi, Stephanie," said Alex, a shy smile forming on his broad, farm-boy face. She smiled back at him, a quick flash of dimples. Jace cleared his throat sharply and narrowed his eyes at Alex, who instantly became busy reading the handout. Fraternization of any sort between operators and their Delta Force military support staff was strictly forbidden. If Steph were a civilian, it would be different. As it was, Alex's puppy love needed to be quashed, and sooner was better.

"Private, why don't you educate us on phosgene?" said Granville.

"Me? Oh, I'm not . . . I mean, I just . . . Yes, sir." She looked down at the printout in her hand. "Um . . . phosgene is a gas. It's, uh, nonflammable, and colorless. It has a molecular weight of . . . well, you don't need to know that. It was used during World War I as a . . . as a chemical agent. It's classified as a choking agent." She stumbled to a halt, glanced at Alex, who nodded encouragingly, and took a deep breath. "Okay. More than eighty-seven thousand people died during the First World War from phosgene gas. That's combined Axis and Allied forces. It's prohibited as a chemical weapon, of course, but it's also legal. Well, I mean it's legitimately manufactured, for a lot of reasons. A billion pounds are produced every year, to be used in the manufacture of pesticides, dyes, and plastics. Pharmaceuticals, too. Synthetic antibiotics, if that doesn't send a chill down your spine." She cleared her throat. "It can be compressed and cooled into a liquid for storage or transport."

Gabe ran a hand along the top of the table. "So, what . . . the vials are liquefied phosgene?"

Granville stuck the cigar back in his mouth. "Believe so. Won't know for sure till that SAS biochemicals guy reports back. We have to make sure we get a copy of that report. Guarantee we'll be asked to help out." He jabbed a finger in Jace's direction. "You know this guy? Be easier than waiting around till someone decides they should fill us in."

"I'll get a copy, sir."

"Good man. Meanwhile, I got a little job for you." He stood

abruptly and paced over to the maps. Jace followed him. "Pagonis is dead, but Malouf is hiding out in a house in Tiqt. Love to have a chat with him. Well, the Yoo-nited States Intelligence and Security Command wants to talk to him. But we're going to go fetch him."

"Yes, sir. When do we leave?"

The commander moved to one of the larger monitors. Without being told, the operator brought up Google Earth and punched in an address. The view shifted and zoomed in, and Jace found himself looking at a run-down neighborhood on the east side of the city. The 3D graphics amazed him. He examined the surrounding buildings and the roads leading in and out.

"Whip up a plan. Transport will be ready by 0230. Quick in and out, a'right?"

Jace acknowledged his boss, jerking his head for his team to gather around.

Ken Acolatse, the Troop's Sergeant Major, joined them. Muscles rippled and flowed under his dark chocolate skin, which gleamed under the artificial lights. His feral grin slashed across a burly face. "You gonna need a second sniper, Jace. I'm bored. Want me to come along and babysit Mace?"

Mace bristled. "Old man, I can outshoot you any day of the week." He straightened up, but his six foot three was still two inches shorter than the giant top sergeant.

"Sure, if the target's standing in front of you." Ken mimed letting the string of a helium balloon go, then blowing it to smithereens with a shotgun. "Time Papa came out to play with the kiddies. Maybe you'll learn something."

"Yeah. Right. Uh-huh. Sure." Narrowed eyes and a flattened mouth marred Mace's good-looking features. "Imma 'bout to hurt you."

Acolatse's eyes gleamed with satisfaction at having gotten a rise out of the younger man.

Jace snorted. Had he ever been as young as Mace? "All right. Archangel and Sandman will be one direct action team. Tag, Alex, and I will be the other. Ken and Mace will provide overwatch. Let's get to work." He was eager to get home and check on Heather.

An hour later, they had a solid plan in place.

"All right, kiddies," said Jace. "Be here by 0200. We depart at 0230. Should be home before dawn." With any luck, Heather would have decided to stay. "Any questions?"

Through the chorus of negatives, he loped out the door.

As he drove, he replayed the events of three weeks ago out in the desert. The original mission, to destroy the newly delivered cache of weapons purchased by this faction of the Kongra-Gel, had been derailed—first by the discovery of the SCUD, then by the need to keep an injured Heather away from the insurgents.

The thought of how close he had come to snuffing out her life, her incredible vitality, made him break into a cold sweat. If he hadn't caught the whiff of perfume, if he had moved just a fraction faster, if his nose had been stuffed up . . .

And that started him on an entirely new train of thought. It clearly hadn't been her own perfume. She had bathed recently, yes. The perfume, though, was pretty standard for Muslim women. Shared with her by one of the females they had seen at the permanent camp? Or forced on her . . . Bile rose in his throat. Whether or not she'd been raped, she'd sure as hell been through some serious shit. She wasn't trained for something like that, whatever she said. How badly would it scar her? The welts raised by the caning would have faded by now. Even the bruises from where someone had beaten and choked her would be nearly healed. The hidden scars, though . . . some of those never healed. She would never be the same; no one who experienced torture walked away from it without damage.

He sure hadn't. The prison camp in Kamdesh, northeastern Afghanistan still haunted his dreams. Dougie had died, and he had survived. The arbitrary nature of it still baffled him, but the experience had made him harder. Stronger.

But would it make her stronger? Or break her?

Chapter Twenty-Seven

September 6. 3:30 P.M.
FOB Hollow Straw, al-Zadr Air Force Base

JACE EASED OPEN the door and shut it just as quietly. He saw Heather at once. She was curled up tightly on the sofa, eyes screwed shut, her deep breathing telling him she was fast asleep. She wore his T-shirt, which suffused him with an absurd pleasure. It had ridden up around her waist, and he took a moment to admire the scrap of peach silk molded to her perfect derriere. She shifted in her sleep, and he caught a tantalizing glimpse of her smooth stomach.

It would be as close to paradise as someone like him would ever get to make love to her. To lose himself in her heat, to have her come so hard and so long she forgot who she was. However, he breathed deeply, knowing it was not going to happen. At least not tonight. Heather was still processing her capture and interrogation. Right now, she was vulnerable, and he would be the worst kind of bastard if he were to take advantage. So, he would take care of her, make sure she was healthy and stable, and then he would drive her home. End of chapter.

That didn't mean he couldn't look his fill, though. Heather was truly beautiful. At five-foot-ten, she was just two inches shy of his own six feet. Her impossibly long legs emphasized her slender build, but her breasts lifted round and tempting. His fingers itched to shape them, taste them.

She shifted, a frown marring her delicate features. Her long hair slid across her shoulders to cascade down her arm, tucked up under her cheek. She jerked, mumbling something incoherent. And then cried out, a sharp sound of fear, tucking her head and bringing her hands and knees up to protect herself.

Without thinking, Jace crossed to the sofa and dropped to his knees beside her. He gathered her into his arms, only realizing his error when she began to thrash in earnest, uttering little guttural cries that tore at his heart.

"Shh," he said. "You're safe. It's Jace. Wake up, baby."

Her eyes flew open. They were huge in her pale face, wild and disoriented. She strained away from him, managing to free one arm and clocking him upside the head. Ouch.

He trapped both her arms by simply wrapping one of his around them. The other he used to smooth her hair back from her face. "Heather. You're safe. You're home." He continued to speak to her, pouring all the calm reassurance he could into his voice. It took quite a few seconds, but he watched as she slowly came back to the present. Jace saw the moment she recognized him.

"Jace."

"I'm here, baby. I've got you." She wriggled her arms, and he loosened his grip. "You were having a nightmare."

She nodded and closed her eyes. "Apparently I'll be having a lot of them over the next few months. The shrink said . . . well, he said I should expect them for a while."

Jace couldn't stop himself from reaching out and touching her cheek. She turned her face into his palm. And his heart did a slow flip.

Fighting his desire to pull her more completely into his arms, to hold her, to reassure himself she was safe, and whole, and alive, he forced himself instead to back away, to go sit in the easy chair next to the couch. Hurt flashed through her eyes, quickly hidden as she sat up and swung her legs to the floor, only then noticing her lack of pants. She pulled his shirt down—it was huge on her—and smoothed it over her thighs as best she could; and Jace watched, fascinated, as color rose in her cheeks.

Heather cleared her throat. "Thank you for letting me stay here and rest. It was kind of you. I'll change and head back to my apartment."

He wasn't ready for her to leave.

"How about you go change, and I take you to an early dinner? It's quarter of four." Maybe he could persuade her to come back here with him afterward. "Or better yet, what if I whip you up a couple of my famous grilled cheese sandwiches? After I go buy cheese, that is. And bread."

Heather shook her head, a faint smile there and gone so fast he might have imagined it. "I'm sure you have more important things to do . . ."

"I have a few hours free."

Standing abruptly, Heather started to move away; then stopped as she realized his T-shirt, while huge over her thin frame, barely covered the tops of her thighs. She tried to pull it down, which only made the fabric stretch tight across her breasts. Jace's mouth was suddenly dry.

She sat back down, which was a shame. Dragging his gaze back up to her face, Jace knew he had failed to hide his hot flash of desire when her eyes widened, and her lips parted on a tiny gasp. She folded her arms across her breasts.

Jace looked away, slightly ashamed of his blatant staring. "Sorry."

"No, I'm . . . I shouldn't have . . ." She exhaled hard. "Jace. You have to know. I can't sleep with you. So if that's the only reason . . ."

"It's not." Jesus. What kind of man did she think he was? "That's not even on the table. Just dinner, okay? No pressure." At her skeptical look, he held up both hands in surrender. "You will never have to be afraid of me, Heather. I'm serious. I'd cut off my own arm before I'd hurt you. If you believe nothing else I say, believe that." Should he back away? Put more distance between them? "I'm really sorry if I . . ."

"Don't be an ass."

What? "I'm just trying to reassure you that I . . ."

She sliced a hand through the air, cutting him off. "Stop it. I mean it." She was annoyed. No, he realized, looking at her. She was pissed. Why?

"I'm not some idiotic swooning debutante. I'm a twenty-six-year-old officer in the United States Army. Stop treating me like a fragile hothouse flower that's going to disintegrate if you look at me the wrong way." She glared at him, planting her hands on her hips, which served to make his T-shirt ride up again. It was distracting as hell. He had to work hard to keep his eyes on her face. "Stop treating me like a damned victim."

Oops. Her words finally penetrated. He stood, hands hanging at his sides, silent; because, really, what could he say? She was right.

She had handled their flight from the camp, in truth, better than many male soldiers he knew. Strong, disciplined, determined . . . there had been no whining, no complaining, no self-pity. Even battered, with internal injuries and a concussion, she had followed his lead, not merely allowing her rescue but participating in it.

"I can't go back to work until the shrink clears me." At first, Heather's words made no sense. How had they gotten here? "If I start thinking, even for one second, that I'm impaired, that I'm weakened, I risk becoming a victim. I refuse to be a victim. I'm a survivor." She glared at him. "So stop being so damned careful around me. Stop tiptoeing, stop apologizing. Just stop."

Silence settled around them. Heather continued to glare, obviously waiting for some sort of response.

He cleared his throat. "Guilty as charged."

She seemed to be waiting for more. Jace wracked his brain. What else did she want?

"I've never met a woman like you," he said at last. "So forgive me if I don't exactly know how I'm supposed to act around you. If you were a man, someone from my team who'd been through a rough time, I'd take you out and get you shit-faced, then I'd start a brawl in some dive so you could work out your anger. That work for you?"

Exhaling a laugh, Heather just shook her head.

"No? In that case, why don't we just go to dinner and forget all this for a while?" Jace would do anything to erase those shadows from her eyes. Whatever she said, however she saw herself, he couldn't forget her terror when she believed he was going to kill her, when she thought they might leave her behind, when the second band of insurgents had cut them off. Was it wrong for him to want to keep her safe?

If so, he was content to be wrong.

Heather abandoned her aggressive stance, walking away from him instead. She headed toward the staircase. "All right. Dinner."

Jace allowed himself to watch her as she climbed the stairs. Damn, she had a body that didn't quit. Her lithe grace hypnotized him. Just watching her walk was a treat. How the men of her unit were able to concentrate with her around boggled his mind. He didn't know if he, consummate professional that he was, would be able to do it. Knowing he was being sexist and unfair didn't change how he felt.

This intense awareness wasn't one-sided. The attraction was mutual. With a little effort, he could talk her into bed. That wasn't ego talking—well, okay, maybe it was—it was experience. But he wasn't interested in a one-night stand with her, or even a short-term affair. Jace wanted her in his life, and that scared the hell out of him.

He was lousy relationship material. He knew that. Delta Force rarely stood still. They were, in fact, constantly in flux. Shorter missions from units Stateside; longer-term deployments like the one his unit was currently on, using the forward air base as a staging area for quick response missions. Most relationships failed within a year or two, the wives and girlfriends unable to handle the long absences, the total secrecy. Even if he wanted to share his experiences with Heather, he couldn't. Heather, at least, would understand the intricacies of his chosen profession. Would she be able to deal with it? Was she interested in trying?

She came back down the stairs, dressed in her own clothes. As he ushered her out the door, he wondered at the hard knot twisting in his gut.

Chapter Twenty-Eight

September 6. 4:00 P.M.
Officers' Club, al-Zadr Air Force Base

JACE WAS DETERMINED to be a charming companion. He'd been told he could be funny, intelligent, and even a gentleman. Chivalry was all but dead in modern society. Men rarely held doors for women any longer, or let them off an elevator before pushing their way on, or any of the other little courtesies women of previous generations had enjoyed. He suspected Heather hadn't paid much attention either way; she struck him as probably more interested in being accepted as an equal in a male-dominated field. But she did not pull away from the hand he placed at the small of her back as the hostess led them to a small table at the far end of the dining room, or wince as Jace held her chair for her.

This area of the Officers' Club was casual and breezy, decorated with seascapes and large paddle fans stirring the air. It was nothing like the formal dining room, with its heavy wood and gold scrollwork. Sure, the fishing net and painted starfish might have been a little hokey, but it had a charm and comfort Jace liked, and a fabulous view. Huge windows spanned the west wall, showing a sweeping valley leading to high, jagged mountain peaks in the distance. Sunsets were truly spectacular. This time of day, it was virtually deserted; too late for the lunch crowd, too early for dinner.

Jace forked a mouthful of his fettuccine. "Mm. This is good." He grinned at her. "So what brought you to the Army?"

Heather toyed with her salad. "College," she said, then shrugged. "My parents had different plans for me, that's for sure. I am a great disappointment to them. But I saw *G.I. Jane* when I was ten, and that was it for me. I watched every war movie I could get my hands on. There were no female role models, you know? Not as soldiers. Sure, there was Wonder Woman and Buffy, but they weren't real. So I decided to be the role model. Show those young girls out there that they could be like G.I. Jane, too." She gave a crooked grin. "My parents wouldn't support my choice, so it was either scholarships or public school."

Jace cocked his head at her. "So where did you end up?"

"Public school. New York. As far from home as I could get. You?"

"Colorado School of Mines." He sipped his iced tea. "Had a view not dissimilar to this one." He gestured out the windows. "'Course, the base of Mines' foothills are covered in trees. Beautiful in the fall."

Heather looked a little wistful. "It sounds like it. I think I've forgotten what a real tree looks like. I'm trying to decide where I want to go after my tour here is up; maybe Colorado or Washington State."

What about North Carolina? Jace closed his mouth over the

words. Heather was ambitious, that much was clear. Even suggesting she follow him home . . . and even if she did, what on earth would he do with her? He was gone more often than not.

And yet, when he was with her, a tiny part of him yearned to put down roots.

"I want to go somewhere where I can really make a difference, you know?" she was saying. "God help me if I get stuck in the bowels of the Pentagon, or at some huge post where I'm a staff officer and not doing any real work." She twitched a shoulder in self-deprecation. "Ego aside, I'm actually sort of decent at my job. And I love supporting the Special Forces. What I do, what I figure out, helps my guys plan their missions better. Keeps them safer. How can any career top that?"

Jace grinned. "I get that. If I couldn't do what I do, I'd slit my wrists."

She cocked a curious head at him. "What happens when you get too old, hotshot? SpecOps is a young man's game. What happens when you slow down?"

Ugh. He got cold chills even thinking about it. "Won't happen. I'm indestructible. Like Superman." He changed the subject. "Have you worked with the 10th Special Forces Group the whole time you've been here?"

"For sixteen of the twenty-two months I've been at al-Zadr. They're debating sending me home early." She frowned. "I have two months left on my tour. I just want to get back to work, no matter where it ends up being."

Jace bit back everything that flashed through his brain. "No" would go over like a lead balloon, and he had no right to say it. "As long as you're restricted to base" would be met by disbelieving laughter. Her job required her to travel back and forth. "Only if

I'm there to protect you" would be met with hostility. He'd never known anyone so persistent in proving herself.

So he changed the subject again. "When you do rotate back Stateside, you going home for a visit? Seeing family is always nice." He stroked his chin, pretending to think. "Let's see . . . I'm going to guess you're from, where? Helena, Montana? Grew up on a farm?" He couldn't keep his eyes from dropping to her mouth, remembering their incredible softness. Their sweet heat. "Your first kiss was at the Homecoming dance, where you and your very lucky escort got crowned King and Queen?" And her date had driven her to a lake and parked, no doubt, and run his hands over that soft skin, maybe fumbled his way inside her bra . . . Heather was looking at him oddly, and he realized he was gripping the edge of the table with both hands, gritting his teeth so hard a muscle jumped in his cheek. Because of a vision of another man touching Heather? Like he was jealous? No way. He wasn't jealous. He forced his hands open and pretended to relax.

Shit.

Heather laughed, and he lost himself in the sound.

"Try Los Angeles. Mother a model, father a screenwriter." She hesitated, then shrugged. "A failed screenwriter, who believed an artist had to suffer, or at least drink, for his art. They weren't A-List, but people recognized them. Got good tables, good seats at events, invites into exclusive clubs. Like that."

"Never would have pegged you for a Hollywood starlet. You also modeled? How could you not, with that body?"

Heather frowned. "Yes. My sister didn't have the height for it. My mother kept shoving me into those stupid beauty pageants." Raising her voice into a falsetto, she said, "My fondest wish is that we are able to achieve world peace in my lifetime."

God. How awful was that? He couldn't picture strong, independent Heather Langstrom simpering across a stage, pretending her body, fabulous as it was, was her only asset. Had anyone recognized or encouraged her keen intelligence?

Still, the devil in him teased her. "I love those shows. Especially the swimsuit exhibi . . . I mean, the part where we hear from all the suma cum laude astrophysicist majors. Did you win?"

She shot him a disgusted look. "I hated it. My mother wanted me to be a professional model, too. An actress, if I could attract the right kind of attention. She couldn't seem to grasp the concept that I thought it was a total waste of time. And yes, I won. I won't trot out my pedigree; it's too humiliating."

Jace laughed and reached across the table and intertwined their fingers. The slide of skin against skin felt more than good. He sobered. "Don't go home yet. I don't like the idea of your being alone."

Heather gave him a who-are-you-kidding look. He laughed.

"Well, of course I'd prefer that. But you're safe with me, I promise."

"But are you safe with me?" Heather snapped her mouth closed. She cleared her throat, looking down at her plate and tugging her hand free. "Sorry. I can't say I'm not going to date you, then flirt with you."

Jace exhaled a soft laugh. "Don't stop on my account," he said, teasing her. "I'm a big, strong he-man. I can take it."

HE MIGHT BE able to take it; but could she? Slouching back into her chair, Heather tilted her head back to watch the fan rotating above her. What was it about him? Why was he different? Because he was. She'd dealt with dozens of Special Forces soldiers—hard, confident, handsome warriors—nearly drowning in a sea of testosterone, and had never once been tempted to break her rule. And yet, now, with Jace . . .

She watched as he tossed back the rest of his iced tea in one long swallow. His head thrown back and the strong column of his throat working had her aching to put her lips where a single drop of condensation slid from the glass to his chin. To lick it off, then lick down his throat, to trace her hands across his collarbone, to explore the muscles of his shoulders . . .

"You keep looking at me like that, I'm going to lose all my noble intentions."

Heather jerked her gaze back to his face, a guilty flush rising in her cheeks. His words had been light, but the expression on his face was intense, his dark eyes probing her, the heat unmistakable.

Rather than answer, she pushed herself to her feet. Walking down to the long windows, she gazed out at the panorama below her. Miles and miles of sand and rock and scrub, then the rising peaks of the bare, jagged mountains. For the first time since she'd been here, she failed to appreciate the raw beauty of the landscape. Instead, it seemed barren and inhospitable. Empty.

Lonely.

A wellspring of realization hit her. An epiphany, lighting her from the inside out. Heather felt desolate, too. She focused on achievement. On success. Not on people, or on relationships.

She felt rather than saw Jace come up beside her. He didn't speak.

"I don't want to be alone," she whispered.

He didn't say anything. He simply dropped cash onto the table, clasped her chilled hand in his warm one, and guided her to his car. Neither said a word as he drove to his little house. God, she was tired. Bone-deep weary.

Maybe she just needed a nap.

With Jace?

No. No, no, no. Down that path lay disaster. Sure, she could sleep with him. Once, maybe twice. And word would get back to her unit, and every testosterone-laden, thickheaded moron whom she had rejected over the past year would be all over her, all over again. She'd get no peace. Her reputation would suffer, and that she could not have. She was under no illusions; her assignment at the 10th Special Forces Group worked only as long as she could command the respect of her superiors, peers, and subordinates. If her commanding officer thought for one second she was a distraction to his men, she'd be rotated back Stateside before she could say, "Unfair."

Jace pulled into his tiny driveway and killed the engine. Turning sideways in his seat, he draped a wrist over the steering wheel. "Hot tea," he said.

Heather nodded, unfastening her seat belt. She would be safe here. She could rest. Nurse her wounds—the ones no one could see—and hide for a while. Just for a little while.

She followed Jace into his house.

He led her into the kitchen, where he put on a kettle. He scrounged through his cupboards, eventually coming up with a box of chamomile tea. "Ha!" he said. "Knew you were still around."

Heather smothered a laugh. "Not a tea drinker, huh? I didn't really think so."

Shaking his head, Jace grinned at her. "Not on your life. Coffee all the way."

"Then who . . . ?" Heather clamped her jaws shut. She turned away and pulled open the refrigerator, peering inside and pretending she hadn't spoken. It was none of her business. None at all.

She didn't hear Jace move across the floor, but his heat blasted her as he stood directly behind her. "My mother," he said softly, sliding his arms around her middle and pulling her back against him. He was solid and warm, and she let herself lean against him, just for a moment. "She visited six months ago. Couldn't get to sleep without the stuff." He shuddered, and Heather laughed.

Jace turned her in his arms and pulled her in more tightly, silently offering comfort and strength. Even knowing she should pull away, put some distance between them, she found herself sliding her arms around his waist and laying her head on his broad chest. Just for a minute. His heartbeat, steady and strong, under her ear.

Something inside her relaxed.

The kettle began to whistle. Heather was all for ignoring it, but Jace eased himself away. Grabbing a cup, he dropped the teabag into it and poured the water. Some splashed over the edge and onto his fingers. He cursed, pulling them away and shaking his hand.

Heather laughed.

He slid a glance her way. "My pain is funny to you?"

Heather shook her head, but snickered. "Kinda, yeah. Three weeks ago, you went out, deep into a hostile area. You fought a ton of bad guys and went on the run for twelve hours straight, dragging me along. All that without ever losing your cool. A little hot water burn just doesn't seem like much next to that."

Pulling a wounded look onto his face, Jace held out his fingers. "It's a big burn. Huge. In fact, I might lose my fingers."

Chuckling, Heather took hold of his hand. A jolt of electricity shot through her. Whew. The man was potent, that was for sure. She bent to examine the burn, finding only a small patch of reddened skin. "Yes, I can see the severity of the wound. We'd better get you some serious first aid." Acting without thinking, she bent and kissed the skin, soothing it. What was she doing? Where was her sanity?

It was Jace who stopped her, easing his finger free and stepping to the refrigerator. He opened the door and stood there, peering inside and not moving. Finally, he cleared his throat.

"Do you take milk in your tea? Sugar, lemon? Actually, I don't have any lemon. And I think this milk expired last May."

Heather let out a breath she didn't know she'd been holding. "Nothing, thank you."

"Why don't you sit out on the couch? Or at the dining room table."

"All right."

How could they sound so normal? She herself felt anything but normal. Jittery, and like her skin was too hot and too tight for her bones. "Sorry."

"No problem. I'll bring the tea out. Go sit down."

Heather left the kitchen. She curled her legs under her on the sofa. Soft music filled the room, some sort of gentle jazz she didn't recognize. Figured a man who couldn't be bothered to buy his own furniture would have a sophisticated sound system. He handed her the cup of tea and perched at the other end. Heather sipped, scalding the tip of her tongue. Good. Maybe it would put her mind right. She was getting in too deep here, and really, nothing had happened. They'd shared a few kisses, that was all.

They sat in a faintly uncomfortable silence. She wrapped both hands around the mug, feeling chilled in a way she couldn't explain. When she finished the tea, Jace took her mug without a word and set it on the coffee table.

"Lie down on your stomach."

Puzzled, she glanced up at him. He met her gaze, his expression unreadable. "You're cold and tense. I promised I'd be good. So turn over, Langstrom. That's an order."

She tried to laugh, but nothing came out. Finally, she simply did as he said and stretched out along the sofa. He sat next to her, his hip nudging her back a bit. She tensed as his hands settled onto her shoulders, but relaxed as he did nothing more than rub.

It felt heavenly. He worked the tension loose from her muscles with a sure touch, avoiding the few remaining yellow patches of bruising. He started at her neck, working his way down her shoulders to her back, kneading along her spine and into her lower back. She groaned in appreciation.

"Pleasepleaseplease, don't stop," she found herself saying.

Jace laughed. "Not a chance, sweetheart."

He worked on the knots in silence, the only noise the soothing music. His touch was leaving little licks of fire in its wake. Her skin came alive, her body humming in anticipation of his touch. When his hands left her, she pressed her mouth closed to prevent herself pleading for more.

He started again, this time at her feet. His fingers pressed along her heels, down the arches, to her toes. She couldn't remember the last time a man had given her a massage. Nor had she realized how tense her muscles clenched until his magic fingers smoothed across her calves and up the backs of her thighs. And while there was nothing sexual or suggestive about what he was doing, her nipples contracted, and moisture gathered at her core.

She kept expecting him to touch her more intimately. Her body was so tuned to his she nearly turned over right then and there and begged him to make love to her. True, she wasn't entirely sure if she would welcome a more intimate touch or not. It was a lousy idea; she'd established that already. Still, she found she was disappointed when he finally got up and went to the coat closet to pull out an extra pillow and comforter. He tucked her in like she was a child, then sat again at the foot of the couch.

"That was amazing." More than amazing. Too bad massages like that didn't come bottled at the store, without the complexity of entanglements like the ones Jace Reed represented. And she definitely wanted more. Wanted his mouth where his hands had been. She blew out a breath, trying to calm her body. "Thank you."

He didn't answer. Puzzled, Heather lifted her head and craned it around. Jace was staring at the floor, a muscle ticking in his jaw. Long moments passed. Finally, he seemed to come to a decision, because he looked over at her. She turned over and scooted back into a sitting position. Whatever he meant to say was obviously important to him.

"Two years ago, we were on a mission . . . somewhere." Somewhere classified, he meant. His voice was low, and she had to strain to hear. "We weren't welcome. There was an al Qaeda presence there, protected by the locals. Our mission was to find and extract a particular person of interest. During the exfiltration, an RPG hit our helicopter. Blew off one of the struts and part of the tail. We went down pretty hard. The impact killed one of my teammates. Three others injured." He took in some air and let it out slowly. "Including me. Broken arm, some cuts." He paused, as though weighing what he should tell her. Or maybe what he was willing to put into words. Heather found herself holding her breath.

"The objective—the person of interest—was unhurt. Our primary mission hadn't changed. Get him out and into American hands. That was the priority." He paused again, struggling with how to tell the story. "There was a firefight. The team needed a diversion, needed time to get away. Dougie and I held the line long enough for a second helicopter to extract the rest of the team."

Jace stared at the floor again, perhaps lost in a haze of memories. Heather could relate. She'd seen that look in the mirror a lot the past few days.

"Dougie and I were captured. It's a hard thing, to capture a Delta Force operator. But these guys were well organized, well armed, trained, and lucky." He shifted so he could rest his elbows on his knees, head down. "They took us up into the mountains, where they had all the advantages. They knew those mountains. All the caves, tunnels, passages. Everything we didn't know." He rubbed both hands over his hair, then laced his fingers behind his head as he stared at the floor. "We figured they would parade us around, show off their prisoners. Make it real public, you know? But they didn't. They wanted information. Hell, maybe they just had a hard-on to crack a combat applications guy." He glanced at her. "Sorry. They wanted to break us."

"I've heard the word before," she murmured, fearing if she spoke louder, he would stop talking.

The ghost of a smile crossed his lips and vanished. "Yeah." He cleared his throat. "It took the Joint Special Operations Command nine weeks to get any information on our whereabouts. It took another two to put together a viable extraction plan. Our guys came for us, but it was too late for Dougie. He died . . . he died three days before rescue came." Jace cleared his throat again, and Heather knew he was trying to control strong emotions. Heather turned her head away, pretending to look out the front window, giving him at least a pretense of privacy as his throat worked convulsively.

"I'm sorry." It was so inadequate, but she didn't know what else to say. Good Lord Almighty. What could she say? It was horrifying. Jace and Dougie had been prisoners for nearly three months. Three months of . . . of what? What had they endured? Compared to what her imagination conjured up, her paltry four days seemed insignificant.

He seemed to sense the direction of her thoughts. "I didn't tell you that to diminish your own experience. I was a seasoned combat veteran. At the time, I'd been with Delta for six years." In other words, he was capable of withstanding capture, and she was not. Heather bit her tongue over her retort. Hell, maybe he was right. She doubted she would have been able to take three months of abuse, especially not after the sheik had proven whatever point he intended to with her body. Not without losing her mind. She swallowed hard.

"I just, I don't know, wanted you to know that yeah, I do get it. Not everyone would. But I do. So, if you want to talk . . ."

"I don't."

"But if you do."

"I won't. But thank you." She scooted back down, tucking her feet up and pulling the blanket over her shoulders. Despite Jace's confidences, she couldn't face her demons. Not yet. Maybe not ever. "Thank you for telling me that. I know it was hard for you. But what I really need is a nap. Is that all right? If it's a problem, I can go . . ."

"No." His voice was absolute. "It's no problem at all. I still want to keep an eye on you. Dr. McGrath didn't want you on your own, you know. I wasn't making that part up. You're not as well as you think you are. You're still in the early stages of recovery." He stood up. "Besides, I need to hit the rack, too. I'm leaving around two in the morning, so I gotta catch a nap. Why don't you take the bed, and I'll bunk down on the couch?" He stood beside her, obviously expecting her to get up.

Heather sat up, but did not relinquish the blanket. "Where are you go . . . oh, never mind. I know you can't tell me, anyway." She sighed. She missed her work. Especially, she missed knowing what was going on in the world. Having insider information, as it were, by reading the intelligence information reports every day, by talking to the locals. "I'm not going to take your bed. If I stay, it's here on the sofa. Take it or leave it."

Jace looked down at her, a soft warmth in his gaze. "I'll take whatever I can get." There it was again. That aching tension between them.

Heather plucked at the blanket, turning away from him. "Go to bed, Jace. Alone." He moved away, regrettably. Why did he pick now to listen to her? "Sweet dreams."

He twisted to see her from the second stair, a roguish grin splitting his face. "Only of you, baby." He bounded up the stairs.

The room was immediately colder.

It was best, she told herself. And repeated it a dozen times. Her body still burned where his hands had run over her body. What would it be like to have him give her the same massage, but linger over the strokes, turning the entire experience unbearably erotic?

Where was he going? Did his mission have anything to do with the Kongra-Gel? The whole situation still bothered her. Everyone at her debriefing agreed that since the SCUD had been destroyed, the threat was over. They discounted the Eshma chief of police's involvement. But they hadn't been there, hadn't seen the antagonism flickering in his eyes. Her gut said he was involved.

Her gut said a threat still existed.

She hoped Jace's mission shed new light on the situation. Maybe he could help her figure out what was going on. He had eyes on the ground, while she was annoyingly all but bedridden. Soap operas, her ass. Maybe she could arrange to have Jace report back to Dr. McGrath that she was fully functional?

And that started her thinking about sex again. Fully functional, indeed! Was Jace in as much discomfort as she was?

Forcing her mind off Jace and his magical hands, Heather stripped out of her clothes and dropped them onto the floor, leaving on only a T-shirt and underwear. She put her attention to untangling the mystery of her kidnapping. And immediately fell asleep.

She was back in her cell. Someone yanked her arms behind her. Cruelly bound them. The dirty cloth pushed past her teeth smelled like goat, and she gagged. Her tormenter glared down at her, one hand tangled in her uniform top, yanking her close enough to smell his fetid breath and see the cracked incisor when his lip curled up. He spoke to her, but she couldn't understand him, and the more she strained to hear, the farther away his voice seemed. Whatever he was saying was crucial, and she had to understand. It was vital she understand. But he began to fade, growing smaller and smaller.

"Wait!" she shouted. "Tell me!"

The ghostly form turned back. "You will die," he said. "You will all die. The debauched places that soil our beautiful country will burn, and you will writhe in agony. Allah has willed it." He faded to smoke.

Heather woke in a cold sweat, thrashing within the snarled binds of the blanket. Where was she? It took her several moments to orient herself. Untangling the blanket and throwing it off, she swung her legs over the side of the sofa, but did not try to rise. At the moment, she was aware of every single one of her nagging bruises.

She tried to lie down again, but it was impossible. What if she slept, and he came again?

The shrink had told Heather to sit with her feelings. Phagh. Why the hell would she want to do that? She never wanted to experience a single one of those emotions again. Sit with her feelings and be an objective observer, understanding they could no longer hurt her. Look at them and let them go.

"Quack," she muttered.

But she knew the approach had merit. Facing her fears head-on had always been her approach, whether it was the fear of heights that had led her to Airborne School, or her fear of snakes that had prodded her through Jungle Warfare School.

This was different. How could it not be? She'd never been so helpless in her entire life. Bound, blindfolded, gagged, unable even to see her captors to defend herself. Until he wanted her. She hadn't lied to the doctors, not really. Their exam had proven no rape took place. And the very thought of facing the man again sent shudders of revulsion and rage through her. If she had the opportunity to kill him, she would do so, without hesitation or remorse.

She shifted restlessly on the sofa. Now too wired to sleep, she looked at the clock. It was barely seven twenty in the evening. The setting sun filtered in around the edges of the shuttered windows, leaving the interior dim. She shivered again. She'd never been afraid of the dark, instead viewing it as an ally. Now, after so many hours restricted by the blindfold, by the perpetual dimness of her cell, she wasn't so sure. Being unable to tell night from day had been psychologically more debilitating than she could ever have imagined. SERE training—Survival, Evasion, Resistance, and Escape—had been rough, the toughest experience of her life. And yet, in comparison to the real thing, it had been fun on a playground.

Her thoughts turned, as they had so often over the past week, to her rescuers, namely Jace. They had all kept her safe, of course, but on Jace's orders.

Jace, who wanted her.

His guilt consumed him, but he had done nothing over which to condemn himself. In the end, he had not killed her. The hated perfume, a humiliating precursor of things to come, had, instead, saved her life. The irony was intense.

The thought that she'd almost died felt surreal, like it had happened to someone else. Supposedly, her life was meant to flash before her eyes, but hers had not. There had merely been a sense of things undone, a life she'd never get to live. And in that moment, she'd wanted things she'd never considered before. A husband. A family. She still could not see herself in any kind of a nine-to-five job. But someone to love, who cherished her . . .

She looked up at the ceiling. Jace's bedroom was right above her.

Without another thought, she slipped from the sofa and padded up the stairs.

Chapter Twenty-Nine

September 6. 7:25 P.M.
FOB Hollow Straw, al-Zadr Air Force Base

THE FOURTH STAIR CREAKED. Just a little. He'd never fixed it because old habits died hard, and he figured it was merely another early warning system in the extremely unlikely event terrorists infiltrated his house on al-Zadr Air Base. Much more likely was that his guest was coming up the stairs, probably to use the bathroom. Jace listened to her attempts to be silent and chuckled. The truth was, she was good. Better than good. But she wasn't an operator. Delta Force operators were the best in the world, despite the SAS and SEALs both claiming the honor. Delta still had the highest dropout rate during Selection. What was it, ninety-four percent, compared to the SEALs' eighty and the SAS's ninety percent?

As expected, Heather went into the bathroom and closed the door. The toilet flushed and the water ran. He waited for her to go back downstairs. When he didn't hear her, he found himself sitting up in bed, straining for a sound. Had she moved, and he hadn't heard her?

No way.

He rolled onto his back and looked at his watch. It was a little before seven thirty, and he had to be conscious at one in the morning and able at two. He was on the verge of investigating anyway, fearing she had fallen, or . . . or what? He flopped back onto the sheets, laughing at himself. She was no longer in any danger. Her injuries had all but healed. He was being an idiot. The truth was, he burned for her to push open his door, get in next to him, and . . .

Holy shit. As though he had conjured it, the knob on his bedroom door turned.

She came through the door like a wraith, drifting closer and closer. Jace waited, curious to see what she would do. Did she want to talk?

What she did blew his mind. She lifted the corner of the sheet, and slid in next to him.

HEATHER SHIVERED. So cold. All she could focus on was Jace's heat. He would warm her. He would make the nightmares go away. He could do it.

Easing under the sheet, she shifted carefully across the mattress until she encountered a solid body. Maybe she could just lie here and get warm, and slip out again in a few hours, before he ever knew she had been there. But strong arms surrounded her, pulling her in close to him. She welcomed the furnace blast of heat as he plastered her against a hard, sculpted chest. *Oh, shit.* Jace slept nude; not something she had even considered before she crept into his bed. Tilting her head up, she met his eyes, black in the dimness.

"I'm sorry," she said, sounding much more breathless than she intended. "I didn't mean to wake you up."

"I wasn't sleeping," he said. "Nightmares?"

How had he known? She nodded, her throat suddenly closed up. Had he also had nightmares after his ordeal? "Do they ever go away?"

His breath was warm against her face. "Eventually. Maybe. Some things never leave your mind, though. Can't exorcise them, no matter what." He ran his hands up her arms, his touch sure and gentle and not nearly as impersonal as it had been in the desert. Or downstairs. "I'll tell you a secret, though. A time-honored way to get rid of them."

"What?"

She felt rather than saw the quick grin. "Have sex with the nearest naked man, as fast as you can. And as often as humanly possible."

She huffed out a laugh and shook her head, but she suddenly knew he was only half joking. As an affirmation of life, as proof she had not died in a prison cell in the mountains of Sari Daru Province, to remember she was not the animal they had tried to make her but a human being of strength and resolve—she clung to him, praying he had not merely been teasing her.

"I kept trying to figure out what I did wrong," she whispered. "If I'd handled things differently, if I hadn't told my boss we needed to talk to the police. If I . . ."

Jace placed a single finger over her mouth. "You can drive yourself crazy with hindsight. No one can know for certain what would have happened. Someone knew something, and thought you knew something as well."

"I still think they're wrong about Sa'id al-Jabr. How could

the Kongra-Gel men have known anyone overheard anything if someone didn't tell them?"

"I agree."

Such simple words. The people who'd debriefed her in the hospital were smart, competent men. And they'd all said she was wrong. They'd found no evidence linking al-Jabr to the Kongra-Gel. But this man believed her. The relief was intense. A portion of her heart melted into a puddle.

"It's my fault Captain Bernoulli is dead. That those soldiers died in the ambush. It's all my fault." The tears leaked from the corners of her eyes before she could stop them.

Jace rubbed small circles over her back. "We'll argue that one tomorrow. It wasn't your fault some terrorist assholes decided to plot whatever they plotted."

Heather hesitated. "What if they're not done? What if destroying the SCUD isn't enough to stop them?"

"Then we'll uncover and stop whatever else they have planned." His calm certainty steadied her. His proximity set her pulse thrumming.

She had shut off her brain when she unlatched his door and invaded his bedroom, but talking caused ugly thoughts to resurface. She didn't want to think. Pressing her face against his neck, swallowing hard, she slid her arms around his neck, wanting only to feel.

Jace tensed, but did nothing. She could feel his restraint, his control. Ignoring the faint trembling in her hands, Heather pressed her open mouth to the pulse hammering in his neck. She wanted the distraction. She wanted to forget, if only for a few moments. Was he really going to say no?

Kissing her way up his neck, she paused to nibble at his chin, and reached for his mouth. He met her halfway, groaning against her lips as he parted them and swept his tongue into her mouth. She made a noise in the back of her throat. Thank God. He wasn't going to turn her away.

It was even better than she remembered. Spicy and hot. Gentle and demanding. This time, she could kiss him back.

She did.

He tasted like safety and freedom and the lick of life. Heather slid her tongue along his and angled her mouth, inviting him to deepen the kiss. He did so with alacrity, causing a flutter of pleasure. Whether he felt her bone-deep chill or her enjoyment, he hauled her closer until there wasn't an inch of her that wasn't plastered against him.

"You're the strongest man I've ever met," she said. He shifted his hands under her shirt, and explored her spine with fingers that touched her lightly, incredibly gently. A small sound escaped. Not a sob. Never a sob. She didn't make a habit of crying, and she had already cried in his arms once. "I need . . . Jace, I . . ." She didn't know what she needed, not really. But he did. He kissed her again, then left her lips to explore her face with his mouth, nibbling, tasting, kissing each eye. Licking his way down her neck, he took his time at her collarbone, hesitating at the small, round scar. Heather didn't want him thinking about it.

Heather grabbed Jace's head and pulled it lower, trying to guide him to her breast. He resisted, hands smoothing the bare skin of her arm, running his fingers up and down it as though he had all the time in the world. It was Heather who grabbed the hem of her T-shirt, pulling it off and dropping it onto the floor.

Jace bent his head to her breasts, hot breath blowing across her nipple before his teeth scraped along it. He drew her breast into his mouth. She arched up, gasping, the pleasure intense. A hand came up to cup her other breast, fingers stroking along the sensitive mound. Shivering, Heather spilled her hands down his back to cup his buttocks, and he reacted with a groan and an involuntary press of his hips. He was hugely aroused, but he quickly controlled himself and pulled a little farther away from her. He was being so careful with her she couldn't stand it. The hell with his restraint. She wanted him as crazy hot for her as she was for him.

Thank God for the darkness. Her bruises had faded to the pale greens and yellows of the almost-healed, but if he was being this careful with her in the dark, God only knew how he would react in the light.

Heather opened her mouth. To say what? I'm all right? She was . . . or as good as. "What he did to me . . ." Her voice cracked. She took a deep breath a tried again. "What I went through was about power and control." Please, let him not ask her again. "Nothing like what we're doing now. At least, what I hope we're doing now."

"Oh, yeah."

His voice was absolute. She smiled in the darkness. "Whew."

He laughed, a soft rumble from his chest. "Do I look like the kind of moron who would walk away from this?" He swept his hand from her shoulder to her hip. Her breath hitched. Fingers lingering on the soft skin just below her spine, he bent to kiss her again, his mouth growing more urgent.

He swept his hands up her back with an eagerness that had her laughing again. But he took his time sliding her underwear off her legs, fingernails scraping across nerve endings that jumped to life, turning her laughter into moans. He had magic fingers. Everywhere he touched her turned to liquid fire.

As he returned to lay next to her again, Heather raked her fingers through his curly hair. It was softer than she had imagined. She touched his face, and he turned it to press a kiss into her palm.

"You're in control," he said. "All right? You say stop, we stop. Anything makes you feel uncomfortable, you speak up. Okay?"

"Okay." But she wasn't in control. Not really.

Wrapping both arms around her, Jace rolled onto his back, pulling her with him until she sprawled across his chest. The incredible sensation dizzied her. Her naked flesh slid along his as he pulled her up, until he could put his mouth against her, and oh, heaven! He kissed her, and the amazing sensation had her pushing against his mouth and closing her thighs around him. He grinned up at her in complete enjoyment. The sight of his handsome face, mouth wet with her juices, had to be the most erotic thing she'd seen in her life. It pushed her dangerously close to the edge.

"Jace," she gasped. "If you keep doing that, I'm going . . . to . . ."

"Yes." He paused only long enough to say one word. And then she rode a helpless wave of pleasure, moaning and gasping and laughing all at once. He continued to lick and suck at her, drawing her orgasm out. Her body was taut, her head thrown back with complete abandon, eyes closed.

Eventually, she pulled away and collapsed, rolling over onto her back so as not to smother him. He rolled with her, pulling her down until they were nose to nose, and kissed her.

He kissed her as though he would be happy to do it forever, with evident enjoyment. In fact, he seemed to enjoy everything about sex so far. She couldn't help herself; she started to laugh.

He just cocked his head and waited.

"That didn't make me uncomfortable at all. We can add it to the can-do list."

His white teeth flashed in the darkness. "Maybe we should make certain. You know, experiment. Do that again, just to make sure." He touched her as though he couldn't bear not to, exploring her shoulder blades, tracing a path down her spine. She did the same, reveling in the incredible contrast between soft skin over hard muscles. Her mouth followed her hands, pressing against his shoulder, up to his jaw, and across to his mouth once more.

He was still hard against her stomach. Heather pressed closer experimentally. His swift intake of breath preceded both hands spearing into her hair to cup her face. She slid her leg over his in mute invitation. Jace pushed forward until he was cradled in her heat, but stayed that way, head down, fighting . . . what?

"I won't break."

Jace groaned. "But maybe I will." He nudged her leg higher, grinding against her. "You're going to be the death of me."

And just like that, she bounced right back to where she did not want to be. Death. Visions of the soldiers around her being cut down. The smell of blood. No.

"Please," she begged.

Somehow knowing where she'd gone in her head, Jace hesitated. "Are you . . . okay?"

"Yes. Jace. Please!"

No longer hesitating, he again went to his back, pulling her with him. Heather ended up straddling him, her long hair framing them both. He reached up to touch it.

"Your hair is amazing. I hope you don't ever cut it."

It was ridiculous how much the small compliment pleased her. But it also had the potential to rip her heart out. Even knowing that, she couldn't bring herself to move away from the sight of him, his masculine perfection, a flawless alpha male lying relaxed, almost submissive beneath her, ready to let her take the lead.

Which she did.

Reaching down, she wrapped her fingers around him, delighting in his sharp intake of breath and involuntary movement. Exploring him, she admitted, "I've been thinking I might cut it short." Ever since her brutal captor had used it to control her movements. No. Don't go there.

"Don't. It's beautiful."

He slid on a condom. Heather lifted her hips over him and pressed down, slowly, drawing it out because there was only ever one time two lovers first came together. Jace gripped her hips, then loosened his hold. She had to admire his self-control. Desire etched his face and tightened his body. His head was thrown back, and she fell onto his chest, kissing the strong column of his neck with an open mouth. His hips pressed up, trying for fuller penetration, but she pulled away, enjoying her momentary power.

"No. My pace."

He immediately backed off, and she realized her mistake. He thought she was uncomfortable with his aggression. So she smiled at him, a sultry siren's smile, and pushed him a little farther inside her. And pulled all the way out. And did it again, a little deeper, all the while looking into his face. His eyes locked onto hers. She saw his struggle. He wanted to slam himself home; and she wanted him to, but she wanted him hotter, wilder, out of control.

"God, Heather . . ." He groaned his frustration. "You're killing . . . me."

"Let go," she whispered.

And he did.

He exploded into action, clamping his hands over her hips and thrusting upwards, pulling her down so her breasts dangled in his face and he feasted on her. His hands roamed over her shoulders and back, cupped her breasts, teased her nipples. Pleasure blasted through her.

Jace sat up, pulling her closer, pressing himself deeper inside her as he thrust his tongue into her mouth. Their tongues dueled and slid together decadently. He touched her, explored her femininity as she gasped and ground against him. This was incredible. There was sex, and there was this. Sex ramped up to a thousand. She clung to him as they rocked together, as she did a slow roll of her hips that wrung a guttural sound from him.

"You are so goddamned sexy," he said, voice hoarse. The heat in his eyes lit her on fire. He touched her, licking and tasting, returning to her lips again and again. Pushing impossibly deep inside of her, he wrapped his arms around her. He had said she would be in control, but despite her position, she rode helplessly along with him as he set a fast pace. She moaned her approval.

And then she moaned for a different reason, as she shattered into a thousand million pieces, head thrown back, face and neck flushed as she spun out of control. He was right behind her, shouting as he thrust, thrust again, and then simply wrapped his arms tightly around her as they shuddered their release.

She wanted to stay there forever in their magical place. Eventually, though, her body reformed and she floated back to earth. Jace held her snugly against him, her head resting on his shoulder. How had she gotten here? She didn't remember moving. Couldn't imagine moving, she felt so boneless. Completely undone.

She rolled her head just far enough to see him. He watched her, male satisfaction stamped clearly on his face. It made her laugh.

"I vote we add that to the can-do list, too," she told him. "Immediately."

Jace laughed, touching her hair with gentle hands, pushing it back behind her ears. "How about in, oh, say, fifteen minutes?" He ran light fingers down her back to her rear, stroking it and cupping it in one large hand. "Make that ten."

Heather let herself enjoy laying entwined in his arms. It was like coming home; completely natural, like she belonged there and nowhere else. Jace moved, though, getting rid of the condom and cleaning himself up. The chill penetrated her fulfillment. When he came back to the bed, her mood had darkened. Even when Jace scooped her back into his arms, even when her head was pillowed on his chest, the mood was broken.

Yes, he had made her forget. She had known he would be able to do it. It had been incredible—breath-stealing—but now the press of tears was hot behind her eyes as reality reared its ugly head.

Heather cleared her throat, cleared it again. Realizing she was tense as a board, she tried to relax her muscles. She couldn't stop the images swirling through her head. Jace's chest rose and fell evenly beneath her ear. Shouldn't she let him get some sleep? He had to be at work in a few short hours. But then he spoke.

"Are you cold?"

She shook her head. Well, yes, but it was not a physical cold. Was she really going to do this? She blew out a breath, hard.

"I was held in a cell," she started. If Jace was surprised, he gave no indication of it. He didn't so much as twitch a muscle to let her know he listened. It was just as well. If he had said anything at all, she wouldn't have been able to continue.

"There was no way out. There was a guard at the door, and another one down the hall. I heard them talking all the time."

That was the easy part to say. "They tied my hands. To keep me off balance." Literally and figuratively. That, and the blindfold, and the jeering comments the guards had thrown at her. "The man who was . . . in charge of my interrogation was . . ." A brute. Cruel. "He was in charge of the camp while Sheik al-Hassid was gone. He liked throwing his weight around. He . . . liked throwing me around, too." She swallowed audibly. Could she squeeze the words past the constriction in her throat?

Jace began to stroke along her back. Up and down, lulling, soothing. His steady heartbeat under her ear gave her the courage she needed to continue.

"He would leave for a while, and whenever he came back, he was mad. It was as though someone else wanted to know if he'd gotten the information out of me yet, and it pissed him off that he had to say no." She tried breathing through her nose. Maybe that would be easier. "He, um, would pin me into a corner." She started shaking, a fine tremor through her limbs she couldn't control. Jace flipped the blankets up and over her, pulling her more firmly into his own heat.

"He would take off the blindfold so I could see him." But not the ropes. He knew she could fight from the ambush site when she'd broken his nose. It had been he who had knocked her out with one blow. "And he would. Um. Press up against me. Rub, you know, himself against me. He did it to intimidate me." No, be honest. "Well, he wanted me, too. It infuriated him, wanting an infidel, so he punished me. And he . . ." Her voice broke.

Jace worked hard to keep his voice even, but she knew him well enough to know he was feeling anything but calm. "You don't have to."

But she did. "If I don't now, I never will." She was silent for a while. Jace just continued to hold her, pretending he couldn't feel the dampness of her tears on his skin.

"I slept on the floor."

She could sense he didn't understand. Shifting a little, Jace brushed a kiss across her temple. "At the hospital, when Christina Madison said she'd had a cot to sleep on, you got really tense."

She remembered. In fact, she'd gotten so lightheaded she'd been afraid she would pass out. She cleared her throat again.

"Yeah." She exhaled. "Because . . . there was a cot. In my cell. Too." She closed her eyes, but that only made it worse. Underneath her, Jace was tight as a bowstring. What was he feeling? Some minor version of the fury burning in her own heart?

"You said . . . Jesus, Heather. Put me out of my misery, here. Did he rape you?"

She shook her head. "Not . . . exactly." God, did this have to be so hard to say?

"What the fu . . . what does that mean? Not exactly?" He sounded pissed, and his breathing had grown harsh. But he tried to temper his reaction; she pulled away from him, and he immediately stilled his body. Slowed his breathing. "Sorry. I'm sorry. I just . . . It's making me crazy, not knowing."

"I know. I'm sorry. It's just hard."

"No. God. You . . . this is harder for you to say than it is for me to hear. And if you've got the grit to say it, I'd damned well better have the grit to hear it."

That quiet statement gave her the courage to continue. He thought she was brave—little did he know how her insides quivered, even now.

She cleared her throat, for what felt like the umpteenth time. Her vocal cords just didn't want to work right.

"The cot . . . he pushed me down onto it." The tears slipped out faster now. Jace rubbed circles on her back, his touch neither light nor gentle. He fisted his other hand in her hair, then, seemingly through sheer force of will, relaxed his hands. "He . . . grabbed me." Hard. Had enjoyed hurting her. Thank God Jace had never seen the bruises the man had left on her breasts. "Straddled me. Um. And, uh . . . he . . . then he . . ." She couldn't continue. "You know."

"Jerked off?" His voice sounded as strangled as hers.

Heather pulled away from him. "Yes."

She sniffed, trying to stem the flow of tears. Maybe he didn't need to know the rest of it. How her revulsion infuriated him, drove him to new heights of rage. How he had screamed obscenities at her, and described in brutal detail how he planned to rape her after the sheik cast her aside. How he would tear her, how he would use her like the dog she was.

Heather stuffed a fist into her mouth to stop the nausea from erupting. No. No more.

Come on, Heather. Get it out there. Start to heal. That's what the damned shrink said would happen, anyway. At the moment, it just felt as though broken glass clogged her throat.

She forced herself to choke the words out. "He . . . he, you know . . . went in . . . in my hair." On her face. "I tried to bite him." Had come damned close. He had slapped her so hard she had nearly passed out. That was the night the sheik arrived in camp.

Jace brought up an arm to cover his eyes. "God damn him," he said, so softly she barely heard him. It was far more frightening than if he had shouted. "I will kill him." There was absolute certainty in his voice. This was no idle threat.

Heather dragged in a breath. "Not if I get to him first." Interestingly enough, she did feel better. Lighter. "But I didn't tell him anything. No matter what he did or threatened." She could be proud of that, anyway. He had not broken her.

Jace didn't move. What was going on inside his head? She raised herself up on an elbow so she could look at him. He still didn't move.

"What, um, are you thinking?" she finally managed to say. Did he think her weak because she let it bother her?

He lowered his arm and turned his head. There were tears in his eyes. Heather's own eyes became huge in her face. Tears. For her.

"I'm so sorry," he whispered. "That any of it ever happened to you. Give me a description. I'll find him. I will kill him for you."

Despite everything, that dragged a smile out of her. "And beat your chest? Hoist me onto your shoulder and claim victory and vengeance?"

Jace didn't return the smile. In fact, he looked as grim as she'd ever seen him.

"Rape is just a word, Heather. Just because there was no penetration doesn't mean what he did was in any way less of a violation."

Heather burst into tears.

Chapter Thirty

JACE GATHERED HEATHER into his arms and rocked her. What else could he do? There was no way he could quell the murderous rage inside him. That bastard had done more than question her. He had deliberately set out to degrade her.

The man was dead. He just didn't know it yet.

"Do you really think so?" She asked the question in a small voice.

Jesus H. Christ. Could she have the slightest doubt? And then he knew. She could and she did. "Heather. For God's sake. He's sick. Twisted and perverted. That wasn't for interrogation. It was to humiliate. Power and control. You used those very words."

There was a nod against his bicep.

"Want to go get drunk and get in a bar fight?" He meant it as a joke. "If I had the time and, you know, you were a guy." He tried a weak smile.

She nodded again. "Does that mean we're a team?" Obviously, she remembered he said that's how he'd handle the emotional baggage of his teammates.

Damn straight. He wasn't letting her out of his sight. It was ridiculous how much he wanted to beat his chest, and, yes, drag her back to his cave and make her his.

"Yeah." He stopped to clear his throat.

"Then I'd rather talk about the SCUD," Heather said.

Huh? Really? That was so far from his own thoughts, it took him a moment to catch up.

"Jace, what if those vials contain an agent so strong the plan was to mix it with some sort of reagent and launch it at a US target? The president's visit has been public knowledge for a long time now. We've intercepted a bunch of chatter supporting killing him." Communications intelligence, she meant. "Nothing credible. We've passed it all on to the Secret Service, of course. But what if we missed something?"

Jace nodded slowly. "I'm starting to think you're onto something. Finding the SCUD with no warhead has been bugging me." He stopped, a comical look on his face. "The courier came from Iran, right? What if the SCUD came from there, too?"

"That's what I'm thinking, too. There's no way to verify—Azakistani military records are unbelievably inaccurate—but if a SCUD was stolen from Iraq, for instance, during Gulf War One or Two, and hidden here, maybe for years, while they waited for the perfect opportunity to use it . . ."

An opportunity like a presidential visit. Heather didn't need to say it.

Jace continued her train of thought. "And they found or stole or bought a SCUD transporter, an erector-launcher. They could hit anywhere in Azakistan. But we took out the SCUD. Until and unless they replace the inertial guidance system, it's useless."

"We need to find out if anyone's found the warhead yet," she said. "That'll give us the rest of the terrorists."

Jace reached for his cell phone on the nightstand. Punching in a few numbers, he waited.

"Yeah, Stephanie. Jace. Need your sharp eyes, Private." He cut off her greeting. "Listen. This isn't about tonight's mission. That's a go. I need to know if any intelligence agency's found a SCUD-b warhead. Unattached. Need that info ASAP."

"I'm on it."

He disconnected. "All right," he said. "We'll know soon enough. Steph's our best researcher. If someone reported it, she'll find it."

Before he could settle back onto the bed, his phone rang again. That was fast. Jace flipped it open and hit the speaker button.

"What'd you find, Steph?"

There was a pause, then a masculine voice spoke.

"Jace? Trevor. We need to talk."

Chapter Thirty-One

September 6. 10:10 P.M.
Starbucks behind Samarra Mosque, Ma'ar ye zhad

HEATHER AND JACE met Trevor at a coffee bar near the city business college. Without preamble, he told them the hard news.

"It's biochemical. It's a toxic gas called phosgene. Dichloromethanal carbonyl chloride. Dreadful news on a grand scale."

Jace nodded. He did not seem surprised.

Heather, however, let out a tiny gasp. "An attack inside the embassy? I didn't even consider that. I was so focused on the president's visit . . ."

"Well, don't discount it yet," said Trevor. "Shelby is notifying the right people at the embassy. She's authorized me to keep you in the loop on this. The amount of phosgene in those five vials could have killed a lot of people, or at least made them very sick. It's quite toxic. One of the things that makes phosgene so dangerous is, by the time you smell it, you've been exposed to four to five times the amount considered an immediate threat to life. Still . . ."

Heather finished the thought. "We'd be naive to think we intercepted the only five vials in transit."

"Right."

"We've gotten indications the terrorists are looking to acquire phosgene," Jace said. "We might know more in a few days. Hopefully. If we can get a person of interest to talk to us."

Heather rolled her shoulders. She hated that Jace couldn't tell them what his mission was tonight. It would be dangerous; Delta would not be sent on a mission that anyone else could handle. A knot of worry formed in her stomach. "I don't know anything about phosgene. Is it like anthrax?" she asked.

Trevor sipped his coffee, grimaced, and put it down again. "Nasty stuff. No, anthrax are bacterial spores." He pushed the cup away. "Thank the news services, I suppose, for everybody thinking all biochemical weapons are like anthrax."

"Phosgene is a gas," Jace interjected. "A choking agent. Used during WWI for chemical warfare."

Trevor looked at him in surprise. "Very good, mate. Enough of it mixed into the warhead of the SCUD you found would cause quite a problem. Launch it onto whatever target they chose. A population center, a housing area. Anywhere there are a lot of people. The warhead explodes, the gas releases. By the time the victims are able to clear the area, they would have been exposed to a toxic level." He pushed the coffee farther away and looked around. "Disgusting swill. I don't hold out much hope for a decent cup of tea, though."

Heather chewed her lip, deep in thought. "Maybe a smaller attack? We don't know who has the warhead, the Kongra-Gel or the seller."

Trevor exhaled an unamused laugh. "The smell is noticeable

at zero point four parts per million. That's already four times the threshold limit value. Look, it's toxic because it affects a person's respiration and causes suffocation. It's true it's not as dangerous as other chemical weapons like sarin, but it's much easier to produce. And we can estimate as many as a hundred thousand people might have died during the Great War from it. Make no mistake, the gas is dangerous."

"If this stuff's so easy to transport, and if there are other foreign national couriers sympathetic to the Kongra-Gel's cause, there could be more vials out there," Heather said.

"Maybe not," Trevor said. "It's not like this stuff is easy to come by in any sort of quantity. Safeguards against accidental exposure are quite stringent. We should check biochemical labs to see if anyone has reported an accident or a theft."

"We also can't assume it's the Kongra-Gel, either," said Jace. "They might have been acting as intermediaries, or even brokers. If they have the stuff in hiding somewhere, if we're right about it, they might just be selling it for their own profit."

Heather shook her head. An absolute negative. "You didn't see the fanaticism on the faces of the men I overheard, or on the face of the man who . . . questioned me. It's them."

Jace nodded, seemingly satisfied. "Then you bring it to the right people."

"The CIA is helping the Secret Service coordinate with whoever they need," Trevor said. "I'd start with Jay Spicer, the CIA station chief."

Heather slapped her legs and stood. "Then let's go."

Jace laughed. "Heather, it's ten o'clock at night. He's at home watching reruns of *Law & Order* by now. Morning will be fine."

He drained his coffee cup. "Thinking tonight's little jaunt might be useful."

The lump in Heather's gut intensified.

September 7. 3:26 A.M.
Tiqt, Azakistan

THE STREETS IN this part of Tiqt were narrow and twisted. There were no less than six avenues of approach to the house in which Omran Malouf was supposedly hiding out. Jace slipped from shadow to shadow. They'd left their Humvee a few blocks away so they could approach silently.

Mace and Ken broke away, heading separately for the rooftops they had selected for overwatch. From there, they would make sure no one snuck up on the A-Team.

At the next corner, Archangel and Sandman turned right, heading toward the back of the townhouse. It was the center house in a row of three. Jace, Tag, and Alex held position while their teammates worked their way into place. By the time the double clicks came over his headset, he was itching for action. Nodding to Tag and Alex, he led the way to the front door. Alex watched the street, which was deserted at this time of the night. Jace placed a hand on the knob and turned it slowly. Locked.

Reaching into his breast pocket, he extracted the proper tools, and in a short time heard the tiny *snickt* as the lock tumbled under his hand.

Jace turned the knob and pushed the door open a little at a time. The house was quiet and dark. He slid inside, with Tag and

Alex shadows beside him. They met up with Archangel and Sandman at the base of the stairs. Gabe gave a slight shake of his head. No, no one was in the kitchen or living room. The five of them slipped up the stairs and positioned themselves outside the three bedrooms.

Jace readied his flash-bang, a grenade that emitted a deafening noise and blinding light when set off. Standing to one side of the door, he eased it open. In concert with the others, positioned at each bedroom door, he pulled the pin and tossed the grenade inside. Turning his face away, he closed his eyes against the flash, and steeled himself for the noise. For the unprepared, it was disorienting, and in this instance, it worked perfectly.

He and his teammates rushed into the bedrooms, shouting orders in both English and Arabic.

"Freeze!"

"Don't move!"

"Hands up! Get onto the floor. Do it now!"

In seconds, the seven occupants of the house knelt, hands laced behind their heads. Archangel and Sandman searched them while the others kept their rifles trained on them. Archangel shoved the documents he found into his cargo pocket. Tag snapped pictures of the occupants with his phone, and sent the photos back to headquarters with a touch of a button.

"Which one of you is Omran Malouf?" Gabe asked in Arabic. "Omran Malouf. That's all we want, then we'll leave."

Alex flipped through the wallets. Only two of the men had identification. "It's him," he said, pointing to the man on the left. Who lunged for the door.

Jace had him on the floor with two blows. He secured the man's hands behind his back with plastic flexicuffs and dragged him to his feet. "Let's go," he said.

His team deployed around him, keeping their weapons up and ready as they backed onto the landing and down the stairs. Jace pushed Malouf ahead of him.

As soon as they turned the corner, Jace heard the men upstairs jump to their feet and rush across the floor. A moment later, a burst of automatic gunfire chased them the last few feet out of the house and into the street. Tag waited by the front door, returning fire as the men came down the stairs. The house's occupants flattened themselves against the walls, giving Jace and his team the precious few seconds they needed to run down the cracked sidewalk.

One man leapt over the stoop and raised a semiautomatic rifle. Before Jace could turn and fire, a sharp crack split the air. The man crumpled. Jace sent a brief mental thank-you to the team sniper.

"You're clear," said Ken. "Haul ass."

Jace needed no second invitation to run. The commotion agitated the neighbors, most of whom had the good sense to stay hunkered down in their homes. A few lights had flickered on. He dragged Malouf along with him. By the time they reached their Humvee, Mace and Ken had joined them. They shoved Malouf into the center of the backseat. Sandman stood up to man the M60 machine gun, and Gabe gunned the engine. In moments, they careened out of the neighborhood and headed back toward base.

Chapter Thirty-Two

September 7. 7:22 A.M.
FOB Hollow Straw, al-Zadr Air Base

JACE PULLED HIS car into his tiny driveway and sat, staring up at his bedroom window. Sunrise had snuck in an hour past, while he handed over their prisoner and debriefed his squadron commander. He hadn't hit adrenaline letdown yet; his bones felt bigger than his skin, and his palms itched. He stank like an open sewer line. Still, he didn't move.

He pictured Heather as he'd left her, curled around his pillow, one hand thrown out as though seeking him even in sleep. Despite the importance of the mission, it had been a wrench to leave her. Would she look at him the same way this morning, languid, contented, with liquid heat simmering in the depths of her eyes?

He wanted that. He ached for it.

He pushed himself out of the driver's seat. Only one way to find out. House dust sparkled in the early morning light as he padded up the stairs. First things first. Entering the bathroom, he stripped out of his boots and combat uniform, peeled off his shorts and socks, and left them in a heap on the floor. He adjusted the spray so that it beat down on him, easing some of the tension knotting his shoulders. The mission had been a success. Omran Malouf had babbled the whole way back to base. Their interrogator would have no problem extracting information from him.

His body still thrummed with combat readiness. He soaped up and scrubbed, trying to ignore his own readiness for action; but, as usual, he couldn't get his body back under control. For hours after a mission, he remained keyed up, on edge. Barely civilized. In the past, he'd head out to one of the rough dives with his teammates, get sloppy drunk, and screw whatever came near enough and willing. Now, the only woman swimming through his veins was Heather. About to turn the water as cold as he could stand it, he instead stilled as the shower curtain eased back, and a lithe figure stepped into the tub.

"Good morning," she murmured.

Heather was gloriously, wondrously naked. Jace's blood leapt in response, heating and thundering through his veins in an instant. She stepped into his body and wrapped her arms around his waist, leaning her head against his chest. The primitive male inside of him howled with joy. He scooped her close, loving the feel of her wet skin against his.

"A very good morning," he agreed. For a moment, he allowed himself to picture coming home after every mission to her warm arms. Reality crashed in when she shifted against him, her nipples rubbing across his chest and the hair at the apex of her thighs brushing against his shaft. *Cheee-rist!* He nearly jumped out of his skin, sensitized to the point of pain in a nanosecond.

"Heather," he panted, trying to push her away. She did not

release him. And then rubbed against him again. Did she know what she was doing? "Heather, you shouldn't . . . don't . . ."

"Shhh," she said. Her pelvis tilted forward as she pressed her hips to his, creating a drag against his balls. He barely stopped himself from grabbing her and slamming her up against the wall. He tried again to speak, to warn her, but his vocal cords dried out, and all he could manage was a croak.

Her mouth found his collarbone. She licked across it to his throat, his jaw. Her tongue swirled around the shell of his ear, then she nipped his earlobe. With the last shreds of his sanity, he grasped her shoulders, forcibly putting a few inches of space between them.

"You don't know the effect adrenaline has on the male body," he gasped out, feeling feverish. "It's too soon after the mission. I can't . . ."

"I don't want you to," she interrupted. "Be controlled. I want you wild for me."

"Oh, Christ, Heather. Do you know what you're offering? I don't want to scare you."

Heather captured his gaze, then deliberately ran her pink tongue over her lips. She cupped his face, pressing a thumb into his mouth. He suckled it. She pulled it across his bottom lip, the wetness causing an erotic drag, then replaced her thumb with her tongue. She had barely nipped him when he gave a feral groan and squeezed her to him, crushing her mouth under his and thrusting with his tongue. She sucked on it, and he groaned again, bringing his hands up on either side of her face and angling her head for better access. She met him kiss for kiss.

He pushed her up against the wall, water sluicing over her shoulders and breasts. His fingers traced the path of the moisture, running down her arms, then up to cup her breasts. His thumbs teased her nipples, and she threw back her head, arching into him and moaning.

"God, Heather. You are so sweet, so ripe. You taste incredible." He replaced his hands with his mouth, licking and sucking and nibbling until her moans became ragged and urgent. He slid his hands down her waist to her hips, then farther, scooping his palms under her knees and lifting her. She wrapped those long, long legs around his waist, and he nearly wept at the feel of her scalding heat, exactly where he wanted it.

And then it wasn't enough. He needed to be inside her, now. He slid his palms over the perfect globes of her ass, squeezing and pulling her in tighter. She responded by pressing her hips forward and grinding against him, which ripped a groan from his lips.

"Now," she urged. He lifted her higher, fingers finding her core. One slid inside, then another. She reached down and encircled him, guiding him to her. One press of his hips, and he slid home. Her slick heat gripped him. She uttered a strangled cry, and began to move on top of him, slamming herself down as he lunged upward. They flew in perfect synchronization, the pounding pace winding them tighter and tighter. He strained, desperate for release, but equally desperate to make it good for her, with whatever control he could muster.

She braced her heels against the edges of the tub, meeting him thrust for thrust, little mewling sounds of pleasure driving him mad with lust. He moaned right along with her, dangerously close to release. As though she knew that, as though she knew he tried to hold on for her, she increased her pace again, bucking against him as he pistoned in and out of her.

Just as the quivers gathered at the base of his spine, her entire body tautened, her heels coming up to lock around his ass, pulling him even farther into her. Her head dropped back, hands braced on his shoulders, and she pitched forward, wrapping herself around him as she quaked and twisted and cried her release. He bucked forward twice, three times, straining as sensation raced down his spine, as ecstasy spasmed through him, as he emptied himself inside her.

HEATHER RESTED HER head against Jace's shoulder, letting her legs drop from around his waist to rest on the edges of the tub as she tried to catch her breath. She could feel his heart thundering in his chest and stroked gentle hands across his shoulders, loving the hard feel of him. He was magnificent.

He tried to speak, but only a dry croak emerged. Heather turned off the water. He snagged a towel, patting and stroking it across her body, lingering over her breasts and belly. He stroked his long fingers across her rear, kneeling before her to dry her feet. She looked down at his bent head. Her warrior. Gentle, strong, fierce, and loving.

As he rose, he buried his head in her smooth belly and clamped an arm across her legs, effortlessly lifting her over his shoulder. She shrieked with laughter, bracing a hand on his butt, her long hair spilling down his back. "Jace!"

He turned his head and bit her hip, then pressed a kiss to the spot. Carrying her to the bed, he released her by sliding her down the front of his body in increments. The friction and drag electrified her. She didn't release his shoulders even after her toes hit the floor. Instead, she nibbled at his chin and licked the artery pulsing under her tongue. He growled, turning to capture her lips with his, and swept his tongue into her mouth. Their ferocious ride in the shower had blunted the first wild edge, but primal hunger still darkened his eyes.

She crawled onto the bed, making her motions sinuous, and looked over her shoulder at him with invitation in her eyes. He was on her in two strides, grasping her ankles and stretching her flat. She gasped and giggled as he flipped her over and tugged her to the edge of the bed. Her breath came in spurts. He draped her legs over his shoulders and knelt between them.

Never had she felt more desired than she did at this very moment. His focus on her was intense and absolute. Her feminine power roared within her. At the first touch of his tongue, her giggles turned to breathy moans. He dragged his open mouth across the tender flesh of her inner thigh, and she cried out, hands flailing for something to grab onto and fisting in the tangled sheets. He kissed her as though he had all the time in the world. As though the roar in his head and the thunder in his blood didn't demand her total surrender. His tongue drew across her slick flesh, and her back bowed.

"Jace! Holy shit, Christ, Jesus."

He chuckled, a smug, masculine sound that shivered across her belly. When his teeth found the core of her, she shot upright with a strangled shriek, grabbing for his hair. His grip on her thighs loosened, and he rolled his eyes up to hers. The molten lava burning in them sent a crash of sensation through her, and she crested on a potent blaze of emotion as foreign to her as it felt right.

She urged him up, and he came willingly, running his hands up under her back and cradling her as he claimed her mouth. She tasted herself on his lips, the flavor at once exotic and familiar. Shivering, she let her legs fall open. He positioned himself between them, then hesitated as she cradled him in her heat.

"Heather . . . are you all right with this? Am I being too rough?"

She groaned and shifted her hips. "I'm massively okay with this. Can't you tell?" She'd meant to sound teasing, but her voice was hoarse with need. The sultry passion in her eyes, the subtle thrust of her breasts, seemed to reassure him. "God, Jace, I need you inside me. Right fucking now!"

He laughed at her obscenity, as she'd hoped he would. This time there was no hesitation as he gripped her hips and pushed inside, one long thrust that buried him to the hilt.

"Uunh," he said, stilling, head hanging and eyes closed. "God, you feel amazing. So hot and tight." His hands came up to cover her breasts, lifting them to his mouth as he suckled first one nipple, then the other. He stroked in and out of her at a leisurely pace, drawing almost all the way out before pushing himself home. The pressure built in her as he continued to lave her breasts, to kiss her, to move inside her so exquisitely. He seemed so attuned to her that he knew what she needed before she did, his attention unwavering. It was quite possibly the most erotic experience of her life, and it pushed her dangerously close to the edge.

He seemed in no hurry to allow her to orgasm, though. Instead, he brought her just to the brink, then backed off, bringing her down slowly before starting all over again. It drove her wild, her head whipping back and forth as she writhed on the bed. She began to beg, sobbing his name over and over.

"Jace, please. Oh, God. Please."

Finally, *finally,* he increased his pace, thrusting now with an urgency she matched. She dug her nails into his shoulders and wrapped her legs around his butt, straining upward as he finally lost control, finally crashed into her with no finesse, desperate and scalding her with his heat. She exploded like a bottle rocket, heels digging and body stiffening as her head blew off, as she arched and cried out and spasmed, fragmenting and re-forming only to fragment again. He shouted, his hips plunging again and again as he pressed his face into her neck and shuddered his release.

She still quivered with aftershocks as he reached between them and pressed his palm against her core, causing the pleasure to spiral up again and transfix her in a place of ecstasy that didn't end. Finally, she slumped back onto the sheets, wrung out and so sated she felt boneless.

"Jesus. I've never come like that in my life," she said.

"Uunh." Jace collapsed onto her, but immediately made to roll off. She stilled him with her arms, amazed again that he obeyed her touch. She loved the feel of his weight on her. Her fingertips smoothed up and down his spine as they caught their breath and their sweat dried. She pressed her nose to his skin and inhaled. His clean, masculine scent was addictive.

Eventually they showered, made love, and showered again. Jace ordered pizza, delivered by a teenager driving an ancient Buick. They argued amicably about which movie to watch, then argued about the movie.

"He should be arrested for leaking the story," Jace said. "He was a classified analyst. He knows he can't discuss what he does."

"Then his friends died for no reason," replied Heather. "If he hadn't told his side, there would be no justice for them." She curled her feet up under her and settled back against Jace as though she'd done it a thousand times before. His arm came around her. A strange feeling settled inside her. Contentment.

Belonging.

Chapter Thirty-Three

September 10. 3:00 P.M.
Delta Force Tactical Operations Center, FOB Hollow Straw

"Okay," boomed the squadron commander. "Let's go around the table and lay out what everyone knows. Fill in the gaps, as it were."

"I'll start," Jace decided. "We know vials of toxic phosgene have been smuggled into the country. We have no idea how many or how long it's been going on. We suspect those vials, at least some of them, have made their way into the hands of the Kongra-Gel, to be loaded into the warhead of a SCUD-b missile. Now that they can't use the missile, we believe the Kongra-Gel either have a Plan B, or are scrambling to develop one in time for the president's visit in two days."

"We know the Kongra-Gel are Salafist jihadists," Heather said. "Their rhetoric is violently anti-Western. They have to know it will be nearly impossible to attack the president without the SCUD missile. Their Plan B has to include another delivery method." She rubbed her forehead. Was her concussion acting up again? The doctors said she was fine, but Jace fidgeted, fighting the need to go to her.

"Phosgene is heavier than air, so it sinks into the low-lying areas," said Trevor. "We need a map of the installation."

The squadron commander snapped his fingers, and three support soldiers jumped to find what was needed. Within minutes, a topographical map of the area overlaid a map of the base.

The five of them stared at it.

"The parade ground is elevated," Jace finally said. What the hell?

"And open," added Trevor. "Which means any breeze will have maximum ability to dissipate the gas."

Christina shook her head. "Without the missile, they have no chance of killing the president."

Archangel studied Christina, then turned to the map. "It's naive to assume that. I agree it's improbable, but what if they have another missile? Anyway, the president isn't going to land a helicopter on the parade ground with hundreds of people milling around. He needs to stage somewhere."

Christina bristled, belligerent eyes boring into his back. "If the phosgene is going to sink away from where the president's going to be, and the wind will probably blow it away entirely, tell me how they're thinking to kill him then. The parade ground might be open to the public, but any staging area won't be. No one's getting close to the president to throw a vial at him. They might harm civilians, but not President Cooper."

Jace blew out a breath. There was too much they didn't know.

Gabe's lip curled. He moved closer to Christina, close enough that she took a step back, lips pressed tightly together. He raked his gaze over her body, radiating his contempt. "A terrorist stupid enough to throw even a bottle of phosgene at a person either doesn't know what he's got or isn't a terrorist we need to worry about."

Jace held up a hand. Gabe, prone to temper, was reacting negatively to the young CIA agent. His lack of trust in outsiders— anyone who was not one of his own teammates—was legendary inside Delta Force. Gabe glared, but finally stepped back. "Phosgene is only dangerous if breathed in over enough time to affect the respiratory system. Is that right?" He directed his question to Trevor.

"Essentially, yes."

"Then we have to assume they have another way of blanketing an area large enough to do significant damage. Airspace is restricted. Other ideas?"

Christina hesitated. "Are there bombs or other munitions on base that could be used as a dispersant?"

"Nothing even remotely close to the parade ground," Gabe said impatiently. He gave Christina a *"What on earth are you doing here?"* look. "Despite the persistent right-wing rhetoric, we don't store munitions underneath the pool house. Or near any public gathering places."

Heather grimaced. Jace sympathized. He, too, was annoyed by the constant blog traffic of anti-Western and antimilitary factions, which postulated with varying degrees of hostility that the US stored munitions near family housing areas.

"Okay," said Bo Granville. "Where are the low-lying areas on base?"

Jace pointed his little finger at one area. "I hate even to say this, but here, and here. The main recreational areas—including the pool house," he said, exchanging an amused look with Gabe and Heather. "And these picnic areas and playgrounds." A small frown appeared between his brows. "Truthfully, these areas are close enough to both the enlisted housing area—Dogwood Beach, right?—and the south side of the town of Garhara, also residential. But it's nowhere near the president."

"We've been assuming the target's the president," said Tag. "What if it's not?"

"Who else?" said Christina. "Nothing else of significance is happening any time soon. Both Garhara's and Ma'ar ye zhad's mayors will be attending the president's address, and some prominent local businessmen, but Prime Minister al-Muhaymin is meeting President Cooper at his palace, not on US soil." She leveled a challenging glare at Gabe, but Jace saw the flash of hurt in her eyes when his team second merely turned away.

"What would be the political fallout of an Azakistani attack on the US president?" Heather asked.

"Get Shelby Gibson on the line," said Trevor. "She'll know."

"IT WOULD WEAKEN public perception," Shelby told them, her husky voice coming through the speakerphone loud and clear. All six paid close attention. "Obviously. It would publicly embarrass Prime Minister al-Muhaymin, who considers himself to be a very progressive, strong ally of the United States in this region." She paused. Heather found herself watching Trevor. She wasn't stupid; Christina had interrupted something between Shelby and him. He looked weary.

"The conservative movement would point to it as weakness on his part, saying he has little control. It would engender a certain level of sympathy for the United States, of course. Post-9/11, our allies and friendly nations don't automatically assume the US can absorb any blow. Still, as with 9/11, some countries in this region would be cheering, either openly or secretly. And there are factions inside the prime minister's own government who would point to the incident as well deserved. Overall, though, if this happened, and I pray it does not, the fallout would center more on negative sentiment against the US, with a bit toward the Azakistani Parliament, as unfair as it sounds."

Gabe snorted. "We get attacked, and we deserve it? Jesus."

"Yes," said Shelby. "It's been the reaction around the world each time someone attacks the United States. Oh, sure, our allies condemn the attacks. But Khobar Towers in Saudi Arabia, the USS *Cole*, the 1998 attacks against the embassies in Tanzania, Nairobi, and Dar es Salaam . . . in each case, after the initial outrage, public opinion in Middle Eastern countries was we deserve it." She hesitated. "And we all remember the celebrations throughout the Middle East, the burning of American flags, the cheering, during and after 9/11. Hatred against the United States is not far from a national hobby in some of these countries. And even the populist uprisings in Egypt and Libya happened in North Africa, not the Middle East."

There was silence around the table.

"The president's visit has been on his public agenda for months, because of the 9/11 commemoration," Heather said. "There's obviously significance to the timing of the attack."

"We should bring in the Secret Service," Jace said finally. "Even if we think an attack would be ineffective, they need to know."

"Agreed," said Granville. He glanced at Heather. "Good work, young lady."

Heather looked around the table. "To all of us. A good team effort."

Bo Granville gave a smug smile that puzzled Heather. Her contribution had been relatively minor. Why did he single her out for praise? She seemed to have caught his special interest. Why?

Chapter Thirty-Four

September 10. 8:15 A.M.
Bachelor Officer's Quarters, al-Zadr Air Force Base

IT WAS GOOD to be back in her own apartment. Heather puttered. She dusted, vacuumed, and took a long, hot soak in the tub. Washed her hair. Napped.

And missed Jace.

Where was he?

It had been less than twenty-four hours, so the empty ache inside her felt ridiculous. But the past week had been glorious, every moment spent with him. They talked, laughed, made love. He took her to a picnic on one of the unused shooting ranges. She showed him her secret place at the edge of Lake Sego, where the rushes met the water and a broad, grassy strip was the perfect place to sit and read. She had shared with him parts of herself she'd kept barricaded inside for years.

No doubt he was busy working with the Secret Service to thwart any possible terrorist attempt to get close to the president.

Her fingers literally shook with the need to get back out there. To help.

Instead, she forced herself to read one of the books Jeremy had lent her. CNN hummed in the background, discussing the president's visit to Azakistan the next day. The visit included a meeting with Prime Minister al-Muhaymin, a town hall assembly with the soldiers of al-Zadr Air Base, then a speech at the al-Zadr parade grounds, thrown open to the public in honor of the event. She shivered.

By noon the next day, she was too restless to sit still. Getting into her car, she headed across base to the headquarters of the 10th Special Forces Group. She needed to clear out her desk anyway; her tour of duty in Azakistan would be up before the doctors cleared her for active duty. And it would be good to see her friends. It had been almost a month since her escape from Sari Daru Province. They no doubt wondered about her.

She was mobbed as soon as she stepped into the building. One after another, friends and colleagues hugged her or shook her hand. It was silly, really, all the fuss. Most of these same people had visited her in the hospital. Still, this was goodbye, so she smiled, thanked them, hugged them back, and shared some tears for their lost comrades.

Finally, she made it to her desk. There really wasn't much to pack—a few pictures, a dead plant, some books. The new regimental intelligence officer stayed with her as she sorted through her drawers, picking her brain on various projects she had been working on prior to her trip out to Eshma. Finally, she stopped in to say her farewells to the battalion commander.

As she made her way out of the building, a uniformed officer hurried after her. "Lieutenant Langstrom. I'm glad I caught you."

Heather smiled at the head of personnel. "Hey, Captain. How're things?"

The officer shrugged. "Same ol', same ol'," he said. "We're sure sorry to lose you."

"No more than I'm sorry to leave."

"Well, you're going from the frying pan into the fire. And in a hurry, too."

Heather cocked her head, her brow wrinkling. "Sir?"

The personnel officer lifted a sheaf of papers in his hand. "New orders. They came in this morning. I was going to have them messengered over to your quarters, but you saved me the courier." He handed them to Heather with something of a flourish. "You must have impressed someone."

Already? She had thought new orders wouldn't come for another few weeks, until her doctors cleared her to return to active duty. Frowning, Heather glanced at them.

What?

Heather did a double take, looking hard at the orders in her hand. Reading them again didn't change the words. She had been reassigned to the 1st Special Forces Operational Detachment-Delta.

Delta wanted her?

An instant of joy washed through her. Jace would work beside her.

Delta Force was, of course, the elite of the special operations forces. Even the SEALs weren't as tough, as trained, as elite as Delta Force operators. To be selected to support them was the highest form of compliment. Delta always got the best. Always. And if they wanted her, that meant they thought . . . she was.

Reality crashed in. Delta didn't want her, Jace did. What strings had he pulled to get her reassigned?

She looked over her orders more carefully. She was being attached to Forward Operating Base (FOB) Hollow Straw, al-Zadr Air Base, pending full medical release. That was, she now knew, where the Delta detachment resided, where she had been spending a lot of time recently. Her orders further stipulated a follow-on assignment to 1st Special Forces Operational Detachment-Delta at Fort Bragg, North Carolina, home to the Special Operations Forces. She was due to report there in a little more than a month, when her rotation in Azakistan ended.

Heather didn't even try to control the hot wash of anger coursing through her. Of all the conceited, arrogant, high-handed actions, this one had to take the cake. How dare Jace mess with her career? Fuming, she walked back to her car. When she eventually accepted an elite assignment such as this one, it would be because she earned it. On her own, with no one's help, and on her merits. Not because someone pulled strings. It galled her.

Without conscious volition, she drove across base to FOB Hollow Straw. The guard checked her ID and her orders, and allowed her, unescorted, through the gate. Heather let her fury carry her into the Tactical Operations Center. Like a laser, she saw Jace at once, bending over a map on the central conference table, deep in conversation with several men. She barreled over to him, interrupting him midsentence.

"Captain Reed. I'd like to talk to you, please."

He looked up, clearly surprised to see her. "Heather. Hi. Can you give me a . . ."

"Now, Captain." She stalked back toward the door and wrenched it open.

Jace straightened, leveling a look at her. After a moment, he glanced toward his men. "Tag, keep working with Mr. Seifert and Mr. Boston. Gabe, get with Private Tams. I'll be right back." He followed Heather through the door, closing it firmly behind him, shutting out the curious faces turned their way.

Heather took a few stiff steps away from the building before turning on Jace. "How dare you?"

Jace's eyes narrowed fractionally. "You're upset. I can see that. Care to give me a hint why?"

Heather waved her orders in his face. "This, you bastard. My reassignment. Here."

His brows pulled together as Jace took the sheaf of papers from her hand. He scanned them, his frown deepening. "What the hell?"

"Exactly!" Heather cried. A passing soldier gave her a curious look. Lowering her voice, she said, no less intensely, "What gives you the right to mess with my career? *I* decide where I go. Or the Army. Not you."

"Look, Heather . . ."

She spoke over him, her volume increasing again. "What, did you think I'd fall all over you in gratitude? Follow you home to North Carolina? What? What could you possibly have been thinking?"

"Will you calm down?"

"I will not calm down. This is unconscionable. Pulling me away from my unit . . ."

Jace got loud. "I didn't do anything of the sort. I had nothing to do with this."

Heather waved her arms. "Oh, and I'm supposed to believe this is all some sort of great coincidence? I meet you, and suddenly I'm assigned to your unit? I'm not an idiot, Jace."

"Then stop acting like one. Let's be rational—"

"Well, guess what, Jace?" Heather interrupted. "Your great plan backfired. 'Cause now? Now we'll be working together? We're not going to get to have any kind of a relationship."

Jace rubbed two fingers along the bridge of his nose. "This is a misunderstanding. Are you really saying you're going to throw away what we've been building?" He exhaled hard, slicing a hand through the air. "Look, let's stop and take a breath, okay? We're not going to get to the bottom of this by shouting at each other."

Heather simply shook her head. "No. We're not. Because I'm going to take this assignment, Jace. This is the chance of a lifetime for me. And as for us? We're through." Her shoulders sagged, and her throat clogged with tears as she realized the truth of what she was saying. "The second the adjutant cut these orders, I became a member of Colonel Granville's support staff. And fraternization between military support staff and operational personnel is prohibited. You and I are done."

Chapter Thirty-Five

September 11. 8:00 A.M.
Ma'ar ye zhad, Azakistan

AA'IDAH TUCKED HER purse into the bottom drawer of her desk and turned on her computer. Shukri disappeared into his own office. Her father was out this morning, at a breakfast meeting with a potential new client. She checked the appointments calendar for the day. Nothing special, just a few clients. She began to sort their portfolios from the file cabinet and put them in order.

Her fingers stilled, the folders momentarily forgotten as she stared at the photograph she'd taken from Shukri's office yesterday. He had framed it in wood decorated with henna designs. Five men stood shoulder to shoulder, smiling into the camera. Two were Zaahir and the sheik. Shukri was on the left. The one on the right had been at her home with Zaahir. She thought his name might be Rami. The fifth man she did not know at all.

She picked up the photograph. If Shukri asked where it was, she could always lie and tell him she wanted a photo of Zaahir on her desk. Once she faxed it to Christina Madison, though, she had stepped over a line she could not uncross. Her stomach fluttered.

A step sounded on the floor an instant before Zaahir al-Farouk appeared. Aa'idah closed her eyes; but when she opened them, he still stood in front of her desk, and he did not look pleased. Neither was she.

She had not seen him since the disaster at lunch four days ago. Both her father and brother had bellowed at her for her rudeness, and her mother screeched that Aa'idah was ungrateful, that Zaahir was a strong and powerful man—and handsome, by Allah's grace—and would provide well for her. Aa'idah had tried to explain the sickness she sensed in him, but her family scoffed.

"You are a silly girl."

For a moment, Aa'idah could not tell if the words came from her mother or from the hulking man in front of her.

"Have you no greeting for your betrothed?" Zaahir asked.

Ice froze her heart. Had her father truly given his consent for this marriage? "You are not my betrothed."

Zaahir waved a hand, dismissing her words. "I soon will be."

"Honored sir, I do not wish to marry. Not anyone."

Zaahir offered a tender smile. "All women must marry and produce children. You will have your own household, Aa'idah, with servants. I will pamper you. You will want for nothing."

Aa'idah stood, unwilling to have him tower over her. "But I do not understand this. Why choose me? There are women more beautiful, younger, more conventional. I'm a modern women, I am educated and intend to work again, to teach. You are very traditional. We would not suit."

For the first time, he displayed to her the arrogance he showed her father and brother. "I will teach you the practices. You are intelligent and will learn quickly. You yourself are both beautiful and desirable. In time, you will grow to love me."

Love? She almost gagged. "What must I say to dissuade you? This cannot happen."

His heavy brows pulled down as he frowned. It made his already-harsh features ferocious. Aa'idah found herself cringing away from him.

"An alliance between our families can be nothing but beneficial to both the Karim and al-Farouk households. Yes, there are other reasons for us to ally, important political considerations. Still, I desire you." His warm gaze moved over her face, then dropped along her body. A small smile played around her mouth. "Very much. I will be a devoted husband to you."

"I do not wish your devotion!" cried Aa'idah in panic. The thought of his hands upon her body had her stomach roiling. The reception desk imprisoned her, she realized abruptly. Maybe she could squeeze past him? "My father is a successful asset manager. He's not political." Her shoulders sagged. She did nothing but fool herself with such thoughts. She knew what these men intended. While the thought of reporting their plan to Christina Madison frightened her, allowing an explosion to harm Americans when she could stop it filled her with repugnance.

Somehow, she would find the courage to try to stop Zaahir.

Zaahir's smile was condescending. Before he could speak, Shukri appeared in his office door. "Father has strong political ties," he said. He gestured between Zaahir and himself. "And we have important work to do."

Aa'idah felt her head spinning. "My father has been funneling money so you can buy guns," she blurted out, then clapped a hand over her mouth. What was she doing? "Is this what you do?" She glared at Zaahir. "Kill?"

His eyes narrowed. "I support jihad as my sacred duty, praise be to God."

"But jihad is for defending against an attack, not to slaughter the innocent," she said. "No one attacks us."

Zaahir scowled. "Every day these nonbelievers befoul our lands, Muslims forget our sacred traditions and responsibilities. It is an attack on our way of life, and I will not rest until every one of them is dead."

Aa'idah pressed a hand to her chest, seeking courage. "Zaahir, you spoke to Shukri about a bomb. What do you mean to do?" She held her breath.

Shukri blew a sound of annoyance, but Zaahir, astonishingly enough, answered her.

"I have a very dangerous gas," he told her. "I intend to mix it with another chemical. The explosion will send a poisonous cloud that will blanket my enemies in death."

"American soldiers?" Even her lungs ceased functioning as she waited for the answer.

"No. I will strike them where it hurts the most. Once their families are gone, they will also leave my country."

She gasped. It took many moments for her to work up the courage to ask, "When will you do this?"

"On the day of the American president's visit, by God's grace."

Her hands pressed together entreatingly. "No, you can't. Please. There will be babies . . ."

"Nonbelievers." Zaahir dismissed them as unimportant. "Your

father has been lax. Once we are married, I will teach you our sacred ways. Our alliance is important."

"But why?" she wailed.

"When we marry, your family becomes my family. Your father will obey me and continue to fund the training of our courageous Muslim youths. I will provide the money, and he will force his government contact to buy necessary supplies."

Since she didn't understand what he was talking about, she turned to what she could comprehend. "So I am a pawn so you can control my father and brother."

"No one controls me!" Shukri said. "I fight alongside my brother."

Zaahir's irritation flickered through his eyes, but Shukri did not notice. "Where can Aa'idah and I be alone?" he asked. Shukri flushed, but pointed to their father's office. "Thank you. Would you be kind enough to bring back some donuts for your sister? The soft white powdered ones."

How had he known those were her favorite?

Shukri's mouth turned down, but he went without comment. Aa'idah nearly called him back; but really, what could he do? His loyalty was clearly to Zaahir.

Who came around the reception desk and hooked a hand around her bicep. "Come, fiancée. I wish to have a few private moments with you."

She tried to free her arm without success, heart pounding loud enough she wondered if he could hear it. "No. I need to stay here. I am the receptionist. I cannot . . ."

He did not speak further, simply pulling her along until they reached her father's office, ignoring her protests. He closed and locked the door, and she backed away from him, putting nearly the width of the room between them. Something primitive and hungry flared in his eyes, and Aa'idah realized her mistake. Her running excited him.

"Zaahir, please do not do this." For she was not a naive young girl. She knew what private moments with him would entail. She would not give in to him.

"We are betrothed. It is the same as being married. I would like to make love to my wife before I begin the jihad against the foul Westerners. Is that so wrong?"

"You cannot force yourself upon me!" she cried. "It is sinful and forbidden by Allah."

"We will wed. You will obey your father." Warmth fled from his tone, leaving it brittle and harsh.

She blurted out the only thing she could think to say. "A virgin cannot be married without her consent."

Something ugly moved behind Zaahir's eyes. "I will have your consent." He stalked toward her, nostrils flared and eyes blazing. She tried to dart around him, knowing he would move faster but determined to fight him until the bitter end.

He caught her around the waist, jerking her back against him. His hands came up to cup her breasts, squeezing them though the fabric of her blouse, pinching her hard enough to hurt. One hand slid down her torso and shoved between her legs. Aa'idah opened her mouth to scream. Sensing her intention, his other hand clamped over her mouth, gripping her jaw. He slammed her forward into the wall, pinning her in place with his body. Her head smacked the plaster, and she cried out under his hand. He began to yank and tug her blouse from the waistband of her skirt.

This can't be happening.

If she did not do something drastic now, he would succeed in forcing himself on her. Nausea roiled in her gut. When his hand loosened on her mouth, she opened her jaws wide and clamped down as hard as she could.

His scream carried through the office. She refused to let go, even when he punched her in the side of the head and she saw stars. He hit her again, but somehow she found both the strength and will to turn in his arms, and brought her knee sharply into his groin. He shouted again, but his hold on her loosened as he collapsed in on himself. Tearing herself him his grasp, she wasted several precious seconds fumbling with the door lock and several more snatching her purse and Shukri's photograph from the desk drawer, Zaahir's bellows of rage following her, before running out into the sunny morning.

She did not stop running until she reached the gates of the American Embassy.

Chapter Thirty-Six

September 11. 1:33 P.M.
TOC, FOB Hollow Straw, al-Zadr Air Force Base

JACE WATCHED HEATHER'S car spin on the gravel and fishtail out of the lot. What the hell was going on? One person would have the answer.

Jace pushed through the door of the Tactical Operations Center harder than he'd intended, much like Heather had done just a few minutes earlier. He found Colonel Granville at his desk at the far end of the TOC, chomping on an unlit cigar and muttering to himself as he sorted through files and folders. His commander looked up as Jace approached and jabbed a finger at one of the two chairs in front of his desk.

"Damn and blast this idiotic paperwork. It's no fit occupation for a SpecOps warrior. Feeling old, Jace. Feeling old. What can I do for you?"

Jace sat, slouching a little. "You can answer a question for me. Did you authorize the reassignment of Heather Langstrom?"

Bo Granville gave a smug smile. "You bet your ass. I snapped her up in a hot minute. We're damned lucky to have her." He shuffled through some folders and finally plucked one from the pile. Handing it to Jace, he said, "Take a gander at her personnel records."

Jace opened the olive green folder.

"Five years in Military Intelligence. Speaks three languages. Airborne, Air Assault, and Jungle Warfare Schools. Hell, if she could, I wouldn't doubt she'd have tried for Ranger School." The commander grinned and shifted his cigar to the other side of his mouth. "Top ten percent of her class at West Point, too. None of that ROTC bullcrap."

Jace looked up. West Point? *That* was the public school she'd attended in upstate New York?

"She's exactly who I need as my operational support platoon leader. An experienced officer who took capture and interrogation like a man and spat on those assholes. From your reports, she all but rescued herself."

"Sir . . ." Jace sighed as he tossed the folder back onto Granville's desk. "I don't think she's ready for another assignment just yet. Her doctors haven't even cleared her for active duty. She's barely out of the hospital, and that's not even bringing up any psychological scars from her ordeal. Wouldn't it be safer to wait? See if she comes through this okay? Send her back to the States for a while?"

Granville took his cigar out of his mouth and jabbed it at Jace. "I got the shrink's report right here. She'll have to go to counseling twice a week for a couple months, but he had no problem clearing her for a desk assignment. I won't send her forward until I'm sure she's ready."

Jace's heart stuttered in his chest. Send her forward? Oh, holy hell. Her orders assigned her to the Operation Support Troop. The intelligence assets Delta employed were not just analysts. They also regularly deployed to hostile foreign countries to gather intelligence, in preparation for Delta missions. Once the psychiatrist authorized her to return to full duty, she would do what every other member of the Operational Support Troop did.

Heather would be in the line of fire.

"No."

The word ripped from him. Granville narrowed his eyes, sitting forward and slapping his forearms atop his desk. He pinned Jace with a laser stare.

"You got special insight, Captain? Spit it out."

Jace hesitated. One word from him, and Heather's orders would be revoked. Granville trusted him, trusted his judgment. If he said Heather couldn't cut it with Delta . . .

Trouble was, Heather trusted him, too. This assignment would make her career and guarantee her promotion. She was ambitious; he knew that. He had no right to derail her because he was afraid for her.

And anything negative he said would be a lie.

He tried to choose his words with care. "Sir. Heather— Lieutenant Langstrom—no doubt performed well for 10th Special Forces Group. But . . . have you talked to her commanding officer? And being an analyst is not the same as being sent into hostile areas. She has no training . . ."

Granville grunted. He was no fool; Jace could see understanding glimmering in the depths of the man's eyes.

"Jace. Is there an *operational* reason why you think Langstrom is unsuitable?"

No. There wasn't. And, "*Sir, I think I may be in love with this woman*," just wasn't going to cut it with his boss, a dedicated and hard-core career soldier. Jace scrubbed a hand down his face.

"No, sir," he ground out.

"Then I expect you to work with her as you would any other professional asset. And to set your mind at ease, her commander at 10th Group sang her praises. She's cool under pressure, has a sharp mind, and knows how to interact with the locals. Disguise herself to blend in. She'll be fine." Granville waved an arm back toward the central table. "Now get back out there and find me a terrorist."

Jace pushed himself to his feet. Could he do it? Work beside Heather, day after day, knowing he couldn't touch her, kiss her, taste her?

No.

The only alternative would be for him to leave Delta. And that was unacceptable.

If she were here, he could at least monitor her whereabouts. Keep her safe.

Shit.

He had to talk to her. Try to . . . what? She planned to accept the assignment. He didn't like it. Not one bit.

But he had to accept it.

If he respected her even a little, if he cared for her at all, he needed to step back, to give her the opportunity to shine. Because she would, without a doubt.

Double shit.

"Jace."

Jace looked over at Tag, at his team, waiting for him. He tried to pry his jaw apart so the muscle in his cheek would stop jumping, but knew he'd failed when Tag cocked his head in a silent, *"Are you all right?"* He gave a slight nod. Yeah. Sure. He was great, as long as having his beating heart ripped out of his chest qualified.

The door to the TOC opened, and Trevor and Christina came in. Their escort nodded to Jace and left. Jace motioned them over to the table.

"Let's make sure we all know one another," Jace said. Damn it. Heather should, by all rights, be here as well. "Brian Seifert and Mike Boston, Secret Service. Christina Madison, CIA. Trevor Carswell, SAS." He glanced around. "Private Stephanie Tams, Operational Research. Need anything found or confirmed, she's the go-to gal." He pointed to each man in turn. "Gabe 'Archangel' Morgan. John 'Tag' McTaggert. Scott 'Sandman' Griffin. Thomas 'Mace' Beckett. Alex Wood, Ken Acolatse. We're working on finding them suitable nicknames." A brief smile lit his face and faded. He looked at the two Secret Service agents. "I know you've got your own men, but you need us, you use us. Okay?"

Mike Boston fingered the walkie-talkie at his hip. "We will. Thanks. The exterior perimeter is still . . ."

A phone chirred. Christina yanked it from her pocket and checked the number. Her eyes brightened. "It's my contact. Aa'idah Karim."

Jace gestured for her to answer it. "Put her on speakerphone."

Christina glanced toward Gabe with a finger to her lips. "She'll spook if she hears you," she said. "Any of you."

Suddenly, the TOC was dead quiet. Jace nodded his thanks to Bo Granville, who motioned for one of the soldiers to go guard the door. No interruptions.

Christina took in a lot of air, let it out in a rush, and pressed the green button.

"This is Christina," she said, dropping into a British accent. Her voice sounded remarkably calm, even soothing. Jace strained for any sound coming from the other end. After what seemed like a very long pause, a voice came tentatively onto the line.

"It is Aa'idah Karim."

Christina grabbed a pad of paper and a pen. Several of the others did, as well.

"Hello, Aa'idah. It's very good to hear from you. How are you? Is your family well?"

There was an even longer pause.

Finally, the woman said, "It is about my family that I contact you. You . . . asked me to be alert for . . . certain activities in the office in which I work. Do you recall this?" Her British-accented English was flawless, testament to her higher education.

"Yes, of course."

Jace worked his shoulders, trying to loosen them.

When the woman spoke again, her voice was stronger, as though she had come to a decision. "I did this. I also overheard a conversation in my own home, between my brother and a man named Zaahir al-Farouk. I confronted Zaahir myself. He is part of a group of men who wish to commit harm against you."

She sighed deeply. "It is with a heavy heart that I pass this information to you. Today, while the American president visits our country, Zaahir al-Farouk, my brother, and two other men intend to gain access to the United States Air Force Base, where they will detonate an explosive."

"Did they mention how they planned to get close to the president?" Christina asked.

"They did not." There was another pause. "Forgive me. They did not intend their target to be the US president. They intend, rather, to harm many people. Women, children. Mothers and fathers. Families. Innocent victims." Aa'idah's voice shook. "I cannot allow this to happen if my report to you can prevent this tragedy."

Christina's voice dropped, became even more soothing. "You absolutely did the right thing, Aa'idah, by calling me. I have a team of people, good people, who want to prevent this from happening just as much as you do. What else did they say?"

"Zaahir al-Farouk spoke of the great shame this would bring to the United States."

Jace glanced around the table, encountering bewildered looks in return. Mike Boston scribbled something on a notepad, and shoved it under Christina's nose. The young CIA agent nodded.

"Aa'idah, did al-Farouk say more about President Cooper?"

"Yes. The explosion is not to look like an attack at all, but like an accident. And . . ." The woman paused. Her distress was palpable, even through the telephone line.

"What else, Aa'idah?" It was funny, really, how a woman as tense and stiff as Christina could sound so reassuring.

Aa'idah sniffed, then sniffed again. Jace realized she was crying. "It is not the explosion itself that will harm the children. The families. Both Azakistani and American. Many of my people will be on the American base. Can you prevent this from happening?"

"I'll do my absolute best." Her British accent faltered for a moment. "But I need to know as much as possible. Is the explosion biochemical? Do you know where they are headed?"

"All I know is the explosion is to be mixed with something else, something which will cause a cloud of poisonous gas to spread across the land."

Stephanie Tams darted to a computer, fingers tapping the keys.

Aa'idah Karim sighed heavily. "I wish my brother to be safe. I wish he did not become involved with these bad men. He is a good man at heart, but very, very angry. Sometimes I think he does not even know why he is angry." She sighed again. "Can you guarantee me my brother will not be harmed?"

Christina rolled her eyes toward the Secret Service agents. Brian Seifert shook his head, once, sharply. Of course she couldn't.

"I wish I could promise you that, but you know I can't. Aa'idah, he's prepared to kill dozens, if not hundreds, of people."

"I understand. I . . . just, perhaps they will be arrested?"

"We're going to do our level best to find them and arrest them, Aa'idah. I promise you. But if they resist . . . you know I can't promise your brother won't be hurt."

Jace grabbed a pen and wrote "Photos?" on the yellow pad, turning it so Christina could see it. She nodded.

"Aa'idah, if I show you some photos, would you be able to identify Zaahir al-Farouk and the other two men? Would you be willing to show me a picture of your brother?"

The young Azakistani woman clicked her tongue against her teeth. "I can do this. I have a picture my brother keeps, of these men with whom he associates."

Christina's eyes snapped with excitement. Again, however, her voice did not reflect it. "That would be a huge help."

"I am . . . at the American Embassy in Ma'ar ye zhad. They have granted me temporary asylum from . . . my family. They will fax it to you. My brother Shukri will be on the left. I don't know the man next to him. I think the one on the right is called Rami. I do not know the other man's name, but he is a sheik. The one in the center is Zaahir al-Farouk."

Jace sent up a prayer of thanks for Aa'idah's courage and foresight. If the terrorist cell had caught her with the photo, there would have been serious consequences for her.

Someone wrote down the fax number, and Christina read it off to Aa'idah. In moments, the machine whirred, and a piece of paper slid forth. Stephanie snatched it up and darted to the photocopier. In thirty seconds, she was back with copies, which she flicked to each of them. The quality of the picture was excellent, the five faces clear and sharp. Christina was still talking to the Azakistani woman, so Jace moved off to the side with the two Secret Service agents and Bo Granville.

"I'd like to take my men up to the parade ground," he said. "Fan out, help you search for these men. You've got the president covered, but if the target's the civilians on base to hear the president's speech, the bomb or bombs could be well away from him."

Mike Boston nodded. "We'll pass it up the chain and make it happen. Be ready to identify yourselves real quick, though. My agents are on edge, and I don't have the time to introduce you. I'll send your photo around, though." He used his camera phone to snap pictures of each of them.

"I'm issuing you weapons," Granville said. "I'll let the base commander know."

Brian Seifert held up a hand. "Wait a minute. That's got the potential for disaster. The Secret Service . . ."

"Are protecting the president," interrupted Jace. "We're responding to a direct threat against a US air base on foreign soil."

Seifert stuck his thumbs through his belt loops. "I know that. I just don't want tensions to run so high we end up shooting at each other. Just remember you won't be able to get within our outer perimeter. If you're challenged, be ready to stand down. All right?"

There were nods all around.

Jace rapid-fired commands. "Christina, get this photo circulated as widely as you can. Military police, Secret Service, CIA, gate guards, everyone. Steph, I need you to identify those last three men in the photo. We need names. Addresses, families who might know where on base they're going to be. Cell phone numbers, if they have them, so we can triangulate in on them. Known associates. We can't assume the four Aa'idah knows of are the only ones."

Trevor poked at the photocopy in her hand. "The one next to Aa'idah's brother is Na'il Fakhoury. He was a classified courier for the Embassy. He's the one who brought the vials of phosgene in, hidden inside the classified materials pouch. He died in a car accident. That's how we found the phosgene."

Gabe peered over her shoulder. "I recognize al-Farouk. He was second-in-command at the Kongra-Gel training compound. Mean son of a bitch."

Which meant he was probably the bastard who had hurt Heather. Jace sprinted out the door, his men hot on his heels. "Someone call Heather Langstrom and fill her in. Have her come in and help ID those last two terrorists." And keep her safely out of the line of fire in the process.

"We're right behind you," said Seifert. "Two minutes."

Jace, Gabe, Tag, Mace, Alex, Ken, and the Sandman jogged over to the armory. It took a few minutes, but at last his men strapped on their sidearms. The decision had been made not to alarm the civilians and guests on the installation by carrying semiautomatic rifles. It potentially put them at a tactical disadvantage if the terrorists had somehow managed to smuggle rifles onto the installation, but sidearms were better than no weapons at all. Finally, they piled into Ken's truck and Jace's BMW.

Jace hit the button for Brian Seifert. "We're heading up to the parade ground. Who're we going to be coordinating with up there?" He listened, then disconnected. "Seifert's on his way now."

Even breaking every speed limit, it took fifteen minutes to get to the parade ground. Silence filled the car. They all knew the stakes, knew the consequences of failure.

They would not fail.

Nevertheless, Jace's heart sank.

Americans and Azakistanis packed the grounds. His half-hearted hopes the area they needed to cover was, indeed, the size of a normal parade ground disintegrated. The area set aside for this celebration encompassed several city blocks. Normally a huge, empty patch of dusty ground, metal barriers had now been erected around it, patrolled by a mixture of Secret Service and military police. A finite number of entry points and metal detectors allowed access onto the grounds; a separate but only slightly smaller area with a newly constructed chain-link fence was further restricted for access to the president.

Many of the Azakistani locals had parked outside the Air Force base's main gate and had been transported by small buses into the area. Security Police directed traffic at each intersection, moving the foreign nationals into the designated areas. Jace showed his identification.

"We're meeting the Secret Service liaison . . ."

"Yes, sir. We've been briefed. Go on through."

With Ken's truck following, he drove right up to the pedestrian barriers. Without waiting for the others, he jogged over to one of the access gates. Brian Seifert was waiting for him.

"Every Secret Service agent knows you're here," he said, by way of greeting. "And the military police. Major Carswell's SAS team, they're here, too. As long as you defer to my agents with respect to direct access to the president, they'll cooperate as far as they can. But you understand, right, their first priority is keeping President Cooper safe?"

"Yeah. And our first priority is stopping an explosion." Jace looked around. "Christ, there are a lot of people."

Hundreds wandered inside the pedestrian barriers, or patiently waited to pass through the metal detectors. Booths had been set up, selling food and T-shirts. A gaggle of teenagers gathered around a dunking booth, shouting with laughter. An inflatable bouncy castle swayed and jerked with the force of tiny feet smashing it. He could even see a tank and two helicopters, their crews patiently explaining the inner workings while wide-eyed children climbed in and around them.

He shaded his eyes, trying to get a good look at the inner parade area. Huge banks of bleachers lined one side of the grassy area. A platform, a raised dais with podium, had been set up across from the bleachers. Secret Service agents stood around the area, keeping the curious at bay.

"All right." Jace pulled the photocopy of the picture Aa'idah had sent from his pocket. "Check perimeter areas. Rest areas with benches, play areas with swings or whatever. Porta-Potties. Even strollers. We don't know how big this bomb needs to be." He looked at each of them in turn. "You know who we're looking for. Go find them."

His team dispersed.

Chapter Thirty-Seven

September 11. 2:10 P.M.
TOC, FOB Hollow Straw, al-Zadr Air Force Base

THE SECOND TIME Heather entered the Tactical Operations Center, she was in control of her emotions. She approached Private Stephanie Tams.

"Can you get me the logs of all traffic in or out of the gates on base?"

"You bet. Gimme two minutes."

Heather sat down at an empty desk, shrugging a little. She had heard Delta operated outside of military norms. They weren't undisciplined—far from it—but the culture was quite different from the strict customs and courtesies of her former unit. Most tended to be on a first-name basis regardless of rank, something that would not normally be tolerated.

"There's no way they're bringing a bomb on base, especially not today of all days," Heather said to Trevor, who scrolled through pages and pages of complex formulae, evidently in a biochemical weapons database. "What if they brought it on in pieces, over the course of weeks?"

Even as she said it, she rejected it. "They didn't have that kind of time," Trevor confirmed. "Jace's team disabled the SCUD not even a month ago. Whatever their Plan B is, they've had to cobble it together in a hurry."

An electronic log popped up on the screen in front of her. Stephanie peered over her shoulder and pointed to it. "This is today's police blotter. It includes traffic onto base. Use this filter to isolate your parameters. Press this icon to break it down to entry activity by gate, or this icon to change the date range."

Heather studied the installation map, finding and marking each of the three gates. Military police manned the gates, logging all traffic onto the base. Unfortunately, only access *to* the base was restricted. Anyone could *leave* the base . . . or not leave.

"Assuming they intend to plant the phosgene bomb near the public areas where the president is speaking . . ." Damn it. Something felt . . . off. Wrong. "The Secret Service and the Security Police are vetting everyone who's coming through the main gate." She clicked her way to the more remote gates. "Ignoring military residents . . ." She scanned through the entries. Foreign nationals who worked on base. Deliveries to the commissary and gas station. Visiting spouses. Nothing jumped out at her.

She did the same thing for the previous day, then went back as far as a week ago, then switched her view to encompass all entries, not just vehicular traffic. The police blotter had the usual assortment of entries for the week: a reported break-in at one of the housing areas; two brawls outside the noncommissioned officer's club; a teenager shoplifting a blouse at the base exchange. A dispute between the entertainment facilities manager and a local company over the delivery of too many boxes of supplies. Too many? Usually the problem was being shorted in a delivery.

The blotter didn't specify the type of supplies or the delivery location. Curious, Heather looked up the facilities manager's number and punched it in. The call went directly to voice mail. Of course. Only essential personnel worked today.

The company providing the supplies sold water treatment products. The delivery agent with whom Heather spoke insisted the order had been completed correctly.

"Yes, madame. One renewal order, an annual delivery of chlorine cakes my company has made every year for the past five years, plus a separate rushed order for enough shock chemicals to clean and sanitize two standard fifty-meter pools, whose filtration system apparently became compromised. We service both community pools on the air base."

The processing agent knew nothing about the subsequent dispute. Thanking him, Heather disconnected. She pushed away from the computer screen, shoving strands of hair fallen out of her French braid back behind her ears. She rolled her chair over to Christina, who watched Trevor clicking the mouse and muttering to himself. The other woman glanced her way.

"Anything?"

"No," admitted Heather. "You?"

Christina shrugged. "Aa'idah didn't know the last name of the man we haven't identified. We're running it through the known terrorist database, but it could take a while."

Heather looked over the young agent's shoulder, and found herself face-to-face with her abductor. Her world tilted. Grabbing the arms of her chair, she fought for a moment to breathe.

The close-up of his face had obviously been cut from a larger photograph. In it, the man smiled, friendly, at ease. It was so far from the terrifying man who had questioned her for days Heather gave her head a sharp shake. Christina gave her a curious look, then understanding dawned.

"Is that him?"

"Yes." Her voice came out as little more than a gasp.

Christina handed her a faxed copy of a group photo. "His name is Zaahir al-Farouk. He's Omaid al-Hassid's second in command. Remember the third email we found, dated to happen today? 'Pick up transportation vehicle and link up with me.' I'm thinking Zaahir al-Farouk is the one calling the shots here, and one of these two men was supposed to get a car. Maybe the bomb is in the car?"

Heather forced herself to take the photo. "Doubtful. I'm still thinking we're missing a big piece of the puzzle here." She examined the men in the photo. "This one might have been at my convoy's ambush. It's hard to remember." Deep breaths. Just keep breathing. Her head cleared.

Trevor joined them. "I'm heading up to the parade grounds," he said. "I'm not getting anywhere here. Maybe if I see something, I'll recognize it. Besides, whoever finds it will need my help neutralizing it."

"Whatever *it* is."

Trevor blew out a breath. "Right. Whatever it is. My team's already there. I'm going to join them." He looked at the two women. "Are you staying here?"

Christina gave an unamused laugh. "Jay wants me back at the embassy, where he can keep an eye on me. I was supposed to be on my way back an hour ago." She forced a smile. "Guess I'll be paying for my mistake for a long time."

She and Trevor exchanged a wry look. He seemed to know exactly what she meant.

"What happened?"

Christina shook her head. "Too long a story. I messed up, my first time out of the gate. My very first mission. That's what Jay meant the other day, in his office. Trevor bailed me out. Tell you the story another time."

"Sure," said Heather. "When this is all over. Cup of coffee, my treat."

The TOC seemed quieter after they left, its hum less intense. She rubbed her arms. She was missing something, she could feel it. Something hovered, just at her periphery. *Damn it!*

She was doing no good here.

Wandering over to Colonel Granville, she waited while he finished being briefed by someone in a T-shirt and cargo shorts, who winked at her as he walked away. She rolled her eyes, and Granville grinned. "Whatcha got, kid?"

Heather couldn't help but smile back at her new boss. "Very damned little, I'm sorry to say. Since I know what Zaahir al-Farouk looks like, and the other two as well, I'd like permission to go help Captain Reed's search team."

He stared at her for several long minutes. Heather had to force herself not to squirm. Granville balanced his unlit cigar across the top of his coffee cup and folded his arms.

"Well, it entirely depends, Lieutenant. You're here in a completely advisory role as long as I think you're not field-ready. And your doctors tell me that might not be for a few months. Convince me." He jabbed a finger at the chair his previous visitor had just vacated.

Heather perched on the edge of the seat. "It's not like I'm going into combat, sir. And I'm one of the few people who will recognize Zaahir al-Farouk without a photograph. Possibly the other two, as well. The truth is, I'm not much use here at the moment, but I can be up at the parade grounds." Granville was still staring at her, so she kept going. What did he want to hear?

"Sir, I'm not going to deny it's been a challenge. It's only been four weeks. I get that. I do. But how many of your operators would just give up? Versus how many of them would just get back up, dust themselves off, and jump back into the saddle?" She met his gaze squarely. "Treat me the same as you would them. No better, no worse. Just the same. That's all I ask."

Granville sat back in his chair, looking smug. "Then what the hell you still doing here, Langstrom?"

Heather dashed to her car. The nagging feeling wouldn't go away, and she knew she wasn't going to find that missing piece in the TOC. What she'd told the colonel was true. The part she'd skipped burrowed a lot deeper. She had to do this. Going after the man who'd hurt her, stopping him, was the best therapy she could think of and the fastest way to heal.

As she drove, she reviewed the information they had. And again. Grabbing her cell phone, she dialed Jace.

"Nothing yet," he reported. "We started near the area the president's going to be speaking at, and we're expanding as we clear each section. It's slow going, and he's due to speak in less than two hours."

"I'm heading your way now," she said. "And Trevor's five minutes ahead of me. Two more sets of eyes to help."

"No!" The negative was an explosion of sound. "Nuh-uh. Your place is at the TOC."

Say what? Had she heard that right? Heather's mouth tightened. Her voice dropped several octaves. "My *place*?"

There was dead silence at the other end.

"My place, Jace? What, exactly, does that mean?" Heather's voice rose, despite her attempts to modulate her tone. "Tell me. 'Cause I really want to know how you feel about me."

She heard him blow out a breath. Then, "Shit. Shit shit shit. This is *not* the time for this conversation."

Heather gripped the steering wheel so hard her knuckles turned white. "Seems to me this is the perfect time. If you didn't want my particular skill set working for Delta Force, why did you get me transferred into your unit?"

Jace gave a frustrated hiss. "I did not have anything to do with your transfer. That was all the colonel's idea. And if I'd known, I'd have nixed it. Fast."

Heather didn't move for several long moments. She stared blankly, unseeingly out of the windshield. Nixed it? Funnily enough, she believed him. Jace *didn't* want her in his unit.

"Why?"

Silence.

Heather slowed at an intersection, glancing around. Which way to the parade grounds? The gas station and mini mart sat on her left. The parking lot was deserted; yellow covered several of the pump heads, indicating they were drained. It seemed everyone was up at the parade grounds for the celebration.

If the gas station was on her left, she needed to turn left. She signaled, spun the wheel with one hand, and pulled out onto the road, still clutching her cell phone to her ear.

"Why?" she asked again.

"Look, Heather . . ."

She cracked her teeth together in fury. And hurt. "Don't 'look, Heather' me," she shouted. "Just say it. I want to hear you say it." He thought she wasn't good enough, tough enough, skilled enough. Which one was it this time?

It didn't matter. Either way, Jace didn't think she could handle herself.

Heather had been hearing it her entire career.

"I . . ."

Heather braced herself.

"I need you to be safe." The admission was almost whispered.

That stopped her cold. "You . . ."

"Want you safe," he growled. "Out of danger. So what if it's not politically correct. So it alters your three-star general career trajectory. I don't care. You asked what I want? That's what I want."

Heather's throat closed up. She couldn't have managed more than a squeak at that moment if her life depended on it.

Damn it. She had gone the wrong way. The parade grounds were behind her.

Heather spun the car around, ending up back at the intersection with the gas station and mini mart. Pulling into the lot, she slammed the car into park.

"I don't suppose I have to tell you," she said, finally able to get her vocal cords working, "what *I* want is a career. The same opportunities men have. I have a place here, too. I'm good at what I do. I'm making a difference. Saving American lives."

There was a long pause. "I know. And I know my views are archaic. And I know I have no right to ask you to do this, but . . . turn around and go back to the TOC."

She clutched the phone. "I won't do that, Jace. I can't."

He sighed heavily. "I know. Just . . . I had to ask."

Heather swallowed the hard knot of disappointment in her gut. "We're going to be working together soon. I have to know if you're going to sabotage me, hold me back."

"No!" He actually sounded shocked. "Of course not. I don't like it, but okay. There it is. There's nothing I can do about it."

Heather rested her head against the window, not really seeing anything. "I don't see there's any 'of course not' to it. So what was all the bullshit about your respecting me?"

Another sigh. "I do respect you. I just also love you."

His words hung in the air between them. Heather chewed on her nail as she fought to find a response. A car pulled in past her and maneuvered over to a gas pump, and immediately pulled ahead as the driver noticed the yellow covering on the pump.

Yellow covering.

"Heather?"

Brows pulled down, Heather looked more closely at the driver, who was now out of the car with the nozzle in hand. The middle-aged woman looked curiously back at her.

Yellow covering.

"Jace, I'll have to call you back." She flipped her phone closed.

Two of the four pumps at the gas station were covered. Empty. But a gas truck had been admitted onto base just this morning. So why was the reservoir almost drained?

Her mind made lightning jumps. Heather dialed the base Security Police. "There was a gas truck let onto base this morning," she said. "I have reason to believe it never arrived at the gas station. I think it might be bringing a bomb onto base."

"Nearly every cop we got is up helping with security for the president," the sergeant on duty told her. "I'll tell my patrol cars to haul ass to find your truck, but I'm really stretched on manpower."

Heather hung up and called Trevor. "We need to find a fuel oil truck that came onto base this morning and disappeared. I think he's our guy. Or guys." She filled him in. "I'm starting to search now."

Trevor swore. "Bollocks. I passed one heading toward one of the housing areas, roughly four miles back. I'm turning around now."

Heather pulled back onto the road and accelerated. "Did you notice the driver?"

"No."

"Damn it. I'm heading your way now." She disconnected, then called the SPs back and filled them in. The duty sergeant promised to send backup. Her next call was to Bo Granville.

"Perfect timing, Langstrom," he thundered. "Omran Malouf talked. Babbled all over the place. He admitted he was in cahoots with that Greek scientist, Pagonis, who was found dead in his lab. They were siphoning off phosgene gas and smuggling it into Azakistan. And you're not going to believe who Malouf says he works for."

"Who, sir?"

Colonel Granville almost crowed. "The conservative party leader and Prime Minister al-Muhaymin's chief rival, Najm al-Najib. Remember his chief of staff? Met with an Iranian conservative in Tehran to talk about importing terrorism?" he asked. "Now we have a direct connection between al-Najib and the planned attack on the US president. Headline-news stuff."

A swell of triumph hit Heather. "That's it, then. The why of all this. If the Azakistani prime minister fails to safeguard his ally, the American president, on Azakistani soil . . . my God! It would at best be an international incident. At worst, an act of war."

"Ya think?"

"Sir, I think one of the terrorists is driving a fuel oil truck, heading toward the . . ." She wracked her brain. "Uh, the Dogwood Beach housing complex. A bomb, more phosgene—I don't know. The warhead? Trevor and I are heading in that direction. The military police are also sending backup."

"I'll let the Secret Service know . . ."

Her call waiting beeped. "It's Trevor," she said. "Maybe he found it. I'll call you back."

"Conference me in . . ."

Heather had already jabbed the buttons to end one call and accept the other. "Trevor?"

"I see it," he said. "It's half a mile ahead of me." He paused. "It's a small one, not one of the huge tankers."

That was good news, at least. Although, if there really was a bomb inside the truck, the size of the tank probably didn't matter.

"I'm pulling across the road," Trevor reported. "Maybe we'll get lucky and the guy's just lost."

"Yeah." But Heather didn't believe it for a moment. She sped up again. She was still at least six minutes from Trevor. There was the sound of a car door slamming shut.

"Give me your cross streets."

He did so, adding, "I'm trying to flag him down." Trevor swore sharply. "He's not slowing. Fekking hell." There was a thump, as though Trevor had fumbled his phone. The unmistakable tearing sound of automatic gunfire ripped through her speaker, a gunned engine, the crash of metal on metal. Silence.

"Trevor!"

Through the tinny receiver, she heard a diesel engine crank over. It whined as the driver put it into gear. The sound slowly faded as the truck moved farther away.

Her heart in her throat, Heather waited. Nothing further came through the phone line.

"Trevor?"

Her call waiting beeped. It was Jace. She hit the ignore button, disconnected her line with Trevor, and called 9-1-1. Her voice was remarkably calm, considering how hard her heart thudded, as she requested an ambulance and the military police.

Finally, *finally* she could see the government car. It was half on, half off the road, and at an odd angle. The hood was crushed. She braked hard behind him and threw herself out of the car.

"Trevor. Trevor!"

A faint voice answered her. "Here."

Thank God!

She ran to the other side of the car and saw him. He sat propped against the front wheel. His face was white, and he held his side.

"Sod it all."

Dropping to her knees next to him, she said, "Are you shot? I heard gunfire." She checked him for telltale blood. There didn't seem to be any. "What happened?"

"Bloody hell," he said, disgust and pain twisting his face. "I cocked it up good. The truck rammed my bastarding car. It spun out, and I caught the back bumper. I've a couple of cracked ribs."

"Ambulance is on its way."

"Help me into your car. Mine's bolloxed. We've got to stop the tanker."

If she took Trevor away from the scene of the accident, he wouldn't get the medical help he needed. And if his ribs were broken rather than cracked—and that was the extent of his injuries—he risked a punctured lung if he moved around.

"I'm good for it. Let's go." Trevor struggled to his feet. "The driver is our terrorist, absolutely no doubt."

"Zaahir al-Farouk?"

"Yes."

"We should wait for the ambulance . . ."

"Not bloody likely." Trevor was walking slightly hunched over, and Heather realized he wasn't just holding his ribs.

"Your arm is broken."

Trevor didn't stop. "Just the wrist. We'll need to find something to splint it with."

Heather trotted around until she was in front of him, forcing him to stop. "The ambulance will have a splint. And a wrap for your ribs."

The British SAS officer shook his head. "We can't wait. Every second we stay put is a second the terrorists come closer to detonating a biochemical bomb among civilians. I'm not willing to risk it. Give me your keys." He held out a hand. His functioning hand.

Heather blew out a breath and popped the trunk of her car. "Is there a first-aid kit in your car? Government vehicles usually have them . . ."

"Bandages and aspirin, I'm afraid."

"Damn it." She rustled around in her trunk, looking for anything that could be used as a splint. Roadside emergency triangles, emergency blanket, emergency flares. Nothing, however, useful for this emergency. Although . . .

She plucked out the emergency triangles. The tough plastic was hard to break. She finally resorted to sticking her foot inside it as though it were a stirrup, and yanking up as hard as she could until it cracked. Repeating the process, she ended up with two roughly straight pieces. Heather tugged her belt free. Luckily, it was one of her stretchy ones.

She set the two pieces of plastic against his wrist, and wrapped the belt several times around them before securing the end. Trevor grunted in pain, his lips white. "Will that do?"

"Yes."

He moved gingerly. Heather could relate. One of her ribs had been cracked—mostly just bruised—and every step she'd taken had been painful. He must be in agony.

A bit of color returned to his face. "All right. Let's go."

Although, what they were going to do when they caught up with the oil truck was beyond her. Neither of them had a weapon of any sort.

Wait . . .

She dashed back to the trunk. The flares. There were three of them. Too bad they were roadside flares and not the kind that could be shot out of a pistol. Still, it was better than nothing.

Maybe not by much.

Chapter Thirty-Eight

September 11. 2:58 P.M.
Main Parade Grounds, al-Zadr Air Force Base

JACE ALMOST THREW his phone against the fence in frustration. Why wasn't Heather picking up? Okay, maybe it was too much to hope that his declaration of love be met with an, "I love you, too," but to hang up on him?

About to shove the phone into his pocket, he paused, then dialed Trevor. Maybe he and Heather had linked up. Again, there was no answer. What the hell was going on?

He'd barely pressed the disconnect button when it rang. "Heather?"

"Do I gotta rattle your teeth, Reed?" Colonel Granville barked. "I need your focus, son."

"Sorry, sir. I can't reach either Heather or Trevor. They should be here by now."

His commander grunted. "Langstrom's after a fuel truck. Says there's a bomb of some sort on it. Heading into one of the housing complexes. Dogwood Beach."

Oh, shit. The bottom fell out of Jace's stomach. She was supposed to have stayed at the TOC, where it was safe. Now she was chasing after the terrorists and their bomb on her own? Damn it all to hell.

"On my way, sir." Jace disconnected.

He caught Tag's eye, and his senior sergeant immediately left the bench he was searching and came to Jace's side. "Whassup, boss?"

"They're not coming here," he said. "Heather found them. Looks like they're going to a housing area instead." He swept the area, hoping to spot the rest of his team. "Fuck. I can't get through to Trevor. He never made it here. I think—hope—he and Heather linked up. Get the team together and haul ass. Dogwood Beach housing area. Got it?"

Tag already had his phone to his ear. "We're two minutes behind you."

Jace sprinted back down to the metal detectors where he'd linked up with Brian Seifert. The agent in charge stepped forward to meet him.

"I expected Trevor Carswell to meet me here," he said, wasting no time. "Did he come through? Anything on the wire about Heather Langstrom?"

"No to Carswell." The agent pulled off his sunglasses. "A call came in to the police station from a Heather Langstrom, in reference to a fuel oil tanker. It's believed to contain some sort of explosive. We have our snipers on the lookout, but nothing so far."

Jace glanced up at the roof of the closest building, where both snipers and spotters swept the area with binoculars. A drop of cold sweat shivered down his spine.

"It's not coming this way. We have it heading into one of the housing complexes. Don't stand down, obviously. We could be wrong. There could be two trucks. I'm going after it."

He made it to his BMW in ten seconds flat and dove inside, foot already jammed to the pedal.

Where was Heather?

He pressed her speed dial again, finding himself holding his breath and praying. "Come on. Pick up pick up pick up."

"Jace?"

The male voice threw Jace for half a second. "Trevor? Where's Heather?"

"Driving. We found a gas truck, a small fuel oil tanker. It's heading southwest, toward the housing areas. Not toward the parade grounds. Do you copy?"

"Copy that," Jace replied automatically, but his heart sank. In retrospect, it made perfect sense. Knowing virtually every law enforcement officer would be protecting access to the president, the terrorists had, instead, chosen a soft target. Civilians. Aa'idah had even said as much. "Families and children," he said, a muscle ticking in his jaw. "We assumed that meant the people up at the parade grounds today. Visitors, families, Azakistanis and Americans alike, doing the whole carnival thing. We were looking in the wrong place."

Trevor made a noise that might have been agreement. "I don't know what the second chemical is. A blast powerful enough could send a plume of poisonous gas across the base. The parade grounds are only a couple of miles away . . ." His voice trailed off.

"There it is!" Heather said in the background.

"Holy Mary, Mother of God," said Trevor. "I know what they're planning."

Chapter Thirty-Nine

TREVOR'S CELL PHONE BUZZED. In reaching for it, he fumbled Heather's phone, which dropped to the floor and went dark. He leaned over carefully, mindful of his broken ribs and wrist, and plucked it from the floor mat. His own phone, damaged when the truck rammed his car, buzzed again. He pressed a few buttons, but the phone didn't respond. Finally, he just dropped it into the cup holder next to Heather's.

The noise stopped, then started again.

"It's Shelby," she told him. "Answer it."

"I think the truck ran over my phone. Let it go to voice mail."

Instead, Heather snatched her cell from his good hand and punched the number in one-handed. "Trevor. We're chasing down what is most probably a bomb on wheels, completely unarmed, heading into ground zero of a biochemical explosion designed to kill hundreds of people. Talk to the woman." She hit the speaker-phone button and handed it to him. When he simply glowered at her, she motioned for him to speak.

"Erm. Shelby?"

"Trevor? Whose phone . . . oh, never mind."

He opened his mouth, but before he could get more than a syllable out, she spoke over him. "I have an update you need to hear. Jay Spicer pressed a few contacts. I guess Heather and Christina convinced him the Kongra-Gel had a Plan B?"

They'd convinced the CIA station chief? That was news to her.

"Anyway, the conservative party leader's chief of staff? He used to be the chief of police in Tiqt. He gave Sa'id al-Jabr his job."

Heather thumped her palm against the steering wheel. "I knew there had to be something. Did he tie al-Jabr to the Kongra-Gel?"

"Heather? Hi. No, but he's convinced there is one. He'll find it. He's very good at what he does. You asked the wrong questions, apparently, and alarm bells started ringing."

Heather and Trevor exchanged glances. She was unsurprised, but hearing it confirmed relaxed something inside her. "Anything else?"

"That's not enough?" Paper rustled. "The meeting in Tehran I mentioned at the briefing, Trevor? Between Najm al-Najib's chief of staff and Iranian fundamentalists? It was to arrange Iranian funds and weapons to support recruiting and training of antigovernment troops. We can't confirm al-Najib's involvement at all, though. He's either covering his tracks really well, or he really doesn't know what his chief of staff is doing."

"How does that tie in to an attack against the American president?" Trevor asked.

Shelby hesitated, as though unwilling to impart bad news. Finally, she said, "If he can embarrass or discredit the prime minister, he can push for a vote of no confidence and force early elections."

Heather furrowed her brow. "Okay. Let's talk this through.

We've been so focused on the president's visit and the families around him, we didn't stop to consider an attack *only* on civilians. Away from the celebrations going on at the parade grounds. So what's the big picture here?"

Trevor shifted the cell phone and almost lost his grip on it. "When we get to Dogwood Beach, we'll be looking for a community center, or some sort of community swimming area. An indoor or outdoor pool."

"Why set a bomb in a pool?" Heather's fingers clenched around the phone. "Or inside the pool supply building, maybe. They're clearly piggybacking on the urban legend that the US military stores chemical weapons under the pool house. Still have a hard time understanding why civilians buy that rubbish, but there you go."

"What does that get them?" asked Shelby. "I mean, if the attack isn't against the parade ground where the president is speaking?"

"Once the SCUD was destroyed, they implemented their Plan B."

"Which is to fake a biochemical leak in the pool house," Trevor said. "Which will then 'accidentally' mix with the chlorine already there."

Heather flashed hot, then cold. "The base police got dispatched because of a dispute between a delivery company and the facilities manager, over a too-large delivery of chlorine cakes. The company delivered hundred-pound buckets instead of the twenty-five-pound buckets he ordered. Ten of them. I . . . I didn't realize . . ." Her voice wobbled.

Trevor swore sharply. "A thousand pounds of chlorine, mixed with God knows how much phosgene and an explosion . . . it will rip the pool house apart. The ones who don't die from the explosion will die from the poisonous gas. The gas will be spread across an exponentially larger area and could reach the parade grounds. They're only, what, a mile or two from here? Shelby, you've got to call the police. The Secret Service. Everyone. Get those people out of there. We'll evacuate this lot."

Heather's heart sank. "There will be a lot of panic."

Trevor furrowed his brow. "Yes. But why bother to make it look like an accident?"

"Think about it," Shelby cut in. "Our treaty with Azakistan specifically precludes nuclear-biological-chemical weapons on their sovereign soil. The discharge of phosgene would cause a serious rift between Azakistan and the United States. The prime minister can't control his own foreign partners? Americans trampling all over their sovereign rights? It gives a huge boost to the ultraconservative right. Look what the evil West is doing. Plus, how many of our other allies suddenly want to rewrite their treaties? You see?"

Heather glanced over at Trevor but addressed her question to Shelby. "So, you think the prime minister's opposition party leader sponsored this whole scenario? He's responsible for the Kongra-Gel and the SCUD?"

"I believe so, yes," said Shelby. "Where are you?"

"We're following a small oil truck . . . look! There it is!" Heather's voice sharpened.

Trevor raised the cell phone to his mouth, but then let his forehead drop forward and rest on it instead. "We found it. Look, I just wanted to tell you . . . in the event that . . ." The car hit a bump, and he grunted, lips whitening.

"What's wrong?"

"Everything's fine," he said. "It's nothing. I . . . just wanted to say there's nothing between Christina and myself. There never was. We're friends, nothing more. She just needed my help the other day, is all. One professional to another."

"It's turning," reported Heather, speeding up. Trevor gritted his teeth and held on.

"Okay," said Shelby slowly, drawing out the syllables. "I hear you. And I heard Heather, too. You're going to try to stop the gas truck by yourself, aren't you? You're saying goodbye to me?"

Trevor cursed. "Look, I need you to call Mike Boston and pass this information to the Secret Service. They have to get the president out of there. There is danger to him, and to all the people in the area. And here. We're in the community pool area, and it's packed."

Heather slowed the car, then pulled off to the side of the road, turning into the parking lot of a building that blocked their view of the tanker. Of course, it also blocked the tanker's view of them.

"They're pulling around to the back of the community buildings," she said, pushing the car door open and alighting. One hand rested on the top of the door, while the other shaded her eyes. The community recreation area consisted of a large outdoor pool, surrounded on three sides by concrete areas full of lounge chairs . . . full, period, with screaming, running children, strollers, parents, teens. The pool was packed, residents enjoying the coolness of the water in contrast to the heat of the day.

"Trevor? Are you . . . still there?"

They had to evacuate this area. If they tried to do that, though, Zaahir al-Farouk would know his mission had been compromised and might start shooting into the crowd. Right now, he might believe he had escaped detection, that Trevor had not been able to call for reinforcements. Which he hadn't. If not for Heather, he would still be lying by the side of the road.

"I'm here."

Shelby's voice was soft, hesitant. "You're hurt, aren't you. I can hear it in your voice."

"I'm all right," he said, tenderness creeping into his tone. "Don't fret." The call waiting beeped. "It's Jace. I've got to go. Get the parade ground evacuated, all right?"

"Trevor . . ."

But he clicked over to the new call. "Go."

"Where are you?" asked Jace.

Heather took the phone from Trevor. "The rec center is about a hundred yards away, over open ground with virtually no cover. There's an indoor pool, and game rooms and meeting rooms. A snack area. It's going to be as crowded inside as out. There are two outdoor pools just south of the rec center. Also basketball, tennis, volleyball courts. This complex is enormous, Jace. And very, very crowded. The truck pulled back behind it. I've never been back there. Probably maintenance areas. Supplies."

"I'm no more than five minutes behind you. Do not engage. Stay where you are. I'll come to you, and we can figure out a plan."

Heather sighed. "Just get here as soon . . ."

"Do *not* engage!" Jace roared. "Trevor, keep Heather away from those animals. Do you hear me?"

Heather raised her face to the sun. A warm breeze wafted the scent of chlorine and sunblock across her nose. The sweet sound of children's laughter brought a smile to her lips. Mothers and fathers. Newlyweds. Precious babies. A picture formed in her mind, of her sitting under one of those striped umbrellas, a chubby toddler with springy dark hair and laughing eyes in her lap. Jace handing her a bottle. Their fingers brushing and entwining. A heart so full of love she thought it might burst.

A sharp pang of regret pierced her. The picture vanished with the reality of their situation. She would likely never experience those things. The only option remaining was to drive forward. To try, knowing her chance of success was slim.

They could not wait. They might already be too late. "Just get here!" She disconnected, cutting Jace off in mid-curse.

She started the motor. "The parking lot is so crowded, we could drive right in and they would never see us. It'll get us much closer."

Trevor climbed in, wincing. Heather glanced at him. "You could stay here," she started, but he cut her off.

"Drive." His voice came out as more of a groan as he banged his broken wrist against the center console. "Shite."

Chapter Forty

To GET TO the parking lot on the west side of the rec center, Heather either had to drive all the way around the south side, past the outdoor pool, and back north, or she could drive past the back end and turn into the parking lot.

"They don't know this car," Heather said. Trevor's face was white as a sheet. Truth was, he barely looked conscious. "Are you up for this, soldier?"

She couldn't do it without him. She didn't know anything about biochemical weapons. Neither did she know what to look for.

"Yes." He took her phone, dialing with his good hand. "Colonel Granville? Major Carswell. I need you to listen closely and disseminate this as far as it needs to go." He listened for a moment. "We're at the community center. There's both an indoor and outdoor pool."

Heather turned her head. "The indoor pool's closed for maintenance. That's a mercy, anyway. Fewer people."

For some reason, this news made Trevor close his eyes and thunk his head against the back of the seat. "We need to hurry.

The oil truck may or may not be carrying explosives, but it is absolutely carrying phosgene gas. A great deal of it."

Heather turned the car toward the back end of the recreation center. With a little luck, she could just drive past as though she were any other resident and turn into the back lot. What they would do once there was beyond her. Neither of them had firearms, and Trevor was badly injured. Against how many men with weapons, what chance did they stand?

She had to try.

She didn't intend to slow down, didn't intend to look for the gas truck as she drove past. Certainly had not intended to meet the eyes of one of the men near the truck. Recognition flashed through the man's eyes, then alarm. He grabbed for something near the back wheel of the truck, brought it up to his shoulder . . . the AK-47 spat a stream of bullets, and Heather yanked the wheel, hard, in the opposite direction. Her foot slammed down on the accelerator. The car slewed around, fishtailed. Leaped forward. Plowed, nose first, into the ditch at the edge of the pavement.

The airbag punched her hard. Dizzy, disoriented, Heather pushed at it, trying to get it to deflate. Trying to get it out of her face so she could see.

"Trevor?"

There was no answer. The bag finally flattened enough for her to look across to where Trevor slumped against the door. He had blood on his face. Heather fought her seat belt free, leaning across to see if she could find a pulse.

Her door was yanked open. A hostile face filled her vision. Rough hands grabbed her, dragging her away from Trevor, who still had not moved. Oh, God, don't let him be dead.

"You stupid son of a camel!" roared a voice from far away. In

Arabic. "Someone might have heard the shots. Do that again, and I'll kill you myself."

It was the convoy all over again. Someone wrenched her out of her seat and shoved her to the pavement. The rough cement ground against her cheek as the terrorist searched her. Another went around to the other side of the car, listing sideways in the ditch. The door wouldn't open. The man, dressed incongruously in jeans and a T-shirt, pressed his face against the window and said, in Arabic, "He's dead. Leave him."

A despairing cry ripped from Heather's throat. "No!"

She kicked and twisted as they yanked her arms up behind her and half dragged, half carried her over to the building, up the stairs, and through the open bay door. The sudden dimness had her blinking. It was clearly a shipment area. Trucks could simply back up to the concrete platform and offload their deliveries. A man waited just inside the door.

Zaahir al-Farouk.

He held a wicked-looking handgun. It was the very distinctive PHP VM-17 pistol, a Croatian-made firearm. As Heather was yanked to a stop in front of him, he raised the pistol, thumbed back the hammer, and pressed the barrel against her forehead.

Chapter Forty-One

September 11. 3:25 P.M.
Recreation Center, Dogwood Beach Housing Area

JACE ARRIVED AT the recreation center just behind the military police. Two cars. Two cops. Jesus. Where was the cavalry? He sprinted across the parking lot to them.

"Get these people out of here!" he shouted.

As one, they took a step back from him, hands dropping to the butts of their weapons. Jace realized what he must look like to them, a madman running full tilt at the cops. He skidded to a stop, hands spread to show he had no weapon. No visible weapon, that is.

"I'm Captain Reed," he said, moving much more slowly but with no less purpose. "There's a bomb on the premises, somewhere. I have to find it. You need to get these people evacuated."

The more senior of the two, a buck sergeant, dropped his hand away from his handgun and saluted, despite Jace not being in uniform. "Yes, sir. We spotted the gas tanker back behind this building. We were just heading . . ."

Jace interrupted him. He had no time for this. "Do either of you have experience disarming bombs or handling biochemical weapons? No? Then the best way you can help is to get these people the hell away from here, without causing a panic."

"We'll take care of it, sir." The younger cop headed toward the crowded pool area. "But you need to be aware there's a car back there, too, in the ditch. There's an ambulance on its way."

Fuck and double fuck. Jace turned and sprinted for the rear of the building. Please let it not be Heather. Please let her be all right.

Please let her be alive.

There was no movement of any kind at the loading dock. Jace didn't bother with stealth; he simply raced at top speed to the car. The driver's side door was wide open. There was only one person inside. It was Trevor. Jace simply slid over the top of the hood to get to the other side. The door was jammed. Trevor slumped against it; but, as Jace yanked at the door handle, he began to stir.

Jace went back around to the driver's side and leaned in. "Trevor. Trev." He shook the other man's shoulder. Trevor groaned.

Checking him for injuries, Jace found the splinted wrist and a gash on the man's forehead. Trevor groaned again. His eyes fluttered and opened. Jace turned the man's head toward him. His eyes glazed.

"Trevor," he tried again. The SAS major's gaze began to focus. Jace knew the exact instant clarity returned; Trevor jerked and looked around. "Where's Heather?"

"Shite. I don't know. She was driving. Someone started shooting at us, and next thing I knew, we ended up in the trench." He touched his head gingerly. "I must've bounced off the window."

Jace tried to calm his racing heart. Despite his overwhelming need to find her, she wasn't his primary concern. She couldn't be.

He had to trust she could take care of herself.

Groaning, Jace thunked his head against the steering wheel, then pushed himself out of the car. "She wouldn't have run off and left you unless she had no choice."

"No," Trevor agreed. "We have to presume she is in the hands of the imbeciles shooting at us."

"Yeah." He helped Trevor over the center console and out of the car. "Stay here and wait for the medics."

Trevor looked at him like he'd grown two heads. "Like hell. You need me to disarm the bomb."

Jace glanced pointedly at Trevor's ribs, which the other man clutched. "I can take care of the bomb."

"And the chemical weapon? Are you equipped to handle that as well?" The SAS major knew the answer because he moved, albeit shakily, toward the loading dock. "We need to stop them from mixing the phosgene and the chlorine, at all costs."

Jace didn't waste any more time arguing. Drawing his Sig Sauer, he sprinted to the loading dock and up the stairs. Trevor was right behind him, which jacked his respect for the man into high gear. Broken ribs hurt like a bitch and a half; the man must be in agony. But there was nothing on his face except grim determination.

Jace risked a quick look into the bay itself.

It was fifty feet across, double that in length. Support girders crisscrossed the ceilings. Pipes ran down the length of the building at the fifteen-foot mark. The faintly purplish epoxy floor was stained from years of dirt and spills. Two blue doors stood across from him.

The bay was empty.

"I'm figuring the left door will lead to the pool area," said Trevor. "That's where we need to get to."

Sweeping his head from side to side, Jace ran in a half crouch across the floor to the first blue door. Flattening himself against the wall to the left of the door, he nodded to Trevor, who had done the same thing to the right. Trevor reached out and gingerly turned the knob. The door was unlocked, which was a mercy, since he didn't have his tools with him. Trevor held up three fingers, lowering them one at a time.

Three. Two. One.

Trevor pushed the door open, and Jace darted inside, weapon out and searching for targets. Left, right, in quick succession.

The hallway was empty.

It was a repeat of the bay—epoxy floor, cinder block walls, and a ceiling crisscrossed with pipes and support beams. A fire extinguisher was strapped to the wall just to the left of the door. Jace handed his weapon to Trevor and unfastened the extinguisher, hefting it like the weapon it could be.

They turned left and crept in tandem past the door to the electrical room, past light switches and electrical outlets. At each switch, Jace flipped the lights off until the hallway was dark. They passed under a large, empty doorframe and followed the hallway as it turned sharply right. An arrow on the wall pointed the way to the pool.

Halfway down the long hallway were two more doors, one on each side of the hall. The helpful arrow told Jace they wanted the door to their right. As they reached it, Trevor and Jace deployed themselves on either side of the door as though they'd done it a million times. Again, Trevor counted down. This time, Trevor eased the door open a few millimeters at a time.

The room beyond was a twenty-by-thirty storage area. Crates and pallets lines the walls. Several boxes had been pulled out into the middle of the floor. Two men dressed in jeans and T-shirts, the ones Jace recognized as Rami and Aa'idah's brother Shukri, struggled to haul huge buckets across the floor. Jace and Trevor looked at one another, completely in sync. As one, they burst through the door, throwing themselves onto the men.

Trevor barreled into Shukri, catching him by surprise. The man smashed into a crate and bounced, already swinging as he launched himself back at Trevor. A quick fist to the ribs and an elbow to the back of his head, and the terrorist went down.

The second man, Rami, shouted a warning. Jace let loose with a stream of carbon dioxide from the nozzle of the fire extinguisher, straight into the man's face. The man howled and clawed at his eyes. Jace slammed his fist into the man's gut. He doubled over.

"Stop!"

The command came from beyond the storage room, into the pool area itself. A figure appeared in the doorway.

Zaahir al-Farouk.

And he was not alone. Held by her hair, gun pressed to her temple.

Heather.

Chapter Forty-Two

JACE FROZE. PROBABLY for the first time in his career, his brain froze, too. He couldn't think, couldn't breathe. Couldn't focus. All he could do was stare at Heather, and think, "Don't die. Don't die. Don't die."

"Relinquish your weapons," Zaahir said, in surprisingly good English. "Or I will blow her brains all over this very clean floor."

Trevor groaned, clutching his ribs and head, and slowly slumped to the floor. He seemed to lapse into unconsciousness. Both terrorists struggled to their feet and eyed Jace warily. At a sharp command from Zaahir, one pressed his fingers to Trevor's throat and shrugged.

"He's not dead. Shall I kill him?"

"No. We must hurry." Zaahir snapped out a stream of commands that Jace could not follow. Shukri snagged the Sig, half-buried under Trevor's bulk. Jace tightened his grip on the fire extinguisher. Zaahir sneered at him and yanked Heather's hair, jamming the handgun up under her chin. Pain flitted across Heather's face, but not a sound passed her lips.

If he surrendered, he was dead. He knew it. They all were. Every fiber of his being rebelled against the notion.

Jace loosened his grip. Forced his body to relax.

He let the extinguisher swing toward the floor. He wasn't going to risk Heather.

Behind him, Rami reached across and grabbed it, growling something in Arabic. He shoved against Jace's back, pushing him toward Zaahir.

Maybe he could use it to his advantage. He let his momentum carry him forward.

But Zaahir backed away, dragging Heather with him, using her to shield his body. She had fastened her gaze on Jace's face, trying to communicate something to him, but his attention was on Zaahir, waiting for the slightest hesitation, the slightest opening. Zaahir didn't give it to him.

He backed all the way into the main indoor pool area and jerked the handgun, indicating Jace should follow him. "Over there. By the stairs."

Jace glanced over to the ladder leading down into the water. It was foul, green, and reeked. Something had caused the filters to stop working. A perfect excuse to close the pool and allow these men to execute their plan.

The pool was a standard-sized lap pool, four feet deep, six lanes. Two lines of triangular flags, even with the lifeguard's elevated seat, trisected the pool. Old Glory hung on the wall opposite him, along with a poster with the words "al-Zadr Field Recreation Division" on it. The leaf skimmer mounted on the opposite wall caught his attention. It would be a bit light and the net would make it unwieldy, but it would make a decent weapon in a pinch.

Not that he would have the opportunity to grab it.

Rami and Shukri came into the main area, dragging Trevor's limp body between them. Zaahir al-Farouk snapped an order. They heaved him close to the nearest starting block and let him drop. His head smacked against the concrete. Was he conscious? Playing 'possum?

Dying?

"Lie facedown on the floor," said Zaahir. "Rami will tie your hands. If you resist in any way, I will kill this whore."

Rami sidled toward Jace, his eyes red and watery from the fire-suppressant chemicals, clearly reluctant to come within range of his fists. Glaring daggers at him, Jace slowly knelt, then lowered himself to the floor. He stretched his arms out in front of him; Zaahir laughed.

"Do you think me a fool, infidel? Put your hands behind your back."

Reluctantly, Jace obeyed. He couldn't keep his gaze from returning to Heather. She was thinking, plotting, waiting. If Zaahir gave her half an inch, she'd take the mile. Jace felt a chill. If she calculated wrong, Zaahir would pull the trigger, and her vibrant light would be snuffed out.

That was unacceptable.

"Come here," barked Rami. Jace allowed the man to wrap his wrists with some sort of thin twine and move him to the starting block where Trevor lay. Heather looked close to tears. He sent her what he hoped was a reassuring smile. They hadn't searched him. Their mistake. He no longer had his Sig Sauer, but he was far from helpless.

Zaahir marched Heather over to the block of concrete, and Rami tied her hands as well. Jace frowned. She had a bruise forming on her cheekbone; Zaahir had hit her. He would pay for that.

"Are you all right?" she asked him.

"Just fine. You?"

She gave him a shaky smile. "Never better. How's Trevor? He has broken ribs and a broken wrist. Did they knock him out?"

Rami tried to tie Trevor's hands, as well. The SAS major hadn't moved. The terrorist had a tough time wrangling the dead weight up behind Trevor's back, particularly with the broken edges of hard plastic acting as a splint; his arms kept flopping to the cement. Something inside Jace relaxed minutely. The Brit was conscious, after all.

Rami finally gave up and tied Trevor's arms over his head, wrapping the twine through the plastic. He hurried back to Zaahir.

As Jace watched, Trevor's eyes cracked open, just a sliver.

"Three tangos," Jace reported quietly. Three terrorists. Trevor did not so much as twitch to indicate he'd heard, but Jace knew he listened. He described their surroundings, the entrances and exits, the tangos' activities. Two of them now dragged the huge buckets close to the edge of the water, while Zaahir supervised. "They're bringing the chlorine to the pool."

Zaahir roared at them to hurry up and issued a spate of directions Jace couldn't follow.

"He's telling them to hurry up and finish," said Heather. "And then to go out and attach the hose to the tanker for dispersal." She listened for a moment, becoming even more grim. "The explosives are attached to the tanker. Underneath the chassis. He told them to take them out and bring them in here." She looked from one to the other. "What are we going to do?"

Chapter Forty-Three

JACE GRINNED AT HER. He actually *grinned*. What was wrong with him?

"We're going to get loose, and we're going to stop them," he told her, utter confidence in his tone. He shifted his knees so his hip was almost in her lap. "Yes, I'm happy to see you, but that really is a knife in my pocket. Would you mind getting it, sweetheart?"

A few feet away, Trevor turned a laugh into a soft cough. Heather risked a peek at Zaahir. He stood in the doorway of the storage area, hands on his hips, Jace's Sig Sauer stuck into his belt, his own weapon in his hand. He stared at them a moment and turned away.

Jace shielded her actions with his body. Heather twisted her torso as far as she could, working her fingers into his front jeans pocket.

Um. That was *not* his knife.

Despite herself, heat rose in her cheeks.

"Ooh, baby," he murmured. Teasing her. Helping to steady her. She had freaked when Zaahir thrust his pistol against her forehead and cocked it. She forgot to breathe, knowing she would die. Her knees shook and turned to water. She had not fallen, though. Somehow, she'd stiffened her spine and faced him squarely. And he had backhanded her, knocking her to the cement.

"You are responsible for the destruction of my camp," he snarled. "The death of my men." He kicked her. "Shooting you is too easy. You represent the corruption of your kind, spreading your pollution and filth in my country. Therefore, you will witness my assault against you who offend Allah." He'd hauled her to her feet by her hair and slammed her against the wall.

By increments, she was able to work the penknife out of Jace's pocket. Just as she pulled it free, though, hard footsteps behind her alerted her. She dropped the knife, praying no one heard the faint clatter as it hit the concrete. Shifting her hip to hide it, she threw her head back to glare at Zaahir. He glowered down at her, fingering the still-healing nose Heather had broken during the convoy ambush.

"It is your fault we lost our missile, whore. But it does not matter. You and your friends will die here, victims of your own government's lies and deceit."

Heather spat at him. "Go fuck yourself, you son of shit." It felt good to curse at him, tied up or not. For some reason, he had fixated on her as the architect of his troubles. His face darkened even more. He pulled back his foot to kick her, and Jace exploded into action. Despite his tied hands, he delivered a side kick that smashed into Zaahir's shin, missing his knee by a millimeter. The man lurched back, swearing.

Zaahir reached into his back pocket and withdrew a black spring baton. With a snap of his wrist, the steel cylinder extended to more than a foot. The terrorist leader whipped it through the air once and circled around to Jace. He didn't bother with finesse. He simply lunged at Jace, striking him with the spring baton. The whipping effect built momentum as the steel slewed through the air, giving it maximum striking power. Maximum ability to hurt. Jace twisted, taking the blow on his shoulder and upper back. He coiled, shooting a leg toward Zaahir's midsection. The terrorist cell leader swung the baton down, catching Jace's calf. Jace hopped straight up, swishing his hands under his legs and landing lightly, hands now in front of him. Zaahir struck again, even as Heather shrieked at him and Trevor struggled to his feet.

Zaahir swiveled his head toward Trevor. Two steps and a solid kick, and Trevor was flung backwards. He hit the surface of the water and sank beneath it. Zaahir drew his VM-17 pistol and fired.

A red stain blossomed on the green surface of the water.

Heather screamed her fear and rage. Zaahir merely laughed at her, turning the pistol to Jace. Heather scrambled forward, trying as best she could to shield him with her own body, while at the same time Jace gripped her arm, trying to push her clear.

"Zaahir, where should I put the bomb?"

To Heather's intense relief, Zaahir hesitated, and finally turned to Rami with a snort of annoyance. He examined the interior, pointing across the bloody water to the far eastern wall. Two sets of twelve-foot windows, with two more sets higher up on the wall, overlooked the outside pool area. Heather could hear, faintly, splashing and screams of laughter.

"There. The blast will push the gas outward, for maximum effect."

Without warning, he spun, whipping the baton around and smashing it against Jace's temple. Who dropped without a sound.

Heather uttered a guttural shriek of despair. "Jace!" She fought her bonds like a wild woman, but only succeeded in digging the thin twine deep into her skin.

Zaahir shoved his handgun into the back of his pants and twisted the baton, collapsing it. Pushing it into his back pocket, he withdrew an Afghan folding knife. Heather shrank back as he loomed over her. Zaahir's thin lips twisted up, enjoying her fear. With one strong stroke, he cut the twine attaching her wrists. Grabbing her, he dragged her to her feet.

"Now you will witness our great strike, deep in the heart of the infidel cowards." He strode toward the storage area, ruthlessly yanking Heather along behind him. She twisted around, trying to see Jace or Trevor, and stumbled. The concrete cracked against her bones as she lost her balance and fell to her knees. She repressed the yelp of pain. She would not give the bastard the satisfaction.

"You're the coward," she spat instead. "Killing innocent women and children? That doesn't make you some brave freedom fighter. It just makes you a murderer."

Zaahir gripped her by the throat and forcibly lifted her to her feet, squeezing cruelly. Black spots danced in front of her eyes as she strained for air. *"Al-jihad fi sabil Allah.* I strive in the way of Allah. Jihad is my sacred duty. I have sworn my life to the struggle, to protect Islam against invaders, unbelievers, and dissenters who renounce the authority of Islam."

Heather tried to force words past the constriction of his fingers. "Butcher."

He let her drop, digging his fingers into her arms instead as he turned her and pushed her into the storage area and beyond. "You are a woman and unworthy," he said. "You will bear witness to my success, then you will die." He shoved her down the dark hallway to the bright spill of light at the door to the loading bay.

Heather blinked several times to clear her vision. Someone had maneuvered the oil truck sideways, so it was parked parallel to the loading platform. Shukri now struggled to connect a long hose to the back valve of the tanker.

She shivered. They had failed. Trevor was dead, and Jace probably was, too. She was helpless to stop these men from mixing together the lethal combination of poisonous gases and slaughtering dozens, if not hundreds. Bile burned at the back of her throat.

She, too, would be dead, soon.

Maybe Jace had just been knocked unconscious. It had been a fearsome blow, but Heather clung to hope anyway. How cruel an irony it was, to have found him, only to lose him a few short weeks later. Jace, the formidable warrior, the tender confidant . . . the man she loved, with all her heart.

She choked back tears.

Shukri still wrestled with the hose connectors. Zaahir barked, "What's taking so long?"

Zaahir yanked Heather with him as he went to investigate. The valve was corroded with age, and he couldn't get a solid seal. The cell leader shoved Heather to the ground. Putting some muscle into it, Zaahir finally locked the valve and the hose together.

Rami appeared on the loading dock. "I placed the bomb, Zaahir."

"Help Shukri."

Rami took the front end, while Shukri hefted the more central portion onto his shoulder. Together, they began to carry the hose toward the pool. And the chlorine.

Chapter Forty-Four

"RISE AND SHINE, Sleeping Beauty."

Something slapped his cheek. Pain exploded in his skull. He struck out, blindly, instinctively. Someone caught hold of his wrist and held it immobile.

"Easy there, mate."

Jace forced his eyes open. He lay half on his side, with Trevor kneeling next to him, sawing on the ropes with Jace's penknife.

"You kiss me, and I'm gonna kick your ass," he muttered.

Trevor's eyes twinkled. The twine parted, and Jace sat up. Too fast. Light exploded behind his eyes, and he sagged. Trevor slipped an arm around his shoulders.

"All right?" he asked.

Jace nodded. Flexing various muscles, he tried to determine how much damage the bastard's steel baton had inflicted. Nothing seemed to be broken, which was a miracle. Mostly, he felt like he'd gotten the shit stomped out of him.

He sat up again, albeit more slowly, and tried his legs. With Trevor's help, he stood. "You were shot."

"Bugger just creased my shoulder." Blood dripped steadily down his arm, though. Jace gestured for his penknife, and used it to hack a strip off his T-shirt. The wound was high on Trevor's arm; tying the strip of material tightly around Trevor's bicep would at least slow the bleeding. Trevor nodded his thanks.

"We've got work to do. All right with that, are you?"

Jace turned toward the door. "I'll kill the bastard if he's hurt her."

Trevor stepped in front of him, a hand on his chest. Jace narrowed his eyes, but the Brit didn't budge. "We have to stop the explosion. That has to be our first priority. Agreed?"

Jace didn't like it. Not one bit. Everything in him screamed to get to her side. Still, he knew Trevor was right. He nodded, exhaling hard. "Yeah."

He heard footsteps in the other room at the same time Trevor did. As one, they shifted to the door, one on either side of it. Rami stepped through the doorway, dragging a hose that had to be three feet in diameter.

Jace didn't hesitate.

Two steps, a hand snaked across the terrorist's throat and another at the back of his neck. An efficient twist. The terrorist dropped without a sound. Jace snatched the man's Uzi from his dead fingers.

Trevor squatted to examine the hose assembly. "I need to cap this," he told Jace. "Or block it off somehow. And disarm the bomb. You go."

Jace popped the magazine, checked the ammunition, and slammed it home again. A quick peek—there was a round in the chamber—and he dashed through the door. The hallway beyond the storage room was still dark and empty. Uzi raised to his shoulder, Jace advanced, body taut, knees bent, muzzle following the line of his body as he hunted for a target.

He stopped just inside the hallway leading to the loading bay, allowing his eyes time to adjust to the bright sunlight. Shukri hefted the wide hose on his shoulder, obviously trying to help pull it all the way down to the pool. His eyes bulged out of their sockets at the sight of the fearsome warrior facing him. He dropped the hose to reach for his rifle.

Jace shot him. Two to the body, one to the head.

The noise rang in the small space, and with his head still throbbing from Zaahir's beating, he doubled over, grunting in pain. Blood spurted from the terrorist's wounds as he jerked backwards, fell over, and lay still. Jace spared a fraction of a thought for Aa'idah. There had been no way to save her brother.

He stepped into the loading bay, weapon up and searching for another target. Zaahir al-Farouk stood near the stairs, looming over Heather, who was on the ground at his feet. Black eyes glittered with hatred as he aimed his deadly handgun at Jace. The two locked gazes for a long moment; one of those seconds ticking away into eternity. Jace knew he could not swing the Uzi to its new target fast enough. Not before Zaahir squeezed the trigger. He had a moment of regret for his missed opportunity with Heather, even as his body dove for cover because he didn't know how to admit defeat.

Heather launched upward, slamming into Zaahir. He stumbled back, his shot pinging harmlessly off the concrete. She flew at Zaahir, using the palm of her hand to smash under his chin, using her elbows, her knees to pummel him. Zaahir retreated, arms up to shield his face. Heather leapt for the gun, still in his hand.

Zaahir swung the butt of the pistol across his body, knocking her arm aside. His other fist smashed into the side of her head. Heather faltered. Zaahir grabbed her by the front of her shirt.

Jace shook his head to clear it. No, that wasn't ringing in his ears. Sirens wailed in the distance, growing closer. The cavalry.

His brave Heather reached across Zaahir's fist, tangled in her collar, and twisted his fingers so he was forced to release her, then pressed her thumbs down along the back of his hand. The wrist lock brought Zaahir to his knees with a snarl of outrage. Quick as a snake, he wrapped his forearm under her knee and yanked. She tumbled to the ground. He was on her in a flash, his gun jammed up under her chin, forcing her head back.

Jace raced toward them, shouting, fearing he was too slow, too late, knowing part of him would die if Zaahir pulled the trigger. With no finesse, with no thought other than to get him off Heather, he slammed into Zaahir like a linebacker.

The handgun discharged next to his ear, deafening him. He rolled over Zaahir and was on his feet in a flash. Zaahir rocketed up; Jace kicked the wrist holding the gun, and it skittered across the concrete. The terrorist cell leader lunged for him, wrapping both arms around his waist and shoving him back. Jace brought his elbow down between the other man's shoulder blades; he responded by slamming his fist into Jace's gut once, twice . . . Jace twisted out of Zaahir's hold and aimed a side kick at the man's knee. He missed but pivoted to kick again, higher, landing his blow straight to the asshole's family jewels. He let his rage wash over him like a cleansing river, his focus sharp and his goal clear: to decimate the man who put his hands on Heather and fear in her eyes.

Zaahir staggered backwards, bending double. But oh, holy hell . . . he wasn't just bending; he was also reaching, into the waistband of his pants. For Jace's own Sig Sauer. Jace leapt for him. Just as he reached the terrorist, he heard the gunshot.

The pain was immediate and overwhelming. Red blossomed across his chest. He reached for the wound with some idea of applying pressure, only to find his arms wouldn't respond. He sank to his knees, struggling to stay conscious, gaze instinctively searching for Heather. Where was she? Was she safe?

He found her gaping in horror in his direction. Don't worry about it, he wanted to say. I'll be fine. But his vocal cords weren't working, either. I love you, he thought. Maybe she knew. He wanted her to know.

Zaahir stepped into view, blocking Heather from his sight. That pissed him off. If he was going to kick it, her beautiful face was the last thing he wanted to see. Jace reached for the Sig, still clutched in Zaahir's evil hands, but the terrorist squeezed the trigger.

Chapter Forty-Five

September 11. 3:55 P.M.
Recreation Center, Dogwood Beach Housing Area

EVERYTHING IN HEATHER FROZE. Jace had been shot. There was blood everywhere. He was on his knees because he could no longer stand.

Zaahir was going to kill Jace with his own gun.

Time slowed down. She seemed to have all the time in the world to dive across the pavement, scoop up the terrorist's PHP VM-17 pistol, and roll out into a crouching firing position. Time to steady her aim, time to squeeze the trigger.

The first shot hit him high in the shoulder. He jerked, but did not fall. The next blew a hole in his face. Heather pulled the trigger over and over, until the steady *click-click-click* finally penetrated the red haze in her brain, and she realized the magazine was empty. Fifteen rounds.

Zaahir sprawled in an expanding pool of blood.

Nevertheless, she crept up on his body, ready for him to leap to his feet and grab hold of her. His sightless gaze reassured her. Backing away from the spreading puddle, she turned and dropped to her knees beside Jace.

"Jace? Jace, look at me!" She gripped the bottom of his T-shirt, already torn, and ripped it further, trying to get a good look at his wound. The bullet had penetrated his upper chest, above and to the left of his heart. Blood poured from his torn flesh. The gory ruin terrified her.

She gagged.

Forcing herself straight, she fought down her nausea. She turned him in order to lay him flat, alarmed at how easily he fell. Placing both hands over his wound, she leaned her palms into it, applying pressure. "You stay with me, Jace, do you hear me?" she said. "Don't you dare leave me!"

Jace's mouth turned up at the corners. "Wouldn't dare," he managed. He tried to raise a hand to her face. She caught it and lifted it to her cheek. His blood and her tears mingled together.

"You know I love you, right?" Her tears dripped onto his hand.

He moved his head in what could have been a nod. He shivered, going into shock.

Police cars and an ambulance veered around the corner, their sirens piercing. They drove almost up on top of them, and suddenly the loading area was swarming with people. Firm hands pulled her away.

She let them separate her from Jace, weeping, panic freezing her insides. The medics palpated the area around the bullet hole, packed it, started fluids, and shifted Jace into a neck collar and spinal board, just to be safe.

"His systolic is above eighty," one told her. "That's the good news. I've called for a life flight. We need to get him to a trauma center."

Heather crept back to his side. He was still conscious, barely, hanging on until he saw her. This time, she got a faint smile.

"Love . . . you," he whispered.

Heather smoothed her hand over his short hair. "Save your strength," she murmured. "I'm not going anywhere, and neither are you. You live for me, do you hear me, soldier? You don't get to swoop into my life, then leave me."

Trevor appeared on the loading dock, hobbling, with a medic hovering at his elbow in case he fell. He made it over to the ambulance under his own steam. "How is he?" he asked.

The other medic scanned the sky. "Better if we get him to the hospital," he said. "His blood pressure is dropping. I've called for an air ambulance."

The Blackhawk medical helicopter took five and a half minutes to arrive. Heather knew, because she alternately scanned the sky and checked her watch. Jace slipped into unconsciousness as the medic labored to keep him stabilized.

The flight medics loaded him onto the helicopter. Medics on the air ambulances were qualified combat medics, she knew. Trained specifically to stabilize and treat battle-wounded men. That didn't stop her from wringing her hands after she scrambled onto the bird behind him. Trevor had been put on another stretcher bed, and the third medic immobilized his wrist and checked his ribs for breaks. She barely spared him a glance. He would live.

So would Jace. He had to.

Running her hands over her knees, she tried to still her trembling. Someone draped a blanket around her shoulders. One of the medics knelt in front of her. "I'm going to cut your pants at the knee, okay?" he asked. "I need to check your injuries."

What injuries? She looked down in surprise. Her jeans were

torn and bloody. It must have happened when she'd fallen, when Zaahir dragged her away from the injured Jace. "I'm fine," she said. "Take care of Captain Reed."

The medic patted her hand. "We're doing everything we can for him. He's as stabilized as he can be until we get to the trauma center. Time to check you out."

Heather pulled away and went to sit next to Jace. "Later."

The medic hesitated. "We're one minute out."

She stroked Jace's hair and held his hand. There wasn't anything else she could do.

The Blackhawk landed on the roof of the al-Zadr base hospital. Several medical staffers waited on the roof; they moved Jace to a gurney and rushed inside. Heather tried to follow him, but a nurse guided her, instead, to a curtained-off area in the emergency room, where she ordered Heather, kindly but firmly, to remove her pants. Heather almost screeched her frustration.

"He's going into surgery, darlin'" the nurse said. "You got a wait ahead of you anyways. Might as well clean out those abrasions."

Sighing, Heather did as she was told. Truth was, the scrapes stung. They weren't serious; the nurse cleaned and bandaged them. Refusing her offer of "something for the pain," Heather instead began to pace.

Chapter Forty-Six

September 11. 8:00 P.M.
Base Hospital, al-Zadr Air Force Base, Azakistan

HEATHER SAT IN Trevor's visitor chair, not saying much. Until someone updated her on Jace's condition, there wasn't much to say. The bullet had smashed into his upper chest, missing his collarbone and his heart by just a few inches. Her worry hung palpably in the air.

"He's still in surgery," she said, as though Trevor didn't already know that.

"We'll know something soon," he soothed, as though he hadn't repeated the words half a dozen times already. He reached for the water pitcher, but Heather beat him to it, pouring it for him and holding it to his mouth. He gave a half grimace and took it from her. "Broken ribs are a pain in the arse," he said, "but my arm works just fine."

"Your left one, anyway," she said. His right wrist rested in a heavy splint until the swelling went down, at which time it would be put in a plaster cast to heal. He didn't seem to appreciate her fussing, so she began to pace instead. "Why isn't anyone telling us anything?"

"Patience, ducks," he said. "Still in surgery is good. Still in surgery means they're fixing him up like new."

Heather threw herself back into the visitor's chair, arms crossed over her chest as she slumped back. "I know."

The Defense Threat Reduction Agency was on its way to take charge of the phosgene in the oil truck. Heather and Trevor had both been furious to discover LTC Louis Jowat, in charge of security into and around the parade grounds, had intercepted and overridden Shelby's order to evacuate the military and civilian visitors at the parade ground. The president had already started his speech, and Jowat decided, unilaterally, the danger at the recreation center was too far from the site of the president's visit to pose a threat, and the president would be gone before any threat from the recreation areas could affect him. The Secret Service was livid, demanding Jowat be court-martialed for endangering the life of the President of the United States. Heather wasn't too broken up about it. The man had made serious errors in judgment.

A figure appeared in his doorway. Heather shot to her feet. "How is he? Is he out of surgery? Can I see him?" It was not, however, Dr. Denby.

It was Shelby.

Trevor sat up, chuffing out a pained noise. Heather shot him a chiding look.

"Your own fault for refusing pain meds," she said.

Shelby trickled a gray silk scarf through her fingers several times. Finally, she took a few small steps into the room. "Am I interrupting?"

"No. Not at all. Absolutely not," Trevor said.

She wouldn't look at him, not directly. Instead, she crossed to Heather and hugged her. "I'm glad you're all right. Both of you," she added, but still wouldn't meet Trevor's gaze.

"We're waiting for Jace to get out of surgery," said Heather, returning the hug. Her eyes filled with tears; she couldn't help it. What would she do if Jace died? Part of her would die, too.

Shelby looked her over, and she realized she still wore her torn jeans. The blood caking it made the denim stiff and uncomfortable. She hardly cared. No way was she leaving before she'd seen Jace.

Shelby wandered to the window and looked out. The late afternoon sun dipped toward the horizon. Shadows lengthened across the hospital grounds. Heather glanced askance at Trevor, and he gave a small nod. *Yes, please leave.*

She started toward the door. "I'm going to get some coffee. And then I'm going to go down to surgery and see if there's any news."

Shelby turned sharply. "Oh . . . no, please. Don't let me displace you."

Heather hesitated. Which friend did she sacrifice for the other?

"You need to stretch your legs, I'm sure," Trevor said. "You've been cooped up in here for quite a while."

She gave a small shrug, cast an apologetic look Shelby's way, and went out the door.

"Nice view," she heard Shelby say. The window looked out over the parking lot, as it happened. The view stunk. Heather wandered down to the nurses' station.

"Any word on Jace Reed?" she asked. The nurse, an older woman with steel gray hair, picked up the receiver and dialed down to the surgical ward without a single comment or reprimand. Heather had asked her the same question twenty times in the past two and a half hours.

"They're still operating," she reported back a moment later. "It's likely going to be another hour, at least."

Breathing deeply, reminding herself that the continued surgery meant that Jace still lived, Heather thanked the patient woman. More coffee was last thing she needed—five cups already swirled in her bloodstream—so she walked back to Trevor's room.

She leaned against the wall opposite the doorway, trying to tune out the conversation between Shelby and Trevor. She couldn't.

"I bet the State Department's in chaos," Trevor was saying. "A lot of political fallout from this."

"Yes, it's crazy. The Azakistani woman, Aa'idah Karim, came to the embassy, asking for asylum. I think she'll get it, too." Pause. "Look, Trevor . . . what happened last week . . . us, um, you know. After the Festival Gala. It was a mistake. I'm sure you've realized it, too. So it shouldn't be a problem, um, for us to . . . just forget it ever happened, right?" The pause felt weighted to Heather. "I mean, it's not like our paths are likely to cross again anyway, right?" Faint desperation tinged her tone.

Heather cursed the poor timing. Two broken ribs, head split open, broken wrist, gunshot to the shoulder . . . Trevor was lucky to be alive. And Shelby chose to dump him now, while he was still in the hospital?

Trevor sighed. "I did not leave your bed to go to Christina's," he said. "She was in trouble."

"Yes, I understand," Shelby spoke over him. "That's not why . . ."

Heather rubbed between her eyes, trying to dislodge some of the pressure there. Not long ago, she might have run from a relationship, too. Now, she just wanted Jace to live. It was vital that he live. Little mattered beyond that right now.

She would do anything, anything at all, for him.

Marine Gunnery Sergeant Hugo Bisantz of the Embassy Security Group strolled up the hall, out of uniform in casual slacks and a black, button-down shirt.

"Evening, ma'am," he said politely.

Until that moment, Heather had not registered that Shelby was dressed in a short, flirty skirt. Dangling earrings. Heels. Careful makeup. And apparently not for Trevor.

"Are you here to visit Captain Reed, Sergeant?" she asked pointedly.

"I'm waiting for Shelby, ma'am."

Heather's heart sank. At least the Marine had the sense to stay out of the hospital room. A tense silence had settled inside. Just as Heather straightened from the wall to go rescue either or both of them, Shelby spoke again, her voice overly bright.

"Well, I just wanted to check in to see how you were doing. Ambassador Stanton inquired, so now I can give him a firsthand report."

"Yeah, you do that." Trevor's voice grew an edge.

"I'm sorry you were hurt," she said. "Truly I am."

"Not your fault," Trevor said. "Not any of it." He sighed, sounding tired.

Shelby hovered by the door, clearly eager to leave. "Goodbye, Major Carswell," she said.

"Yeah."

But as Shelby passed through the doorway, Heather saw the anguish, the unshed tears, the sorrow in her eyes. And even as Hugo placed a hand at the small of her back to lead her away, she glanced longingly back toward Trevor.

Sometimes life just sucked.

Chapter Forty-Seven

September 14. 3:15 P.M.
Base Hospital, al-Zadr Air Force Base, Azakistan

JACE KNEW INSTANTLY he was in a hospital. If the familiar smell of antiseptic and Band-Aids didn't orient him, the wretched throbbing did. He flexed various muscles to check the severity of the damage. And immediately stopped.

Oh, yeah. He'd been shot. Pain in the . . . well, chest, in this case.

He opened his eyes. Why did they have to paint hospital walls stark white? And keep the lights so bright? Squinting a little, he looked around at the tubes and wires attaching him to various machines. Bandages covered his chest and shoulder. And then he forgot those trivial details.

Heather slept, her head near his thigh. She had pulled the visitor's chair close to him and sort of doubled over to get close enough to lay her head on his bed. It looked uncomfortable, but he didn't wake her. He remembered drifting in and out of consciousness;

each time, the gladness in her eyes enveloped him. She stroked his hair, held his hand. Coffee cups littered the table and floor, too. How long had he been out?

She stirred, as though sensing his wakeful state. He couldn't not touch her; he shifted his hand by increments to her hair. It had fallen out of whatever twist she'd put it in and cascaded over her shoulder onto the bleached white sheets. Exhaustion smudged her elfin face, streaks of dried tears leaving a path of clean down her grimy cheeks. Her eyes opened, lit up when she saw him.

His heart did a slow flip.

"Hey," she said, voice rough from sleep.

"Hey, yourself." He wiggled his fingers, and she obliged by twining her hand into his. He tugged, and she shifted onto his bed next to him until they were nose to nose. "How long have you been sitting there?"

She shifted her shoulders, looking away, which meant she'd been here since he'd gotten out of surgery. "Let me go get the doctor."

"I don't need a doctor. I need you."

That coaxed a smile out of her. "I'm all yours. How do you feel?"

"Like I was shot in the chest." Her smile disappeared, and he kicked himself for the thoughtless response. "Heather, really, I'm going to be fine. That's what the doctor said, too, right?" He vaguely recalled someone in a white coat reassuring him he would make a full recovery. Heather nodded, frowning, clearly unconvinced. She slid off his bed.

"I'm at least going to tell the nurse you're awake."

He tightened his grip on her fingers, then reluctantly let them slide free. The truth was, he didn't want her out of his sight. They both had come too close to death.

The room seemed dim and cold after she left. The other bed in the windowless room lay empty. He sighed, looking at the television mounted high on the wall. CNN was reporting on a mudslide in Ecuador. When a commercial came on, he let his eyes close again. He dozed until the doctor entered. He took Jace's pulse and blood pressure and made some notes on the clipboard at the foot of his bed.

"How's your pain level?"

"I'll live," Jace said. The mass of agony in his chest would ease eventually, right? The doctor gave a disapproving shake of his head and adjusted the drip running into Jace's arm.

"I get you're tough," he said. "But you don't get brownie points for suffering needlessly. I'm giving you fentanyl."

The narcotic worked fast, and Jace felt himself fading. "Make her go eat," he slurred.

AT THE DOCTOR's insistence, Heather returned to her quarters on base, showered, changed, and ate. Feeling more human, she tumbled into bed.

And couldn't sleep.

What was she doing? Everything in her demanded that she return to Jace's side. It had taken nearly losing him for her to acknowledge how vital he'd become to her. Whatever her love meant, wherever it took her, she needed to be with him like she needed to breathe. He filled her life with color and joy, things she'd never even realized were missing.

If she stayed with Delta Force support, they could never be together. Only civilians could fraternize with military operators. An obscure paragraph in a regulation that was going to force her to make the hardest choice of her life.

Was she really willing to give up her ambitions for him? Yes, her heart sang. Not so fast, her brain countered. Following a man from military base to military base, surrounded by what she'd chosen as her career, what she loved . . . could she bear it?

No. She had to be honest with herself. To sit on the sidelines and watch while Jace put himself in harm's way, unable to help, unable even to know where he was going or what his mission was, would be unendurable.

There had to be an answer. She frowned unhappily. The Finance guy and the woman in charge of the Research arm were both civilians. Maybe she could take accounting classes? It would be better than nothing. Or she could ask Colonel Granville to transfer her to another unit on base, and hope the Army was nice enough to move them together when it was time to permanently change duty stations.

Finally, *finally*, she drifted to sleep. She didn't dream at all.

When she awoke, she felt strangely calm. At peace, because she knew what she needed to do. Four in the morning in Azakistan made it—she did some quick calculations—more or less four in the afternoon, yesterday, at Fort Bragg. She picked up the phone.

An hour later, she had a job.

Fort Bragg hosted special operations units, yes, but also the Special Warfare School. Which needed trainers. Starting next month, she would support the instructors teaching the Special Forces Operations and Intelligence Course, and would also teach the six-month Arabic language course. For whatever time Jace spent at his home base, they could be together. It was enough. It would have to be enough.

Slipping into her favorite cotton sundress, the one with the scooped neckline and yellow abstract poppies along the bottom of the skirt, she left her hair down for once, letting her natural curl give her a windswept look. Her pale pink t-strap wedges pushed her height above six feet. A swipe of mascara to enhance her eyes, and she was ready.

She knew her efforts had been a success when Jace saw her and nearly spit out the juice he was sucking down.

"Holy Jesus!" he croaked. "Wow." His gaze incinerated her. "Come over here so I can strip that off you."

Heather laughed. "That would earn you another week in the hospital."

"It would be worth it."

He flapped a weak hand, and she went to him. Without thinking, she bent down, her lips touching his. He snaked his palm around the back of her neck, opening his mouth and slanting it for better access. She leaned into him, the electric slide of his tongue against hers sending thrills down her spine. Both hands came up to frame his handsome, precious face. She traced his lips with her tongue, let him suck it into his mouth, let him nibble her chin and kiss each eye closed. His fingers scalded her skin, the rasp of calluses causing goose bumps to rise. She didn't want to stop. "Careful of your stitches.'

He groaned. "Don't wanna." But he slumped back against the raised bed, tugging her down to sit beside him, looking tired. His obedience told her more than anything else how much he was still hurting.

"When did you have your last pain meds?"

His gaze softened and turned tender. "I'm okay."

"You will be, and that's all that matters." The words she really wanted to say stuck in her throat. Now she was here, doubts assailed her. What was she doing? What if she was making a terrible mistake? Once she sounded the bell, there was no unringing it. What if Jace . . .

"Whatever it is, just tell me." Worry replaced the tenderness in his eyes. His hands clenched the blanket, and he looked ready to leap out of bed. "You're scaring me."

It terrified her that, in such a short space of time, this man had become so critical to her happiness. She had never been cowardly about going after what she wanted, so why now?

"Heather?" Jace interlaced their fingers, tacitly offering his strength. It steadied her. She blew out a breath.

"I'm not going to take the assignment," she blurted out.

He cocked a head at her, clearly not understanding.

"My new position supporting Delta," she clarified. "I'm going to refuse the orders."

Jace couldn't have looked more shocked if she'd told him she was secretly a nun. "What?"

She tried to rise, to move away from him, but he refused to let her go. "Heather? Talk to me. You can't refuse orders. You know that."

She swallowed hard. "I can if I resign my commission."

The declaration lay between them. The silence stretched out past the point Heather could stand.

"Jace?"

His eyes became solemn as he looked at her. "I'm going out on a limb here—are you doing this for me? For us? So we can be together?"

She couldn't seem to speak above a whisper. "Yes. If that's . . . if that's something you would want."

He laughed, a sudden burst of air that became a groan of pain. "Hell, yeah, that's what I want."

Something deep inside her relaxed. "Then . . . it's settled. I'm going to resign my commission."

"I accept your resignation," boomed a voice from the doorway. Heather jumped. Bo Granville leaned against the doorjamb, not bothering to conceal he had been eavesdropping. Heather tried to untangle her feet to rise, but he waved her back down with a casual hand. "Sit, sit."

Heather pressed her hands together in her lap to still the faint trembling. It was done. There was no going back now. "Thank you, sir."

Colonel Granville guffawed. "Don't thank me yet, missy. You haven't heard my conditions."

Conditions? Ultimately, he could not truly prevent her from separating from the Army. He could, however, draw out the process and make it miserable if he so chose.

"Sir, being offered the opportunity to work with Delta is a dream come true—an amazing privilege, and I recognize the compliment." She glanced at the man in the hospital bed. "But accepting this honor would mean Jace and I can't be together. Frankly, sir, my career doesn't mean much if I can't share it with him."

"That your final word, Lieutenant?"

Heather opened her mouth and killed her career.

"Yes, sir."

He nodded and crossed his arms across his massive chest. "Okay. Get your paperwork together, and I'll muster you out." He rolled his mouth, looking for his cigar. Even Bo Granville wasn't allowed inside a hospital with tobacco, lit or unlit. "But I got me a problem, kid."

He looked at her expectantly. Heather wrinkled her brow. "Sir?"

"I visited one of my soldiers in the hospital, who was careless enough to get himself shot while he was saving the life of the President of the United States and the lives of hundreds of Americans and Azakistani civilians." He jabbed a thick finger at Jace. "Guess what he said to me?"

Heather had no idea where the colonel was going with this. "Don't know, sir."

"Well, see, here's the thing. He gave me an ultimatum. He said there was this girl he wanted to marry. He told me to find a way for y'all to be together, or he would quit my team." He frowned at Jace, annoyance and displeasure clear. "It's an ultimatum a man can make exactly once in his career," said Granville. "If he weren't one of my best officers, I'd have booted him out in half a heartbeat. But, since the Army's spent a bucketload of money on his ass . . ." Granville yanked a manila envelope from inside his uniform jacket and presented it to her with something of a flourish.

Heather took it, not sure what it might be. She tore open the flap and pulled out several sheets of paper. As she read, her eyes widened.

It was a job description. For a civilian intelligence support role with Delta Force. She would be doing exactly what she was doing now, except she would no longer be an Army officer. And there were no restrictions on relationships between the military and civilians. She and Jace could be together.

"You game, girl?"

Instead of answering, she turned to Jace. "This is a full operational intelligence position," she told him. "You have to understand that. It means I'll be sent forward, in advance of Delta operations. I'll be sent into potentially hostile areas to gather intelligence."

Jace swallowed hard but met her gaze steadily. "I won't lie to you, Heather. It's going to be tough for me. I'm going to want to protect you and keep you safe. But I won't stand in your way. I promise I'll support your career. On one condition."

Her heart clogged her throat. "Anything."

"Marry me."

Tears rushed to her eyes. Gazing at Jace, letting him see her tears, she spoke to Colonel Granville. "I accept the job, sir." She leaned toward Jace. He met her halfway, capturing her lips as surely as he had captured her heart.

When she surfaced many moments later, she realized they were alone. And together.

Did you enjoy Leslie's alpha heroes and strong heroines?
Don't miss the next book in her thrilling
Duty & Honor series

BAIT

Coming April 28, 2015 from Witness Impulse!

About the Author

LESLIE JONES has been an IT geek, a graphic designer, and, much like her heroine, an Army Intelligence officer, bringing her firsthand experience to the pages of her works. She's lived in Alaska, Korea, Belgium, Germany, and other exotic locations (including New Jersey). She is a wife, mother, and full-time writer, and splits her time between Scottsdale, Arizona, and Cincinnati, Ohio.

Discover great authors, exclusive offers, and more at hc.com.